FRANCESCA'S KITCHEN

Books by Peter Pezzelli

HOME TO ITALY

EVERY SUNDAY

FRANCESCA'S KITCHEN

Published by Kensington Publishing Corporation

FRANCESCA'S KITCHEN

PETER PEZZELLI

KENSINGTON BOOKS
http://www.kensingtonbooks.com

For Andrew and Gabriella

FRANCESCA'S KITCHEN

CHAPTER I

There was no point in taking chances, so the first thing Francesca Campanile did after boarding the plane and finding her seat by the aisle was to open her pocketbook and take out her rosary beads. Rolling one of the dark, smooth beads between her thumb and forefinger, she whispered a quick Hail Mary and made the sign of the cross, while ahead of her, at the front of the cabin, a smiling stewardess was just beginning to give her cheerful recitation about what everyone should do in case the cabin lost pressure in flight or the plane plummeted into the ocean or crash-landed after takeoff. The knowledge that there were little air masks that popped out of the ceiling and flotation devices under her seat did little to reassure Francesca that she hadn't been completely out of her mind just stepping on board. In truth, as whenever she flew, which wasn't often, it almost seemed as if the stewardess was telling them all these things just to make the passengers like Francesca feel even more scared out of their minds before take-off—if that was possible. It was like a cruel joke.

Francesca sat there, pondering her rosary beads, until the jet engines began to whine and the plane suddenly lurched forward, giving her a start. As the plane pulled away from the terminal, the stewardess up front babbled on, pointing out all the emergency exits, while one of her co-workers marched up the aisle, telling everyone to put their seats in the upright position. Francesca reached into her pocketbook, pulled out a set of photographs, and placed them on her lap next to the rosary beads. The plane taxied toward the runway, the cabin gently bouncing to-and-fro. It was a crystal clear January day outside, perfect for flying. Just the same, the motion of the plane and the anticipation of their imminent takeoff was profoundly unsettling to Francesca. She clutched the photographs to her heart and looked anxiously about at the people all around her.

The plane was packed, not an empty seat to be seen. It had probably been a mistake taking the seat by the aisle, Francesca told herself; she would probably get trampled if something bad happened and everyone had to get off in a hurry. As it was, people practically knocked each other down to get off the plane even on the best days. It was like the running of the bulls. She could have easily taken the window seat. The nice young man sitting next to her had offered it to her when she had come on board, but she had politely declined. Francesca dreaded flying and was just as happy to be as far away as possible from the window. Somehow, despite the threat of being trampled, it made her feel safer. Besides, she had no intention whatsoever of even looking at the window, never mind looking out of it , so why deny someone else the nauseating pleasure of enjoying the view from thirty thousand feet? The flight from Tampa would take close to three hours, and she intended to spend every second of that time in prayerful meditation, until the plane safely touched down in Providence. Till then, the window was all his.

The young man, who until this moment had been leafing through a magazine, happened to glance her way and notice the rosary beads and photographs.

"A little nervous about flying?" he said with a kind smile.

"Eh," Francesca replied with a shrug. "I'm an old lady, so who cares if I die, right? But if you ask me, this thing is nothing but a big sardine can with wings. It's a crazy way to get from one place to another."

"Well, I guess you have a point there," the young man laughed. "But it's still the *fastest* way to get from one place to another."

"Ayyy, there's more to life than speed," answered Francesca with a wave of her hand.

"Not when you're in a hurry," the young man kidded her. "Besides, they say flying is the safest way to travel—you know, statistically anyway. So you shouldn't worry."

"I'm a grandmother. All I do is worry."

"You sound just like *my* grandmother."

"We're all the same."

The young man laughed again before nodding at the photographs in Francesca's hand. "Your family?" he asked, as if he sensed that it might make the old woman feel better to show them to him.

"My grandchildren," said Francesca, smiling for the first time since she had come on board. She knew the young man was just trying to be nice by asking, but she was grateful for the distraction. "See," she said, passing one of the photographs to him, "those are my two grandsons, Will and Charlie. Look how big they've gotten. They live out in Oregon with my daughter Alice and her husband, Bill. That's them in this other photo. They all moved out west a few years ago, after Bill took a job with some big company out there." She paused for a moment and let out a sigh. "Seems silly to pick up your wife and children, and move so far away from all your family and friends just for a job," she went on, "but he makes lots of money—I guess. What do I know?"

The engines gave a brief roar as the pilot maneuvered the plane along the runway into its position behind with the other planes waiting to take off. The sound gave Francesca another start, and she clenched the rosary beads tighter in her fist.

"And who's in the other pictures?" asked the young man, trying to keep her focused on her grandchildren.

"My daughter Roseanne's three kids," she replied, passing

him another photo. "Rosie lives down here in Florida with her husband, Frank. That's Dana and Sara, the two oldest girls. Dana's a teenager now, and Sara's not far behind. And that's little Frankie; he's the youngest. They all came out to the airport today to put me on the plane. I hated to go. I spend so little time with everyone nowadays. Breaks my heart to say good-bye."

"I'm sure they must come home sometimes to visit you," offered the young man. "That must make you feel good."

"Oh, sure," said Francesca, heaving another sigh. "I fly out to see all of them once or twice a year, and sometimes they fly home to Rhode Island to see me, but it's not the same as having people close to you all the time. You never feel like you're a part of each other's lives, the way you're supposed to feel about your family. It always feels too rushed, too confused."

Francesca paused and let her thoughts drift back to the two weeks she had just passed at the home of her daughter and son-in-law. Roseanne was her oldest daughter, and Francesca missed her terribly when they were apart, just like she missed all her children and grandchildren. They were much alike, she and her daughter, both headstrong and independent. Consequently, they had spent the better part of the two weeks quibbling over just about everything. The way Rosie had decided to wear her hair these days—so short, instead of beautiful and long, the way it used to be. What was that all about? And the scandalously skimpy bikinis she let the girls wear to the beach. Francesca would never have let her daughters out of the house wearing such things! The late hour Frank inevitably returned home from the office, and the way he was always too tired to take care of some of the things around the house that she had noticed needed fixing. Maybe he should get up a little earlier in the morning. And the television shows she let Frankie watch, and those crazy video games she let him play. And the way Rosie made her marinara sauce or fried up the eggplant, which wasn't at all the way she had been taught by her mother. From the moment she had awoken every day to the moment she had gone to bed, it seemed as if Francesca had spent her entire visit bickering nonstop with her daughter.

It had been wonderful.

Francesca understood, of course, that her daughter and son-in-law had built a life of their own together. They had discovered their own ways of doing things, their own ways of raising their children, keeping their house, sharing their meals. They were a family, and their life together had acquired a unique rhythm, which was beautiful and perfect in its own way. Francesca knew that it was she who was out of step with it, she who was disrupting the ordinary ebb and flow of their days. She knew that she made all of them a little crazy whenever she visited, or when they visited her, but wasn't that what grandmothers were for? Besides, she knew how to make it up to them. When things started to make everyone a little too frazzled, she would offer to stay at home with the kids so that Rosie and Frank could have a night out together just by themselves. When she wasn't babysitting the kids, she took them to the mall and bought them anything they wanted. She pitched in by helping Roseanne keep the house clean, sweeping the floors and making the beds (which were supposed to be the kidss' jobs, but she didn't mind), and anything else she happened to notice that might need doing. Most of all, she cooked.

Francesca loved to cook, and she loved to watch people eat what she had cooked. It was one of her greatest pleasures in life. She had that special touch that some people have in the kitchen. She didn't need to go shopping to prepare a meal. Given five minutes to poke around in the cupboards and the refrigerator, Francesca could always roust up enough ingredients from whatever happened to be on hand to make something that would set mouths to watering. What was to be had? A clove of garlic and a little bit of olive oil? An old box of spaghetti or a leftover piece of meat? A single egg left in the carton? Maybe a bag of spinach or a couple of zucchini that had been forgotten on the bottom of the vegetable drawer? A block of cheese? A can of tomatoes that had been sitting on the back of the shelf for who knows how long? Some crusty old bread that even the birds wouldn't want?

Nothing went to waste.

Francesca would just add a little of this and a pinch of that to whatever creation sprang from her imagination, sauté it up in the pan or let it simmer in the pot, and before you knew it, dinner was served. Bring her to the grocery store, of course, and the possibilities were endless. Then, if she had a notion to bake a cake or a pie or a batch of pizzelle or a tray of biscotti, and the house suddenly took on the sweet aroma of a bakery on Sunday morning—well, a lot could be forgiven.

And so, when it came time for Francesca to go home, when they all drove out to see her off at the airport, there were hugs and kisses and tears galore. There were promises to call as soon as she made it home and promises to visit again soon. She had looked back only once when she had finally pulled herself away from everyone and made her way to the gate where the plane waited. Little Frankie had been draped over his father's shoulder. He had waved his little hand and called, "Bye-bye, Nonna," to her, the sound of his voice so sweet that it had brought the tears anew to her eyes.

Now, as she sat there with the photos in her hand, knowing full well that she must be boring this poor young man to tears of his own, she felt a wave of sadness wash over her, the same one that had washed over her when her grandson had waved goodbye.

"Anyway," she finally said, "that's about the best I can do right now: see my family whenever I can, and be happy for what I've got instead of sad for what I don't. So that's why I get on these stupid airplanes and fly all over the country even though they scare me to death." Francesca allowed herself another smile. "And that's why I carry my pictures and these rosary beads with me," she added. "So that if the worst happens, at least I won't be all alone."

The young man cast a bemused glance at the crowded cabin before handing the pictures back to her. "I don't think you'll have to worry about feeling all alone," he said, "at least not on this plane."

"Don't be so sure," said Francesca. "You'd be surprised at how easy it is for someone to feel lonely even when there are people all around."

With that, she let the young man go back to reading his magazine. She was grateful for the conversation, for it had made her feel a little better. Just the same, as the engines roared and the plane began its takeoff, Francesca took hold of her rosary beads and the pictures of her grandchildren, and began to pray.

There was no point in taking chances.

CHAPTER 2

No one was there to greet Francesca when the plane arrived at T.F. Green Airport in Warwick, a few miles outside of Providence. This had been the cause of no small amount of consternation on the part of Roseanne, who had wrung her hands about it the entire day before her mother flew home. Wasn't there anyone who could give her a ride from the airport, her daughter had asked? Who would carry her suitcase, and who would make sure she got safely in the door? And what if something was amiss in the house? It was winter back in the Northeast, cold and snowy. What if she slipped and fell walking up the steps? Why didn't she move out of that stupid old house and into an apartment in a nice building where they made sure the walks were always shoveled and clean? Or why couldn't Francesca just move to Florida or Oregon, where at least one sister or the other could look after her?

It was always the same for Roseanne, and for her sister, Alice, as well. No matter how well or poorly a visit with their mother might have gone, the day of parting was inevitably one filled with pangs of regret and guilt at the thought of the old woman being forced to fly all the way home by herself. The one consolation was always that their brother, Joey, could be counted on to be there at the airport to pick her up. Thirty-two and unmarried, Joey was the youngest of Francesca's three children and the only one to stay close to home. This time, however, Joey himself was away on vacation. He and his rugby friends had decided to take a trip to Australia, to see, his sisters and mother could only surmise, if banging into one another's heads felt any different in that part of the world than it did in New England. In any case, Joey would be gone for the better part of a month, so Francesca was on her own.

Not that she minded.

When the plane landed and Francesca began to make her way out with the rest of the herd, she knew that she would be perfectly capable of carrying her one small suitcase out of the airport, of finding a taxicab to carry her home, and of negotiating the perilous ten paces up the walkway to her front door. Of this she had tried in vain to assure her daughter that day she flew home from Florida. She was a big girl, she told her. And so, when she finally collected her suitcase and made her way to the exit, Francesca was unperturbed by the bone-chilling blast of cold air that swept across the parking lot like a wave of ice water to welcome her when she stepped outside. It affected her little that the bright Florida sunshine and warm, caressing breeze was replaced by the pale gray shroud of a January sky hanging gloomily over the city as she rode home in the taxi. She didn't mind trudging through the crusty snow that blanketed the walkway to the front steps; the cab driver, after all, was kind enough to carry her suitcase for her. These were all things for which Francesca had prepared herself. How could she have done otherwise? She was a New Englander born and bred.

There was, however, one thing for which Francesca was never quite ready, something that always took her by surprise whenever she came home. That particular day, as was so often the case, she encountered it in that very first moment after she stepped inside the house. Francesca set her suitcase on the floor and closed the door behind her. Somewhere in the back of her mind, of course, she knew that it had been there all along, bid-ing its time, waiting for her return. Still, she chose to forget about it, to push even the thought of it as far back into her sub-conscious as she possibly could, for it was the one thing that made coming home very difficult, the one thing that, if she dwelt on it, was able to let the harbingers of despair creep into her soul.

The silence.

Alone in the hallway, unwinding the scarf from around her neck, Francesca felt the heavy stillness of the house pressing in all around her, squeezing the breath out of her, keeping her from moving further within. It was like standing in the middle of an elevator that was becoming more and more crowded at each successive floor. Except here, there were no people crush-ing in on her, only the memories of those who had once hap-pily occupied that same space with her and the echoes of their voices. The joys and sorrows, the laughter and tears, the tranquil and chaotic moments alike, all rushed in and smothered her, like little children greeting a work-weary parent at the door.

Francesca stood there for a time, listening intently. The house, she soon realized, was not completely silent. From the kitchen came the humming of the refrigerator, and from the living room the relentless *tock tock tock* of the clock on the mantel. Added to these was the low grumble of the furnace in the basement. The monotonous tones, however, did little to dispel the gloomy quiet. There was something unsettling about them that served only to deepen her sense of isolation, and in their monotony, they drove home all the more emphatically the point that there was no one there but her.

Francesca tugged off her overcoat, hung it in the closet, then reached down to collect the pile of bills and solicitations that the mailman had deposited through the slot in the front door. Everything was still addressed to Mr. and Mrs. Leonard Campanile. Leo had been gone for over eight years, but Francesca had never bothered to change the name on her mailing address to reflect the fact that she was a widow. Somehow, seeing their names together on the envelopes kept a glimmer of hope burning inside that her husband, even though she could no longer see him, was still in the parlor watching television while awaiting her return, or sitting at the kitchen table reading the paper like he always did, or perhaps upstairs on the bed taking a nap. She half-expected to find him there waiting for her every time she walked through the front door; that half of her felt it keenly when, inevitably, she did not.

Sifting through the mail, Francesca's spirits brightened, when she spied a postcard nestled between the electric bill and a credit card offer. It was from Australia. The front side of the card showed two photographs side by side. Francesca regarded the pictures uneasily. The one on the left was of a young man standing atop the railing of what appeared to be a rather high bridge. Around his ankle was tied some sort of rope. Behind him, a group of smiling onlookers seemed to be cheering the young fool on. The photograph to the right showed the man in midair, his eyes and mouth as wide as saucers as he plummeted off the side of the bridge toward the water far below. The caption on the card read: TAKING THE PLUNGE DOWN UNDER!

Francesca shuddered at the thought of her son doing such a thing. She made the sign of the cross and flipped the card over. It read:

Hi Mom!
Having a wonderful time! Just as well you're not here.
Joey

"*Dio mio!*" Francesca exclaimed, looking up to heaven. "What an idiot!"

Refusing to give it another thought, for the whole idea of her son jumping off a bridge just for fun gave her the jimjams, Francesca dropped the postcard back in with the rest of the mail and went to the kitchen. Along the way, she paused to check the thermostat, which she had left set at fifty-five degrees. It was now only slightly warmer than that in the house, and Francesca considered nudging it up a few degrees. She paused and considered the newly arrived gas bill. Pulling the collar of her sweater more tightly about her neck, she decided to leave the thermostat just as it was.

Once in the kitchen, she set the mail onto the table in a neat stack and turned to look out the window over the sink. If the interior of her home seemed gloomy to her, the exterior was positively bleak. It was late afternoon, and the barren trees and shrubs swayed back and forth in the cold wind, while the sun slowly fell off to the west. A thin cover of hard, frozen snow lay across most of the backyard, though here and there a patch of ground managed to show itself. The picnic table at which Francesca liked to sit during the warm weather was blanketed, as were the nearby gardens in which she occasionally liked to putter around. Across the yard, a bird feeder clung to a tree branch. Francesca had filled it before leaving for Florida, but now it was empty, swinging to-and-fro like a pendulum in the wind, not a bird in sight. This saddened Francesca, because she welcomed the sight of the birds happily pecking away at the feeder. They were a sign that life was still close by even though it was the dead of winter.

Francesca gave a little sigh, turned away from the window, and went to the refrigerator. It was several hours since she had last eaten. The stewardess had offered her a snack during the flight home, but Francesca had said no. She had been too nervous to eat. Besides, Roseanne had packed a pepper-and-egg sandwich for her in case she really became hungry. She had ended up giving it to the young man sitting next to her. He had never before tasted a pepper-and-egg sandwich, so the look of surprise and pleasure on his face when he took his first bite had been the only bright spot of the journey. The rest was just a long blur of nervous anxiety.

Now, peering into the refrigerator, Francesca realized that

the anxiety had all passed, but she still did not feel hungry, or if she did, she didn't care. There was plenty on hand in the refrigerator for her to whip up something quick, but the thought of eating alone at that particular moment took away any satisfaction the meal might have given her. Added to that was the sudden weariness that settled in on her like someone had just handed her a sack of potatoes. She was too tired to cook.

Francesca closed the refrigerator door and walked out of the kitchen to the front hall. Her daughter, she well knew, would be waiting by the telephone back in Florida, anxious to hear that her mother had made it home safely. Francesca would call her from the bedroom and then lie down to rest. She took hold of her suitcase and turned toward the staircase.

"Leo," she called as she started up the stairs, "I'm home."

CHAPTER 3

"Tony, you call these tomatoes?"

Tony, the grocer, who at the moment was putting out cucumbers on the shelf across the aisle, looked over at Francesca and gave a shrug. "Well, that's what it said on the carton they came in, Mrs. Campanile," he replied with a good-natured smile. Francesca had been coming to the market for years, and Tony had long since become accustomed to her occasional criticisms of the produce selection.

Francesca picked up a piece of the fruit, breathed in what little she could detect of its scent, and made a face that suggested her assessment of it had been less than favorable. She dropped the tomato back in the bin with the others and shook her head in disdain.

"The cardboard boxes these came in probably have more flavor," she suggested ruefully. "I should find another market."

"Ayyy, what do you expect?" laughed Tony. "Nobody has good tomatoes this time of year."

"Ayyy, and that's what you always say," replied Francesca, shaking her hand at him for emphasis. "What are you doing? Hiding all the good tomatoes for yourself? I should go to the supermarket down the road. *They* probably have some nice tomatoes there that actually taste like tomatoes. These things don't even *look* like tomatoes."

Tony chuckled, for this was a scene that had been played out many times there in his little corner market just down the street from Francesca's house. Inwardly, Francesca gave in to a smile of her own. Both of them knew full well that, despite the lower prices and the greater selection to be found in the huge super-markets, Francesca preferred the comfort and convenience of her own little neighborhood market. It felt almost like a part of her home. Why would she go anywhere else when Tony carried just about everything she needed? Sure, the detergent and paper goods were a little more expensive, and the store didn't stock fifteen brands of every item, but nobody anywhere had a better meat selection than Tony's Market, and the produce, despite her occasional gripes in the winter, was the best around. But there was more to it than just the meat and the fruit and the vegeta-bles that kept her coming back.

Though she would not have admitted it at the moment, Francesca stayed away from the big markets for one simple rea-son: They made her dizzy. They were all so big and impersonal. Too many people, too many products, too many aisles. Too many everything. Here, everyone knew her. When she walked into the store, she was always greeted with a "Hello, Mrs. Campanile!" or a "What will you have today, Mrs. Campanile?" It was nice to come to a place where you always found the same faces and everybody knew you. Francesca rarely had to waste time look-ing around for help if she couldn't find what she was looking for on the shelf or if it was up out of reach. It seemed as though someone would always be nearby looking out for her. "Oh, we moved the spices yesterday to the next aisle over," Tony might tell her before she needed to ask. "Let me get that for you, Mrs. Campanile," one of his sons might say before she had a chance to lift her hand. "Try this new brand of pasta we just got in, Mrs. Campanile. I think you'll like it," Tony's wife, Donna, might sug-gest. Those little gestures of familiarity meant a lot to Francesca. They were the primary reason she always returned. Then, of course, there was the pleasure of knowing that if she was in the mood to complain about anything, a not-uncommon occurrence, she didn't need to go searching all over creation for the manager. Tony, or Donna, or one of their sons, was always right there every day. There was nothing she liked better than to give one or all of them a good earful now and then, just to keep them on their toes. It made her day. In an odd sort of way, it made theirs as well. They all knew that her occasional outbursts were nine-tenths playful bluster.

The dearth of decent tomatoes, however, was a source of true consternation to Francesca. Not that she blamed Tony for it. She well understood that, no matter where she shopped, the bland, flavorless pieces of near-plastic grown hothouses or shipped in from somewhere overseas were all that she would find in the middle of the winter. There was nothing to be done about it. But how she longed for those beautiful native tomatoes of late summer! Gazing at the pile of (not) cheap imitations, she tried in her mind to replace them with the sweet, succulent varieties from the local farms she would find there in the balmy days of August. The cherry tomatoes, bursting with sweetness at the first bite. The big beef tomatoes, so luscious and heavily laden with flavor that just one was a meal in itself. And her favorites, the oval-shaped plums. It was enough to bring tears to her eyes.

Leo, of course, had kept a tomato garden for years, spoiling Francesca. How could these pale things before her even compare? There were not words enough to describe the scent and taste of a sun-warmed tomato just plucked from the vine. Sinking your teeth into it, letting the sweet juiciness fill you up, renewed the life inside you. It was like eating sunshine. There was no end to the uses to which she would put those beautiful sun-ripened tomatoes from her husband's garden. Marinara sauces, pizza, salads, sandwiches. Her favorite, though, was a simple tomato salad. Francesca would start by cutting up the tomatoes and tossing them into a bowl with a healthy dose of virgin olive oil. Next, she would add a clove or two worth of diced garlic, some chopped basil and oregano picked fresh from her own little garden, then pinches of salt and pepper. Finally, she would toss it all together once or twice, and she was done. The addition of a loaf of fresh-baked bread and maybe a nice piece of cheese was all anyone needed for dinner on a hot summer's evening. If she and her husband were really hungry, they found that nothing went better with those tomatoes than a thick juicy steak hot off the grill. That was Leo's favorite meal in the summer. He loved to scoop up the tomatoes and drizzle the juice and olive oil and bits of garlic onto the meat. It brought a contented smile to his face every time. Despite the paltry selection of produce before Francesca, the memory brought a wistful smile to her face. She let out a long sigh.

"Cooking for the family tonight?" asked Tony, bringing her back from her reveries.

"Eh, I wish, Tony," she answered, shaking her head. "No, it's only me tonight. I was just in the mood for some nice tomatoes, that's all. Something to make me forget about all this cold weather." She cast another baleful look at the tomatoes. "But I can't bring myself to do it," she said glumly.

"I know what you mean," Tony confessed with a nod of his head. "Tell you the truth, I won't eat those things myself. But I suppose they're better than nothing in the winter. Just be patient. It'll be summer before you know it, and we'll have some nice tomatoes in. By then, of course, we'll all be complaining because it's so hot outside."

"And by then you'd better make sure that *inside* you have that air conditioner working again," she admonished him. "Not like that time last summer when it broke and it was a hundred degrees in here."

"Ayyy, don't worry," sighed Tony. "My wife has already reminded me a thousand times about that. You two are a lot alike; you never forget anything."

"It comes with being a woman."

With that, Francesca continued on to collect the few things that she needed from the market that day. In truth, she could have managed quite well with what she already had at home. But it had been two days since she had returned from Florida, and this was the first time she had stepped outside. Already it felt as though the walls were closing in around her, so a trip to the market had been a good excuse to get out of the house. The previous day had been spent unpacking, washing her clothes, getting her closet back in order. Then there were the bills to be paid, and the appointments to be confirmed to have her hair done and to get a checkup from the doctor. Francesca liked to have everything in order. She started each day by making a list of things she needed to do. While she sipped her morning coffee, she would check the list from the day before to see if there was anything she had forgotten. She lived alone, so it was easy to forget things. Organizing her day in this way made her life easier. It kept her busy and made the days when she was alone pass more quickly.

The only items on the list for her excursion to the market were a half gallon of milk and a loaf of bread. The tomatoes had been an afterthought. A few other odds and ends caught her eye as she made her way up and down the aisles. She tossed them into the cart and ambled along. Francesca took her time; there was really no hurry. She had no place else in particular to go and nothing else to do that day. Now and then, she cast a glance over to the entrance, hoping to spy a familiar face coming in, one of her market friends, as she liked to call them. Most of her old friends from the neighborhood were gone, some having moved to warmer climes, some to retirement centers or nursing homes, and some directly to the next life. Still, there were new faces she had come to know, younger couples who had moved in to take the place of the old. Francesca enjoyed seeing these new people, exchanging a few moments of pleasant conversation with the younger women, commenting on the price of this or that, complaining about the weather. Most of all, she loved seeing their little children, especially the newborns. It gave her hope.

On this day, however, there was no one in the store she recognized, so she pushed her cart up to the checkout counter, where Tony's wife, Donna, waited by the cash register.

"Find everything you need, Mrs. Campanile?" she asked. "I see you have your milk and bread. That's good. They say we might get some snow later today."

"Oh, yes," Francesca replied as she started to put her groceries up on the counter. "I heard the forecast. I've got everything I need, not that I'm one of those nervous Nellies who thinks the sky is falling every time she sees a few snowflakes, but it never hurts to be prepared."

"They say we might get six or seven inches," Donna said as she scanned the groceries. "Sounds like it will be a good night to just stay home."

Francesca nodded and smiled. "What else would I do?" she thought.

CHAPTER 4

A few fragile flakes from the approaching snowstorm were already drifting down when Francesca left the market and started on her way home. It was late morning, nearing lunchtime, and the cars zipped up and down the road as she walked along the sidewalk. There was a palpable feeling of nervous tension in the air; she could see it in the faces of the passing motorists as they hastened along, almost frantic to run their errands before the real snow started to fall. Watching them go by, seeing the impatient frowns of the men and the worried looks of the women chirping away on their cell phones instead of paying attention to the road, Francesca could not help but laugh. It was always the same whenever the weathermen predicted a winter storm. The specter of a few inches of snow put everyone in a tizzy.

Clutching the handles of the cloth bag in which she carried her groceries, Francesca made her way along the sidewalk, keeping a watchful eye on the pavement lest she slip on a patch of ice. That was all she needed to have happen. God forbid she should fall and hurt herself; she would never hear the end of it from her son and daughters. Francesca might just have easily taken the car to the market instead of walking; she was a perfectly capable driver. But she liked the exercise and enjoyed being out in the open air. Besides, in her mind, the world was already going by much too fast. As far as she was concerned, people spent too much time hurrying from one place to another, from one task to another, without ever taking a moment to appreciate the journey. People, she often observed, would be far better off if they could only learn to slow their lives down a bit, but they were generally in too much of a rush to give the idea much thought.

An added benefit of walking to the market was the opportunity it afforded Francesca to monitor the comings and goings in the area. Hers wasn't what one might call a tough section of town by any means, but some of the shine had gone off the neighborhood since she and Leo had first moved there years ago. The main avenue down which she was walking was lined with two- and three-decker tenements, where generations of predominately Irish and Italian families had once lived together. They had been proud people who had kept their properties immaculate. It grieved Francesca to see the dilapidated condition into which many of those beautiful old homes had descended since the old families had moved out. Not that it was the fault of the new Hispanic and Asian families that had taken their place. Francesca blamed the landlords from whom the new families rented the houses. Had they lost all their pride? She was heartened, though, by the new shops and little restaurants and other businesses she saw the newcomers opening here and there. The neighborhood, as she saw it, was in transition. In time, these renters would become owners, and then those houses would be restored to their proper states. It was inevitable. Nothing instilled pride in a person more than owning his own home.

Francesca rounded the corner off the main road and walked up the street to her house. The street climbed a considerably steep hill, but her legs were more than equal to the task. Over the years, she'd made that climb more times than she could remember. When she finally made it to the house and through the front door, Francesca hurried straight to the kitchen, to put away her groceries. Her haste was not due to any great concern about the food spoiling. She kept the temperature so low inside that even if she left it all out on the counter, everything would probably stay fresh for days. Her real purpose in bustling so purposefully through the hallway to the kitchen was the reassuring noise that it created. It dispelled some of the quiet in the house and made her feel like less of a ghost rattling around within its walls.

The little red light on the telephone answering machine was flashing when she came into the kitchen. She gave the button a tap and listened to the messages while she sorted out the groceries on the table. The first was from Alice: "Hi, Mom. It's me. Just wanted to see how you were doing. I talked to Rosie yesterday. She said you guys had a good time together at her house. Hope you're all settled back in, now that you're home. We were watching the Weather Channel last night, and they said a big storm is heading your way. Looks like you might get a lot of snow. Make sure you stay inside. Don't try to shovel the walk or clean the car by yourself. Get one of the neighborhood kids to do it. You don't want to slip and fall. Anyway, no snow out here, just a lot of rain this week. So, that's all. I just wanted to say hi. Hope to see you soon. Yesterday, Will and Charlie were wondering when you were going to come out to visit us again in Oregon. They miss your lasagna. Give me a call when you get a chance. Love you."

A beep, then the next message, this one from Rosanne: "Hi, Mom, It's me. You home? What are you doing? Out gallivanting again, or are you just screening your calls? No? Not there? Okay, just wanted to see how you're doing. I talked to Alice yesterday. Told her about your trip. Heard you guys might get a bunch of snow up there today, so I hope you get home soon before it starts. Call me."

A succession of beeps without messages followed, then: "Hello. This is the West End Public Library calling to let you know that some books you reserved have come in. We'll hold them here for a week. Thank you."

Francesca hurriedly put the groceries away and picked up the telephone to call Alice in Oregon. She was a little concerned because, given the time difference, her daughter ought to have been at work. Was something wrong, something she hadn't mentioned in her message? Francesca was always trying to read between the lines in this way, wondering how much her children didn't tell her about what was going on in their lives. It troubled her deeply. True, her children were all adults now. But even though they were all grown up, they still had a lot they could learn from their mother. There were still lots of ways she knew she could help them if they would only let her. Francesca knew that Rosie and Alice did their utmost to withhold from her anything that they thought might make her worry. But that only made her worry all the more! In her mind, it would be better to know the truth and play a part in dealing with it.

As was most often the case, though, there was nothing for Francesca to worry about. Alice had stayed out of work that day simply because her son Will had a case of the sniffles. Francesca was relieved. Just the same, she lectured Alice on making sure that her son got plenty of rest and drank enough fluids. A nice bowl of chicken-and-escarole soup would probably do wonders. She gave her daughter the recipe. For her part, Alice lectured her mother on the dangers of the ice and snow sure to accompany the storm the weathermen were predicting. Rosie did the same when Francesca called her a little while later. Francesca assured both of them that they needn't worry; she wasn't about to taking any chances with the weather. It gave her a modicum of satisfaction to know that now *they* were worrying about *her*. What goes around always comes around.

When she was finished talking to Rosie, Francesca hung up the phone, erased the messages on the answering machine, and paused to look out the back window. The kitchen was her favorite room in the house, not so much because of her love of cooking, but because of the beautiful view it afforded of the city. When the leaves were off the trees, like they were at this time of year, you could look out across the backyard and see all the way downtown, to the dome of the State House, and beyond, to the houses up on the East Side. Turning over in her mind the third message on the answering machine, she stared thoughtfully at the drab shroud of gray clouds that had covered the sky over the city since her return from Florida. The snowflakes, she noticed, were coming down now with greater urgency, in a light but steady flurry. Deep within herself, part of Francesca was urging her to just stay inside, to curl up on the couch and take a nap. Another part of her, though, longed to be out of the house once more despite her daughters's advice to just stay put. She fretted about it for only a minute before deciding to pull her overcoat and hat back on.

"This is New England," she told herself while she fished the car keys out of her pocketbook. "It's supposed to snow in the winter."

CHAPTER 5

The librarian was gazing out the window at the thickening snowfall when Francesca walked in. A small, handwritten sign on the young woman's desk announced that, due to the approaching storm, the weekly book club meeting had been cancelled for that afternoon. Francesca was not particularly disappointed by the announcement; she hadn't planned to attend the gathering. Still, she could not suppress a sigh of consternation at the thought of it. The library, she guessed, would be closing early as well. The coat and pocketbook resting to the librarian's side confirmed her suspicions.

"Hello, Rebecca," said Francesca.

The young librarian turned to Francesca with fretful eyes. "Oh, hi, Mrs. Campanile," she said, taking nervous note of the snowflakes on the shoulders of Francesca's coat and hat. "It looks like it's really starting to come down out there. Are the roads getting bad?"

"Treacherous," Francesca fibbed. "My car barely made it up the hill to get here."

Rebecca cast an anxious glance at the clock on the wall. "We're closing in a half hour—at two—today," she advised her. Then, worriedly, "Is it really that bad out?"

The mischievous side of Francesca wanted to string the girl along a little further, but she thought better of it. "No, honey," she answered with a smile. "I was just having a little fun with you. Trust me, if an old lady like me can drive through this weather, so can you. You're too young to be so worried about a few flakes of snow."

"Ugh," the young woman sighed. "I hate driving in the snow."

Francesca set a cloth bag atop the desk. It was one of many she kept at home, in the closet by the front door. She had a sturdy bag ready for every occasion; this one she used to tote her books to and from the library. "I understand you have some new books for me," she said, nodding to the bookshelf behind Rebecca.

Rebecca found the three items reserved for Francesca—two books and a set of Vietnamese language tapes—and placed them on the desktop next to her computer. She opened the cover of the first book and passed a handheld scanner over the bar code on the inside of the front cover. "Hmm, what are you studying this time?" she said, looking over the book's cover with curiosity. *"Perspectives on Vietnamese Culture,"* she read. "Sounds interesting. Plus a Fodor's guide to traveling in Vietnam," she noted as she scanned the next book and then the language tapes. "Looks like someone is getting ready to take a trip to Southeast Asia."

"Just in my mind," chuckled Francesca. "Flying to Florida was far enough for me. I just like to study new things now and then, especially during the winter. It passes the time and keeps my brain from drying up inside my head."

It was true. Francesca sometimes enjoyed watching television to pass the long, lonely nights at home, but more often than not, she preferred to put her mind to a more active use. She never quite understood why, but there was something about learning new things that gave her a warm feeling inside and always made her feel better about herself, especially whenever she was feeling a little down. For Francesca, to learn something new was to become a child again. Whether it was dabbling with a foreign language, or delving into ancient history, or struggling to understand the basic principles of physics, there seemed to be nothing that didn't pique her curiosity. When she tired of one subject, she simply moved on to the next. Her son, Joey, had often suggested that she might enjoy taking some night courses at one of the local colleges, perhaps work toward a degree in some field of study that she found interesting. Francesca, though, had always decided against it. Why should she pay all that money to take a course when she could learn everything she could ever want to learn for free right there at the local library?

"Well, learning to speak Vietnamese should keep you busy for a while," said Rebecca, handing her the books and the tapes.

"We'll see," said Francesca, tucking everything into her bag. "Not that I ever expect to use the language. It's just fun to know a little about these things sometimes."

"Hey, you never know," said Rebecca. "There are lots of Vietnamese people living in this part of the city now. Maybe you'll make some new friends."

"Maybe," said Francesca with a laugh. "I suppose there might be some old Vietnamese ladies around for me to talk to."

"Or maybe a Vietnamese man," said Rebecca playfully. "It won't be long before it's Valentine's Day, you know."

"Oh, please," laughed Francesca. "That's all I need right now." She turned and nodded to the clock. "So I guess you'll be chasing everyone out in a few minutes, right?"

"Sorry," shrugged Rebecca, looking only slightly sincere.

"Okay," sighed Francesca. She had collected her things and was just starting to go when someone called to her from the back of the library.

"Frannie, is that you?" came a familiar voice.

Francesca looked about and saw Peg, one of her library friends, beckoning to her from the little computer room in the back. The library offered seniors free classes in Word and Excel, whatever they were, but Francesca rarely set foot in that room.

When she wasn't taking out a book during one of her frequent visits to the library, she preferred to sit with the other library regulars in the periodicals section, perusing the nice variety of journals and magazines on display there. Now and then, though, she peeked into the computer room just to take a look at the monitors, which seemed to glow at her like giant square eyes. Though curious about the machines, she had yet to put her fingers on a keyboard. Francesca knew that everyone, even old biddies like Peg, were learning how to use computers, but something about even going near them made her uneasy. There was something threatening about the way they looked at her. Just the same, she nodded a thank-you to Rebecca and strolled over to talk to her friend, who had slipped back into the room.

"Come here, Frannie," whispered Peg when Francesca stepped through the door. "You have to take a look at this."

Francesca saw that Natalie and Connie, another two of her library friends, were seated at the other computer terminals. They both waved hello. The three old women, all of them bundled up in bulky sweaters despite the warmth inside the library, had their eyes glued to their respective computer screens while they pushed around a little plastic device that Francesca had heard them refer to as a mouse. That was another thing that gave Francesca pause. Why would she want to spend her time holding something named after a rodent? Nonetheless, she came closer to Peg and looked over her shoulder. Francesca had heard that people could find all manner of interesting things on the Internet; a world of information was right there at your fingertips, at least so they said. She was prepared to find Peg poring over an article about some new medical discovery, or perhaps reading up on investment advice for seniors. Instead, much to her embarrassed surprise, she found herself gazing at a full-screen photograph of Brad Pitt wearing little more than a pair of undershorts.

"Look at those abs," enthused Peg. "Ooh, what I wouldn't give to be thirty years younger!"

"Thirty? Try forty," suggested Natalie. She tugged her knit hat down further over her ears to stay warm before turning her attention back to the chat group she had logged on to.

"While you're at it, why not go for fifty?" added Connie, who was logged on to a chat group of her own. "I just told this guy that I'm blonde and twenty-one. He wants to do lunch."

Francesca gave a little cough to clear her throat. "My," she said, trying not to stare at the picture. "All this time, I thought you three were learning about word processing and spreadsheets and the rest of it."

"Ayyy, forget that stuff," huffed Peg. "It's boring. The Internet is where all the fun is. You can find just about anything or anyone you want to look at. All you have to do is Google them."

"Goo-goo?" said Francesca. "What's that all about? Babies?"

"No, silly," laughed Peg. "Goo-*gull*, not goo-*goo*. Don't you know anything?"

"Afraid not," sighed Francesca. "At least, not about these things."

"You should give it a try," suggested Natalie. "It's a cinch."

"What for?" replied Francesca. "What am I going to find out there with that thing that's so wonderful? I'd rather read a book."

"Don't know what you're missing," said Connie. "Besides, what else is there for old bats like us to do? It's fun, and e-mail's a great way to keep in touch with people."

"Ayyy, that's what they invented stamps and envelopes for," said Francesca. "There's nothing like getting a nice handwritten letter."

"*Letter?*" Peg laughed along with the other two women. "What century are you living in? Nobody writes letters anymore."

"Yes, I know," said Francesca grumpily. "That's another thing I miss these days." She gave another sigh. "Well, at least I know how to use the telephone whenever I want to hear someone's voice."

Peg pulled her eyes away from Brad Pitt long enough to give Francesca a thoughtful look. "What's with the puss on your face today, Frannie?" she asked after a moment. "Everything okay?"

"Oh, yeah," said Francesca, giving a shrug. "Just feeling a little blue, that's all."

"What about? You just got back from Florida, right? Everything okay down there with your family?"

"Yes, of course," Francesca replied. "They're all fine. It's just that . . .'" She paused and looked away, her hands fidgeting with the straps of her book bag.

"What?" said Peg.

By now, Natalie and Connie had turned away from their monitors and were listening to what Francesca had to say. Francesca looked back at them, unable to suppress the glum expression on her face.

"I don't know," she finally answered, giving a shrug. "It's just that I keep thinking about my daughters and my grandchildren. They're all so far away. I miss them, even more since I just saw them. Who knows, my son will probably move away somewhere next. You'd think that after all these years, I'd be used to it by now, but it just seems to feel worse every day. Lately, I just feel useless."

"Don't we all," sighed Connie.

"Don't worry, Frannie," said Peg kindly. "It's just the winter getting you down, that's all. It's cold and dark outside, and we're all cooped up inside. What, you're supposed to be dancing a jig every minute of the day? But I know what you mean. It happens to me sometimes too, especially in January."

"Me too," Natalie added.

"Nighttime's the worst for me," said Connie, nodding her head. "Sometimes all I do is sit in my kitchen and think about my children."

"It's so strange, isn't it?" said Francesca. "I can remember a time when I couldn't wait for mine to all finally grow up and move out of the house and just stop driving me crazy. Now, a day doesn't go by without my wishing that I could have them all back upstairs at night, sleeping in their beds. I'd pay anything to have them small like that again for just one more day, to see them wake up and come downstairs for breakfast in the morning."

"Who wouldn't?" said Peg. "But life goes on. You can't waste your time wishing you could turn back the clock. You should be happy just for the time you do spend with your children because, let me tell you, no matter where they live, there are no guarantees. My kids all still live in Rhode Island, and I hardly every get a chance to see them. I'm thinking about moving down to Florida. At least then, maybe they'll want to visit me with the grandkids more often in the winter. You haven't got it so bad. Besides, you still have your son close to home."

"Ayyy, that one," scoffed Francesca. "He might just as well be living on the far side of the moon. The only time I get to see him is when he's hungry or he wants me to do his laundry for him. The kid needs a wife."

"Yeah, but then what would there be for you to do?" asked Natalie.

"You know, you're not being very helpful," replied Francesca ruefully.

At that, the four women all laughed.

Feeling a little better, Francesca looked across the library to the front desk, where Rebecca was pulling on her overcoat. "Well, I guess I better get going. Looks like Chicken Little's getting ready to throw us all out any second."

"Bah," huffed Natalie with a wave of her hand.

"Let her try," Connie chimed in.

Francesca turned to go.

"Hey, Frannie," said Peg, patting her hand, "try not to worry about it, okay? Before you know it, it will be spring, and things will look a lot brighter."

"Sure, I guess," said Francesca. "But what do I do in the meantime to keep myself from going crazy?"

"You have those," said Peg, nodding to her book bag.

"And if they don't do the trick?"

"Then you can always try what I do on those days when I'm a little bit down in the dumps."

"What's that?"

Peg smiled and nodded to the monitor. "I check out those abs."

Later that evening, Francesca stood at the kitchen counter, beating some eggs in a bowl. She stirred in a little milk and some bits of cheese before pouring it all over a batch of ground beef and onions she had sizzling in a frying pan atop the stove. While everything simmered, she threw together a quick salad of lettuce and cucumbers, with a little oil and vinegar as a simple dressing, then she turned her attention back to the eggs, moving them around with a spatula to keep them from sticking to the bottom of the pan. When they were cooked, she pushed them onto a plate, added a splash of Tabasco sauce, and poured herself a little glass of red wine. The addition of the heel of a loaf of bread made it a simple but hearty meal, more than enough to warm her up a little on a cold winter's night. Francesca put everything onto a dinner tray and carried it into the den.

Francesca set the tray on a TV table and sat down on the sofa, listening all the while to the intensifying storm. For once, the weathermen had gotten it right; it was snowing like crazy outside. In fact, it had already started to come down quite heavily by the time she had left the library earlier that afternoon. The snowplows had not yet cleaned the roads, and it was a slick, jittery ride home after brushing off the car; she had regretted being so smug with Rebecca, the librarian. The wind now had started to howl and to toss great handfuls of icy snow, which sprittered against the windowpanes like grains of sand. The sound of it made Francesca shiver, and she pulled a throw over her legs and feet. As she contemplated her dinner, her thoughts drifted to Florida and Oregon and Australia, all of them nice warm places far from the cold and the whirlwinds of snow that were spinning wildly across her backyard like drunken dancers. She looked up and let her eyes scan the photographs of her children and grandchildren covering virtually every square inch of the den's walls. She gazed longest at a photograph from Christmas two years earlier. It was the last time that she had had everyone all together at the same time. It had been a wonderful day for, her and the memory brought a brief smile to her face.

Francesca reached over and popped the first of the language tapes into the cassette player on the table by the sofa. As the tape started to play, she lifted her wineglass to her family.

"*Salute,*" she told them. "Sleep tight tonight, my sweets."

Then she took a sip of wine and began to eat her supper.

CHAPTER 6

The telephone rang first thing the next morning. It was Rosie, of course, checking in to see if her mother had survived the big storm. It wouldn't be long before Alice awoke out west and called as well. Though she would never have let on to her daughters, Francesca had already been up since the crack of dawn. The moment she had gotten out of bed that morning, she had dressed quickly, pulled on her boots and coat, and headed outside.

The raucous winds of the previous night had diminished to barely a whisper earlier that morning when Francesca had stepped out the front door and surveyed the scene. It seemed to her then that the entire world had gone white, as if overnight the skies had chosen to blanket the earth and the roofs of the houses inches deep with baby powder. The low-lying bushes and shrubs to either side of the front stoop had disappeared, and the branches of the evergreens drooped beneath the weight of the snow that clung to them like enormous cotton balls. As she waded across the yard to the driveway, all was quiet and still, every sound softened in that way it usually is after a heavy snowfall. Even the engine of a passing sander was muffled to a low grumble, the sand whisking out the back sounding like the bristles of a shoe brush moving against leather. There was something peaceful and soothing about it all, the quiet and the frozen landscape. It was as if nature had chosen to take matters into her own hands and slow the world down, if only for a short while.

It was difficult to tell precisely how much snow had fallen. In some places, the wind had sculpted it into fanciful wavelike drifts that curled up as high as four feet, while in other spots, it had left patches of ground completely bare, hardly a flake to be seen. Francesca guessed that at least a foot or more of the white stuff had come down. One thing was for sure: There was far too much snow for her shovel. The front walk was buried, and the passing plows had left a small mountain at the end of the driveway.

Francesca assessed the situation and let out a grumble at the thought of her son, who was off, at that moment, somewhere on the far side of the world, soaking up the warm Australian sunshine. Joey usually stopped by to dig her out on days like this. Arranging for someone to take over for him in the event of snow while he was gone was the one item she had forgotten to put on her list of things to do before she went to Florida. Francesca cast an annoyed glance at her driveway. It was obvious that she wouldn't be driving anywhere that day. Just the same, she brushed off the driver's side door, started the engine, and left it running to warm things up while she cleaned off the rest of the car.

By the time Rosie called, Francesca was already back inside, warming her toes by the kitchen radiator while percolating coffee on the stove.

"Yes," Francesca told her after she answered the phone, "it really came down last night. There's definitely no school in Foster-Glocester. The Weather Channel said we got how much? Eighteen inches? Wow. I don't know. I think we got more than that around here, but it's hard to tell just from looking outside."

Then, "No, now don't worry. I'll find someone to shovel me out. What? No, I haven't got anywhere to go today."

Rosie was in a state, lecturing Francesca as if she were bundling up a child before sending her off to school on a cold, blustery day. How did she get to be such a bag of nerves? One would never have guessed that she had grown up in New England.

"Yes, yes, yes," Francesca assured her daughter. "I'll probably just stay right inside today. The car's snowed in, so where would I go?"

The conversation went much the same when Alice called a little while later. While they talked, Francesca sipped her coffee and eyed the patches of blue breaking out across the morning sky. The sun was finally getting ready to show its face again.

"It's about time," she said to herself, interrupting Alice, who was in the middle of warning her against trying to shovel the driveway by herself.

"Say that again, Mom," said her younger daughter.

"Never mind. It was nothing," replied Francesca. "Just talking to myself. You were saying . . ."

By late morning, the clouds had drifted away, leaving behind clear skies for as far as the eye could see. The January sun was not nearly strong enough to melt away any of the snow; it was still quite cold outside. Nonetheless, the brilliant sunshine reflecting off the snow and through the windows brightened even the rooms on the north side of the house, which were normally left in shadows throughout the day. It almost hurt to look outside.

Francesca sat in the living room, flipping through an old photo album. She was trying to find the pictures from the great Blizzard of '78, a vicious nor'easter that had struck the region with sudden and startling fury. Packing hurricane-force winds, the storm had unexpectedly hit with full power at midday, downing power lines and sending cars skidding into each other on the highways. There were dozens of accidents, stalling traffic in every direction and blocking roads all over the state before the snowplows had a chance to clear them. Stranded motorists were forced to abandon their cars wherever they happened to find themselves on the highways and take their chances trudging home through the gale. Several people died, and the entire state, for all intents and purposes, was paralyzed for the better part of a week. After all the years, that blizzard was still the gold standard, the storm by which all other winter weather was measured in Rhode Island. It was as deeply etched into the memories of Rhode Islanders as any great historical event. Those who lived through it could tell you exactly where they were and what they were doing when the storm first blew into town.

Searching through the album, Francesca was curious to see if nature's latest effort measured up. One look at the first photograph she came to was enough to remind her that the previous night's storm wasn't even close. In the photograph, Leo was standing in the driveway up to his waist in snow. With shovel in hand, he gestured to an enormous snowdrift behind him that climbed all the way up the front of the garage to the bottom edge of the gutter. To the side of the drift, a single corner of the rear bumper of the car was the only evidence that anything at all lay beneath. It jutted out of the mound of snow like it was part of a giant piece of marble out of which a sculptor had just begun to chisel an automobile.

Francesca found other pictures from the storm, and even the yellowed front page of the newspaper she had saved from the day after. Reminiscing about the days that had followed, she recalled that, despite all the inconvenience the storm had wrought, it was still one of the most pleasant times she had ever experienced in the neighborhood. As so often happens, the worst of times brought out the very best in people. Neighbors, some of whom had rarely spoken to one another, had gone out of their way to help each other dig out of the mess. Children had frolicked without fear in the middle of the streets because the roads virtually everywhere had been impassable. With their cars all buried and the roads unplowed, people had actually started to walk from place to place near their homes, no small matter for those normally accustomed to automatically jumping behind the wheel for any trip farther than two doors over. Complete strangers had greeted each other with smiles, stopping in the street to chat like old friends as they passed one another. In an unexpected way, people who had lived in the area for years ahd rediscovered their neighborhood, their neighbors, and the warm feeling of community that came from acknowledging that they were all in it together.

Such would not be the case with this storm, Francesca well understood. While ferocious enough in its own right, it had not inflicted anywhere near the mayhem as that storm of 1978. School had been cancelled throughout the state, and many stayed home from work for the day; the weathermen had predicted the snowfall early enough so that this time, people had been well prepared when it hit. With the populace cooperating by staying off the roads, the snowplows and sanders had passed early and often.

It was something of a disappointment to Francesca.

Closing the photo album, she stood and gazed out the front window for a time. From outside, she could hear the scraping of snow shovels and the roaring of a power snowblower somewhere nearby. It might take most of the day to clean things up, probably well into the night, but as soon as people shoveled out their driveways, life would very quickly resume its former frenetic pace. Turning away from the window, she began to walk about the house, looking for something constructive to do to pass the time. All the while, the voices of Rosie and Alice kept echoing in her ears. They were right, of course. She shouldn't even think about going outdoors again. Just the same, Francesca had been born with what her own mother had called *una testa dura:* an exceedingly hard head. Such being the case, she was finding it very difficult to resist the temptation to take a stroll around the block, just to see how the rest of the neighborhood had made out after the storm. It occurred to her that the bill payments neatly stacked on the kitchen table provided a convenient excuse; it was time to put them in the mail. What harm would there be in a quick jaunt down the street and around the corner to the nearest mailbox?

Francesca pondered the answer to that question a short while later while picking herself up out of a snowbank on the side of the main road. The walk down her hill had proven to be more treacherous than she had imagined. True, the road had been plowed well enough, but the snow had been pushed up onto the sidewalks, forcing her to walk along the road's edge. When she rounded the corner at the bottom of the hill onto the main street, she had found that the cars and trucks were already whizzing along, often within inches of her elbow. Determined to reach the mailbox a few hundred yards or so down the road, Francesca had been looking back over her shoulder for approaching cars when she had suddenly lost her footing and toppled sideways into snow. She has landed in a snowbank with a less-than-graceful flop and let out a string of Italian epithets she had learned from her mother. As she stood and tried to brush herself off, furious at the conditions of the roadways, no public official save the Pope was spared her wrath. She trudged on, the snow caked on her hat and up and down her entire backside so that, to motorists overtaking her, she appeared to be a very grumpy walking snowman.

The humor of the sight was not lost on a group of teenaged boys milling about on the front steps of a tenement house as Francesca trod by on her way to the mailbox. They all looked to be of Asian descent, some wearing similar jackets, which suggested they were part of a gang. Fuming as she was, Francesca took little note of them when she first passed. She dropped the bills into the mailbox and turned to go back the way she had come. As she passed the boys once more, one of them stepped closer to the old woman and gave her an impertinent look. He held out his hand, as if asking her for money, then he turned to his friends and said something that made them laugh. Francesca had no idea what the young man had said, but she was reasonably sure that it was not a compliment.

Now, an onlooker to the scene would certainly have been forgiven for thinking that perhaps a very unpleasant confrontation of some sort was about to take place. Francesca herself considered the possibility, but she was not one to be easily cowed. She stopped in her tracks and faced the young toughs.

"*Cam on ong, toi manh*," she said, eyeing them sharply. It meant, "Thank you, I am fine." It was the only phrase she could remember from the language tapes she had been listening to the night before. Judging by the startled, wide-eyed looks on their faces, she knew that she had guessed right that the young men were Vietnamese.

Clearly mortified at the prospect that the old woman might have understood what he had said, the boy who had made the remark that so amused the others flushed with embarrassment. The others, even the gang members, bowed their heads or tried to look in the other direction. Seeing that she had managed to chase some of the bravado out of the boy and his friends, Francesca walked right up to them. She wasn't about to give up the initiative now that she had seized it.

"You speak English?" she asked of the boy who had first addressed her. He was standing there now with his hands in his pockets, trying hard to avoid the gaze of Francesca's blue eyes, which had lost none of their piercing inquisitiveness in her old age.

"At school," he replied sheepishly. Then, trying his best to regain his lost self-assuredness, he rushed to add, "But here we speak our own language."

"There's nothing wrong with that," said Francesca in a mild voice. "It's good that you speak your own language sometimes. It keeps you from forgetting your roots. That's important."

Then she looked past him to the house. "You live here?" she asked.

The boy gave a nod. "Second floor," he said.

"Tell me," said Francesca, "does the dining room still have that nice cabinet built into the corner, and that pretty crystal chandelier hanging over the table?"

Suspecting that perhaps he had unwittingly crossed paths with some sort of witch, the boy gaped at the old woman, as did the others.

"How—how do you know this?" he asked warily.

"Ayyy, because I've been in your house a thousand times," Francesca told him. "This house used to belong to Doctor Ricci and his family. I was good friends with his wife, Dee."

"A doctor lived here?" said the boy incredulously.

By now, the other boys had started to gather around to listen more closely to what Francesca had to say.

"Of course," she went on. "Doctor Ricci had an office on the other side of the city, but sometimes he would come to our houses when one of us was sick, or we'd come by to see him right here. He never charged anyone a penny." Francesca paused and looked about at the surrounding houses. "You'd be surprised; all sorts of important people have lived in these houses," she told them. "Like there, across the street."

"That's my house!" exclaimed a small boy, who until this moment, had been hiding behind the others. He looked no more than nine or ten.

"Well, that's where Judge McCarthy and his family lived for

the longest time," she told the lad. "He was very strict with his children, but he was a good father and one of the nicest gentlemen you'd ever want to meet."

Francesca turned back to the older boy who lived in the Riccis' old house. "What's your name?" she asked him.

"I am Phoung," the young man replied respectfully.

"Hello, Phoung."

"And I'm Tai!" cried the small boy.

"Well, hello, Tai," she answered with a smile.

"I'm Cam," said one of the other boys.

"Bay," said another.

One by one, each of the boys introduced himself.

"Well, it's nice to meet you all," said Francesca. "You remind me of the old days, when my own children used to play with their friends around here. The kids were always in and out of each other's houses and yards. It seemed like everybody knew each other. That's the way it was around here back in those days."

"Pardon me, but what is *your* name?" asked Phoung with great deference. He was still quite chagrined at his earlier misbehavior, and now he was trying his utmost to show respect.

"My name is Mrs. Campanile," said Francesca. At seeing the strained look on their faces, she decided to sound it out for them. "Like this: Com-pah-*neel*-ay."

"Comma . . . ?"

"Oh, just call me Mrs. C," she laughed. Then she let a stern expression come over her face, the same expression she used to wear whenever she gave one of her children a good talking to. The boys all stood rapt.

"I want all you young men to do me a favor," she told them with great solemnity. "I can tell that you are all good kids, so I want you to promise me that you'll always look after the old folks and the little children around here. This has always been a good neighborhood, so now it's your turn to do your part to keep it that way. Can you do that?"

All of them nodded.

"Good," said Francesca. "Now show a little pride. You can start by going home and shoveling off the sidewalks in front of all your houses. How's an old lady like myself supposed to get around the neighborhood without slipping and falling?"

The snow from her recent tumble on the side of the road was still caked on Francesca's coat and hat, so the remark elicited a round of giggles, the boys glancing at one another while trying their best to not laugh out loud.

Not wanting to press her luck further, for in reality they were actually a pack of tough-looking customers, Francesca decided that it was time to go. First, though, she wanted to impress them one last time.

"*Chao ong*," she called over her shoulder as she turned to go, quite pleased with herself for having remembered how to say good-bye. Then she went on her way.

"*Chao ong!*" they all called back..

As she walked away, Francesca heard Phoung say something as if he was giving some sort of an order to one of the other boys. She waited until she came to the corner of her street before casting a quick glance back. To her surprise, she saw that the small boy, Tai, was doing his best to follow her at a discreet distance. At seeing her stop, he ducked behind a telephone pole. Francesca pretended not to notice and proceeded home up the hill.

Back inside the house, Francesca pulled off her coat and boots, and hurried to the front window. She parted the curtain just enough to get a view of the street. Tai, she saw, had followed her all the way home. The small boy walked up the street to the front of the house and stood there for just a moment, before running off back the way he had come. Francesca wondered what he was up to. As she went about her business the rest of the day, she worried all the while that perhaps she had gone too far with those boys, and that they might have some sort of mischief planned for her. Perhaps, she told herself, she had made a mistake in even talking to them, instead of just walking away and keeping her big mouth shut. The thought shadowed her the rest of the day and into the evening while she prepared for bed. It didn't leave her until she awoke the next morning to discover that someone, during the night or the early morning hours, had shoveled out her driveway and cleaned off the front steps and walkway.

CHAPTER 7

"Bless me, Father, for I have sinned."

It was Saturday afternoon, and Francesca was making her confession, as she often did before evening mass. Something about acknowledging her sins, however great or small they might have been, had a way of lifting her spirits and getting her through the week to come. A lift was what she sorely needed, for at the moment she was in decidedly ill humor, and had been all day.

By now, the pleasant glow from Francesca's encounter with Phoung and his friends earlier in the week had faded away, only to be replaced by some considerable soreness in her hip and shoulder, the result of her encounter with the snowbank that same day. Francesca felt certain that she hadn't done herself any serious harm, and indeed, she hadn't. Just the same, she squirmed uncomfortably as she knelt in the confessional. The jolt from the fall had strained her hip and back muscles; they would be tender for the next few days. A few doses of even a mild pain reliever would have done wonders for her. Francesca, however, usually disdained taking medicine of any kind; she preferred to just grit her teeth and bear it. Two nights of poor sleep, though, had left her tired and irritable. She would have to give in later on and take something before bed. Otherwise, she would be tossing and turning all night again. A few aspirin and a good night's rest after confession and mass were sure to chase away the pain and brighten her mood by morning. Till then, though, she was as amiable as a lioness with a thorn in her paw.

"It's been six weeks since I last confessed," she continued, a distinct edge in her voice.

"Ah, Francesca, where have you been?" Father Buontempo said pleasantly from behind the thin little curtain inside his cubicle. "It's been so long, I was beginning to wonder what had become of you."

"*Hey*," Francesca snapped, "you're supposed to at least pretend not to know who I am when I'm giving you my confession. What kind of priest are you?"

"Sorry," he replied, rolling his eyes, knowing she wouldn't see. This wasn't the first time he'd had an exchange of this sort with his parishioner. Experience had taught him that there was no point in arguing with her. Still, he couldn't help himself from adding, "But how could I not know it's you? You're one of my best customers." Then he let out an audible sigh before adding, "Sometimes you're my only customer. Do you know what it's like just sitting in here all by yourself all afternoon?"

"Never mind about that," Francesca grunted. "I've got problems of my own."

"All right," he relented. "What have you been up to now?"

"I took the Lord's name in vain," Francesca answered, getting straight to it. "I didn't mean to do it, but it just slipped out, more than once, after I fell down in the snow."

"Were you hurt?" asked Father Buontempo, sounding truly concerned.

"Mostly my pride," admitted Francesca. "I guess having too much of that is something else I should confess."

"Anything else?"

"Yes. I lied to my children."

"Don't worry about it. Everybody lies to their children."

"Father!"

"Well, I know how difficult having children can be, even

after they've grown up. It's just that I think stretching the truth is the only thing that gets parents through their days sometimes, so I try not to be too hard on them." Then he corrected himself. "But of course, it *is* something a father or mother should refrain from doing when at all possible, even when they think they're doing it in their children's best interests. The truth is always the best way."

"Whatever."

"Is that all?'

"No," said Francesca after a moment's pause. "Something else has been on my mind."

"What is it?'

"Well, it's hard to explain."

"Give it a try."

Francesca took a deep breath. "Like I said," she finally replied, "it's hard to explain, but lately, God has been getting on my nerves. Is that a sin?"

"Hmm, that's a new one," replied the priest. "I guess it depends. Why don't you tell me what you mean when you say God is getting on your nerves."

Francesca hesitated for a time, trying to put into words exactly the way she felt. It had been building for some time now, and she wanted desperately to get it off her chest.

"I just don't know what He wants from me lately, that's all," she finally lamented. "I mean, I feel useless these days, and I can't get rid of the idea that it's all His fault. What is my life supposed to be all about now that He has taken my husband and my children have grown up and moved away? What am I without my family? I know that I'm old, but does that mean that everything's over for me? Have I already done whatever it was that God intended for me to do in this life, and I'm just killing time now until it's all over? It's starting to really annoy me."

"Those are hard questions," answered Father Buontempo, "questions that all of us ask ourselves at different points in our lives. God's will isn't always immediately clear to us, so there's certainly nothing sinful about seeking to understand it. Accepting His will once we understand it can be the hard part." He paused to assess whether his words were helping her. Then he continued, telling her, "But you ought to remember that even though your children might be far away, they love you and think about you every day, just like you love and think about them. You're always all together in your thoughts and prayers. That's how you stay close despite the distance."

"It's not enough," said Francesca, shaking her head. "I need more from my family. *They* need more from me, even if they don't know it."

"Perhaps. But maybe it would help to consider the possibility that your children and grandchildren are not your only family. You're also part of God's greater family. Everyone you meet is a son or daughter or sister or brother, or even a father or mother, regardless of your age. They're all there, all about you, everywhere you go. In a special way, each of them needs you, and you need them."

"Maybe," muttered Francesca, not completely convinced.

"Be patient," the priest told her kindly. "When God is ready, He'll make whatever it is that He wants you to do next clear to you."

"No chance He could give me a little hint in the meantime?"

"Sorry, I don't think He works that way. You'll just have to wait."

"And what do I do while I'm waiting."

"For starters, you can say three Our Fathers," he told her, "and you can try to stop lying to your children."

Then he absolved Francesca of her sins, real and imagined, and sent her on her way.

After mass, Francesca stopped by the market to pick up some vegetables and a few pieces of meat to put in a soup she was planning to make. She liked soups, especially in the winter. They were so easy to make, and one good-sized batch cooked on a Saturday night would last her through the weekend and for several meals beyond. As she looked over the selection of stew beef and other meats, Francesca's eye fell upon the butcher's weekly special: a nice pork tenderloin roast that would be perfect for a Sunday dinner. In her mind, she could already see the entire meal on the table, the beautiful roast at the center, beside it some roasted potatoes and a platter of sautéed rabe, and maybe a fresh-baked loaf of bread. She could almost taste it all. The beautiful vision quickly faded, though, as the realization that there would be no one there to share such a meal with her once again invaded her thoughts. Just the same, Francesca picked up the roast and put it in her basket along with the vegetables and meat she had chosen for her soup.

"That's a nice price for that roast, isn't it?" said a smiling Tony when Francesca brought everything to the cash register."

"Too good to pass up," Francesca agreed.

"Cooking for the family tomorrow?" he asked as he tied the roast up in a plastic bag to keep it separate from the rest of the groceries.

"Nope," replied Francesca, shaking her head. "Just me."

"That's a lot of meat for just one person," Tony joked.

"Oh, no," explained Francesca. "This is going in the freezer for someday and somebody, who knows when or who."

"And what about you in the meantime?"

"Me?" she said with a shrug. "I guess tonight I'll just make myself some soup . . . and then I'll wait."

CHAPTER 8

"**B**lood pressure is fine," said the doctor. He removed the cuff from Francesca's arm and scribbled the numbers down on her chart. Then he took the stethoscope and listened to her heart for a few moments, before placing the cold metal disk on her back. "Big breath, please," he asked.

Francesca took a deep breath.

"Now out," said the doctor. He moved the stethoscope to another part of her back. "Again."

Francesca had come in for her yearly checkup. She didn't care much for going to the doctor, but it kept her son and daughters from nagging her about taking care of her health. But wasn't it her job to nag them, she wondered as the doctor continued his examination. Francesca had been in such gloomy spirits earlier that morning that she had almost canceled the appointment. The thought of having to listen to the children carry on to her about it was the only thing that had motivated her to get in the car. She looked back at the doctor, who was now leaning back against the examination table. He was a young man, late thirties at the oldest, she guessed, though a few flecks of gray on his temples suggested he might be slightly older. If she had to go to the doctor, Francesca ordinarily would have preferred to be examined by someone closer to her own age. Doctor Johnson, however, to whom Francesca had gone for years, had retired the previous spring, leaving this new doctor, Doctor Olsen, to take over the practice. Though she did not yet trust him, trust being something that did not come easily to her, she could not help but like his pleasant manner and the way he took his time with her. He seemed competent enough. Francesca decided that he would do for the time being.

"Let's see," the young doctor continued as he scanned his notes, "your heart sounds good, weight's just where it should be—though it wouldn't hurt to be a little heavier, believe it or not—and all your blood work looks fine."

"So I guess that means I'm going to live, Doctor Olsen?" she asked, not particularly cheered by his findings.

"If I had to put it into medical terms, I'd say that you're healthy as a ,horse."

"Then how come I feel so rotten all over?"

"Well, I'd say it's because of that fall you told me about," he explained. "You'd be surprised by how long it takes to fully recover from a jolt like that. It might not have seemed so bad to you at the time, but you probably gave yourself a good wrench. Just that little bit of constant achiness you've been experiencing catches up with you. Add in a few nights of poor sleep on top of that, and you're not going to be in the mood for turning cartwheels."

"I guess," said a glum Francesca. In her heart, she knew the doctor was right. She also knew that there was more than just the fall that was making her feel so down. She had already confessed all that, however, so she saw no point in bringing it up again here.

The doctor tapped his pen against his clipboard and eyed her thoughtfully for a few moments. "You know, I don't think there's anything wrong with you other than what I've told you, but this time of year can get you down as well. We call it seasonal affective disorder. SAD."

"Sad. That sounds about right for what I have," said Francesca, chuckling for the first time since she came to the office. "What causes it?"

"Lack of sunlight this time of year," he explained. "It's more and more unheard of the closer you get to the equator, where the daylight remains fairly constant. Up north where we live, though, as the days get shorter, so do our tempers, if you know what I mean."

"What do you do for it?"

"Try to get out in the sun for a few minutes each day," he recommended. "Or even just sit in front of a sunny window whenever you can. Getting more sleep will help as well. Perhaps even taking an afternoon nap every day if you don't already take one. You're a very healthy person, so you should try to find something to keep your mind active to pass the time. That's always important."

"I'm tired of just passing the time," Francesca told him with a sigh. "I want to fill it and live it." She sat there sulking for a time. "Maybe I should get myself a job," she suggested.

"There's no reason why you can't still work if you want to," said the doctor.

"Really?" said Francesca. She had made the suggestion as a joke and was much surprised by his response.

"I mean, just part-time," he said. "I wouldn't want to see you working more than a few hours here and there every week. Not that you couldn't, but unless you need the money, why would you?"

Francesca turned the idea over in her mind. By a strange co-incidence, while she had been straightening up the kitchen after supper a few days earlier, she had happened to notice an article on the front page of the career section of the Sunday newspaper. The article was titled "Getting Back into the Job Market: A Guide for Older Workers." At the time, she hadn't given it much thought. She hadn't bothered to read the article, but instead used that section of the newspaper to wrap up the food scraps from dinner.

Looking back now, though, she wished she had saved the article. For a moment, it seemed like an intriguing possibility. But then another thought brought her down.

"It's been years since I worked outside the house," she told him. "Last time was before I had my children. Who would hire me now, and to do what?'

"I don't know," admitted the doctor. "But it's never to late to learn something new, something that you might enjoy, and at the same time be of use to an employer. I guess you'll just have to keep your eyes open and wait to see what comes up."

"Wait," Francesca muttered. "You sound an awful lot like someone else I know. Seems like all I do these days is wait."

The doctor gave her a kind smile. He helped her put on her coat and then held open the door. "See you next year, Mrs. Campanile," he said pleasantly.

"If God wants," Francesca replied, giving him a nod. Then she picked up her pocketbook and headed out to the front desk to schedule next year's appointment

CHAPTER 9

The newspaper lay in an orange plastic bag at the bottom of the front walk when Francesca looked out the window early the next morning. The sun had only partially risen, so the front yard was still in shadows. From where she stood, the newspaper looked like some sort of small, bright orange creature curled up asleep on the icy pavement.

Francesca let out a grunt of consternation. Once upon a time, the paperboy would have at least made certain that he tossed her morning newspaper up onto the front step so that, one, it would stay dry, and two, she wouldn't need to go traipsing through the snow or rain to retrieve it. She remembered Jimmy, their paperboy when she and Leo had first moved into the house. Jimmy had been up every morning at the crack of dawn, his sack of newspapers slung over his shoulder as he pedaled his bike from house to house before school. In those days, *The Providence Journal* also put out an afternoon edition, *The Evening Bulletin*, so Jimmy would come around again after school. He was the nicest, most polite young man she had ever met, and she always gave him something extra when she paid him each week.

Nowadays, though, there was no longer an afternoon edition of the newspaper, and one person in a car did the job of ten paperboys. This arrangement, she presumed, is what some people referred to as progress. Francesca did not think of it that way. Whoever it was that drove by every morning at five a.m. had no time for niceties such as making it easier for an old lady to pick up her newspaper. She often awoke to the sound of the newspapers plopping against the sidewalks on her street. As best as she could discern, the driver never stopped, but simply flung the papers out the window as the car passed, letting them land wherever. Sometimes hers came to rest within easy reach; sometimes it landed in the middle of a puddle on a rainy day. Francesca was lucky, she supposed, that her daily newspaper had not yet ended up stuck in a tree someplace—but then again, it was probably only a matter of time.

At lunchtime, the newspaper still rested on the same spot. Lately, the headlines had been proclaiming nothing but gloom, something that Francesca felt she already had in ample supply; there was no need to hurry out to get more. Besides, it was a bitter cold day, and she had been disinclined to brave the elements that morning. Instead, she had spent the early part of the day upstairs, rummaging through the bedroom closets. It always amazed Francesca to discover how much clutter her children had left behind. No matter how many times she straightened out the attic or closets, she inevitably found something that she had previously overlooked. Truth be told, much of what was left was old clothes that were beyond use. Many of these she simply tossed out from time to time, when she had the chance. The clothes that were out of style but still in good condition she usually gave away.

Certain things, however, were still too precious to Francesca to give away when she came across them. Whether it was a dress Rosie had once worn, or perhaps a bonnet Alice had adored as a little girl, the clothes from when her children were small were always the ones that affected Francesca the deepest. On this particular morning, she held up a little blue cardigan sweater that she happened to pull out of Joey's closet. Her son had last worn it, she well remembered, for Christmas back when he was all of four years old. Hanging beside it was the shirt and the pair of corduroys Francesca had dressed him in that day. Down below on the floor, she found the tiny pair of shiny black shoes in which he had clomped about the house so proudly. She knelt to take a closer look at them. Holding the shoes up, she recalled how he had looked so adorable that day that everyone had just wanted to pick him up and hug him for all they were worth. Joey was too much of a little boy, of course, to let anyone hold him, so he inevitably managed to squirm out of their arms before long.

Now, as she knelt there thinking back on that day, remembering her son and daughters as they were, wishing for all the world that she could have them back like that again for just a little while, Francesca breathed in the scent of the wool and squeezed the little sweater to her heart. In her mind, she understood that time marched on, that these things for which she sometimes yearned could not and should not ever be. Still the tears ran freely from her eyes, until she carefully placed the sweater back on its hanger and tucked the shoes back in their place. Then, drying her cheeks with the back of her hand, she closed the closet door and returned downstairs.

Later, Francesca finally went out for the newspaper while the last of the soup she had made the previous weekend was heating up on the stove. Muttering something uncomplimentary about whoever it was that had delivered her newspaper, she hurried back inside with it, hoping she wouldn't slip and fall in the process. A shiver raced up her spine when she finally made it back into the front hall. She shook off her coat and went into the kitchen to warm up.

Francesca looked over the newspaper while she sat at the

kitchen table, eating her soup. As she often did, she gave the front page only a cursory examination before going directly to the obituaries. Perhaps it might seem odd that someone who was feeling so gloomy would be so anxious to read the death notices. In truth, though Francesca read them with dread, praying that she would not find the name of anyone she knew, it seemed like wakes and funerals were the only time she saw her old friends anymore. In an odd sort of way, they were something to look forward to. Besides, when Francesca was feeling glum, as she did at this particular moment, the fact that she did not find her own name listed there was something of a consolation.

Relieved to find that none of her acquaintances had chosen to leave this world, Francesca turned her attention back to the front page and looked over the headlines of the day. As she leafed through the rest of the paper, she found little that held her interest among the usual accounts of scandal and calamity. She set the paper down for a moment and gave a sigh; she just wasn't in the mood for it all. Francesca often wondered why they called it the news when it seemed like nothing truly new ever happened. With each turn of the page, she always hoped to find some newsworthy item that would spark her imagination, something that would inspire her and snap her out of the doldrums. As she stared blankly across the room, her gaze fell on the clock above the stove, and suddenly she became acutely aware of the passage of time. It was then that Francesca realized that what had been troubling her most that day was the feeling that she had grown weary of reading about what other people were doing, of watching them on television, and of hearing of their exploits, as if her time had passed and now she was only a spectator and not a participant in life. She was sick of the feeling that she was just sitting on the sidelines, watching it all go by. She longed to get back in the game—for however long God would allow her to play.

Francesca looked down at the newspaper. She was just about ready to fold it all up and toss it into the recycling bin when she noticed the classified section peeking out from the bottom. Not sure of exactly what she was looking for, she pulled out the section and opened it to the help-wanted ads. Her gloom turned to dismay when she beheld the columns of employment opportunities. As she scanned the page, she found nothing for which she was even remotely qualified. Francesca was good with numbers, but she was certainly no accountant. She was as good a cook as any restaurant could hope for, but she had no formal training or license. She possessed no bachelor's degree in any subject, nor did she have any computer skills. She would have loved to offer her services to the local school distract as a substitute teacher, for she was certain that there was a lot she could teach the kids, but even those temporary positions required a degree and certification from the state.

Francesca sighed and put the paper down again. She had just made up her mind to forget about the whole thing and toss the paper out when her eye spied a very small help-wanted ad near the bottom of the page. Her first inclination was to skip over it, but then she leaned closer and gave it a quick read. Then she read it again more carefully. Somewhere inside the back of her mind the light of a new idea suddenly flickered to life. At first, she tried to dismiss the notion, but try as she might, it only seemed to glow that much brighter. Francesca sat there for a time, wondering what she should do. It would help to talk to someone. She *needed* to talk to someone, but who? Rosie and Alice were sure to have a conniption if they found out what she was contemplating, and Joey was off to the other side of the world. She stayed there, turning the matter over and over again in her mind, until at last she came to a decision and stood. A few minutes later, bundled up in her coat and hat and boots and gloves, Francesca grabbed her book bag and opened the front door. She stood there for a few moments, wondering if she was doing the right thing.

"I've waited long enough," she finally muttered. Then she stepped outside, locked the door behind her, and went to the car.

CHAPTER 10

"**Y**ou want to do *what?*"

Peg gaped at Francesca with wide-eyed incredulity. Francesca had found her, as she had hoped she would when she had left the house, back in the library computer room. Natalie was there as well, gazing at Francesca with much the same look. Connie, Francesca suspected, would have been making the same face had she not been off in some other part of the library, looking for a book.

"Frannie," Peg continued, "I can understand you want to keep busy, but do you really want to be a nanny for someone else's brats?"

"Really," Natalie chimed in. "Are you crazy?"

"It's not really a nanny the ad said she's looking for," Francesca tried to explain. "It's more like a babysitter, 'a responsible person' is what it said, to look after a couple of children at their home for just one or two hours after school every day. What's so bad about that?"

"Ayyy, that's how it starts," warned Natalie. "Trust me, you don't know what parents are like these days. First they tell you that they'll be home at five, next they ask if you would mind staying a little later because they're busy at work, and before you know it, they're out till all hours, gallivanting around every other night, while you're stuck there watching *their* kids. Believe me, I've seen it happen, so I know what I'm talking about."

Peg nodded her head in agreement. "She's right, Frannie," she said. "These people will take advantage of you every chance they get. It happened once to my daughter, Judy. She agreed to watch one of her neighbor's kids one day after school. The mother said she had some big important thing to do at work, and that neither she nor the husband would be able to get home on time. The next day, she asked my daughter to do it again. At the time, Judy figured it was no big deal, since the little girl went to the same school as my granddaughter and they were friends. All of a sudden, though, the mother's calling Judy from work practically every day, asking her to watch the little girl for her. Naturally, Judy always winds up having to feed her supper too, and even helping her with her homework. She was more of a mother to the little girl than her own mother! Well, before long, the kid was showing up at the front door even when the mother didn't call. They sucked Judy right in. It went on for quite a while like that, until one night when the parents didn't pick her up until almost ten o'clock. That's when my daughter finally got up the nerve to put a stop to it."

"How sad for that little girl," said Francesca.

Her two friends were not telling her anything that she didn't already know. It was nothing new. She was well aware of how selfish some parents could be, of how indifferent they often behaved when it came to caring for their own flesh and blood. They looked upon parenting, she could only assume, as some sort of chore that had to be avoided whenever possible or, at best, squeezed in somewhere between their busy work and social lives. In truth, Francesca had always believed that such people had no idea of what they were missing. It was the plight of the children, though, that saddened her most. In a land of plenty, there were so many, rich and poor alike, who went without the simple things that counted most in life.

"Forget about it," Natalie advised. "Why would you want to do it in the first place?'

"I don't know," Francesca admitted. "I guess it's almost like asking me why I breathe. I don't understand how or why it happens, but I know if I stop doing it, it's all over for me. That's kind of the way I feel about this whole thing. It's just a way to keep me breathing."

"If I were you, I'd stop and take a deep breath, and then think about this some more before I went ahead with it," said Peg.

Just then, Connie appeared at the door. Peg and Natalie soon filled her in on Francesca's plan.

"What are you? Crazy!" she exclaimed.

"They've already asked me that," replied Francesca. She was finding it hard to suppress a smile, because the more they all tried to dissuade her, the more she felt convinced she was doing the right thing.

"But who are these people?" asked Connie. "What do you know about them?'

"Nothing," replied Francesca with a shrug. "The ad just said, 'Working mother seeks responsible person,' to watch her kids after school. That's all I know."

"All the more reason why you shouldn't do it," said Natalie. "You never know what kind of creeps you might end up involved with."

"Oh, don't worry, girls," Francesca told them. "I know how to take care of myself. Besides, who's to say that I'll even get the job? And there's nothing that says that I have to take it even if they offer it to me. I just want to give myself the chance, that's all."

"Well, it's your life," said Peg, turning back to her computer. "But if you asked me, I'd say that you're just looking for trouble."

"Maybe, but what else is life for?" she replied.

Later, Francesca left the others to their computer fun and stopped by the front desk to check out some books she had found on babysitting. She tucked them into her book bag and headed to the exit, where she saw Connie waiting by the door.

"Need a ride home, Connie?"

"No," her friend answered. "I'm on my way to do some grocery shopping. That's if my idiot husband can manage to find his way back here without driving himself into a snowbank someplace. God forbid."

"I'm sure he'll make it," laughed Francesca. "Just be careful out on the roads when he does."

"And you be careful too," said Connie. "You know what I'm talking about."

"I will," Francesca promised.

With that, she nodded good-bye and walked out to her car. Once inside, she started the engine and sat there for a moment, turning things over in her mind. Francesca wondered if perhaps Peg and the others might be right. Maybe it was a crazy idea to respond to the ad. But then she began to wonder about the person who had placed it, and a thousand intriguing questions danced in her head. Where did this woman live? What kind of person was she? Why did she need someone to help her? What were the children like? Could Francesca help them?

There was, Francesca well knew, only one way to answer any of these questions, so she took a deep breath, made the sign of the cross, and started on her way back home.

CHAPTER 11

"Mom?"

The voice came to Loretta Simmons from someplace far, far away, like an echo in a canyon.

"Mom."

It came round again, this time closer and more insistent. There was something tormenting in the sound of it, the way it sought her out no matter how she struggled to escape it.

"Come on, Mom."

She was hiding now at the bottom of what she could only perceive as a deep, dark well, a well from which someone, very much against her will, was trying to pull her up and into the light. She did her best to resist, to stay burrowed in the darkness, but she knew it was of no use. No matter how hard she struggled against it, she was being borne inexorably to the surface.

"Come on, Mom. We're gonna be late!"

Face down in the pillow, clenching the bedsheets beneath her, while a cold rivulet of drool seeped from the corner of her wide-open mouth, Loretta Simmons opened her eyes. She tried to move, but it felt as though she were lying beneath an anvil that was pressing her deeper and deeper into the mattress. She was too tired to even yawn. Wearily, she lifted her head off the pillow, pushed aside the hair hanging over her eyes, and looked into the face of her son, standing at the edge of the bed. Wiping the side of her mouth with the back of her hand, she glanced at the clock. Seven twenty-five. God, she had forgotten to set the alarm again. There was no way the kids would make the bus; she would have to drive them to school again. Dropping her head back onto the pillow, she let out a sorrowful groan and squeezed her eyes shut once more.

Up to that point, Loretta had been lost in a very pleasant dream, the last remnants of which were now quickly receding from her memory like smoke up a chimney. Desperately, she tried to pull it all back, to piece together the remaining fragments, before it disappeared forever. It was the type of dream she seemed to have with growing regularity lately. Whenever she had it, there was always something oddly familiar about it, like she was acting out the script to a play that had essentially all the same dialog and characters but was constantly being set in some place new. This time around, she recalled standing on a balcony overlooking a shimmering, moonlit bay. A warm, gentle breeze caressed her face and hair, while from down below, the sound of calypso music rose above the sighing of the gentle surf. She wasn't alone, of course. Standing there with her on that beautiful balcony was a man. There was always something very familiar about him as well, even though she never could quite make out his face.

"Tell me you'll stay," she recalls saying to him in the dream.

"Of course I will stay," he had told her, reaching out for her hand.

"Tell me you'll never leave."

"Never."

"Tell me you love me."

"With all my heart."

It was all something right out of a romance novel, but just the same, it all came out so heartfelt, so dramatically real to her. It swept her away. The secret passion, the longing in her heart. It was all ready to burst forth, like the sun emerging from the clouds.

But then, just at the moment when the man finally took her in his arms and began to bring his lips to hers, that climactic moment when the music swelled and the violins began to play, the voice had come and chased the whole magical scene away. Now, try as she might, there was no way to put herself back into it, no matter how tightly she squeezed her eyes shut.

"Get up, Mom," insisted her son, nudging her in the arm. "We're going to be late for school!"

"Go get dressed, Will," Loretta grunted. "I'll be up in a minute."

"I'm already dressed," he replied. "When are you going to make breakfast? I'm hungry."

"You're nine years old," she complained. "Can't you make your own breakfast? Do I have to do everything? Pour yourself a glass of juice. Have a bowl of cereal. Make yourself some toast."

"We have no juice, there's no clean bowls, and the toaster is broke, remember?" her son impishly reminded her. Then, in a more pleading tone: "Come on, Mom. I'm really hungry."

Loretta let out another groan and rolled over onto her back. She rubbed her eyes and stared forlornly at the ceiling. "Is your sister up?" she said.

"In the bathroom, brushing her hair, where else?"

"Okay," his mother yawned, dragging herself from beneath the covers. "Go. I'm up."

Loretta set her feet on the floor and rolled her neck and shoulders for a minute to shake out the cobwebs. Despite the urge to crawl back under the covers, she stood and shuffled out into the hallway. As she passed the bathroom, she rapped her knuckles against the door.

"Don't be all day in there, Miss America," she warned her daughter. "Get a move on. Somebody else might need to get ready, you know." Then she trudged downstairs to the kitchen to make herself a cup of instant coffee. Loretta preferred fresh-brewed, especially in the morning, but there was no time to make it, and in any case, the coffeemaker was broken as well.

Will was already sitting on the end of the living room couch, playing a video game on the television, when Loretta came downstairs. Beside him, on the end table, rested a paper plate holding several saltine crackers. Next to it, a butter knife rose from an open jar of peanut butter. His eyes glued to the television, Will munched away on the peanut butter crackers he had made, oblivious to the crumbs falling onto the couch and rug while he manipulated the game controller. It wasn't the breakfast of champions, thought Loretta, but she supposed that her son could eat worse in the morning. It would have to do. Just the same, she couldn't suppress her exasperation at the mess he was making.

"Watch what you're doing!" she cried. "You're getting crumbs everywhere! Why is it that no matter how hard I try to keep this place clean, it still ends up a mess?"

"Cleansing breath, Mom," said Will placidly, without looking away from the video game. "You're starting to get worked up again."

"Don't give me that," she snapped in reply. "Turn that thing off and finish eating your breakfast at the table. And get your backpack ready for school. Who said you could sit around wasting time playing those games when we're all going to be late? And have you even looked at that science project you had me working on for you till all hours last night?" She followed that up by screaming upstairs, "Penelope Simmons, get yourself down here. *Now!*"

Penny descended the stairs a few minutes later. She was a pretty girl with blue eyes and dark, straight hair like her mother's. However, her choice of attire that morning—a flimsy blouse and a skirt much too short for a sixth grader—elicited sharp criticism from her mother. The daily dress review before school had become something of an ordeal ever since she had turned eleven.

"Absolutely not!" cried Loretta. "Where did you even get that outfit?"

"My friend Jenna let me borrow it. We're the same size."

"I don't care. Give it back, because you're not wearing it to school."

"But why not?"

"Well, for starters, you're too young to dress like that, young lady."

"But this is the way *all* the girls are dressing today," Penny insisted.

"I don't care. And besides, it's the middle of winter. At least put a sweater on. You look ridiculous."

"Tell me about it," chimed in Will, always willing to add fuel to the fire.

"Shut up, game boy," sneered his sister. "Try minding your own business."

"Whatever."

As it usually did on a school day morning, the decibel level continued to increase as the time to depart for school drew nearer. By the time Loretta managed to get herself dressed, collect her own things for work, and bustle with them out the door, she was in full throat, leading the chorus of bickering and mutual recrimination. She glanced inside just once and gave a dismayed sigh at the untidy state of things in the living room and kitchen. There was nothing to be done about it now, so she slammed the door shut and hurried them all off to the car. With barely a look in the rear viewmirror, she backed the car out of the driveway, and tore off down the road.

"Now remember," she told her two children a short while later, when she pulled the car up to the school's front door, "you'll have someone new staying with you today until I come home. Please try to be nice to her. Be polite. Especially you, Penny. Got it?"

"Yeah, sure," said Penny, stepping out of the car.

"And that goes for you too, mister."

"You know me, Mom," said Will, dragging his backpack behind him as he slid out the door.

"Hey," Loretta called after them as they began to walk away. "Don't I get a kiss from either of you anymore?

"When you get home, Mom," Will called back, waving over his shoulder.

Loretta watched until the two of them were safe inside before tearing off again down the road. With any luck, she would be only fifteen or twenty minutes late for work.

CHAPTER 12

Had it not been for the Snickers bar in her desk drawer, Loretta would have eaten nothing at all at lunchtime. Her head was banging and her stomach growling, but she had no time to eat anything more substantial; having arrived late that morning, she was behind in her work and needed her lunch break just to catch up. With just about everyone else gone to lunch, it was quiet enough for her to focus all her attention on the tasks at hand.

Loretta worked in downtown Providence as a legal assistant in the law offices of Pace, Sotheby, and Grant. Much of her day was spent typing up and reviewing for accuracy contracts, articles of incorporation, and other such legal documents. She had discovered early on, when she was first hired, that it was a fast-paced office that demanded the antagonistic attributes of speed and attention to detail. Arnold Grant, for whom Loretta did most of her work, might forgive her for arriving a few minutes late every now and then, but he would never tolerate any diminution in the quantity or quality of her work. He was one of those bosses who was always pleasant but had no time for pleasantries. Dexter Sotheby was cut from much the same cloth. Loretta learned right away that she didn't dare disappoint either of them.

Bill Pace, the founding partner of the firm, was her favorite of the three. A sweet, avuncular old gentleman, he had reduced his role over the years to simply overseeing the operation and occasionally schmoozing with the clients, leaving the hands-on work to his junior partners, who were just as happy to have the amiable codger out of the way. A widower for some years, he had no children or grandchildren to occupy his days, so the office was something of a second home to him, the staff a surrogate family of sorts. That, at least, was the way that Loretta saw him, for he certainly seemed to treat her and the rest of the staff like family. Pace passed the bulk of the workweek in his office, perusing the *Wall Street Journal* when he wasn't working on his putting game. On this day, as occasionally happened, a stray golf ball came rolling out of his office door and across the lobby floor, evidence that the firm's senior partner had once again misread the cut of his office carpet. The ball caromed off the leg of a chair and rolled along the floor, its momentum slowly waning, until it finally came to rest by the wastebasket next to Loretta's desk.

Loretta leaned out from her cubicle and looked down the hall to his office. "Too much club!" she called out playfully to him.

With shirtsleeves rolled up and one suspender slipping off his shoulder, Pace emerged from his office, examining the club head of a new putter he had recently acquired. He gave it a dubious look, which that suggested his evaluation of it was less than favorable. The old man stopped at Loretta's desk, rubbed his chin, and regarded the ball for a moment, noting with consternation its proximity to the wastebasket and Loretta's legs.

"Looks like an unplayable lie," he grumbled before discreetly stooping down to pick it up. "I suppose I'd better take a mulligan. Otherwise, it's a one-stroke penalty."

With that, he sauntered off, the putter riding atop his shoulder. Loretta assumed that he was heading back to his office, to further refine his golf game, but he returned a short time later, bringing with him a cup of coffee, which he placed on her desk. "That's for not reporting me to the rules committee," he said, giving her a wink.

"Why thank you, Mister Pace," said Loretta, delighted to have something to perk her up and perhaps relieve her headache. "But *I'm* the one who should be getting the coffee for *you*."

"Bah," he replied with a wave of his hand. "That's about all they'll let me do around here these days. A man needs to keep himself busy doing *something* useful—at least now and then."

Noting that his tie was hopelessly askew, a not-uncommon state of affairs with him, Loretta clicked her tongue and crooked her finger for him to come closer. He leaned over the edge of the desk and looked pensively at her while she fixed it for him.

"Tell me, Loretta," he said genially. "How did a nice girl like you end up working in a place like this?"

"Why do you say that?" she laughed. "I think this is a very nice place to work, don't you?"

"Hmm, maybe," he grunted, "if you like swimming with sharks. Trust me, they're out there, and they're always watching. Be careful, is my advice."

"Oh, I always stay out of the water," she replied with a smile. "If you know what I mean."

"Smart girl," he said, straightening himself up. He rolled his neck back to help it adjust to the tie's snugger fit and beamed her an affectionate smile. "How are your children?" he asked. "Growing up fast, I bet."

"Too fast," Loretta sighed. She paused and smiled again. "But then again, there are some days when I think that they're not growing up fast enough, if you know what I mean."

"What you need is a good man in your life, to help you ap-

preciate it all," said Pace. He patted his midsection and gave a little cough to clear his throat. "I'd, uh, offer myself, but I'm afraid
these old bones are just about fully depreciated."

"Oh, I wouldn't say that," she replied, playfully batting her
eyes for him before adding, "but *you* could use a good woman to
look after you."

"Have anyone in mind?" he said, playfully batting his eyes in
return.

"Sorry," she shrugged. "I'd offer myself, but unfortunately,
while a good man would be nice, I think what I could really use
right now is a wife."

"Hmm, can't help you in that department," chuckled her
boss. "But I'll keep you posted." He patted his tie and gave her a
nod. "Thanks for keeping me presentable." With that, he tossed
the putter over his shoulder once more and strolled back to his
office.

"Hit 'em straight!" she called after him. "And thanks for the
coffee."

Loretta sighed and turned her attention back to her computer. She had been making excellent headway in catching up
on her work, but now that her concentration had been broken,
she had lost all her momentum. It was then that she remembered that she had several bills to pay. Of course, there were *always* several bills to pay. Loretta could never seem to find time to
do them when she was at home. Between Penny and Will, there
was always one thing or another going on to distract her. On
those few occasions when she did have the time, it seemed like
there was never enough money in the checking account to cover
everything. Where it went, she could not understand. Loretta
earned a good salary and did her best to watch her spending, but
the well just always seemed to keep running dry. She was per-
petually juggling her finances. It was like she was slowly hemor-

rhaging dollar bills, always trying to stop the bleeding by tapping into one of her lines of credit, whose outstanding balances grew inexorably larger with each billing cycle. It was a problem she knew she needed to address, but it was also just one of a million other things that she had on her mind. With another sigh, she logged onto the Internet and navigated to her bank's web site for a few minutes, to see if she could juggle her way through the latest financial crunch until her next paycheck came along.

Later that afternoon, after finally getting her work back up to speed, Loretta allowed herself a brief break and took a walk to the ladies' room. On the way back to her desk, she stopped to chat for a few moments with Shirley, one of the other legal assistants in the office. Like Loretta, Shirley was single and in her early thirties. The two often talked during their break times, swapping tidbits of company gossip, lamenting the dearth of eligible men in the firm, and occasionally confiding in one another about each other's ailments, real and imagined. Loretta had a great propensity for fretting about her health and that of her children. In this regard, she and Shirley were kindred spirits.

"So, how goes the rat race?" Shirley asked when Loretta settled into the chair next to her desk.

"The rats seem to keep getting farther ahead," said Loretta wearily. "Why is that?" She closed her eyes for a moment and massaged the sides of her forehead "Uff, and I have such a headache today," she added

Shirley looked at her with concern. "Is it really bad? I mean, you don't think you're having a stroke or something?"

"No, silly," laughed Loretta. "I know I'm a worrywart, but I'm not that bad. I think I'm just hungry."

"Hey, don't laugh about these things," replied Shirley. "I just read about a woman in Oklahoma who told everyone at work that she had a headache. Someone gave her some aspirin to take, and two hours later, she dropped dead from a brain aneurysm."

"I saw that story too," said Loretta shuddering. Then, with a chuckle, "But I'm pretty sure this isn't an aneurysm. I just need something to eat."

"I'll say," said Shirley. "You're so skinny, it makes me sick. All I do is look at food and I get fat. How do you stay so thin?"

"I don't know," shrugged Loretta. "I guess I just don't look at food that often."

Though she had said it in jest, it was really quite true. Loretta seldom had time for more than a cup of coffee and a piece of toast for breakfast. Lunch generally consisted of a small sandwich and another cup of coffee, purchased in the deli downstairs. She rarely ate anything else between meals. By the time Loretta staggered home from work most evenings, tired and often stressed out, the best she could manage for herself and the kids was to bring home takeout from a restaurant or to heat up frozen dinners out of the fridge. Loretta would have liked to do better, at least at supper time, but more often than not, she simply didn't have the energy.

"So, how are your kids doing?" asked Shirley. "Find them a new babysitter yet?"

"She starts today, thank God," answered Loretta. "I was beginning to think that I'd never find someone. "

"Who is she?" said her friend, always eager to know everyone else's business. "Where did you find her?"

"I put an ad in the newspaper," explained Loretta. "It ran for a week. Do you believe that only two people responded?"

"Who did you hire?"

"A grad student from New York who goes to school at RISD," said Loretta. "Her name's Brenda. She's a little young, but she seems dependable enough."

"Who was the other one?" Shirley pried. "Why didn't you hire her instead?"

"The other one was nice too, I guess," answered Loretta. "But she was this old Italian woman, and I just wasn't sure she could handle the kids. Not that they misbehave or anything like that—I mean, not any more than anyone else's kids—but I thought it would be good for the kids to have someone younger there, someone they might have a little more in common with." Loretta paused for a moment. "Plus, I don't know," she continued. "It's hard to explain, but there was something about her, something that made me feel . . ."

"What?" said Shirley.

"She made me feel guilty," Loretta finally confessed.

"How on earth did she do that?" laughed her friend.

"Well, when I asked her if she had any experience with children, she started to tell me about her own children and her grandkids, and a little about the rest of her family. It sounds like she's very close to them all."

"What's wrong with that?"

"Oh, nothing at all," said Loretta. "It just made me wonder about a lot of things, that's all. As you know, my family life has never exactly been an episode out of *The Brady Bunch*. And then, of course, there was the look on her face when she asked about Will and Penny's father, and I told her that David was long gone and that the two of us had never married. You know, she didn't say anything, but I could tell that she didn't approve, like I had done something wrong. I think she's an old Catholic, just like my mother."

"Old Catholics tend to be like that," opined Shirley.

"I suppose," said Loretta. "But I just don't need that whole guilt scene right now. In any case, I decided to hire the girl."

"I'm sure she'll work out fine," Shirley told her.

"Me too," said Loretta, brightening. "At least that will be one thing off my mind."

With that, she stood and walked back to her desk. It was nearing three thirty. The first thing she planned to do before getting back to work was to call home to see how things were going with Brenda and the kids. When she settled back into her chair, however, she noticed the red light on her telephone, blinking telling her that someone had a left a message.

CHAPTER 13

There were moments—and lately, they seemed to arise with increasing frequency—when Loretta was reminded that the framework of her life was constructed with all the stability of a house of cards. Touch it, remove one single card, take away one support, or subject the fragile structure to the faintest puff of wind, and everything would come toppling down into a heap.

It was a state of affairs of which she had grown acutely aware over the years since David had gone, leaving her to raise two children by herself. The pebbles that dropped into the pond in which she lived didn't cause ripples; what they cause was more like a tsunami. And so, Loretta lived in dread of the multitude of common everyday occurrences, with their inevitable cascade of consequences, that could wreak havoc on her life. What if the car broke down? How would she get to work? Who would come to get her? What if Will or Penny had a doctor's appointment or someplace else they needed to be? What if the heat stopped working? It was the middle of winter. She knew nothing about such things. Who would she call to fix it, and when would he come? How much would it cost to repair? Money—or more accurately, the lack of it—always weighed heavily on her mind. What if she should get so far behind in her bills that the telephone company or the cable television company or the electric company disconnected her service? What would she do? Where would she go? Who would she turn to? What if one or both of her children were to get sick, and Loretta, having no one to rely on, was forced to stay home to take care of them? How long would they tolerate her absence at work before they fired her? Or what if any of a million possible other things went wrong? Like on this particular day, what would she do if she called home and discovered that the baby-sitter she had just hired had not yet shown up to look after the kids when they got home from school? She was at work. Her children were home all alone. What would she do?

"What do you *mean* there's no one there but you and Will?" said Loretta in a panicked whisper when she returned Penny's call. "Brenda should have been there a half hour ago."

"Well, Brenda's not here, Mom," replied Penny. "I had to get the key from behind the mailbox to open the door."

Loretta put her hand to her forehead and squeezed her eyes closed. Her head was beyond aching now. It felt like it was caught in a vise. She took a deep breath to calm herself down while trying to decide what to do. She opened her eyes in time to see the door to Arnold Grant's office open. Her stomach tightened into a knot. Grant emerged from his office and began to walk her way. Though she felt more like crying, Loretta turned the telephone receiver to her shoulder and forced herself to give him a smile. This she did despite having taken note of the file folder he carried in his hand. She knew what was coming next.

"Loretta, would you be able to take a look at this for me and write it up right away? I need it in an hour for a meeting." Grant never gave orders; he always asked. To Loretta's knowledge, no one had ever declined one of his requests.

"Of course. I'll get right to it, Mister Grant," said Loretta, se-cretly wincing inside, hoping he couldn't hear the muffled voice of her daughter coming from the telephone receiver against her shoulder. When her boss had left, she put the receiver back to her ear. Penny was calling to her.

"Mom? Mom? Are you still there?"

"Yes, Penny, I'm here," Loretta said wearily. "Sorry about that. Okay, let me think for a minute about what to do."

"But Mom—"

"Please, Penny, just let me think for a second."

"Mom, don't worry about it," her daughter insisted. "Brenda just walked in."

"She's there?" said Loretta, half in relief, half full of ire.

"Yes. Do you want to talk to her?"

"I most certainly do," said Loretta. "But I can't do it right now. You and your brother go do your homework. I'll talk to Brenda when I get home."

Brenda had a plausible excuse for her tardiness when Loretta finally returned home and spoke with her that evening. Something about an important meeting with her academic advisor that had run longer than she had anticipated. Loretta was too tired to attend to all the details. Brenda apologized profusely and assured her that she would not be late again. At moments such as these, Loretta often felt like Blanche Dubois, except in her own case, she relied not just on the kindness of strangers but also on their honesty.

She gave Brenda a second chance.

To Loretta's relief, she found no messages from home on her voice mail the next afternoon at work. Someone was home, of that she was certain. When Loretta tried to call to double-check that Brenda had arrived on time, all she managed to get was a busy signal. It was possible that one of the kids was on the Internet; it was usually the first thing they did when they got home. The way it tied up the telephone line was becoming a problem. Loretta had considered subscribing to a cable or DSL Internet service to free up the line, but it was just one more thing that she could never seem to get around to doing. Besides, God only knew how much extra she would have to pay each month. It always sounded reasonable until you started adding it up from month to month. In any case, she felt certain that everyone was safely home. Just the same, she fretted all afternoon at the persistent busy signal that greeted her every time she called. It wasn't until she returned home that night and let Brenda go on her way that Will informed her that neither he nor Penny had been on the computer. Brenda had spent the entire afternoon talking on the telephone.

Loretta's blood pressure inched up another notch.

The following morning, before driving to work, Loretta left a note by the telephone, asking Brenda to please leave the line free unless it was for something urgent. To her relief, the line rang when she called home that afternoon. Brenda answered it right away and let her know that Will and Penny were home. Everything was fine. That night, however, her son and daughter had little to say as they sat in front of the television, eating the pizza Loretta had just had delivered. There was something odd about the way they ignored her when she asked them about how their days had gone. She suspected that something was wrong, but try as she might, she could pry nothing out of them. It troubled her all that night, until she collapsed onto the bed and fell fast asleep. It was there again when she rose the next morning, made the kids breakfast, and saw them off to school before getting herself ready for work.

A nagging worry persisted inside her throughout the rest of the morning, until she finally decided to do something about it. Loretta worked through her lunch break and later asked for permission to leave work early that afternoon. When the time came, she pulled on her coat, grabbed her purse, and hurried out to her car.

Loretta was alarmed to see a second car in addition to Brenda's parked out front when she arrived home. She drove up behind it and turned the engine off. She stared at the house for a moment. It was nearing four o'clock, and the sun was falling away fast. The lights in the upstairs bedrooms were lit. Will and Penny, she guessed, were in their rooms. As she stepped out of the car and began to walk up the driveway, Loretta happened to look up in time to see Will gazing down at her from between the curtains of his bedroom window. At seeing her look up at him, Will stepped back quickly from sight. Something was definitely going on, and she was going to get to the bottom of it right away. She strode up the front steps with the key to the door ready in her hand. Before opening the door, though, she leaned over the railing to get a look in through the front window.

Then she understood.

There on the living room couch lay Brenda with a young man, another grad student, Loretta could only surmise. Thankfully, though well on the way, the two had not fully disrobed, but they were obviously giving each other a very extensive anatomy lesson. Oddly enough, when she finally threw open the front door and walked in on them, Loretta did not give in to the urge to scream or carry on in outrage. Instead, she stared at the young man with icy malice, until he hastily managed to collect all his belongings and escape out the door. Then she turned her glare to Brenda, who was red-faced, as one might expect of a young woman caught in such circumstances.

"I can explain, Mrs. Simmons," Brenda said anxiously as she tried to straighten herself up.

"I'm sure you can," replied Loretta. "But don't bother."

"Um . . . I'm . . . sorry," Brenda stammered. "I promise, this will never happen again."

"You're right," Loretta answered cooly. "It won't happen again, Brenda. Let me tell you why . . ."

Later, after she had written Brenda a check for the days she owed her and sent the young woman packing, Loretta sat on the bottom of the stairs and stared forlornly at the floor. She wanted to cry out from frustration, but long experience had taught her that it never helped. She let out a sigh, rested her elbows atop her knees, and propped her chin up on her hand.

Will and Penny came down and sat side by side on the stairs above her. They had been hiding out upstairs until Brenda had gone.

"We didn't want to have to tell you, Mom," said Penny, putting her hand on her mother's shoulder. "We know how hard you tried to find somebody."

"I know," said Loretta. "I'm sorry about all this."

"We don't need anybody," said Will, trying to cheer her up. "We're old enough to stay by ourselves."

"He's right, Mom," his sister agreed. "We can do it."

Loretta reached back for their hands and pulled them down closer to her. She gave each of them a kiss on the head and squeezed them tight.

"Thanks, guys," she told them. "But I'm never going to leave you all alone. Never." She took a deep breath and stood.

"What are you going to do?" asked Will as his mother walked away to the kitchen.

"The same thing I always do," she told them. "Go to plan B."

"What's plan b?" he said.

"I'll tell you when I know for sure," Loretta answered. Then she walked into the kitchen and sifted through the papers on the counter until she found the one she was looking for. She picked up the telephone and dialed the number she had scribbled on the paper. It rang only twice before the person she was calling answered.

"Hello, Mrs. Campanile," she said. "Sorry to bother you. This is Loretta Simmons . . ."

CHAPTER 14

One Sunday afternoon many years ago, just after Francesca and Leo had become engaged to be married, Leo decided that it would be a good thing if his future spouse learned how to drive an automobile. In those days, Leo worked as a mechanic at a local service station. He was a whiz at repairing cars and had dreams of one day soon owning a station of his own. It seemed only reasonable to him that he should want his bride-to-be to know at least a little about how to handle a car.

Up to that point, despite her fiercely independent spirit, Francesca had never summoned up the nerve to get behind the wheel of a car. It wasn't so much that she was afraid to drive, but she had always been content to simply walk wherever she had to go or, if necessary, take a bus. Besides, if she ever needed a ride, she knew she could depend on her father or one of her brothers or Leo himself. And so, learning to drive became one of those things that Francesca was just as happy to keep putting off for some other time; it hardly seemed worth the trouble to her. And what of it, she often said, if she never got her driver's license? She knew plenty of women who left the driving to the men in their lives. Until that Sunday afternoon, Francesca would have been content to let herself be one of them if her fiancé had not finally pestered her into giving it a try.

It was a beautiful October day, that Sunday afternoon. When

she stepped outside, Francesca was greeted by a sparkling blue sky and brilliant sunshine. The air had just a hint of that pleasant autumn crispness in it, just enough to make her pull on a light sweater as she descended the steps to Leo's car. It was the kind of day on which Francesca would have enjoyed just being a passenger if Leo had suggested ride out to the country to take in the colorful spectacle of the changing foliage. She loved taking Sunday rides in the fall. Still, if she had to learn how to drive, this was a perfect day to start. Though quite uneasy about the whole thing, Francesca could not help being a little excited as well, like a child on the first day of school. As Leo hurried ahead to open the driver's side door for her, she smiled despite the nervous pang in her stomach. He seemed as excited as she.

When she slipped in behind the steering wheel, the first thing Francesca did was turn the rearview mirror toward her so that she could assess her appearance before they got started. For a moment, she scrutinized her shoulder-length hair, which in those days was a warm amber color. She decided to tie it back with a ribbon before her driving lesson commenced.

"Come on, beautiful," Leo playfully chided her. "Let's get a move on before the sun goes down."

"Hey, do you mind? I want to look good on my first day driving a car," she told him, straightening the collar of her sweater before turning the mirror back to its original position.

"You always look good," said Leo, kissing her hand. "Now can we please get started?"

And so the lesson began. As Francesca sat there, doing her best to listen to Leo's instructions, she was struck by the difference sitting just two feet to the left of where she normally sat in the car made in her view of the world. There was something thrilling about being behind the wheel of the car, something that gave her a sense of power and freedom. The nervous tension of just a few moments earlier suddenly vanished, and she couldn't wait to get started. Francesca tried to pay close attention while

Leo explained all the details on where the brake pedal was, and how the clutch worked, and when to shift, and how much gas to give it when stepping on the accelerator. Try as she might, though, she found herself simply staring at the key to the ignition, wishing all the while that her fiancé would just stop yacking and let her get on with starting the engine. After all, how hard could it be?

Francesca's first impression, after Leo's dissertation finally ended and at long last he allowed her to start the engine and attempt to put the car in gear, was that there was not an engine beneath the front hood of the car, but some sort of wild beast that was straining to break out. She let loose a scream after her first attempt to let out the clutch succeeded in advancing the car all of three feet. The engine gave a mighty roar, and the car lurched forward, stalled, and then screeched to an abrupt halt, tossing the two forward. Each ensuing attempt to put the car in gear brought the same result. The beast would rear up like a bucking bronco, bouncing them up in the air like rodeo cowboys. Such was the ferocity of the jolting that the ribbon in Francesca's hair came undone and her hair fell wildly about her face.

"What's the matter with this thing?" she screamed at Leo. "What am I doing wrong?"

Fortunately, her future husband had been born with the patience of a saint.

"It's okay," he told her gently. "Don't get nervous. Let's just try again letting the clutch out a little bit slower and giving it just a little gas. You'll get the hang of it. . . . "

And so it went for the next several minutes, before Francesca finally began to understand the subtleties of coordinating the clutch and the accelerator. It wasn't long before she finally managed to find first gear and set the car in motion. The car lurched fitfully but steadily down the road, and the two were on their way.

"Relax," Leo laughed at seeing the death grip with which she held the steering wheel. "There's no point in choking the wheel. Trust me, you're doing great."

Francesca let out a nervous laugh. She tried to relax, but as the car gained momentum, she became aware of the growing roar of the engine.

"Don't worry about that," said Leo. "It's just time to put it into second."

The thought of changing gears sent a stab of fear through Francesca. To her surprise, though, the car shifted easily into second gear as it rolled along. Emboldened, she stepped slightly harder on the gas pedal and was thrilled to feel the car accelerate.

"Now you're getting it!" enthused Leo.

Everything was going swimmingly, until an uphill section of road presented itself to her. Francesca navigated the car toward the top of the hill and came to a halt at the stoplight just before its crest. It was a busy intersection, and within moments, there were several cars lined up behind her. Francesca gave the rear-view mirror a nervous glance.

"Don't worry about them," Leo assured her. "Just remember what I told you to do when the light changes, and everything will be fine."

But everything wasn't fine when the light changed. Francesca depressed the clutch, as Leo had instructed, but the instant she let her foot off the brake, she was alarmed to find that the car began to roll backward before she had a chance to step on the gas. Panicked, she slammed her foot on the brake to keep from rolling into the car behind her. She tried again, but with the same result. As the line of cars on the opposite side of the intersection began to pass by, the line of cars behind Francesca began to grow longer. Suddenly horns were blaring and motorists behind were yelling at her out their car windows.

"What's happening?" she yelled at Leo. "Why can't I do this?"

"Stay calm," Leo told her in that same gentle voice, which at that particular moment Francesca suddenly found very annoying. "Just let the clutch out a little bit before you give it the gas."

Francesca did as he told her, but the beast beneath the hood would have none of it. The car bucked forward into the middle of the intersection and stalled. Fortunately, it went far enough over the crest of the hill so that it no longer rolled backward. By this time, though, Francesca was so rattled that she couldn't remember how to get the car into first gear without stalling again. They were stuck in the middle of the intersection. Cars swerved around them to either side, their drivers making unkind remarks about Francesca's driving abilities as they passed. To make matters worse, the light changed once again, so that now she was blocking traffic coming from the left and right. Francesca tried frantically to get the car going, but each attempt ended with the car stalling and more horns blaring.

"This is all your fault!" she screamed at Leo, furious at the spectacle she was making of herself.

Leo, who by now was wearing an expression that suggested that he was doing his best to not burst out laughing, threw open his door and stepped out into the street. For a fleeting moment, Francesca thought that he was so embarrassed that he meant to abandon her right there on the spot. How, she wondered in anguish, would she explain to her family and friends that her fiancé had called off the wedding because he didn't want to be married to someone who couldn't find first gear? This ridiculous notion vanished when she saw Leo gesturing to the surrounding motorists to just stay calm and be patient as he hurried around to her side of the car. He opened the door and nonchalantly advised her to move over. This heroic rescue made the situation all the more humiliating for Francesca.

"We'll practice some more tomorrow," Leo promised her,

giving her hand another quick kiss. Then, with insulting ease, he put the car in gear and cruised away from the intersection. He assumed a nice drive out into the country to look at the trees in all their autumn splendor would be just the thing to make her feel better. He was right, but several miles would pass before Francesca's ire finally abated enough for her to see the humor in her first adventure behind the wheel.

Now, so many years later, Francesca was not quite sure why the memory of that particular day should come to mind at just that moment. She sat there at the kitchen table and dwelled on it for a time after she hung up the telephone. The call from Loretta Simmons had taken her by surprise. It was a Thursday evening, and over a week without any word from the young woman had passed since their interview. Francesca had assumed, quite reasonably, that the position had gone to someone else. Not that she had expected things to be otherwise. Francesca and the woman had not exactly hit it off when they had first met. There was much Francesca had wanted to say about herself, and many questions she had wanted to ask about the mother and her children, but she had been afraid of being too nosy right off the bat. So, instead of prying, she had tried to answer the woman's questions as succinctly and politely as possible without saying or asking too much. It had made for an awkward conversation, and afterward, Francesca knew that she had not come across very well.

As the days went by and it became obvious that the woman must have chosen someone else to look after her children, Francesca had finally decided that perhaps it was all for the best. Peg and the others were right; she probably wasn't ready for this sort of thing. Besides, she told herself, there were plenty of other things she could find to fill up her time. She would just have to accept things as they were and make the best of it. Something about coming to that resolution had made her feel better. Just that night, while she had sat at the table eating a bowl of mine-strone, Francesca had decided to forget all about it, to put the whole matter out of her mind—and then the telephone had rung.

To say that she had been caught off guard when the Simmons woman had asked her if she were still interested in the position would have been a great understatement. More startling, though, was when she had asked Francesca if she would be able to start Friday, the very next day! Asking for a day or two to prepare herself would have been a sensible idea, but Francesca had been so astonished by the whole turn of events and the woman's re-quest that she couldn't bring herself to say no. Yes, of course she could come tomorrow, Francesca had told her.

As Francesca mulled the whole thing over, she regretted re-plying so hastily. She ought to have said that she could not pos-sibly start until Monday. At least that would have given her the weekend to get her thoughts together. An odd feeling of dread mixed with anticipation filled her as she stood to take her empty bowl to the sink. There was something familiar about it that puzzled, Francesca until she understood why the memory of that day in Leo's car had come to mind. Thinking back on it, she realized that she was now filled with that same odd blend of nervous excitement as on that day when she had first gotten be-hind the wheel of the car. At the same time, though, she recog-nized that same feeling of helpless panic that had overtaken her when she had become stuck at the intersection and the car had begun to roll backward, that sinking feeling in her gut that she had gotten herself in way over her head. The difference this time was that she was all alone. There would be no one to rescue her if things went wrong.

"What did I just get myself into, Leo?" she said aloud as she washed the bowl and deposited it into the dishdrainer. "Am I crazy, or what?"

With that thought in mind, she went upstairs to get an early night's rest. A big day lay ahead of her, and she wanted to be ready. Francesca fretted about the whole thing while she changed into her pajamas, but when she finally put her head on the pillow, she was comforted by one thought: At least now her car was an automatic.

CHAPTER 15

Francesca found the key to the house tucked behind the mailbox, just where Loretta had said she would leave it. Standing in the cold outside the front door, she breathed a sigh of relief. There was much about this undertaking that made her uneasy, but for some reason, the one thing she had fretted most about all day was the fear that the key would not be there when she arrived. Her active imagination had conjured up a multitude of scenarios on how she would respond in such an event. The most extreme had her kicking in a basement window and climbing through. This particular contingency plan posed several problems, not the least of which would have been her lack of agility. Also to consider was the arduous removal of the snow piled up against the house outside the window. Lastly, her skulking about in this manner would have most likely invited the attention of the local police, who would no doubt be informed by the neighbors that a would-be elderly burglar was prowling about the outside of the Simmons home. Reason had mercifully returned to Francesca's anxiety-filled mind when it had come time to drive across the city that afternoon. In the end, she had come to the sensible conclusion that, if the key were not there, she would simply sit in her car and wait for the children to come home.

With that fear now dispelled, Francesca hesitated at the front door. There was, she fully realized, no one home, but just the same, she wanted to present herself well when she stepped inside. It might have seemed a silly notion to others, but she wanted to make a good impression entering the house by herself for the first time. Francesca had always believed that every home has a personality all its own, its own soul almost, something that radiated its own energy apart from the people who inhabited it. It was more than just the style of the windows facing the world outside or that of the furnishings inside. Some houses, she often noticed, made her feel welcome the moment she walked in regardless of how well kept or decorated they might be. Then there were others that seemed to give off a more forbidding air, something that made them feel more standoffish, almost aloof, as if they would have preferred it if you simply went away and didn't bother to come in at all. As she inserted the key and turned it, Francesca sensed an air of shyness and uncertainty in this home, something that gave the impression that this was a place still not quite sure of itself. That being the case, she chose to enter slowly and respectfully, giving it time to grow accustomed to her presence.

Francesca stepped inside and closed the door behind her. She stood there for a time, surveying the interior of the home while she removed her coat and hat. Little had changed since her initial visit to the house, when she had first interviewed for the position. It was not dirty by any means, but the place had the look of organized disarray, which one would expect in a house presided over by a working mother raising two children on her own.

Francesca removed her boots and slipped on her house shoes before stepping into the living room, where she cast a trained eye upon the surroundings. Though almost the end of January, holiday decorations still adorned the windows, and an artificial Christmas tree still stood in the corner with an assortment of toys and games scattered about on the floor around it. The pillows on the couch were tossed helter-skelter, and several days worth of what looked to be unread newspapers were strewn across the coffee table. Some of these had slipped off onto the floor and been kicked underneath, where they were trying to hide along with a stack of magazines.

Francesca turned her gaze to the end table by the arm of the couch. There she spied a small pile of crumbs, evidence that someone recently had been munching on a snack while watching the television. The couch's stained arm cover indicated that this was a popular dining spot, most likely for one or both of the children. She leaned closer and observed that the remote control for the television had slipped down between the cushions. Her first instinct was to extract it and place it in plain view, but she decided that, for the time being, it would probably be better if she just left everything as it was.

The kitchen was a disaster. When she walked in, Francesca found the counters littered with school papers, mail, and a variety of other clutter, leaving little room for food preparation. The table was in much the same state, though it appeared some effort had been made to push some of the mess out of the way. The sink was piled with dirty dishes, cups, and utensils from the previous day, but no pots or pans. This puzzled Francesca, until she noted that the top of the stove was covered with paraphernalia. From the looks of things, it was rarely used. She clicked her tongue and shook her head.

Francesca gave only a passing glance at the downstairs bathroom as she made her way out of the kitchen to the back hall, where she found a washer and dryer surrounded by baskets of clothes, some dirty, others clean but in need of folding. She came back to the front and looked up the staircase.

The first few steps presented a narrow passage, as there were pairs of shoes, hairbrushes, books, and other items piled there. Though curious to go upstairs to see the rest of the house, Francesca decided against the idea. She didn't want to risk tripping over anything to do it, and in any case, she had explored enough for the first day. Besides, she had already seen enough to understand what this mother and her children were up against. With nothing else to do, Francesca went back to the living room, where sat she down on the couch and settled back to wait for the children to come home.

CHAPTER 16

Francesca jumped up when she heard the sound of children's voices outside the front door. In the process, she knocked several sections of newspaper off the coffee table. It had suddenly occurred to her that she wasn't sure of what she should be doing when the children came in. First impressions meant a lot, and she wanted the one she made to be a good one. With no time to waste picking up the papers from the floor, she kicked them under the table with the others. Given the state of things, she doubted anyone would ever notice.

As the doorknob began to turn, Francesca started toward the door, but then decided that she didn't want to appear to be accosting the boy and girl the moment they stepped inside. It would probably frighten them. Instead, she went to sit back down, but then thought better of it; she didn't want them to think that she was lazy. By the time the door swung open and the two youngsters stepped inside, Francesca had finally settled on a position by the end of the couch. There she stood like a lady in waiting, her hands curled into one another in a gesture of respectful anticipation.

The boy and girl eyed her warily as they stood in the front hall, peeling off their coats and hats.

For her part, Francesca's heart melted the moment she first

beheld the two children. They were adorable! The girl, she could see, was just on the cusp of adolescence. With her long, dark hair and slender features, she was destined to be a beautiful young lady someday, but for now, she was still very much a child. The boy was considerably smaller than his big sister. His hair was equally dark, but full of delightful curls, which rolled and tumbled over his forehead. His big, inquisitive eyes peered at her through the wire-rimmed eyeglasses he wore, and he looked for all the world like a professor of entomology who had just come across a rather interesting-looking bug. Gazing at them both, it was all Francesca could do to keep from taking them in her arms and squeezing them for all she was worth.

"Hello, children," she said in a hesitant voice. "My name is Mrs. Campanile, your new babysitter."

The girl gave her a haughty stare. "*My* name is Penny," she replied with a tone of youthful defiance, "and I'm not a baby, so I do not need a babysitter."

"*Penny*," the boy whispered harshly, "be nice. Remember what Mom said."

"Oh, that's quite all right," Francesca assured the boy. "My mistake. It's just that the two of you are so much more grown up than I had anticipated." This remark seemed to put his sister a bit more at ease. "I suppose your sister is right," she went on. "We'll have to come up with something else to call me besides your babysitter." This she said while moving ever so slightly toward the front of the coffee table, to block their view of the manual on babysitting sticking out of the bag of books she had brought along to keep her occupied while she waited alone. To her relief, neither seemed to notice.

"And what is your name, young man?" Francesca asked the boy, even though she already knew.

"I'm Will," he said.

"Well, how nice," she told him. "I have a grandson named Will who's just your age. It's a pleasure to meet you both."

"Yeah, I guess," said Penny, walking past her to the kitchen. Will followed close behind, giving Francesca a quick glance over his shoulder as he passed.

"If there's anything you need . . ." Francesca called after them, but neither of them replied.

Not wanting to interfere in their after-school routines, Francesca simply watched them go. She stayed there in the living room, listening to them exchange whispers as they rummaged through the refrigerator and cupboards. She smiled, for it was a scene, she well knew, that was being played out at that hour in homes all around. Many things had changed since Francesca was a young mother raising her own family, but one thing had remained a constant: children always come home hungry from school.

A few minutes later, Will and Penny re-emerged from the kitchen. To Francesca's dismay, Penny carried with her a bag of potato chips, and Will a bowl of ice cream. There was nothing wrong in having an afternoon snack, but she wanted with all her heart to tell them to have something more wholesome. She understood, however, that it was not her place to do so. Besides, who was to say that there was anything more wholesome to be had in the kitchen at that moment. In any case, the two children paraded by her again and, without a word to her, marched directly upstairs to their rooms.

Not sure of what to do next, Francesca returned to the couch, took a seat once more, and pulled out the book on babysitting. She had always considered herself an old hand at taking care of children, but her first encounter with Will and Penny had left her with the impression that perhaps there might be something new that she needed to learn.

★ ★ ★

"Sorry I'm getting home a little late," said Loretta when she bustled through the front door, clutching a grocery bag in one arm and a cloth bag containing her work shoes and purse under the other. She dropped the cloth bag onto the floor, kicked the door shut behind her, and hurried toward the kitchen.

The clock on the mantel read five forty-five. Loretta was fifteen minutes late, but Francesca didn't mind. In truth, she had become engrossed in one of the books she had brought along—the babysitting manual had held her attention only briefly—and the time had gone by quickly.

"The market was *such* a zoo!" the younger woman lamented as she hurried past Francesca with the grocery bag.

"Eh, Friday night. What did you expect?" said Francesca, strolling over to the kitchen door. She peeked in, curious to get a look at what Loretta had brought home. "Planning to cook for the family tonight?" she asked.

"Oh, no," said Loretta with a laugh. "Who has time to cook? Besides, I can just about boil water."

"It's not so hard to learn," said Francesca.

"Maybe someday, when I have the time. But for now, why bother? They have some really nice prepared food at the markets these days. It's so convenient. You just bring it home, toss it in the microwave to warm it up, and dinner's served. No mess. No fuss. No pots and pans to clean up. Can't beat that."

"I suppose," said Francesca with a doubtful look as she watched the young mother take the plastic containers out of the bag and put them on the table. "What did you decide to get?"

"Meat loaf," said Loretta, opening one of the containers to show her. "Plus some mashed potatoes and vegetables. It's really good."

"That's nice," said Francesca, knowing full well that the expression on her face conveyed a different opinion. "Well, I'm sure you and the children will enjoy it," she added before turning back to the living room to collect her things. By the time Loretta came out of the kitchen, Francesca had already pulled on her boots and overcoat.

"I hope they weren't any trouble for you," said Loretta, rummaging through her pocketbook while the older woman tugged a hat over her ears.

"Oh, no," said Francesca, giving her a smile. "They were perfect. We had a nice chat when they came home, and then they went straight upstairs to . . . well, I guess to do their homework." She started for the door.

"Oh, don't go yet," said Loretta, still searching through her pocketbook.

"Why not?"

"Because I haven't paid you for today," she said. "Where *is* that checkbook?"

"Please, don't worry about it," Francesca told her. "Today was a chance to introduce ourselves. This one's on me."

"Oh, no, that's not right," protested Loretta. "It's the end of the week, and you deserve to be paid for your time today."

"Believe me, it's really not necessary," Francesca assured her.

"But—"

"Make it up to me next Friday," said Francesca, giving her a pat on the hand. "Now, go have supper with your children. That's more important."

With that, Francesca bid her good night and went to the door.

Later, after she had traversed the front walk—which was barely shoveled—and settled into her car, Francesca hummed a tune to herself as she buckled up and put the key in the ignition. When she turned it, the engine coughed like a smoker in the morning before rumbling to life. It occurred to Francesca that she ought to have come out earlier to give the car a chance to warm up, but at that particular moment, the cold didn't bother her. She gave in to a little yawn, though, for it had been a long day. Putting the car in gear, she pulled away from the house, unaware that all the while, three pairs of curious eyes were watching her from the windows.

CHAPTER 17

Loretta stood at the window and watched until the old woman had driven off into the cold night. When the car was out of sight, she turned from the window and started back to the kitchen, biting her lip all the while. She was furious at herself for not having had her checkbook ready. What must the woman have thought of her? That she was some kind of charity case? Her ruminations on the matter grew even darker when she re-entered the kitchen and regarded the cluttered table and the sink full of dirty dishes, which she had meant to take care of that morning before work, but for which there simply hadn't been time. Loretta had purposefully bustled into the house and hurried to the kitchen when she had come home. She had hoped against reason that Mrs. Campanile would stay put in the living room for two minutes and spare her the humiliation of seeing the disaster all around while she put out the food for supper. Instead, the old nosebag had waltzed right over to see what she had brought home, forcing Loretta to feign blissful ignorance of her surroundings. As if that weren't insult enough, there was the not-so-subtle dig about learning how to cook! That's all she needed right now: to have a guilt trip laid on her by her babysitter.

Steaming, Loretta poked her head out the kitchen door to call the kids for supper, but by then, they were already on their way down. Struggling as always to be the first wherever they happened to be going, the two siblings squeezed and pushed and elbowed their way down the staircase. Despite his sister's size advantage, Will managed to squirm away and leap the last three stairs to victory. He struck the landing like a gymnast and raised his arms in a victory salute, a gloating smile across his face.

"Cheater," muttered Penelope, giving her brother an elbow to the midsection as she passed. Will doubled over and let out a howl of pain, but in truth, she had given him little more than a nudge. Her brother's dramatic sufferings were all an act.

"Hey!" cried Loretta. "How many times have I told the two of you, no roughhousing on the stairs?"

"She started it," complained Will, his face contorted in phony agony. "Plus she just punched me in the stomach. You must have seen her do it. Aren't you going to do something?"

"Yes," replied his mother. "I'm going to give both of you a good wallop if you don't learn how to behave." In all her years as a mother, Loretta had never once made good on her threats to use corporal punishment on her children. Such being the case, Will and Penny had long ago stopped paying any attention to them. Loretta herself paid them no heed, but it made her feel better to utter them from time to time. "Just go wash your hands and sit down for dinner," she told them in exasperation.

"Oh, my God, Mom, *where* did you find her?" exclaimed Penny a short time later when the three had gathered at the table to serve themselves. "She must be like—I don't know—a hundred and *fifty?*"

The young girl served herself a helping of mashed potatoes and carried her plate to the living room to watch television while she ate.

"Really, Mom," Will chimed in just before stuffing a forkful of meat loaf into his mouth. He took a couple of loud, unpleasant-sounding chomps and swallowed before adding, "Where did you find that Mrs. Compa-bompa-whatever-her-name-is anyway? At a nursing home?" With that, he took his plate and sauntered off to join his sister.

"That's enough from the two of you," his mother called after him. "She seems like a very nice woman. And her name is Mrs. Campanile, Mister Eats-Like-a-Horse. Try closing your mouth when you chew. You can call her Mrs. C if that's too hard for you to remember. And don't forget, we're lucky to even have her, especially since she came here on such short notice."

This last remark sounded even less convincing to Loretta than it did to the children. Loretta did not feel lucky at all. She felt penciled into a corner, like she always did. It was a state of affairs she had grown too weary to bother fighting or even lamenting anymore; these days, when time and circumstances conspired against her, she simply adapted herself to them. Experience had taught her that it was generally the most efficient course of action. Not wanting to dwell further on this particular subject, she decided to change the conversation to another.

"So, I hope no one has any big assignments due on Monday," she told them. "If either of you do, get working on it now, because I'm not going to want to hear about it on Sunday night at ten o'clock. Don't leave it until the last minute, like someone I know does all the time." This comment was aimed at her son, who pretended not to hear as he came back into the kitchen with his empty plate. Instead, he set his sights on another helping of meat loaf. The container of vegetables never once caught his eye.

"I have a team project I'm working on with Jenna," announced Penny. "So I'll need to use the computer tonight."

"But I was going to go online to check out the Yu-Gi-Oh Web site!" cried Will.

"My schoolwork is more important than your stupid game-card thing," replied his sister.

"It's not fair, Mom," he protested. "All's she gonna do is instant message her friends."

"Enough!" pleaded Loretta. "This nightly bickering over who gets to use the computer is enough to drive a person to drink. I have half a mind to throw the whole thing out the second-floor window. Let your sister do her work for a little while, and then you do whatever you want on it later. The two of you are old enough to sort this out between yourselves. If you can't do that and this constant commotion continues, I'll just get rid of the computer, and that will be that."

This was another of Loretta's occasional threats that she and her children well knew she would never make good on.

"Whatever," said Penny.

"So, what's the deal, Mom?" asked Will. "Is she coming back on Monday?"

"Mrs. Campanile? I certainly hope so."

"How come?"

Loretta gave a sigh. "Because at the moment, I don't have a plan C," she told him.

"Sounds like Mrs. C *is* plan C," chuckled Will, quite amused with himself.

"Very funny," said his sister, rolling her eyes.

After they finished eating, Loretta closed up the leftovers and put them in the refrigerator, while Penny logged on to the computer upstairs and Will settled in to play a video game on the television. It had been a long day—a long week, for that matter—and the urge to lay down and sleep was weighing heavier and heavier upon her. She cast a forlorn look at the growing pile of dirty dishes in the sink. Her kitchen was crying for attention, just like everything else in her life, but at the moment, she had no energy for it. The lure of relaxing in a nice hot bath while the kids were quiet coaxed her away. She had earned it, she told herself, and besides, the dishes would all still be there in the morning.

CHAPTER 18

"She didn't *pay* you?" cried Peg.

"Didn't I say she was crazy to do it?" added Connie.

"This is exactly how it starts," concluded Natalie.

They were in the library by the collection of movie videos and audiobooks. It was early Saturday afternoon, and Francesca had stopped by to drop off the books on babysitting she had taken out. She had read about as much of them as she could tolerate; they weren't much help. Peg and the others had been there when she had walked in, each of them browsing through the videos for something to watch on television later that night. Francesca had hoped not to encounter any of her three library friends that day, for she had anticipated what their reaction to the account of her first day as a babysitter would be. The three of them, though, had spied her the moment she had walked through the front entrance. There was no way to escape giving a full report.

Francesca shrugged and gave a sigh. "She wanted to pay me," she insisted. "It's just that it was late, and I wanted to go home, and she couldn't find her checkbook. Besides, it was only one day."

Peg wasn't buying any of it. She stood there, gaping at her friend. Rolling her eyes, she clicked her tongue and shook her head as if to say that Francesca had just set a world record for gullibility.

"Oldest trick in the book," clucked Connie.

"Told you something like this would happen," added Natalie.

"Well," Francesca groused, "at least I didn't have to do any cooking or cleaning—not that I wasn't tempted. And I was so *bombalit'* yesterday morning, trying to get myself organized, that I didn't even think to make a little something for the kids to eat after school. You should have seen the junk they ate!"

"So what?" said Peg with a dismissive wave. "Let them eat what they want. You're better off. You do it once, and they'll expect it all the time. Besides, you never know if one of them might have a food allergy."

"Food allergy?"

"That's right," agreed Natalie. "Didn't all those babysitting books tell you anything? Lots of kids these days are allergic to peanuts and God knows what else. You've got to be careful what you give them."

"That's all you need to have happen," added Connie. "One of the little brats goes into anaphylactic shock, and then what do you do?"

"So, give us the rest of the dirt," said Peg. "Was the house really a mess?"

"Oh, not so bad," Francesca told them, trying to put the best spin possible on the situation. "I never got a chance to see the upstairs, but things were a little lived-in downstairs, if you know what I mean. I thought about straightening up a little before the mother got home—"

"Don't you dare!" huffed Peg.

"Don't worry. I didn't lift a finger," Francesca assured them. "But it wasn't easy. It was all I could do to just sit there on my hands."

Connie leaned closer and gave her a nudge. "So, what about

the kids?" she said with a twinkle in her eye. "What were they like?"

"Oh, my God, you should have seen them!" cried Francesca, holding her hands over her heart.

"Really cute?" sighed Natalie.

"You would pinch their cheeks for an hour if you saw them."

"Hey, cute is what cute does," warned Peg. "It's the cute ones that are always the most trouble."

"Well, you might have a point there," said Francesca. "I didn't exactly hit it off with the two of them. I don't think they're bad kids—I didn't get that impression at all—but they need something."

"What?" her three friends asked in unison.

"I don't know yet," said Francesca with a shrug, "but I'll figure it out."

"So, you're going back there again on Monday?" said Peg.

"Of course."

"But why?"

"It's hard to explain," she said thoughtfully. "I guess it's because I think they need somebody—maybe not me, but somebody. And *I* need to be needed. I need to be doing something useful. It's like I told you once before: It's a way for me to keep breathing."

"And like I said before," sighed Peg with another shake of her head, "I think it's a good way to give yourself a big pain in the backside. But what can I say? It's your backside. Just make sure you get your money next week."

"Ayyy, don't worry, I will," Francesca assured her friend. Then, with a sly a grin, she added, "And if she doesn't pay up, I'll send you three to collect for me."

At that, she and her friends all laughed aloud, until they were shushed by an annoyed library patron hidden somewhere among the book stacks. The librarian herself would have also done so, but she knew better than to tangle with the four biddies.

"Okay, girls," whispered Francesca. "Guess we better quiet down before they call the cops on us."

"Now wouldn't *that* be exciting?" whispered Peg in return, and the four covered their mouths to stifle their giggling, like schoolgirls sharing a private joke.

Francesca went to church later that afternoon. She arrived early enough to go to confession before the start of mass, but she chose instead to stay in her pew and pray the rosary. It was something she did quite often. Francesca loved the quiet, contemplative minutes in the church before mass, especially when things were weighing on her mind—as they so often did For a few tranquil moments before the celebration began, she would let it all go. Her worries for her children. Her fears for the future. Her occasional anger over trivial things that she knew, in the final analysis, really didn't matter, but tormented her still. All these she handed over to God for a time, to let Him sort out the whole thing, while she allowed her mind a brief, refreshing rest. She often emerged from her weekly hour in church feeling far more renewed than she ever did after a month of vacation.

On this particular evening, however, the rosary and the mass did not prove to be the elixir to her spirits that they normally were. From the opening prayers through communion, Francesca struggled to pay attention, her mind dwelling on her first day with the Simmons children. She was feeling a little guilty about not telling her own children what she was up to, even though she was of the firm opinion that it was her business and none of theirs. She felt an additional twinge at not having been completely forthright with her friends at the library. There was more to why she had not cooked or cleaned up the house for the Simmons woman than she had let on to Peg and the others. They all were right, of course, that there were people out there who would not hesitate to take advantage of someone caring for their children. Somehow, though, Loretta Simmons did not strike her as being one of them. From the little Francesca had, to this point, seen of her, the young woman simply seemed overwhelmed by all she was facing, but was too proud to admit it. Pride was something about which Francesca knew more than just a little, and the last thing on this earth she would intentionally do is wound that of another. She understood that, until she knew the young mother and her children better, she would have to tread lightly. It would be a challenge, one she wasn't completely certain that she was up to.

Feeling a bit glum, Francesca gave only a brief hello to Father Buontempo when she walked out of the church after mass was finished. The winter night had fallen like a dark cloak over the city, a cold sliver of a moon rising in the east, and she shivered as she picked her way across the parking lot to her car. When she installed herself behind the steering wheel and turned the key, the engine did not turn over right away, adding a layer of apprehension to her ruminations. On the third try, it roared to life, and Francesca put it in gear before it had a chance to stall. The car gave her no trouble on the way home, but the thought that it might traveled with her the whole way.

When she pulled up to the house, Francesca was surprised to see a car parked out front. She pulled into the driveway, collected her things, and hurried up the front walk to the door. When she stepped inside, she threw off her coat and hat, and went straight to the kitchen. There she found a young man sitting at the table, perusing the newspaper. Her hands on her hips, Francesca stood in the doorway, tapping her foot as she gloated at him. For his part, the young man said nothing, but merely looked up, gave her a nod and a smile, and went back to reading the paper. Peeved at such a complacent greeting, Francesca tried to force herself to frown at the young man, but it was no use, for inside, her heart was soaring a mile high. How could it not?

Joey was home.

CHAPTER 19

Francesca filled a pot with water and put it on the back burner of the stove. She threw in a pinch of salt, turned the heat up high, and covered the pot. While she waited for the water to come to a boil, she began to peel and dice two cloves of garlic on her cutting board. Annoyed at the dull edge of the knife she was using, she impatiently tossed the knife into the sink and drew out another from the utensil drawer by her waist. This one, to her satisfaction, performed much better than the first, and she made quick work of the garlic. When she was done, she slid the diced garlic into a frying pan already coated thick with olive oil. She added a pat or two of butter and a sprinkling of crushed red pepper before setting the heat on low to let the garlic simmer. This accomplished, she looked over her shoulder at her son.

Joey was still at the table, looking over the sports section. He had barely spoken two words since his mother had first walked in to find him there. This reticence was not due to any particular indifference on his part. Joey, Francesca well understood, had simply inherited his father's preternatural state of perpetual calmness. He never seemed to get too worked up about anything, at least not so that it showed. In all the years since he had been a toddler, Francesca had rarely known her son to raise his voice in anger or to fly off the handle the way his mother and sisters were prone to do; he always seemed to be in control of himself. When he so chose, Joey could be a lively conversationalist. Growing up with a mother and two sisters, though, the opportunities to practice the art had been scant. Getting a word or two in edgewise had always been a challenge, and he had had to learn how to make every word count. Not that it mattered very much, for also like his father, Joey could usually convey more with a simple nod or gesture than most people could communicate with a mouthful of words. But for all his placid facade, Francesca knew, he had a lot percolating beneath the surface.

"All I have is a pound of linguine, and some lettuce and cucumber for a salad," she told him. "If I'd known you were coming, I would have stopped at the market."

Joey shrugged and jutted out his chin slightly, as if to say that whatever she made would be more than sufficient. He flipped to the next page of the paper.

Francesca turned back to the stove and took the lid off the pot on the back burner. The water had come to a rolling boil, and she was greeted by a great puff of steam, which quickly dispersed into the air. Francesca ripped open the package of linguine and dumped the long, brittle strands into the hissing water.

"Go get some cheese out of the fridge," she said over her shoulder as she stirred the linguine with a big fork. "Get the Romano. I like that better than the Parmesan. And don't forget the grater."

"You're the boss," said Joey, finally opening his mouth. He pushed away from the table, stood, and walked to the refrigerator with a slight limp, evidence of a recent rugby injury, which immediately caught his mother's notice.

"I wish you would give up playing that crazy game of yours," she told him. "You're getting too old, you know. One of these days, you're going to really hurt yourself. Then you'll be sorry."

In all the years that he had played rugby after college, Joey had managed only once to talk Francesca into stopping by to watch one of his club's matches. She had been aghast at what she had witnessed. From what little she could discern of the mayhem on the field, the game involved little more than thirty grown men doing their utmost to tear each other limb from limb just to gain possession of the ball, which resembled a lop-sided balloon. Any player who happened to have the misfortune of carrying the ball soon found himself attacked by a pack of maniacs. As for Francesca, she had found herself closing her eyes whenever Joey touched the ball, for she was certain that her son would be torn to shreds if he didn't have the sense to immediately pass it to someone else. It was even worse for her than when Joey had played high school football. At least then, he had worn pads and a helmet. These ruminations were unsettling enough for Francesca, but then another thought occurred to her.

"Hey," she said. "I hope you didn't get that limp by jumping off one of those bridges like that fool on the postcard you sent me."

"Wouldn't you like to know," replied Joey, the corner of his mouth turning up into an impish smirk. He poked his head into the refrigerator to find the cheese. Not finding it immediately, he looked back to his mother.

"It's in the drawer on the left, where it always is," she said before he had the chance to ask.

"Got it," said Joey. He limped back to his chair, set the cheese on the table, and picked the sports section back up.

"Tell me the truth," said Francesca, now with a worried strain in her voice. "Did you get that limp on the playing field or by jumping off one of those bridges with the rest of the idiots?"

Joey sank slightly lower behind the newspaper. "Do you know," he began without looking up, "that an object falling to the earth accelerates thirty-three feet per second every second until it reaches terminal velocity?" Then he said no more.

Francesca scowled at her son. This was precisely the type of answer Joey gave whenever he was trying to avoid answering a direct question. It was another modus operandi that he had inherited directly from his father. It was enough to make Francesca scream—and like his father, Joey knew it—but she didn't. Instead, she took a breath to compose herself, turned back to the cutting board, and began to slice the cucumber for the salad.

"I'm not going to hit you right now," she told him calmly, "because you're expecting it, and I'll only end up hurting myself. I'm gonna wait."

Behind the newspaper, Joey's face broke out in a smile. How many times as a child had he heard his mother utter that same warning whenever he or one of his sisters had talked back to her or misbehaved in some other way? More than he could possibly remember. As children, Joey and his sisters had learned to fear that calm pronouncement, for they well knew that their mother was as good as her word. Sometimes days or even weeks would pass with nary a word on her part about whatever infraction one of the three might have committed. To all appearances, Francesca would forget about the whole thing. Lulled into a fall sense of security, the children themselves would forget all about it. Then, on no day in particular, perhaps some quiet afternoon as they all sat in the dining room enjoying Sunday dinner together, her open hand would flash out unexpectedly from across the table and smack the offending party full force across the mouth.

"That," she would explain to the aggrieved recipient, "was for talking back to me that last time."

For his part, Leo would always look with pity on the red-faced child, but only give a shrug in response to his or her lamentations, as if to say, "What did you expect?"

Nothing warms a child's heart like the spectacle of an errant sibling being brought to justice, and such moments would inevitably elicit stifled giggles from the innocent. But no one was spared from her just punishments whenever one of them got out of line. As the baby of the family, Joey sometimes managed to get away with a few more shenanigans than his older sisters, but even he had often enough found himself on the receiving end of one of her wallops.

When the linguine was finished cooking, Francesca poured it all into a strainer in the sink. She gave the strainer a shake to rid it of the excess water before depositing the steaming strands into the frying pan. There she tossed them with a big wooden spoon and fork to mix them with the garlic and olive oil.

Joey eagerly folded the newspaper and put it aside when he saw his mother carrying the frying pan to the table. She set it in the center of the table on top of an oven pad, and nodded for him to help himself while she finished preparing the salad. Joey filled one bowl for himself and another for his mother before digging in. Francesca was happy to note that, by the time she sat down to eat, he was already working on a second helping.

"I missed this," he sighed contentedly as he twirled the linguine onto his fork.

"How was the food down there?" asked Francesca.

"Eh," grunted Joey with a shrug, enough of a response to tell his mother that the cuisine had not been up to her standards.

Narrowing her gaze at him, Francesca reached out and pushed some of Joey's curly hair away from his forehead to reveal an ugly-looking lump.

"Uff," she grunted in consternation. "Look what you do to the beautiful face your father and I gave you. How did you manage to get *that*?"

"Don't worry. I didn't get it falling off a bridge," he told her. "I just caught somebody's boot when I went down to get the ball during the match against—"

"Stop. Don't tell me anymore. I'm sorry I asked."

Joey shrugged and turned his attention back to his bowl of linguine. Francesca studied him for a few moments while she grated some cheese onto her own bowlful.

"So," she asked him, "Did you find it?"

Joey looked up at her with a questioning look. "Find what?" he said.

"You know, what you've been looking for," she answered. "Did you find it down there on the other side of the globe."

"What makes you think that I'm looking for something?"

"Everybody's looking for something," his mother told him. "It what life is all about. Searching for the right things to make you feel whole, especially when you've lost something. But you know, you can run around the world all you want, but what you're looking for is right here," she said, poking his chest above his heart. "That's what will tell you what you really need to know—what to look for and when you've found it—if you just pay attention instead of running away." She paused. "It's been almost four years, you know. It's time to start listening again."

Joey gave another one of his shrugs, telling her there was no use in pursuing this particular subject at the moment. He was not of a mind to discuss it. Instead he glanced to the bowl on the counter.

Francesca shook her head, let out a low grumble, and stood. She gave him a gentle slap across the top of his head and went to get the salad.

"It's good to have you home," she told him.

"It's nice to be home," he said. "So, what have *you* been up to while I've been out of town? Find what *you've* been looking for?"

"And wouldn't *you* like to know," answered his mother with a smug grin as she set the salad bowl on the table. "Now shut up and eat."

As a young man who liked to keep his own counsel on matters close to his heart, Joey was not one to pry into those of someone else, not even his mother's, so he did as he was told and helped himself to the salad.

Joey stayed for a while after dinner, telling Francesca about his trip to Australia, the places he had seen, the people he had met, and the long flight home, until the jet lag suddenly hit him and his eyes began to droop. Francesca knew there was little use in trying to convince him to just stay and sleep in his old bed that night, so before it got too late, she shooed her yawning son out the door; she didn't want him falling asleep at the wheel on the way back to his apartment. Before Joey left, she instructed him to return the next day for Sunday dinner—and to bring his laundry, if he wanted. She stood at the door and watched him drive off, until his car was out of sight. Then she went back into the kitchen. As always, it made her sad to see him go, but at least now she finally had an excuse to thaw out that nice pork roast she'd been keeping in the freezer.

CHAPTER 20

"**M**y, aren't we looking bright-eyed and bushy-tailed this morning," said Shirley, a knowing grin curling her lips as she passed Loretta on the way to her desk on Monday morning.

In reply, Loretta let out a low grumble that conveyed, despite its lack of words, a message of deep malice at her friend's annoying perkiness at that hour.

"Coffee should be ready any minute," Shirley called cheerfully after her.

The morning was never a happy time for Loretta. The first thin sliver of sunlight to arc over the horizon each dawn pierced through the tiny gap between her window's drawn curtains and greeted her weary eyes with all the soft subtlety of a javelin. It was always a shock, one seconded only by the shrill cry of the alarm clock, which inevitably followed just a minute or two later. Monday mornings in the winter posed a particularly daunting challenge to her spirits. She dreaded the miserable first few moments when she awoke to the cold darkness of those early hours and lay there pondering the long workweek stretching out before her. It was like the dawn of the dead.

Somehow, despite her best intentions, the weekends never seemed to provide Loretta with the extra hours of restorative sleep that her body craved. The one just past had been no different. Instead of sleeping in on Saturday morning, Loretta had dragged herself out of bed and set about straightening up the house before the kids awoke. She was determined to get things in better order before Mrs. Campanile returned on Monday afternoon. Why she should be concerned with the old woman's opinion of her housekeeping, Loretta could not quite say. Nonetheless, the thought of it was enough to prod her into action.

Operations commenced in the living room, where at long last she boxed all the Christmas ornaments, dismantled the tree, and carted it all back to the basement. The removal of the tree and the rest of the holiday paraphernalia created a pleasing increase in floor space, which inspired Loretta to break out the vacuum cleaner and really give the place a thorough going-over. It wasn't long, though, before the howling of the machine shook the children from their slumber. Will and Penny soon descended the stairs and started their Saturday morning ritual of lying around watching cartoons, while their mother tried her best to work around them. By the time she had finished in the living room and set her sights on the kitchen, her son and daughter had already made themselves toast and Pop-Tarts (she had bought a new toaster at lunch the day before) and Nestles Quik, which they proceeded to eat and drink in front of the television. Mesmerized by the tube, the two munched away, oblivious to the crumbs dropping onto the couch and floor where Loretta had just vacuumed. Equally maddening, their cups and plates later found their way right back into the sink, which she had only just emptied. The whole cycle began anew as the weekend progressed, and come Monday morning, as she stood at the doorway trying to herd Will and Penny out to the car, Loretta realized with dismay that the downstairs was in much the same state that it had been in on Friday night. She let out a weary, exasperated sigh as she slammed the front door shut. It was like swimming against the tide—and the tide always won.

Once settled behind her desk, Loretta let out a yawn while

she waited for her computer screen to come aglow. Shirley soon appeared with the promised cup of coffee, and the two chatted about their weekends.

"So, how's the RISD girl working out as a babysitter?" asked Shirley, sitting back on the edge of Loretta's desk.

Loretta took a sip of her coffee and rolled her eyes. "Didn't I tell you?" she replied. "I had to get rid of her on Thursday." At her co-worker's behest, she recounted the dismaying circumstances that finally led to the young grad student's untimely dismissal from her babysitting position at the Simmons home.

"What a little tramp," huffed Shirley with some conviction after Loretta had finished her recitation of the whole miserable incident. "You're better off without her."

"That was pretty much the conclusion I came to," said Loretta with a shrug. "Not that it made things any easier for me."

"So, who's going to watch the kids after school now?"

"Guess."

"Not the old Italian lady you told me about," laughed Shirley. "I thought you said you didn't like her because she made you feel guilty."

"She does," answered Loretta. "But it wasn't like I had a lot of other options. Besides, at least when I called her, she showed up on time. She'll have to do for now."

Shirley was about to pry more details about the babysitter situation out of Loretta when the two were surprised to see Mister Pace walk through the door into the front lobby. It was quite early for the senior partner to arrive at the office; most mornings, he didn't saunter in until well after ten o'clock.

"Good morning, Mister Pace," they said in unison.

"Good morning, ladies," the old gentleman said amiably as he stood by the closet, pulling off his overcoat. "Please, don't look so surprised to see me. I do have to work sometimes, you know." He took out a hanger, stuck it inside the coat, and stuffed the whole thing haphazardly into the closet. "That coffee looks wonderful," he added hopefully.

"I'll get you a cup," said Shirley, and off she went.

Pace strolled over to Loretta.

"Sounds like no golf today," she said, giving him a smile. "Busy day planned?"

"Well," he harrumphed, "at least by my standards. New client coming in today. New England Trucking. It's a family business. The Hadleys. Known them for years, so the powers that be pulled me out of the mothballs to make it look good." He sat back against the desk in just the same spot Shirley had vacated and straightened his tie. "Funny," he went on in a wistful tone, "but I can remember back when the Hadleys first started the business. They used to be just a little mom-and-pop operation back in those days. You could do that back then, just run a nice little business. Now, of course, the son's taken over, and they're buying up other small companies all over the region. It seems that's the way it is today in business: you either have to get bigger or sell out. I guess there's a certain logic to it that some people call progress. Anyway, we're helping them close on two deals just this week alone."

Loretta immediately grasped the meaning of this last remark. Multiple closings meant multiple hours, usually extra hours, to prepare the required piles of legal documents. She'd be going home late at least one night that week.

"Sounds like we're all going to be busy," she said, trying her best to hide the faint air of dread in her voice.

"I'm afraid so," sighed Pace. "Isn't work awful?"

Loretta was about to offer her own opinion on the subject, one not greatly at variance with that of her employer, but just then Shirley appeared with a cup of coffee in hand. Pace accepted it with sincere gratitude and ambled off to his office. Shirley likewise repaired to her own desk to start her day.

Alone at her desk, Loretta eyed the calendar. The week ahead now looked even longer to her than it had just a few moments earlier. Occasionally being obligated to work some late hours came with the territory, and Loretta was not one to complain. She accepted it as part of the job. Her only concern now was that her new babysitter would not feel the same.

CHAPTER 21

Francesca went to the window, parted the drapes, and peered out to the street. It was nearing four o'clock on Wednesday afternoon, and the winter sun was already dipping toward the tops of the leafless trees. Soon, she noted with consternation, the neighborhood would be lost in the shadows of the gathering twilight.

The old woman folded her arms and tapped her foot. Standing there, fretting about Will and Penny until she saw them come into sight, had in just three days become something of a daily routine for her. The school bus, according to their mother, dropped them off at the corner up the street at three forty-five each afternoon. Given a few minutes to traverse the sidewalk home, the children should have arrived at the doorstep by ten minutes to four. Francesca understood, of course, that the bus was not always on time, and that the two youngsters could not always be expected to come directly home without stopping to chat with their friends or frolicking in the snow for a few minutes. They were just kids after all. Just the same, the minutes passed at an excruciatingly ponderous pace while she waited for them to appear.

Francesca turned away from the window for a moment and regarded the interior of the house. Things in the living room remained very much in the same state of organized disarray, and the kitchen was still a catastrophe, but it had not escaped her notice when she arrived on Monday afternoon that over the weekend, the Simmons woman had at least managed to put away the Christmas decorations and toss out some of the old newspapers on the coffee table. She appreciated the effort the younger woman had made and the pride it displayed; maintaining an orderly household on a daily basis was challenging enough, never mind trying to do it all alone while holding down a full-time job and raising two small children. It was all Francesca could do to keep herself from pitching in and helping. Whenever she was seized by the notion, however, Peg's stern admonition to not get too involved echoed in her ears until she came to her senses.

At the sound of voices out on the doorstep, Francesca whirled around just in time to see the door swing open and Will and Penny come bustling into the front hall. There, as they did every afternoon, they unceremoniously dropped their backpacks. Weighted down with school books and whatever else they carried inside, the sacks thudded against the floor, their buckles and straps and zippers chinking at the abrupt halt.

"Hello, children," Francesca greeted them as they peeled off their coats and hats. The hair on both their heads was matted down into snarled messes, but their cheeks were bright red from the cold, giving their faces irresistible glows.

"Hello," they mumbled in reply after tossing their hats and coats onto a nearby chair already piled high with sweaters and jackets and who could say what other types of clothing. The whole thing looked ready to fall over onto the floor. Without another word, as had been the case every other day since Francesca had first come to the house, the two children went straight to the kitchen to scavenge for their after-school snacks. This was always a particularly painful moment for their new afternoon governess, who could do nothing but look on helplessly as they marched back out with their treats in hand. That Will and Penny should have craved something sweet after a long day at school was perfectly understandable to Francesca; she had, after all, raised three children of her own. What grieved her was that, in her mind, what they ate was nothing but processed junk. It made her shudder to watch.

As she did every afternoon, Penny headed directly upstairs. "I have to get on the computer, so don't bother me," she warned her brother as she climbed the staircase.

"I don't care what you do," Will replied, starting to follow her. Halfway up, though, he changed his mind, turned around, and came back down. At the bottom step, he stopped and gave Francesca a cautious, questioning look. "I'd like to watch some TV," he said. "Is that all right?"

"Of course," said Francesca, inwardly delighted that one of the children had finally said something to her other than hello or good-bye. She stepped aside to let him pass.

Will slouched over to the couch and plopped down. Holding in one hand the little wrapped snack cake he had pillaged from the kitchen, he reached around with the other, searching between the cushions for the television's remote control. Not finding it right away, he scanned the floor by his feet.

"I believe it's right there," said Francesca, nodding to the end table at his elbow. "Right under the TV section from Sunday's paper."

"Oh," muttered Will, extracting the remote from its hiding place beneath the newspaper. He eyed her suspiciously for the briefest of moments before adding, "Thanks."

"You're welcome," Francesca replied. She watched him turn the television on and scroll through the channels until he found one of those crazy animated adventure shows Rosie and Alice let her grandsons watch after school. Just looking at the screen was enough to make her dizzy, never mind the noise. Just the same, Will settled back with that vacant look of rapt, total absorption that only the television seemed able to induce in children. The young boy breathed an audible sigh of relief and began to tear the plastic wrap off his snack cake. Francesca recognized that sigh, that unmistakable signal children gave after six hours of school-day stress—and children's days, she well understood, could be just as stressful as those of their parents—when they finally could ease back and unplug their minds for a while in the safe refuge of their own home.

"Tough day at school today?" said Francesca, hazarding an attempt at a conversation.

His eyes glued to the television, Will squirreled up the corner of his mouth and gave a shrug in reply. For a moment, Francesca expected him to say something, but to her disappointment, he instead took a bite of the cake. She took a seat on the chair adjacent to the couch and reached into her book bag for a magazine to peruse.

"I got a fifty on my math quiz," Will suddenly confessed in a dejected voice, his gaze never straying from the television. "And Tubs Bennett hit me in the head with a snowball at recess."

"Which felt worse?" asked Francesca She was pleased to observe that her query, as intended, elicited the hint of a smile from the boy.

"Good question," he replied.

"Who is this Tubs Bennett," asked Francesca, pressing ahead, "and what made him hit you in the head with a snowball?"

"He's a big goof in the sixth grade," lamented Will. "He likes to push around little kids, especially me, because he says my glasses make me look like Harry Potter."

"What grade is Harry in?" Francesca asked, feigning ignorance.

"He doesn't go to *our* school!" exclaimed Will, his face brightening at the ludicrous question. "You *know*, he's the wizard, from the stories! Haven't you ever heard of Harry Potter?"

"Hmm, a wizard," mused Francesca, hoping to string the boy along a little further. "Well, if that's the case, perhaps we could get him to turn Tubs Bennett into a toad."

"Ha!" laughed Will. "That would be great. Maybe while he's at it, he could change the grade on my math quiz too!"

"I'm afraid you'll have to accomplish that trick on your own," suggested Francesca.

This idea was not so well received, and the boy turned his attention back to the television.

Upon hearing the sound of their voices down in the living room, Penny came to the top of the staircase and beckoned Will to come up for a moment to look, she said, at something on the computer. Her tone, however, indicated that she had another motive for wishing to speak to her brother right away. His curiosity piqued by his sister's rare invitation to do anything at all with her connected to the computer, Will stuffed the rest of the cake into his mouth and bounded up the stairs, leaving a trail of crumbs in his wake.

From where she sat, Francesca could hear, but not quite make out, the whisperings of the two siblings. Not wanting to give herself away by going to the hallway to listen, she cocked her head in that direction, hoping to catch at least a snippet of what they were saying. This effort met with no success, and she could only sit and wait to see what they would do next. Will descended the stairs a few minutes later. Judging by the look on his face, Francesca surmised that his older sister had advised him against saying too much to their elderly babysitter. He came back into the living room, reinstalled himself on the couch, and lost himself once more in his television show.

Francesca was a bit disappointed that things had taken this turn. Nonetheless, she was pleased to have finally initiated some repartee, however slight, with one of the children. She was just about to congratulate herself on this feat when the telephone rang.

"I'll get it!" shrieked Penny, warding off the others lest it be a call for her. To her disappointment, the caller turned out to be not a friend, but her mother, calling to speak with Francesca.

After grilling her mother for a few moments on what time she could be expected to come from work and what her plans were for dinner, Penny went to the top of the stairs. "It's for you, Mrs. Campa-Compa . . . Mrs. C," she called down.

"Hello, Mrs. Campanile," Loretta began when Francesca picked up the telephone in the kitchen. "I hope the children are behaving for you today."

"Of course," said Francesca, casting a glance back into the living room, where Will was still as one with the television. "They've been perfect."

"That's good," she said, "because I was wondering if you might be able to stay a little later today. It looks like I'm going to busy here for a few more hours. Would that be all right?"

The request came as no surprise to Francesca. Loretta had told her on Monday that there was a chance she would need to work late at the office at least one night that week. Francesca had told her not to worry about it, that she could stay later if the occasion should arise. Just the same, she detected a nervous edge in the young mother's voice, as if she half-expected Francesca to refuse.

"Yes," Francesca assured her, "of course it's all right. Don't worry. I'll stay with them until you come home."

"Thank you so much," said Loretta. "That's a big relief to me."

"Oh, don't mention it, Mrs. Simmons, but there's just one thing," Francesca added, for just then an intriguing thought had come to mind. "What about dinner for the children?"

"Actually," Loretta said meekly, "I was going to ask you that next. Do you think it would be a problem . . . I mean, if it wouldn't be too much trouble, would you mind making dinner for them?"

Francesca could scarcely contain her glee. If not for her advanced years, she might have turned a cartwheel right on the spot.

"Of course I wouldn't mind," she replied eagerly, her thoughts already racing through the possibilities, for surely there was something on hand in the cupboards or fridge that she could whip up for the two youngsters. "I'd be happy to do it."

"Great," said Loretta. "We should have plenty of frozen dinners to choose from. The kids can have whatever they want."

Francesca was not certain that she had heard correctly.

"Frozen dinners?"

"Yes, they should be right there when you open the freezer."

Still not quite grasping the concept of what the younger woman was proposing, Francesca went to the refrigerator. With the telephone in hand, she opened the freezer door and peered in. She extracted one of the frost-covered boxes and wiped clear the label. "Salisbury steak with potatoes and vegetables," she muttered to herself. Francesca tried to gather her thoughts, but her mind was reeling. "You want me to cook these?" she finally asked, her face blanching.

"Oh, it's not hard," Loretta assured her. "All you have to do is pop them into the microwave for a few minutes. Do you know how to work the microwave?"

"Oh, yes," Francesca replied, trying her best to maintain her composure even though it felt as though someone had just thrust a dagger through her heart.

"I'm sure you'll be hungry too, so just help yourself to whatever you like," Loretta added brightly. "I think there might be a fettuccine Alfredo in there."

Francesca swallowed hard. The young woman could not possibly have imagined the pain this suggestion, so cruel in its innocence, had inflicted on her. "Thank you," she said after pausing for a moment to chase the image of it from her mind, "but I'll probably just wait to have dinner at home."

Francesca stared forlornly at the refrigerator door after she had finished receiving her instructions for dinner and hung up the phone. She turned and cast a miserable eye about at the seldom-used oven, the cluttered counters, and the inevitable sink full of dirty dishes. But frozen dinners! Her spirits sank, for she could not recall having ever been brought so low in a kitchen. But then the voices of Peg and Connie and Natalie resounded once more in her ears, reminding Francesca that this was not *her* kitchen, this was not *her* house, and these were not *her* children. She was there to do a job, and that job entailed doing whatever their mother asked. Blindly following orders had never been one of Francesca's strong suits—at her age, she didn't take orders from anyone—but she saw the wisdom in their advice, though it gave her little comfort. And so, her heart grieving, Francesca called for Will and Penny to come to the freezer to pick out their suppers.

If preparing the frozen meals had not been painful enough, watching the children eat them, sitting as they were on the living room couch instead of at the spots she had cleared for them at the table, was pure torture. It seemed to Francesca that she was being punished for some crime of which she had no recollection committing. Or perhaps it was some sort of penance she was being forced to perform, to cure her of her pride and stubbornness. Whichever the case, she turned away from the two children and looked upward.

"Forgive them, God," she sighed under her breath. "They know not what they do."

Later, Francesca was sitting in the living room, doing a crossword puzzle, when a weary-looking Loretta finally walked through the door. The children, who had ensconced themselves upstairs after dinner, descended to greet her, while Francesca pulled on her overcoat and collected her things. She glanced back to the kitchen, where she had set out on the table a plate and utensils for their mother. The choice of frozen dinner she had left to her employer's discretion.

"Thank you so much for staying, Mrs. Campanile," said Loretta, smiling gratefully. "I'm sorry to be getting home so late."

"Oh, it's not so late, Mrs. Simmons," replied Francesca. "The time passed quickly. It was a chance for the children and me to get to know each other a little better."

Given that barely a word had been exchanged between the two and the old lady since before dinner, Will and Penny looked at each other with sideways glances before retreating to the upstairs.

"I hope dinner wasn't too much trouble," said Loretta, dropping her own coat atop the chair with those of her children. That the pile held there without slipping to the floor struck Francesca as somewhat miraculous.

"Dinner was no trouble at all," she answered, not anxious to revisit the memory of her most recent culinary adventure. "Do you think you will be working late again tomorrow?"

Loretta let out a long, weary sigh. "I'm afraid there's that possibility. I'll understand if it's going to be a problem for you to stay again. Just let me know, so that I can make some arrangements."

"Oh, no," Francesca smiled, "it won't be a problem, but would you mind if I ask you a question?"

"Go right ahead," said Loretta, curious to hear what it might be.

"I was just wondering," Francesca began, ignoring the voices of her library friends screaming in her ears, "do your children have any particular food allergies?"

CHAPTER 22

When Will and Penny came home from school the next day, Francesca was not at the window, waiting for them as they traipsed up the front walk, nor was she standing in the hallway to greet them when they walked through the door and dropped their backpacks to the floor. The two puzzled over the old woman's absence but for a moment, for upon entering the house they were immediately distracted by a delightful and unexpected smell wafting from the kitchen. The two tore off their hats and coats and boots, and followed their noses to the source of the warm, sweet aroma that had welcomed them home. Standing in their stockinged feet at the kitchen door, they looked in just as Francesca was removing a tray of freshly baked homemade chocolate chip cookies from the oven. She had made the cookies from scratch, mixing all the ingredients at home, and brought everything, tray and all, with her, so that all she needed to do was toss it into the oven when she arrived.

"Hello, children," Francesca said, setting the tray atop the stove. Seeing the eager, inquisitive looks on their faces, she smiled inwardly, for she knew what it meant to come home on a cold day to find something warm and delicious waiting inside. Earlier that day, she had considered making something other than the cookies—a tray of biscotti or perhaps some pizzelle—

but in the end, she had decided to go with an old standby. "I hope you both had a nice day at school today."

"Wow, those smell good, Mrs. C.," said Will, taking a step into the kitchen. Before he could go too far, Penny caught him by the back of his shirt.

"That's okay, honey," Francesca told her. "You can both come and take a look."

Penny regarded her with a cautious gaze, and the two drew nearer to the counter by the stove. There, she and her brother watched with the sort of rapt attention they usually reserved for television viewing as Francesca took a spatula and transferred the cookies one by one onto a plate. The children's eyes grew as wide as doughnuts as they beheld the mouthwatering sight. When it came to baking, Francesca never did anything small; the dark, steaming cookies were each the size of an espresso cup saucer, all of them bursting with melted chocolate.

"Who did you make those for?" Penny inquired, her chilly demeanor of just a few moments earlier starting to melt.

"Yeah," added Will, licking his lips, his gaze never leaving the plate. "They really do look good."

"Oh, I was just trying to pass the time until you two came home, so I decided to bake these and take them home in case my son stops by tonight," Francesca told them. "He loves chocolate chip cookies."

"Oh," said Penny very softly, trying hard to hide her disappointment but failing miserably. For his part, Will made no effort whatsoever to conceal his utter disheartenment at this letdown. His chin sank to his chest as he continued to gaze longingly at the pile of cookies. He was standing so close that the steam still rising off them fogged his glasses.

"But you know something?" Francesca said, anxious to keep their attention now that she had captured it. "I think maybe you both could have one, if you like. I mean, I'm sure my son wouldn't mind."

"Are you sure?" asked Penny, her face brightening at the prospect.

"Who cares?" said Will, reaching for the plate.

"But first," interjected Francesca before he could lay his hand on a single morsel, "that table needs to be cleared off and these counters straightened up. Do you think you two could do that for your mother while I let these cool?"

Despite the old woman's smile, there was a certain sternness in her eye and in the tone of her voice as she proposed this bargain, neither of which seemed to cause the boy any great concern. His sister, however, paused to consider the whole thing more carefully.

"Is there anything *else* we have to do?" Penny asked.

"Yes," said Francesca, confirming the young girl's suspicions. "You have to wash your hands after. *Then* you can have a cookie."

"That's good enough for me," enthused Will. "Let's get going!"

It didn't take long for the two to clear the table. Most of the mess was old schoolwork and junk mail that had been allowed to sit there collecting dust. Just about all of it, to Francesca's way of thinking, should have gone directly into the trash. She knew that over time, such messes took on lives of their own, and it was hard to displace them once they had established themselves, unless you attacked them ruthlessly every day. Still, she didn't want to run the risk of the children throwing out something of importance without their mother's permission, so she pulled a chair away from the table and had the children stack everything neatly on its seat. It was not the best solution, but at least it was a start. At long last, it might be possible for people to sit at the table and eat.

The counters were a bit trickier. Most of the heap, from what Francesca could see, was useless clutter. Just the same, she was aware that, between the catalogs and pamphlets and sticky notes and announcements from school and old envelopes with hastily scrawled notes across their backs, there was bound to be at least one item of import. That being the case, she directed the children to simply organize everything as best they could, to at least create a little working space for food preparation—if any such thing were to ever happen there again. Francesca briefly considered prodding them to take on the sink full of dishes— after all, doing the dishes every night after dinner had been one of her primary duties as a young girl—but she decided it would be best not to push her luck at that particular moment. Finally, when the children had finished, she reminded them to wash their hands and, true to her word, let them both try one of the cookies, but not before pouring each of them a glass of milk and making them sit at the table.

"Sit, and eat those right there," Francesca told them. "I don't want you getting crumbs from my cookies all over your mother's carpets. And make sure you drink all that milk." She took a seat at the table and watched them, delighted at the looks of pleasure on their faces as they munched away. Perhaps they weren't listed on the food pyramid that people were always talking about, but as far as she was concerned, warm cookies and cold milk were essential nutrients for children. It occurred to Francesca just then that hot chocolate would have gone even better on that winter's day. She filed the idea for future reference.

The rapidity with which the cookies disappeared into their mouths convinced Francesca that to not allow the two children a second cookie each would be cruel. Besides, with Will looking up at her with that irresistible Oliver Twist look on his face, how could she refuse? Before they had a chance to ask, Francesca suggested that, if they liked, they could each take another. The words had scarcely left her lips before two more cookies were swiped from the plate.

"*Dio mio*, chew those slow!" Francesca exclaimed as she watched the two youngsters gobble them down. "I don't want you both to choke, God forbid." As at all kitchen tables at which children sit, the words fell upon deaf ears. All Francesca could do was look on and smile.

"So, what do you think?" she asked when they had both swallowed their last bites. "Were there enough chocolate chips? My son likes lots in his cookies."

Before Penny or Will could answer this dismaying question—for the thought of Francesca taking the remaining cookies home to her son filled them with despair—the telephone rang.

"I'll get it!" cried Penny, springing from her seat.

"You always have to answer the phone," muttered her brother.

"No," said Francesca, motioning for the young girl to stay put. "*I'll* answer the telephone."

Penny stiffened.

"Don't worry," Francesca told her, unmoved by the indignant look with which the child fixed her. "If it's for you, I'll tell you."

As she stood and reached for the phone, Francesca knew that she was crossing a line, but sooner or later, it had to happen. Since she began watching the two children, and against her better instincts, she had allowed Penny a free hand to answer the telephone, and to make calls of her own from time to time, without question. This the young girl inevitably did upstairs, out of the range of the old woman's still-keen sense of hearing. Francesca had never felt comfortable with this arrangement, for she felt an obligation to know who was calling the house and to whom the child was speaking. Besides, she had never allowed her own children such latitude at home, at least not at such an early age. Why would she do so now with these two? Loretta had not advised her one way or the other on the children's use of the telephone. That being the case, Francesca decided it was time to set her own rules. She picked up the receiver.

"Hello," she said with Penny and Will hanging on her every

word, the way children always do when a grown-up gets on the telephone. "Oh, hello, Mrs. Simmons. Yes, everything is going just fine." Francesca put the phone to her shoulder. "It's your mother, for me," she told them before putting the phone back to her ear. "What's that, Mrs. Simmons? Oh, yes, they've been angels. They just had a little afternoon snack, and now I think they're just about to go do their homework." Francesca gave the two children a furtive look when she spoke this last statement. Reluctantly, Penny and Will slouched away from the table and trudged into the living room to find a spot where they would still be close enough to eavesdrop. "You think you might be late again this evening?" said Francesca, a smile breaking out across her face as she watched them go. "No, don't worry, Mrs. Simmons. It's no bother at all. Yes, of course I can take care of dinner . . ."

"Where are you going?" said Will when Francesca emerged from the kitchen a few minutes later and went to the front hall to put on her coat.

"Just out to the car for a minute," she replied. "I'll be right back."

Francesca returned shortly, carrying two plastic grocery bags. She set the bags down on the floor for a moment while she hung up her coat. Then she picked the bags back up and hurried past the two children.

"What's that you got?" Will called after her.

"Frozen dinners," Francesca breezily replied. "Go do your homework. I'll call you when it's time to eat."

Once in the kitchen, Francesca put the bags on the counter and, from one of them, pulled out two half-gallon plastic containers. The tubs, two of the many old ice cream containers she saved to store leftover food in, held the extra tomato sauce and meatballs she liked to keep on hand in her freezer at home. Solid as rocks, they thudded against the counter when she set them down. She peeked in the other bag to make sure it still held the box of spaghetti and the little container of grated cheese she had also brought along just in case she had been called upon to cook dinner. That little bit about frozen dinners had only been a white lie, Francesca reflected as she pried off the tops of the sauce and meatball containers. Most of this dinner was frozen at the moment—but it wouldn't be for long.

There were a thousand other meals Francesca might have conjured up for dinner that evening, but to her recollection, no child she had ever encountered disliked spaghetti and meatballs. Like the chocolate chip cookies, it was a safe bet. Just the same, she held her breath when she called the children back to the kitchen and set the pot of steaming, sauce-drenched noodles and meatballs on the table. She would have liked to serve it in a nice big pasta bowl, but there was none to be had. Presentation, however, was not something that overly concerned her. The food was what counted. And besides, throwing the spaghetti back into the same pot in which she had boiled it would make for less work when it came time to clean up. It had been enough of a job just cleaning one side of the sink so she could strain it all.

Any misgivings Francesca might have had about the meal she had prepared were instantly dispelled when she saw the hungry looks on the children's faces when they came to the table. "Get some clean plates—or bowls would be better," she said, giving Penny a nod. To Will she said, "And you get some forks and spoons."

The two did as they were told and watched eagerly as Francesca filled their dishes. To her chagrin, however, the two took their dinners and waltzed away toward the living room.

"Ayyy!" Francesca exclaimed, stopping them dead in their tracks. "Where are you two going?"

"To watch TV while we eat," said Will, not at all understanding the look of outrage on his babysitter's face.

"In my house," Francesca replied cooly, "when I cook a meal, people sit down at the table and eat it together."

"Well . . . this is not your house," said Penny in a much meeker tone than she had hoped for. She was summoning up as much defiance as she could, but she was finding it quite difficult to do, given the fact that she was dying to get a taste of the spaghetti.

Francesca cowed the girl with a withering look. "This might not be my house, but that's my food I just cooked, so you do what I say if you want to eat it."

"But you didn't say anything last night," countered Will, who was no less anxious to set his teeth into one of the meatballs on his plate.

"That's because I didn't cook that meal," Francesca replied. "I just thawed it out, which is not the same thing. This one's all mine—so back to the table, you two."

Seeing her resolve, and realizing that they were not making their case, the two siblings looked at one another for a moment and reluctantly trudged back to the table. Francesca filled a plate for herself, and the three sat down together to eat.

"Now, isn't this nice?" said Francesca, all the time feeling more and more in her own element. She waited for an answer, but the two children already had their mouths full. "Here, put a little cheese on that," she said, opening the container of grated Romano and reaching for the spoon. "And sit up straight when you eat. And chew that food good before you swallow it. Then both of you can tell me all about your day at school."

CHAPTER 23

"Am I a bad mother?"

It was lunchtime, and Loretta was sitting at a little table in the deli on the first floor of the office building where she worked. Her chin propped on her hand, she took a disinterested bite of her tuna salad sandwich and stared forlornly at the building's main entrance, where people were bustling in and out through the big revolving door. It was another bitter cold day, the latest in a long line. Everyone inevitably walked in from the outside with their shoulders hunched, their hands buried deep within their pockets, and their chins tucked low against the collars of their overcoats. Those walking out assumed the same posture as they approached the door, always hesitating for just an instant before passing through it, as if they wanted to brace themselves before braving the icy air's impending assault. Watching all of them come and go sent a chill up her spine, and Loretta wished for all the world that she could be someplace, anyplace, warm.

"Bad?" said Shirley, who was sitting opposite her, pondering her own tossed salad and low-cal dressing with a less-than-enthusiastic eye. "Of course not. What on earth makes you ask such a question?'

"My babysitter—my nanny—whatever you want to call her," muttered Loretta in reply. She dropped her sandwich onto her plate, dabbed the corners of her mouth with a paper napkin, then started to tear the napkin bit by bit into little pieces.

"Oh, boy. What's happened now?" said Shirley. "Don't tell me you caught *her* making out on the couch with some guy."

"Oh, shut up," huffed Loretta, flicking a piece of torn napkin at her friend. "How could you even think such thing? I mean, she looks good for her age, but not *that* good."

"Well, it is the twenty-first century," offered Shirley with a mischievous twinkle in her eye. "Anything's possible."

"Please. That's all I need."

At that, Loretta tried to go back to sulking in silence. Shirley's curiosity, however, had been piqued.

"Come on," she prodded Loretta, "tell Auntie Shirley all about it. What happened? What did your nanny do that's got you looking so blue?"

"No," said Loretta. "You'll just think I'm an idiot if I tell you."

"Perish the thought. Come on, let's have it."

Loretta let out a long, weary sigh. "Okay, you want to know what happened?" she finally said. "Last night, she cooked the kids spaghetti and meatballs without even asking me."

"Uh-huh," nodded Shirley thoughtfully. "And how was it?"

"What?"

"The spaghetti and meatballs."

"Delicious," griped Loretta, then added, with another sigh, "So were the cookies."

"She made cookies?"

"Homemade chocolate chip."

"I see," said Shirley. "Was that all?"

"No," answered Loretta ruefully. "Before I came home, she made the kids straighten up after dinner so that the whole kitchen was the neatest it's ever been when I got home."

"What a witch," said Shirley deadpan. "I can understand why you're so upset."

"It's not funny," cried Loretta. "I know it sounds stupid, but I felt embarrassed, almost . . . I don't know . . . humiliated."

"Oh, come on," said Shirley with a dismissive wave. "Why on earth would you feel that way? After all, it was only a plate of pasta."

"I told you, she's an old Catholic," Loretta sulked. "They're all the same. They have this way about them. Without even trying, they make you feel guilty for no good reason, like you're doing everything wrong. Trust me, I know. My mother is an old Catholic."

"And what does she have to say on the subject?"

Loretta rolled her eyes and shook her head. "Oh, never mind," she sighed. "Don't even go there. That's another story all by itself."

"Loretta," said Shirley after a time, looking at her friend with a kind grin, "hasn't it occurred to you that maybe, just maybe, all this nice lady wants to do is help? You know, if you were to ask me, I'd say that she's just what you need right now."

Loretta slouched back in her chair and pouted. Deep in her heart, she knew that Shirley was probably right. Thinking back to the previous evening, even she wasn't quite certain just what it was that had caused her so much grief when she had come home to find a nice plate of leftover spaghetti and meatballs waiting for her at the place her children had set for her at the table. Mrs. Campanile had covered it in foil to keep it warm, as she did with the leftover chocolate chip cookies. She even left some leftover meatballs and sauce in the fridge. Walking through the door, cold and weary, Loretta could not have denied that there was something wonderful about that delicious smell of food that greeted her. Later, though, after Mrs. Campanile had gone on her way and she sat down to eat her supper, Loretta had wanted to break down in tears when Will said to her, "Isn't that spaghetti and meatballs delicious, Mom? I wish you could cook like that."

"I don't know," Loretta admitted gloomily. "Maybe you're

right. I know my life is a mess, but it's *my* mess. It's the only thing I have. I'm a grown woman. I feel like I should be able to sort everything out by myself, without needing someone else to do it for me. God, I just need a little break, that's all. A chance to catch my breath. Then I could finally get things in order. Instead, I just bounce from one thing to another, and I feel like . . . like . . ."

"Like you're doing everything wrong?" Shirley finished for her.

Loretta narrowed her eyes in an icy glare. "You know," she grumbled, "you're not being very helpful."

"Sorry," said Shirley. "Just joking. But I wish you would stop and listen to yourself for a moment. You just got finished saying that all you need right now is a break. Maybe this Mrs. What's-Her-Name is it. Why not let her try to help?"

Loretta was about to try to explain why when she looked past Shirley and caught sight of someone stepping out of the elevators. She leaned forward to get a better view. Her spirits suddenly began to rise, and a faint smile came to her face.

At seeing her changed demeanor, Shirley turned around in time to see Ned Hadley, the scion of New England Trucking, for whom the firm had been doing so much work that week, stepping into the lobby. "Well, well," she said at seeing his now-familiar face. "Look what the cat's dragging out."

As Hadley turned and hurried toward the revolving doors, he happened to glance toward the deli, and the two women caught his eye. At seeing them look his way, he nodded a greeting and gave them a wink before slipping out the doors.

"God, he is *so* stuck up," said Shirley, her voice dripping with disdain.

"Yeah, I guess you're right," said Loretta, nodding in agreement, even though she was inclined to a slightly more favorable opinion of the young businessman.

Now, at hearing Loretta's less-than-convincing tone of

voice, it was Shirley's turn to let out a grumble. "Don't even think about it," she warned her friend.

Loretta smiled and gave a dismissive wave of her own. "Who, me?" she said, trying her best to act as though she had no idea at all of her friend's meaning. She knew full well, though, that it hadn't escaped anyone's notice, least of all Shirley's, that the young Mister Hadley had shown a particular interest in her during the past few days. Whenever Loretta came into the room or passed him in the corridor, he was sure to give her a smile and make some pleasant, casual remark that, while harmless enough, perhaps bespoke more familiarity than that to which he was entitled.

"How's my girl today?" he might say with disarming charm as he passed her desk. Or at seeing her approach, he's say "Here's some sunshine coming my way!"

Loretta was too old and too wizened from experience to be taken in by his artful banter; as an attractive woman in a business dominated by men, she endured it almost every day. As a single, stressed-out mother, however, one who could only faintly remember what it was like to hold a man, she was still too young not to be flattered by the attention. Besides, the thought of someday having a knight in shining armor show up to rescue her, a prince to take care of her and allow her to finally bid farewell to her dread of the monthly electric bill's arrival, was a pleasant daydream.

"Get those little notions right out of your head, young lady," said Shirley, bringing her back. "That man has the word 'cad' stamped all over his face."

"Oh, come on," laughed Loretta. "Why do you say that?"

"Don't you know anything?" puffed Shirley. "The guy just got divorced three months ago. Don't ask me how I know this. Anyway, from the stories I hear, he's probably on the make for whatever he can get. Trust me, I've seen his kind in action. He's just out looking for an easy score."

"Gee, thanks a lot," said Loretta, even though she had heard some of the very same stories. "I didn't know I was so easy."

"You know what I mean," Shirley replied with a huff. "Just be careful, is all I'm saying, and make sure you give him the brush-off if he comes on to you."

Loretta settled back in her chair and smiled. "My word of honor," she said with fingers crossed.

"Good girl. So, anyway, what are your plans for your terrible nanny now that she has offended you with her cooking and cleaning?" asked Shirley, returning to the original subject.

"Oh, I don't know," confessed Loretta, "but it's Friday, and I'm going home on time for once. And for tonight at least, *I'm* taking care of dinner—somehow."

Shirley chuckled and gave her an impudent grin. "KFC, here you come," she said brightly before taking a bite of her salad.

Later that afternoon, after the firm had finished up the closings for the New England Trucking deals and the inevitable blizzard of papers flying back and forth between the attorneys had mercifully subsided, Loretta was finally free to go home. Anxious to beat the traffic, she hurried to the closet to get her coat and hat. On the way, she mulled over the options for dinner. Shirley's last little dig at lunch had ruled out fried chicken as a possibility; Loretta wouldn't give her the satisfaction of being able to needle her about it on Monday. Pizza or Chinese food seemed the most likely alternatives, she decided as she pulled on her coat and headed for the door. She was trying to remember which restaurants she might pass on the way home when she happened to walk by the glass walls of the conference room, where the last of the closings had just taken place. The room was now empty save for Ned Hadley, who was seated alone at the head of the table, talking a mile a minute on his cell phone. His brow was furrowed, indicating that he wasn't entirely pleased about whatever the topic of the conversation might be. At seeing Loretta, his faced brightened. He flashed a winning smile and beckoned her to come in. Putting the phone briefly to his shoulder, he mouthed the words, "One minute."

Loretta was anxious to get going, but all things considered, she could see no harm in waiting one more minute. Despite Shirley's admonitions at lunch, Loretta returned his smile and stepped into the conference room. Perhaps her friend was right. Maybe doing so wasn't the best idea. But Loretta was curious, and as far as she knew, curiosity killed only cats.

CHAPTER 24

"Tomorrow night?"

"Just for a few hours," said a hopeful Loretta. "Maybe seven to ten?"

They were standing in the front hall by the door, where Francesca was just getting ready to leave. Will and Penny were off in the kitchen, tearing open the boxes of Chinese food their mother had just brought home. As she wrapped her scarf around her neck, Francesca leaned over to get a peek at them. The two were kneeling on their chairs across the table from one another, quarreling over who would have the spring rolls. Even though she had looked forward to cooking once more for the children, it had been only a minor disappointment when Loretta has called earlier that afternoon to tell her that there was no need to bother, that she herself would be bringing dinner home. As things worked out, Joey had called Francesca just that morning to tell her that he might be stopping by in the evening to pick up some laundry she had done for him. Given that she had yet to breathe a word to her son and daughters about what she had been up to these days, Francesca had fretted all afternoon that Joey would arrive at the house before her if Loretta was forced to work late again. Not at all anxious to endure the inevitable questions that would have arisen about her whereabouts and ac-

FRANCESCA'S KITCHEN   149

tivities, she was just as happy to go home on time. This new request, however, posed something of a predicament.

"I know it's kind of last minute, asking you to babysit tomorrow night," Loretta went on. "I totally understand if you already have other plans, or even if you're just not up for it, so don't feel obligated." Then, in a meek voice, "I, um, just thought I'd ask."

The pleading look in the younger woman's eyes gave Francesca reason to suspect that a date with a promising gentleman was hanging in the balance. Other than five-thirty mass, Francesca had no plans whatsoever for Saturday night and would have been delighted to say yes right away, but again, her thoughts turned to her son. Occasionally, he came unannounced for dinner on Saturdays, before going out for the night. Alarm bells were certain to go off from Providence to Oregon if he called and she didn't answer, or worse, if he came home that night to find her gone.

"I don't want to say no," she told Loretta after mulling the situation over for a moment, "but I can't say yes just yet. Could I let you know tonight, or maybe tomorrow morning?"

"Of course," said Loretta in that desperately hopeful tone that a parent acquires when the opportunity to socialize with another adult finally arises for the first time in ages. "Please, call me as late as you want tonight or any time tomorrow. I'll wait to hear from you."

Francesca patted Loretta on the hand, promised she would let her know as soon as she could, and then went on her way.

Although she was anxious to get home, Francesca did not drive directly there after leaving Loretta's house. Instead, she headed first for the library, to pick up some new books being held there for her. She might just as easily have put off the errand until Saturday, for there really was no hurry, but for reasons of her own, it was important that she not wait. As she drove her car along the darkened streets, listening to the tires grinding through the salt and sand, Francesca tried to imagine what type of man Loretta—or the 'Simmons woman,' as she still thought of her—was planning to go out with on Saturday night. Was he someone of her age? Was he handsome? Did he have a job? Whoever it was, she hoped he was someone worthwhile. From what Francesca had seen, a good man was something that little family desperately needed.

These ruminations were interrupted by a sudden hesitation in the engine, something Francesca had noticed happening with increasing frequency lately. Though it passed quickly and the car accelerated back to its former speed, it still caused her heart to skip a beat. Francesca knew that the car was past due for service; judging by its occasional coughing and sputtering, especially whenever she turned the ignition, it seemed to have developed the vehicular equivalent of a cold. Sooner or later, she would have to get it looked at, but with her new responsibilities as a nanny, finding the time to do it was something of a challenge.

"I could use a man of my own," she muttered as she pulled into the library parking lot. She parked near the entrance and left the car running while she hurried inside to retrieve her books.

Later, when Joey arrived at the house, Francesca was in the basement, pulling the last of the two big loads of clothes she had just washed for him out of the dryer. At hearing the front door open, she called for him to come down to give her a hand. Joey descended the stairs and paused for a moment on the bottom step. He clicked his tongue and shook his head as he came over to help her.

"I don't know, but the service isn't as good here as it once was," he joked in that quiet, gentle way of his, the one that always reminded Francesca of her husband.

"Oh, really," she said with a harrumph. "And how is that?"

"Well, I never used to have to carry my own laundry upstairs," her son explained. "Somehow or other, it all just ended up back in my bedroom drawers. It was like magic."

"Hey, you want that kind of service again, you'll have to get yourself a wife," observed his mother.

Joey let out a harrumph of his own and picked up one of the clothes baskets.

Back upstairs, Francesca instructed him to dump the clothes onto the kitchen table and set the baskets on the floor. She took a seat and began to fold the clothes, while Joey stood at the sink, staring out the back window.

"You know, if you weren't so lazy, you could sit down and help here," she chided him.

"You want me to?" said Joey. "I don't mind."

"No, just go back to what you were doing," said Francesca, peevishly shooing him away.

She was more likely to stand on her head than let her son fold the clothes; she just enjoyed heckling him about it. With a mischievous smile, Francesca hummed a tune to herself as she got to work.

"My, you're sounding rather chipper tonight," said Joey over his shoulder.

"Why shouldn't I be chipper?" she answered. "What do I have to be sad about?" Then, changing the subject, "You hungry? I have some leftover 'scarole and beans in the refrigerator, if you want to heat it up while I do these clothes."

"Nah, thanks," said Joey with a shake of his head. "I'll get something to eat later on."

"Plans for the night?"

"Nothing special."

"Good," said Francesca. "Does that mean I'll be seeing you this weekend?"

"Well, not tomorrow night," he said.

"No, why not?"

"I'm going out."

"A date?" said Francesca with interest. "Who is she? Anyone I know?"

"No, she's nobody," Joey replied, still staring absentmindedly out the window. "Just someone I met."

Francesca let out a huff as she set about matching up the socks. "You know, that's what you always say. 'She's nobody.' It's about time you stopped wasting your time with nobodies and started trying to find yourself a *somebody*, somebody you can settle down with and start a life together and maybe raise a family—or at least, somebody you could bring home to meet your mother one of these days."

Joey turned from the window and leaned back, his arms folded against his chest. "You know I tried all of that once already, Ma," he said, not a hint of impatience in his voice, even though this was a well-worn topic of discussion. "Didn't work out for me," he went on. "And it was probably just as well. I like things better this way."

"What's better about going through your life without someone who really loves you and wants to take care of you?" said Francesca. "That's no way to live."

"Well, it works for now," said Joey. With that, he brought the subject to a close by turning back toward the window. In so doing, he noticed the message light blinking on the telephone answering machine. "Looks like you have some messages. You wanna hear them?"

"No, leave them," said Francesca, perhaps a little more sharply than she had intended, for Joey looked back at her in surprise. "I'll listen to them later," she added quickly.

"Whatever," he answered with a shrug. Then, giving her a quizzical look, "You know, I didn't leave a message, but I tried to call you myself this afternoon, and yesterday too. You've been out and about a lot lately. Anything up?"

"What, are you writing a book?" snipped Francesca, intending to cut off this line of inquiry before it went very far.

"Nope," said Joey, ever placid. "Just asking."

"Well, don't ask me about my business, and I won't ask you about yours," she told him.

"But you ask me about my business all the time," Joey pointed out.

"That's because I'm your mother and it's my right! Now shut up and let me finish what I'm doing here."

"You're the boss."

Francesca waited until later on, after she had seen Joey off at the door, before checking the answering machine. As she had suspected, there were messages from Alice and Rosie. The two had both called earlier in the week, and Francesca had yet to get around to calling either back. It happened all the time, but her daughters inevitably went into a tizzy if they couldn't track her down right away when they wanted to talk. Listening to their voices, she could detect the telltale sound of unease that pointed to trouble in the near future if they didn't hear *her* voice. Now that she was certain that Joey would be occupied on Saturday night, she was anxious to let the Simmons woman know that she would be available to babysit. First, however, she had to call Florida and Oregon.

Francesca picked up the telephone and dialed Rosie's number first. To her relief, she heard her daughter's answering machine come on.

"Hi, everybody," Francesca said after the beep. "It's Nonna, returning Mommy's call. Where are you guys? I just got back from the library . . ."

It was barely a white lie—she really *had* just returned from the library—nonetheless, Francesca felt a little guilty about it, especially since she would have to spin the same tale to Alice.

But it was, she decided, the best approach, even if it wasn't exactly the truth. For the time being, she pushed the nagging thought to the back of her mind. If her conscience bothered her too much, she could always take it up with Father Buontempo next time at confession.

CHAPTER 25

One need not have been a psychic to perceive a certain feeling of high anxiety in the air at the Simmons residence when Francesca arrived the following evening a little before seven. Will answered the door and let her in before fleeing to the relative quiet of the living room couch, where he safely lost himself in a video game. The situation upstairs was not so tranquil. As Francesca stepped inside, she heard a good deal of commotion on the second floor. Voices were raised, particularly that of the Simmons woman, who was no doubt hurrying to get ready for her evening out. At issue seemed to be the location of a pair of earrings that *someone* must have misplaced when she was snooping around in her mother's jewelry box, even though she had been told a thousand times not to. For her part, Penny was denying the accusations with shrill professions of innocence.

It was, a chuckling Francesca decided, just a typical mother–daughter melee. She had endured enough of them through the years with her own daughters to recognize the signs.

"Staying out of the line of fire?" she said to Will as she passed through the living room on her way to the kitchen with the big paper bag she had brought to the house.

The boy rolled his eyes and raised a finger to the side of his head, where he made circles in the air to indicate his assessment of the emotional state of his mother and sister. "It's like this every time when she's getting dressed to go out," he sighed.

"Does your mother go out a lot?" asked Francesca.

"Hardly ever," answered Will. "But it's always a disaster." Then, nodding to the bag, "Whatcha got?"

"Just a few things for later on," she replied. "Nothing special. But come and see if you want."

Will paused the video game he was playing, tossed the controller aside, and jumped off the couch to follow her into the kitchen. He came to the table and stood by Francesca's side, his eyes full of eagerness as she reached into the bag. The old woman looked down at the boy and smiled. Much in the world had changed since she had been a young mother, but without fail, children everywhere were still always fascinated to see what treasures an adult might have brought home for them at the end of the day.

"I thought these might come in handy in case anyone wanted to play a game," said Francesca, pulling a deck of playing cards out of the bag. She handed them to Will, who considered them for a moment with a look of faint disappointment before putting them aside.

"What else?" he asked.

"And I brought this in case we watch a movie or something good on TV," she continued, producing a bag of popping corn. She gave him a conspiratorial wink. "It's the only thing I'll cook in the microwave," she confided.

The prospect of hot, buttered popcorn seemed to spark some interest, but only a little. "Anything else?" he asked, standing on his toes to get a peek inside the bag.

"Just this," said Francesca, reaching deep to get a good hold of the bottom of the glass-covered cake dish resting inside. Slowly she lifted it out, set it on the table, and lifted the cover to reveal the chocolate cake she had baked just that afternoon. She hadn't bothered to frost it, but instead had sprinkled the top with ground nuts and confectioners' sugar. The sight of it elicited the hoped-for look of approval on Will's face.

"Now you're talking," he said happily.

"I hope you ate your dinner already tonight," Francesca said.

"Yup," the boy assured her with an enthusiastic nod of his head.

Having perhaps decided that her best course of action would be to come downstairs and get out of her mother's way, Penny suddenly made an appearance at the kitchen door. She gave an anxious look over her shoulder—her mother was still carrying on upstairs despite her disappearance—before stepping closer to the table to take a look.

"What's all that?" she said with the same look of eager curiosity as her brother.

"Just a couple of treats for later," Francesca told her. "That is, if you're both good. Maybe we'll make some hot chocolate too."

The idea seemed more than agreeable to the two youngsters. Francesca was about to suggest some games they might play to pass the time when they heard the front doorbell ring. All conversation ceased, and Will and Penny exchanged nervous glances. Francesca looked up at the clock and arched an eyebrow. The Simmons woman's gentleman friend was not due until seven fifteen, or so she had said, but it was barely five minutes past. Had this person no sense, Francesca wondered. What kind of man came ten minutes early to pick up a lady on a first date? The two children fell in behind her as she marched off to the front door to find out.

"Hi, Ned Hadley," said the young man straightaway when Francesca opened the door. She looked past him to the driveway, where a sleek black sedan was idling.

"Francesca Campanile," she replied, unimpressed. "Come in."

Before Hadley had finished stepping across the threshold and into the front hall, Francesca had already scrutinized him from head to toe. She noticed everything: the cut of his clothes, his shoes, the way he carried himself. He was handsome enough, she thought, with his sandy brown hair and regular features, and he obviously had more than a few dollars in his pocket, but there was something vaguely annoying about his smile and the easy manner with which he nodded and winked at Will and Penny, who were keeping their distance a few steps back.

"Hi, kids," he said with a smarmy grin. "Where's Mom?"

"You're early," Francesca told him. "Why don't you come in and have a seat for a few minutes?"

"That's okay. I'm ready," came Loretta's voice from the top of the stairs. She was standing there putting on an earring. "I'll be right down."

Francesca shrugged and stepped aside. She would have liked to have had the opportunity to grill Mister Hadley a bit before letting him back out the door, just to find out what sort of man he was. But it was probably for the best, she told herself. It really wasn't any of her business.

A few moments later, Loretta descended the stairs. Wearing a very feminine but conservative black dress, she looked quite lovely. Will was too much of a little boy to pay any attention, but Penny looked up at her mother with unabashed admiration.

"Wow, you look pretty, Mom," she told her as she came into view.

"Ah, here's my girl," added Hadley, eyeing Loretta in a way that struck Francesca as somewhat less than wholesome.

"Thank you, Ned," Loretta replied. "I guess you didn't have any trouble finding the house."

"No problem at all," he said easily. "I just punched the address into the navigation system in the car and let the lady inside tell me where to go."

"Ladies have a way of doing that," said Francesca, though she had meant only to think it.

"Have you met my children, Penny and Will?" said Loretta, beckoning them to come closer.

"We were just saying hello," said Hadley to the two children, who stepped only slightly nearer.

"Say hello, guys," said Loretta. "Why are you hiding over there behind Mrs. Campanile?"

Their reluctance to come much closer did not escape Francesca's notice, and she was certain that it had not escaped Loretta's either. Still, Loretta wasted no time putting on her coat and gloves, and hurried to give each of the kids a kiss.

"Promise me you'll be good," she said, squeezing them both.

"I'm glad you found your earrings," Penny whispered to her.

"Me too," her mother whispered back.

"Will you be home late?" asked Will, a nervous twinge in his voice.

"Not very," his mother assured him, "but when I get home, you should already be asleep. Okay?" With that, she let them go and turned to Francesca. "We won't be late," she said. "Maybe around ten thirty? Eleven the absolute latest."

"That's fine," said Francesca, shooing her to the door. "You two go and have a good time. Just drive carefully. It's dark and icy out there."

"Don't worry," said a grinning Hadley. "She'll be in very good hands." He nodded to the door. "Shall we, Loretta?"

The moment their mother and Hadley stepped outside and the door closed behind them, Penny and Will hastened to the window to watch them go. Francesca came up behind the two children and looked out the window with them. The trio stayed there, keeping watch, until the car backed out of the driveway and sped off into the night.

"Nice car," opined Will once the car was out of sight, "but I think that guy is weird."

"Me too," nodded his sister.

"Me three," thought Francesca. Then, aloud, "Well, now, anybody in the mood for popcorn?"

CHAPTER 26

Francesca took a card from Penny, on her left, and passed one of her own to Will, on her right, who in turn passed one to his sister, on *his* right. Francesca let out a grunt of displeasure. She was on the lookout for a queen, but it was proving elusive. Like a poker player in a saloon, she narrowed her eyes to slits and looked about the table at the children. The two of them were holding their cards tight to their chests, stealing glances at one another, while trying their best to keep a straight face. The decisive moment was almost upon them. On the count of three, they passed cards once again. This time, Francesca's eyes lit up when the hoped-for queen finally appeared in her hand. Without pause, she thrust her hand out into the middle of the table to grab one of the two spoons resting there.

Too late!

With screams of delight filling the air, two smaller hands shot out first and snatched the spoons away. Will threw his cards on the table to reveal four jacks. Penny showed four kings. Gloating in their victory, the two burst out in laughter and waved the spoons at her.

"Cheaters!" cried Francesca. She threw her palms down on the table and glared at the two with mock indignation.

"Uh-uh," said Penny, shaking her head smugly.

"She's right," agreed Will. "We won fair and square. Now you've got to pay up!"

"Hmm, I don't know about that," answered Francesca. "I think maybe I was just hustled by a couple of cardsharps. I should probably just take that cake and head on home."

This suggestion elicited a howl of playful protest. The bowl of popcorn was empty, and the two youngsters were eager for their next treat.

"Okay, okay," laughed Francesca, getting up from the table. "*Mannagia,* my ears! If the two of you are going to carry on about it that way, I guess you can have some. What do you want with it, milk or hot chocolate?"

Hot chocolate having won the vote hands down, Francesca fished a pan out of the cupboard beneath the counter and placed it atop the stove. She filled it with milk, turned up the heat, and ordered Will to find the Nestlé Quik and Penny some clean cups, plates, and forks. Her arms folded, Francesca watched the two children. She was very pleased with herself, for the night was turning out far better than she had expected. After their mother had left for the evening, Francesca had feared that the children would immediately retreat to their usual sanctuaries of the upstairs computer and the television. Instead, they had followed her into the kitchen and waited while she prepared the popcorn in the microwave. To her surprise, it was Will who suggested they play a game of cards. Spoons just happened to be an old favorite of Francesca's.

When the hot chocolate was ready, Francesca filled three cups and set them on the table. "Careful, those are hot," she warned them, before turning her attention to the utensil drawer, through which she sifted around until she found a suitable knife for the cake. She cut three slices and transferred them to the plates using the flat side of the knife. She was about to set the plates down in front of the children when she hesitated and regarded them with a skeptical gaze.

"You did say that you both ate your dinners, right?" she asked.

"Yes, we did," nodded Penny. "We had the leftovers from the other night."

Will took a big bite of his cake. "Yeah, that spaghetti and meatballs was really good," he enthused between chomps, "and the cookies too." He washed this statement down with a gulp of hot chocolate.

"Well, thank you," said Francesca.

Penny cast a wistful look at the stove. "Will you ever cook supper again for us?" she asked.

"Oh, we'll see," Francesca replied. "I suppose if your mother has to come home again late some night after work, then maybe she might ask me."

"Mom's been coming home late from work a lot lately, hasn't she?" said Will, his upper lip now covered with a milky brown mustache. He dragged the back of his hand across his mouth, but only partially succeeded in wiping it clean.

"Uck, you're so disgusting," noted his sister.

"Here," said Francesca, handing the boy a napkin. "Try one of these."

Penny took a bite of her own cake. "That's just the way her job is sometimes," she said of her brother's observation regarding their mother. "Mom says that sometimes they give her a lot of work right at the end of the day."

"Your mother works very hard," Francesca told them, nodding her head to show that she understood how things were. "She does it for you two, to keep a roof over your heads, and food on the table, and shoes on your feet. And I'm sure that sometimes she comes home very tired. That's why you and your brother should do all you can to help out around here, picking up after yourselves and keeping things in order. That's a big job all by itself, you know. Your mother can't always do it all by herself."

"Did you ever have to work late when you had kids like us?" asked Will in a small voice, his eyes peering at her through his wire-rimmed glasses. Looking at him, Francesca had to chuckle to herself, for she realized that Tubs Bennett was right; sometimes Will really did look like Harry Potter.

"Well, I didn't have a job outside the house," she replied, amused by the children's surprised looks. "My husband had his own business fixing cars, and sometimes I would help him by taking care of the books and paying the bills. Things like that. But my most important job was taking care of my house and my family." She paused and gave the two of them a warm smile. "That was another day and age," she went on. "Life was different then."

"I bet things were really hard back in the old days, when you grew up," mused Penny, sounding as if she considered Francesca's "old days" to be centuries ago.

"Well, in some ways I guess they were," said Francesca. "When I was a little girl, we didn't have a lot of the fancy gadgets and appliances that we have today. I had to wash my own clothes by hand and hang them out to dry, because we didn't have a washer and dryer. And we didn't have automatic dishwashers, of course. Everything was done by hand. But in a lot of ways, things were easier in those days, I think—or at least, a little simpler."

"Like how?" asked Penny.

"Yeah," said Will. "Tell us what it was like to be a kid in those days."

"Well, for one thing, families stayed a lot closer in those days," explained Francesca. "At least, mine did. When I was little, my grandparents lived upstairs from us, and my aunt and uncle lived next door. And we had relatives all around the area. It seemed like I couldn't walk anywhere in the neighborhood without seeing someone who wasn't a cousin or whose family came from the same *paese* as my grandparents."

"The same what?" asked Penny.

"*Paese*," said Francesca. "The same town or village back in Italy. Didn't you ever hear the word *paesan*? That's where it comes from."

"I thought it meant someone who likes to eat pizza," said Will.

"Well, I suppose that might be partly correct," chuckled Francesca. "But the long and the short of it was that I could walk anywhere I wanted without worrying because there were always people watching out for me. I think that's what the problem is today. People are always moving around all over the country these days, never setting down the roots of their families, and never really getting to know who their neighbors are, because families come and go so often. You never grow to trust and depend on one another, because no one's ever around long enough."

"You sound just like Grandma Jane," observed Will. At the mention of the name, Penny gave a little cough and cast a sharp look at her brother.

"I didn't know you had a grandma," said Francesca, pretending not to notice the young girl's sudden discomfort.

"She lives up in New York," he said, "so we don't see her much."

"That's too bad," replied Francesca. "I'm sure she must miss you both a lot."

Penny fidgeted with her hands. "She and Mom don't get along," she said awkwardly.

The subject was one that clearly distressed the young girl, and though curious to know more, Francesca decided to save it for another time and move the conversation back to more comfortable terrain. A pall had come over the table, and she was anxious to recapture the light spirits of just a moment ago. It was Will, however, who pressed the issue.

"She never liked Dad," he went on matter-of-factly, "especially since he went away. And Mom never liked Grandma's husband, and so they argue all the time whenever she comes." He might have said more had his sister not silenced him with a shush.

"I see," said Francesca, nodding her head. "But you know, you shouldn't worry too much if your mother and grandmother don't always seem to get along. Mothers and daughters have been arguing with one another ever since . . . well, ever since there have been mothers and daughters, I guess. It's natural. It doesn't mean that they don't love each other, so don't worry too much about it. You should see the way I yell at *my* daughters."

"Where do your daughters live?" asked Penny, taking the opportunity Francesca had given her to move on to another topic.

Francesca gave her a smile. "Oh, I'll tell you all about them some other time," she replied, taking the deck of cards in hand. "For now, how about you finish your cake, and we'll play another few hands before it's time for bed. I want you both asleep before your mother gets home."

And so, as the children ate their cake, Francesca replaced the spoons in the center of the table and shuffled the cards.

"Okay," she told them as she started to deal, "this time, no cheating."

CHAPTER 27

Despite ample experience to the contrary, Loretta always hoped for the best. Life had left some deep scars on her psyche, especially when it came to love. Whatever luck she might have once had in that particular field of endeavor had, it seemed to her, vanished with the dinosaurs. Perhaps it was because she was a single mother and, as such, viewed as easy prey by the men she met, but all her romantic endeavors since David had left her inevitably seemed to end up as fiascoes. Each dismal encounter left a painful mark on her, but hope had a palliative effect. It dulled the sting and helped her forget the mistakes of the past. It was a powerful elixir without which she would have long since succumbed to despair and given up the dream. And so, whenever she met a man who offered the slightest prospect of bringing a measure of warmth and love and stability to her life, she pushed the hard lessons of experience from her mind and let hope have its day.

Such being the case, Loretta told herself that Ned Hadley had many appealing qualities. He had a good head of hair, a reasonably handsome face, and bright, playful eyes that never seemed to stop darting about. He had a pleasant enough personality and a certain charm about him, that easy air of confidence that comes from having money. He had excellent taste in clothes, and dressed every bit like the up-and-coming businessman he

was. He had a great car. He had a membership at a private country club, to which he took Loretta that night for dinner. And
there, it seemed, he had many friends, for as the host escorted
them to their table in the dining room, couples inevitably
looked up and greeted him as he passed.

"Hey there, Ned. Good to see you. How's your mom and
dad?"

"The Nedster! How's it going?"

"Looking good, Nedley! When are you heading south to
play a few rounds?"

These salutations came from the men, all of them exchanging winks and approving nods with him, as if they were acknowledging a shared secret or some private joke. For their part, the
women generally just looked on, smiling vacuously while size-
ing up Loretta with cool, calculating eyes, much the way a sci-
entist might regard a lab rat. Hadley greeted them all, tossing out
casual banter to anyone who might say hello, as he and Loretta
took their seats. He had a cheerful riposte for each of them.

As she settled in at the table and the busboy filled their
water glasses, Loretta looked about at her surroundings. The lighting was a trifle too bright, she thought, and the tables, in her es-
timation, set too close to one another. The former gave the
room a louder, less formal ambiance than it deserved. The latter
gave those with big ears—and she guessed that there were more
than a few in attendance—easy audience to private conversations
other than their own. It was not an intimate room by any means.
Still, with its richly paneled walls and great, lovely windows that
looked out onto to the now-darkened golf course, it had a simple, understated elegance to it, one that Loretta supposed was
much in step with the old-moneyed members who dined there.
She could imagine herself sitting there with them some summer
evening, enjoying an early dinner while watching the players
strolling down the course toward the clubhouse as the sun set
behind them.

All in all, she had to admit that it was a nice place to have dinner on a first date, and Loretta reflected that this was another of the many marks she might record on the credit side of Mister Hadley's ledger. Just the same, as she took her menu in hand and tried to listen attentively to the waiter's recitation of the evening's specials, Loretta could not escape the feeling that all of Hadley's assets were offset by one annoying liability.

His cell phone.

Although recently divorced, Hadley still seemed very much married, but to his personal communication device—and she was a jealous, clinging wife. From the moment they left the house and Loretta first set foot in his car, it seemed hardly two minutes at a stretch passed without them being interrupted by the ringing of his telephone. She might have found that easy enough to live with if Hadley had simply chosen to ignore it. Instead, he invariably picked up and began chatting away, as if suddenly Loretta were not even there. He was doing so just at that moment at the club, while the waiter did his best to explain the dinner specials to Loretta. The young man soon gave up the effort and promised he would return shortly to take their orders.

"Sorry," said Hadley after finally hanging up. "Just business. You know how it is. It never ends."

More than one of his cell phone conversations had ended with hushed "I'll-call-you-laters," leaving Loretta to wonder about what kind of business he was talking, and if perhaps she wasn't the only item on his agenda for that night. Despite these misgivings, she still held out hope that the evening would turn out better than it had started.

"You know, Ned," she suggested playfully, "it might be easier for us to talk if maybe you just . . . I don't know . . . turned that thing off?"

As he tucked the phone into his jacket pocket, Hadley chuckled and gave her an odd sort of half smile, as if to say that he wasn't sure of just exactly what she meant. He picked up his menu and began to peruse the entrées.

"So, sunshine girl," he said easily, "what looks good tonight—besides you, of course?"

Loretta flashed a perfunctory smile in reply even though she did not feel the least bit flattered. She was, in fact, beginning to feel that she would rather go home. Had she not been famished at that particular moment, she might have suggested it. Instead, she returned her gaze to her menu and kept it there until she saw the waiter returning to take their orders.

"Has everyone made up their minds?" he asked pleasantly.

Loretta closed her menu and gave a barely audible sigh.

"Well, I don't know about you," she said to Hadley, a thinly masked hint of disappointment in her voice, "but I think I've just about made up mine. . . . "

CHAPTER 28

After dinner, as Hadley drove her home from the club, Loretta sat quietly in the seat beside him, listening absentmindedly to the soft growl of the car's engine and the hum of the tires against the road. Her companion was, of course, once again engaged in conversation, but not with her. As annoying as the constant interruptions had been, Loretta now reflected that they had in some ways been a blessing. Throughout dinner, whenever the two had had the opportunity to actually converse with one another for any length of time, Hadley had seemed incapable of discussing anything other than the glories of golf and the trials and tribulations of his family's trucking business. Loretta put every fiber of her being into trying to look interested, of trying to *be* interested, but the effort extracted a terrible toll on her patience and, before very long, she lapsed into something akin to melancholy. She had started the evening with high hopes, but soon found herself longing for it to end, to simply go home and just get in her bed. As the night wore on, the thought of curling up and falling asleep was all that had sustained her.

As they drew nearer to home, Loretta began to turn over in her mind her options for bringing the evening to a graceful conclusion. Given that Hadley was an important client of her law firm and a family friend of Mister Pace, there was every reason to expect that their paths might cross once again in the not-too-distant future. She had to be careful. It was just then, as she was deciding how best to send him on his way, that they arrived at the house, and Hadley abruptly ended his conversation, snapped the telephone shut, and tossed it aside.

"I'm sorry," he said in a heavy voice after a moment's hesitation. "I'm afraid I haven't been very good company this evening. Here I am with a beautiful woman, and all I've done all night is talk to other people on that silly phone. I don't know why I get like that. It's just everything, I guess. I've had a lot going on, you see. The business. My divorce . . . "

Hadley proceeded to explain at some length that, despite his outward bravura, he was on the inside the most wretched man on the planet. Since the breakup of his marriage, he told her, he had known only sadness and loneliness. His spirits were in perpetual darkness, and it was all he could do just to get out of bed each morning to face the day. He went on for a time in this same vein, until finally his voice trailed away and he gazed straight ahead down the road, a forlorn expression coming over his face.

Loretta didn't know what to say, for he had taken her very much by surprise. For the first time all evening, Hadley was suddenly behaving like something other than the self-assured boor that she had become convinced he was. He was acting vulnerable and human. His changed demeanor gave her to wonder if perhaps she had been mistaken, that she had judged him too harshly and too quickly. He was now showing himself to her in a different light, one that rekindled in Loretta the hope that had all but flickered out just a short while ago. She realized that this new person, for Hadley did indeed seem to her a new person, might be one worth getting to know better. With that in mind, she no longer felt so anxious for the evening to end.

Loretta, however, said nothing until they came to the house and Hadley pulled into the driveway. As they sat there in awkward silence, the car's engine idling, she let a dramatic moment pass before finally turning to him.

"Would you like to come in, and maybe we could talk for a little while?" she asked softly.

Hadley turned grateful eyes to her. "Are you sure?" he asked.

"Yes," Loretta told him. " I'm sure."

"Okay then," he said, a smile curling the corners of his mouth as he turned the engine off. "In that case, I'd love to come in."

Francesca greeted them at the door when the two walked up the front steps. Loretta laughed to herself, for she had noticed the older woman standing at the living room window, keeping watch like a nervous mother waiting up for a teenaged daughter.

"I hope the children weren't any trouble, Mrs. Campanile," said Loretta when she and Hadley came inside.

"No trouble at all, Mrs. Simmons," she assured her. "They both went right upstairs to bed like little angels. I haven't heard a peep out of them since." She began to put on her coat. "Did you have a nice time tonight?"

"Very nice," said Hadley before Loretta could make her own reply.

"Oh, good," said Francesca, giving him a suspicious, sideways glance. She buttoned up her coat and pulled on her hat, and was just opening her mouth to say something else to Loretta when Hadley leaned over and touched her elbow.

"Shall I walk you to your car?" he asked with a grin. "As you said before, it is a bit dark and icy out there."

"No, I'll be fine," Francesca told him. Then, turning to Loretta, "Well, good night, Mrs. Simmons."

"Good night, Mrs. Campanile," replied Loretta, holding the door for her. "Thank you so much for coming tonight."

"Anytime," the older woman answered kindly. "I was happy to do it. I'll see you on Monday." With that, she went on her way.

Loretta stood at the door and watched while Francesca got into her car.

"Alone at last," said Hadley behind her as he ambled into the living room. He took off his coat and casually tossed it across the arm of the sofa.

"Why don't you sit and relax," suggested Loretta once Francesca had driven off and she had closed the door. "I'll get us something to drink. Some wine or maybe coffee, if you like."

"Please, don't go to the trouble," said Hadley, settling onto the sofa. He looked up at her and patted the seat cushion beside him in a gesture of invitation. "Why don't you just come and join me?"

What happened next was, for Loretta, a disheartening scene that had been played out more than once before in her life. No sooner had she seated herself at a discreet distance from him than without warning, Hadley suddenly reached out and took her in his arms. Professing an uncontrollable passion for her, and obviously under the mistaken assumption that his feelings in the matter were somehow reciprocated, he pulled her close and pressed his mouth to hers in the most awkward and offensive way. Stunned by this clumsy amorous assault, Loretta did her best to fend off his advances, but he was stronger than she had imagined and quite intent, it seemed, on his purpose.

"What are you doing?" she hissed at him, trying to squirm out of his embrace. In that moment, it all became clear that his contrite confession in the car on the drive home had been nothing but a ploy aimed at winning him an invitation to come inside. Loretta was furious at herself for not having seen through the ruse. How many more times would she fall for it?!

"Come on, Loretta," Hadley implored her, holding her tighter. "The kids are asleep upstairs. They'll never know."

"Never know *what*?" answered Loretta, even though she understood his meaning all too well.

"You know," said Hadley, pausing to ogle her with a ridiculously furtive expression as he pressed himself closer. "We're both grown-ups here. We both want the same thing. You know how much you—"

"Mom?"

The small voice coming from the top of the stairs froze Hadley. To Loretta's great relief, he had enough decency to immediately release her at the sound of footsteps descending the staircase. By the time Will came into view and peeked over the railing into the living room, Hadley had retreated to the opposite end of the sofa, where he sat in sullen silence, his ardor of just a moment earlier snuffed out like a candle.

"What is it, Will?" said Loretta, straightening her dress as she jumped up. She hurried over to him, mortified at the prospect that her son might have overheard the goings-on in the living room. As embarrassed as she felt, Loretta had never been more grateful for having one of her children intrude on her social life.

"It's Penny," Will explained. "She says she's sick. I think she's gonna throw up."

Loretta turned to Hadley, who was doing his best to avoid eye contact with the boy. It gave her a certain pleasure to note that he looked exquisitely pained by the turn of events.

"I'm sorry, Mister Hadley," she told him in a tone that conveyed not the slightest bit of warmth, "but I think you'll have to leave now."

Hadley cleared his throat. "Yes, of course," he said, getting to his feet. "I understand completely." With that, he took his coat in hand and made haste for the door, never once looking at Will. "Could I call you again sometime?" he asked with astonishing boldness.

"How about if I call you?" snipped Loretta, holding the door open for him.

Hadley stepped outside, then suddenly stuck his head back in through the door. "But do you know my number?" he asked.

"Doesn't everybody?" said Loretta. Then she unceremoniously pushed his head out and slammed the door shut. Feeling like every drop of energy had been wrung out of her, she turned to Will and slumped back against the wall.

"Is he gone?" said Penny, coming to the top of the staircase. She looked down at her mother with worried eyes.

"I guess you're not getting ready to throw up," Loretta observed.

"I'm feeling a little better," her daughter said sheepishly.

"Sorry, Mom," said Will. "We couldn't think of anything else to do to make him go away."

"Thanks, guys," said Loretta, putting her arm around her son to lead him back to bed. "Sorry for all the fuss."

"He's not coming back, is he, Mom?" Penny asked as the three climbed the stairs.

"Nope," said Loretta. "That's one thing I can promise you."

Later, after she had tucked the children back in bed and gotten herself undressed, a discouraged Loretta collapsed into bed. For a time, she lay there simply staring at the ceiling, her mind turning the evening's events over and over, until she could think about them no more. Her heart heavy, she rolled onto her side and wept softly while she waited for sleep to overtake her and erase the hurt of it all from her consciousness. As she had too many times come to know, hope's triumph over experience was very often short-lived.

CHAPTER 29

"Good weekend?" said Shirley.

The inevitable cup of coffee in hand, she was sitting back against the edge of Loretta's desk, looking down at her co-worker, who was doing her best to get herself organized. It was Monday morning, and Loretta was in her usual state of near-despondency, a mood that descended on her at the start of virtually every work-week.

"Let's just say it was forgettable," she replied with a weary sigh, "and leave it at that."

"Oh, come on," prodded Shirley. "You can do better than that. Tell me all about how Saturday night went with *You-Know-Who*."

Loretta gaped at her friend.

"How on earth did you know about that?" she exclaimed.

"Oh, I have my ways," said a smug Shirley. "But I can never reveal my sources. You know how it is, attorney–client privilege. So, go on. Tell me what happened!"

"Nothing happened," said Loretta with grim firmness, "absolutely nothing." Then, rolling her eyes, she added, "Thank God."

"Ooh," cooed Shirley, her curiosity even more piqued. "Sounds like an intriguing tale. I did warn you, of course, but you wouldn't listen. So, come on. Let's have it. Enquiring minds need to know." She looked at Loretta with pleading, inquisitive eyes.

Loretta gave a little laugh. She considered spilling all the beans, for she could see no harm in it, but in truth, she simply was in no mood to relive Saturday night's escapade. It was all still too fresh in her mind, and she was trying her best to forget it.

"Some other time," Loretta finally told her. "Maybe someday when you start writing for the tabloids."

"Oh, you're no fun," Shirley pouted. She looked ready to nag her some more on the subject, but instead leaned closer and looked with concern into Loretta's face. "Hey, kid, you look a little peaked today," she said. "Are you feeling all right?"

"Just really tired," said Loretta with a shrug, "but that's nothing new."

Shirley reached out and put the back of her hand against Loretta's forehead. "I don't know," she said thoughtfully. "You feel a little warm. You better be careful, I think you might be coming down with something."

"Thanks, Mom," Loretta smiled. "I'll remember to button up my overcoat."

"Hey, it's no joke," said Shirley. "You have to take care of yourself this time of year. There's all sorts of stuff going around." Shirley could not help but share with Loretta a horrendous story she had recently read about a woman somewhere out in the Midwest who had succumbed to a mysterious respiratory infection that still had all her doctors baffled. After imparting this happy tale, she eventually went on her way to start her own workday.

A short while later that morning, Mister Pace happened to amble by Loretta's desk. On his shoulder rode a new putter he was intending to put to the test when he reached his office.

"Good morning, Loretta," he greeted her in his always-pleasant way.

"Good morning, Mister Pace," she said brightly, though she was feeling anything but. "Planning to play eighteen today?"

"I think I'll only have time for nine," he confided with a wink. "It's kind of tough this time of year."

"Sounds like a good time for a trip to Florida," she suggested.

"Ah, now there's an idea," he replied with a wistful sigh.

Instead of moving on to his office, Pace lingered there for a few moments, whistling softly while casting a glance about the office. Looking vaguely ill at ease, he fidgeted with the handle of the putter and cleared his throat, as if he wanted to saying something but couldn't quite get up the nerve.

"Was there something you wanted, Mister Pace?" Loretta asked, hoping to put him at ease.

Pace leaned closer.

"Actually," he began in a tentative voice, "I just thought I'd mention that I heard through the grapevine that you and Ned Hadley had dinner Saturday night." At the look of chagrin on her face, he quickly added by way of explanation, "I have one or two friends at that club, you see."

"Ugh," Loretta groaned, for she wanted to crawl under her desk. Was there anyone who didn't know about her pathetic attempt at a social life? Though it had no exact written policy, it was common knowledge that the firm frowned upon romantic liaisons between employees and clients. Worse, she had—almost—had one with a personal friend of the firm's senior partner. She cringed as she waited for the expected reprimand. To her surprise, however, none was forthcoming. Instead, Pace looked down at her with fatherly concern.

"I, um, hope all went well," he said delicately.

"It depends on how you'd define the word 'well,'" answered Loretta. She looked up and gave him a dejected shrug.

Pace let out a grunt of consternation. "I've known the Hadleys for years," he said. "Wonderful, good-hearted people, but I'm afraid the son is a bit of a . . . well, let's just say that he has something of a reputation."

"Don't worry," Loretta told him with a rueful smile, "I managed to keep *my* reputation intact—just barely."

"Good girl," said Pace, seeming much relieved. Then, in a

regretful voice, "I have to apologize, though. I really should have said something to you much sooner when I first saw him taking an interest, but I thought it best to not interfere. Besides, nobody likes it when the old man goes around butting his nose into other people's business."

"Well, from now on, feel free to butt your nose into my business any time you want," Loretta assured him. She started to stand, intending to fix Pace's tie, which was once again dreadfully askew, but suddenly feeling light-headed and weak, she plopped right back down in her chair.

"Are you not feeling well?" said Pace, coming to her side. "Your face has gone very pale."

"I don't know," said Loretta anxiously. "I was feeling all right just a minute ago. Now all of a sudden, I'm cold all over, and it feels like my head weighs a thousand pounds. You don't think I'm having a stroke, do you?"

Pace gave her a bemused look. "Did you get a flu shot this year?" he asked her.

"The kids got them, but I didn't bother," said Loretta, starting to shiver. It felt like she was sitting in the middle of a walk-in freezer.

Pace clicked his tongue and shook his head.

"You should have bothered," he told her. With that, he took her gently by the arm and helped her stand. "Come on," he said, "I think we'd better get you home."

Despite Mister Pace's fretful pleas to let him or someone else take her home, Loretta insisted on driving herself. It was foolish of her to do so, for she was feeling very unsteady, but Loretta possessed a rather pronounced stubborn streak, which often chose to surface at times like these. It was, she supposed, some sort of deeply ingrained survival instinct that kept her fighting when the chips were down. Nonetheless, she was grateful for Pace's kind attention as he walked her out to the car, all the while making her promise that she would drive carefully.

By the time she made it home, Loretta had neither the energy nor the inclination to do anything other than drag herself upstairs and drop fully clothed into bed. She tugged the blankets over her, intent on burrowing herself in and staying there to keep warm, but then she let out a sorrowful groan, for she realized there was something she needed to do first. Rolling onto her side, she feebly reached for the telephone and brought it onto the bed. With great exertion, she dialed a number.

"Hello, Mrs. Campanile. It's Loretta Simmons," she said with a dry cough when Francesca's answering machine picked up. "I'm home sick with the flu today, so there's no need for you to come. In fact, it would be much smarter if you didn't. I don't want to spread this around. I'll call you tomorrow." Then she hung up the phone, dropped her head back onto the pillow, and promptly fell off into a fitful sleep.

CHAPTER 30

When she opened her eyes many hours later, Loretta realized that she had lost all conception of time since she had put herself to bed earlier that morning. At the moment just before she awoke, she had been having a rather bizarre dream in which her bed had somehow been transported to the middle of a barnyard, where a great clutch of chickens was running about on the floor all around her. It was the sound of the hens's clucking that Loretta remembered most vividly, and she was alarmed to find that she still heard it, or at least something of a similar nature. She peered about the bedroom to find its source. By now, all was plunged completely into darkness, save for the softly glowing computer monitor in the corner, where she discovered Penny sitting—tapping away at the keyboard. The mystery solved, Loretta put a hand to her forehead. Shirley had been right; she was definitely burning up. Summoning all her will, Loretta tried to sit up, but her head was throbbing, as were her back and legs. She felt as though she had been run over by a train.

At hearing her stir, Penny jumped up and came to the side of the bed. Looking down with worried eyes, she reached out and touched her mother's face.

"Hi, Mom," she said, stroking her hair. "I was waiting for you to wake up. Are you okay?"

It was all Loretta could do to keep her eyes open. "I will be," she moaned in frustration. "That is, if this doesn't kill me first—which honestly doesn't sound all that bad right at the moment."

"Don't say that!" exclaimed her daughter, who looked like she was about to burst into tears.

"Calm down. Don't worry," Loretta told her, forcing a smile. "It's just the flu. I'll be okay in a couple of days." She looked around the room. "Where's your brother?"

"Downstairs, doing his homework."

"His *homework*?" scoffed Loretta. "Is he feeling sick too?"

"Doesn't look like it," shrugged Penny

Loretta settled back and closed her eyes. "Do me a favor, sweetie," she said. "Go into the medicine cabinet and get me the bottle of Tylenol and a cup of water."

"I think there's already some right there," answered Penny, nodding to the bedside table.

Loretta lifted her head off the pillow and looked at the table. Sure enough, a bottle of Extra Strength Tylenol stood there along with a small teapot and cup, neither of which she could remember having used in years.

"Now, how on earth did that get there?" she wondered.

"Probably Mrs. C," offered Penny.

"No," said Loretta. "I left a message for her not to come today."

"Guess she didn't get it, because she came," said Penny, walking over to the other side of the bed. She put a hand on the teapot. "It's not hot anymore."

"That's okay," said her mother, scratching her head. "Do me a favor. Pour a little bit into the cup and give me the bottle of medicine."

While Penny poured the tea, Loretta opened the bottle of pain reliever and shook out two tablets. The tea her daughter offered her was cold and bitter, but it served to wash the pills down. When she was certain that she had completely swallowed them, Loretta lay back again and closed her eyes. It occurred to her then that she did indeed have some vague recollection of someone coming into the room and tucking the blanket around her earlier that afternoon. In her fevered state, Loretta had imagined it to be her mother. She had dismissed the memory as a dream, but now she realized that it must have been Mrs. Campanile.

"Are you guys hungry?" Loretta asked feebly.

"No," Penny answered. "Mrs. C cooked us supper."

"She did?" said Loretta, not sure if she felt consternation or gratitude. She was grateful to Francesca for having taken care of supper, but the last thing she needed was for the older woman to catch her flu and leave them high and dry for a babysitter. "What did she make?" she asked, too weak to contemplate the repercussions.

"It was this kind of weird pie thing she made in the frying pan," said her daughter. "She called it a frittatt or something like that."

"Frittatt? What was in it?"

"I don't know," shrugged Penny. "Different stuff. Potatoes and eggs—and onions, I think."

"And how was it?" asked her mother.

"Not bad, actually. She left some on a plate for you and said I should bring it up to you if you were hungry when you woke up. Want me to go get it?"

"No, that's okay, honey," said Loretta thoughtfully. Then, with a yawn, "I think I'm just going to rest for now. Do me one more favor and set the alarm clock for me so that I can get up and help you guys get ready for school tomorrow."

"Oh, don't worry," Penny assured her. "Mrs. C already made us get our clothes all ready for tomorrow morning."

"She did, huh?" said Loretta. She wanted to query her daughter further about what else her babysitter had been up to, but she felt the heavy weight of fatigue pulling her back into sleep. "I guess I'll have to talk to her about it tomorrow," she said with a weary yawn. And then she was out.

CHAPTER 31

"Mrs. Simmons?"

No answer.

"Hello, Mrs. Simmons?" Francesca called softly again. "It's just me, Mrs. Campanile."

Still no reply.

Standing at the front door, a bag of groceries clutched in her arm, Francesca pushed the door further open and peeked inside. It was late in the morning and, to all appearances, no one was home, a circumstance she found quite puzzling. Just the previous day, the poor Simmons woman had been bedridden; it astounded Francesca to think that she might have recovered so quickly and gone to work that day. Just then, another thought occurred to her. What if the young woman had become so ill overnight that she had ended up in the hospital? And what of the children? As it was, Francesca had fretted about them all night, worrying about how they would manage to prepare their own breakfast and get themselves ready for school. The idea that they too might come down with the flu preyed equally on her thoughts. She was just beginning to cycle through the endless list of alarming possibilities she had stored in her mind when she suddenly heard what she thought might be the stirring of bedclothes from one of the upstairs bedrooms. Francesca leaned in through the door and listened more closely. Yes, she heard it again, then all was quiet once more.

Breathing a sigh of relief, Francesca tucked the house key back behind the mailbox and stepped inside. As she stood in the front hall, removing her coat and hat, she noted that the children's backpacks were nowhere in sight, a sure sign that the two had made it out of the house to school that morning. Stepping near the staircase, Francesca leaned over and gave a glance up, recalling the previous day, when she had ventured upstairs for the first time to check on the Simmons woman. The children's bedrooms, she had discovered, were in astonishing disorder. The floor in Will's bedroom was littered with LEGO building blocks, magnets, miniature planes and race cars, game cards, action figures, a football and a baseball, comic books, and a variety of other paraphernalia, all strewn helter-skelter. The bed itself looked as though it had not been properly made in weeks. Francesca had been sorely tempted to make it herself, but reaching it to do so would have been like crossing a minefield. Conditions were only slightly better in Penny's room, where much of the mess consisted of shoes and clothes, stuffed animals, and magazines. Francesca clicked her tongue and shook her head at the thought of it all. She surmised, quite rightly, that things had not improved in the last twenty-four hours. Restoring some semblance of order in the children's rooms was a project she longed to tackle, but for the moment, she had other plans, and in any event, she did not wish to disturb their mother's rest any more than she already had with her entrance into the house. And so, Francesca moved stealthily to the kitchen, set the bag of groceries on the counter, and went straight to work.

Sometimes when she was alone at home and she had things on her mind, a not-uncommon state of affairs, Francesca tended to talk to herself as she went about her business. In truth, she wouldn't talk so much to herself as she would to her husband,

Leo, who despite having passed on to the next life, remained for her every bit as good a listener as he had been in this life. Though she herself was quite often unaware that she was doing it, anyone who might have chanced to overhear Francesca as she walked about the house rambling on about whatever happened to be preoccupying her would have sworn that she was carrying on an actual conversation with her deceased spouse. It was like listening to a person speaking over the telephone to someone else.

And so it was a short while later on this particular day after Francesca had commenced operations in the Simmons kitchen. It was nearing noon, and she had been talking a blue streak for quite a few minutes, when she was surprised to hear the sound of footsteps slowly descending the staircase. By this time, Francesca had already straightened up the counters and washed the children's breakfast dishes, she had been pleased to note the telltale crumbs on the table and the plates and bowls in the sink, evidence that they had managed to make themselves some toast and cereal. A simple broth mixed with pastina and some sliced carrots simmered on the stove's back burner. Wiping her hands on her apron, she turned just as Loretta trudged into the kitchen and deposited herself in one of the chairs at the table. The younger woman was a pitiable sight, her hair a matted mess and her face dreadfully drawn and wan. Two dark semicircles, like smudges of charcoal, shadowed her eyes.

"Oh, it *is* you, Mrs. Campanile," she said feebly. "I thought I heard your voice. Were you on the phone?"

"Oh, you poor thing," said Francesca, coming to her side. "I feel awful. I must have been talking to myself again. Kids and grandkids will do that to you. I'm so sorry for waking you."

"Oh, no, it's okay," Loretta told her. "I needed to get up for a little while."

"But how are you feeling?" said Francesca. "You really shouldn't be out of bed."

"And you really shouldn't be here," answered the younger woman. "I'd feel even worse than I already do if you caught this from me."

"Oh, don't worry about me," Francesca assured her. "I got my flu shot back in October."

The younger woman gave a sigh. "Did everyone but me get one of those?" she said ruefully.

Francesca gave her a kind smile, patted her on the shoulder, and turned back to the stove. "How's your stomach?" she asked over her shoulder. "Think you could manage a little something to eat? I made some soup."

"I guess it's worth a try," said Loretta in a hesitant voice. "But please, Mrs. Campanile—"

"Francesca," the older woman interrupted her as she ladled out the broth and pastina into a bowl.

"Oh, okay. Francesca," Loretta continued. "It's very kind of you to do this, coming to the house so early today, and staying late with the children last night, but I really don't think I can afford—"

"You want cheese on that?" asked Francesca before Loretta could finish whatever she meant to say.

"Cheese?" she said.

"On your soup," said Francesca, her back still to Loretta. "I always like to have a little grated Romano on mine, but everybody's different. It's up to you."

"Um, no thank you," said Loretta. "I don't want you to go to any more trouble."

"What trouble?" said Francesca, finally turning back to the table with the steaming bowl of soup and a soup spoon in hand. She set both before Loretta and stepped back.

"There you go, Mrs. Simmons—"

"Loretta," the younger woman interrupted her. She looked up at Francesca with tired eyes and mustered a weak smile.

"Okay, Loretta it is," said Francesca, returning her smile. "Now just eat this slow, to warm you up inside a little bit, while I finish what I'm doing here."

"What exactly are you doing?" inquired Loretta before taking a spoonful of the broth. The taste seemed to please her, which in turned pleased Francesca.

Francesca returned to the counter and began to dice up some garlic. "I'm making some sauce," she explained, the knife clopping against the cutting board.

"What kind of sauce?"

"Tomato sauce," answered Francesca. "Of course, some people around here call it gravy. I'll make enough for one or two meals."

"But how do you make the sauce?" said Loretta, sounding sincerely curious. "I mean, if you don't mind my asking."

"Oh, it's the easiest thing in the world," laughed Francesca. "Just watch while you eat your soup."

When she was finished slicing the garlic, Francesca slid it all into a pot with some olive oil and turned up the heat. In a few moments, the garlic's strong but pleasing aroma was wafting through the air, giving the kitchen the warm smell of a trattoria. Francesca loved that delicious, distinctive smell as much as anything else in life, other than her family and friends. It was a simple thing, but something about it always filled her with hope and optimism. Breathing it in, she hoped it would do the same for Loretta. She gave a quick glance over her shoulder to see if the young woman was still paying attention. To her satisfaction, she noted that Loretta had already consumed most of the soup.

"Now what?" asked Loretta.

"Now a little bit of meat so that the sauce is nice and thick," she replied.

Francesca opened a small package of ground beef she had purchased that morning and took a fistful of the cool, red meat.

Holding it over the pot, she crumbled the meat in her hand and let it drop bit by bit into the pot with the simmering garlic.

"All you have to do is brown it a little," Francesca said. When the last of the meat had fallen from her hand, she threw in a little salt and pepper, and stirred it all around with a spoon. Then she went back to the cutting board, sliced up a piece of pepperoni, and pushed that into the pot as well. "I like to add that for flavor," she explained, looking back once more at Loretta.

Loretta seemed to be watching with interest, but Francesca could see that her energy was waning fast. She hurriedly opened two cans of kitchen-ready tomatoes and poured them into the pot before adding a sprinkling of basil and oregano. She gave it all a good stir, covered the pot, and turned the heat down low.

"And that's that," she said, wiping her hands on her apron. "Now we just let it cook on its own for a while. All that's left to do is boil some pasta when it's time for dinner." She went to the table and sat next to Loretta. "What did that take? Five, ten minutes?"

"You make it look easy," Loretta said wearily. "I wish I could cook like that."

"It's not a matter of wishing, honey," Francesca told her. "*Wanting* is what's important. If someone wants to learn how to cook, they can. Anyone can do it. You just have to have a little patience. Make it fun, and don't be afraid to make a mistake. I think it's like that with most things in life."

"Maybe," said Loretta, sounding less than convinced.

Francesca folded her hands on her lap and sat in silence for a few moments. There was something she had been itching to ask Loretta, even though she knew that it was none of her business. Curiosity finally overcame her, so she looked up and gave her a nod.

"So, how was your date on Saturday with you gentleman friend?" she asked very tentatively. "Will you be seeing him again?"

"Oh, God, no, not if I can help it," groaned Loretta. "He was a total creep."

"Hmm," grunted Francesca. "I thought as much when I first met him, but I didn't want to say so. Nobody likes it when an old lady interferes."

"You know, you're the second person to tell me something like that," griped Loretta. "Do me a favor. In the future, feel free to interfere."

"I'll try to remember," Francesca told her with a kind smile.

Loretta slouched back in her chair. A sad, weary expression, a look of utter discouragement, came over her face. "Are there any good men left out there for someone like me?" she lamented.

"Oh, they're out there . . . somewhere," Francesca assured her. "There's someone for everyone."

"But where do you find them?"

"Oh, there's no point looking," said Francesca. "From what I've seen in life, the harder you look for something, the harder it is to find it. I think that's especially true for love. You have to just let go and let love find you. Just be patient. You're a young, attractive woman. The right man will show up at your door someday."

"Yeah, but then how do you get him to stay?" said Loretta. "It's not easy these days."

"I don't know," Francesca replied, "but in my day, the first thing you did when you met an attractive man that you wanted to keep was to sit him down and give him something good to eat. You know, a lot has changed in the world since I was young, but that old saying about the way to a man's heart is as true now as it was then. Sounds silly, but it works."

"It would be nice to have a man cook for *me*," Loretta opined, her face brightening a little.

"Well, that's a nice fantasy," chuckled Francesca, "but I wouldn't hold your breath waiting for it."

"I guess you're right," sighed Loretta. "So that leaves it up to me. Maybe you could show me the ropes someday."

"Any time," said Francesca, and she truly meant it. "But for now, you should get right back in bed. You look ready to fall out of that chair."

"Yes," said Loretta, giving her a tired nod. "I think it's that time." She stood and started to reach for her spoon and bowl.

"Leave those," Francesca told her. "Just go and rest."

Loretta hesitated for a moment, her lips pursed. "Thank you so much for the soup," she said, her voice quavering ever so slightly. "I know I don't act it, but I really appreciate—"

"Come on now," said Francesca, gently taking her by the arm before she could finish. "You need to get your rest. We'll talk again later."

With that, she guided Loretta to the bottom of the stairs and watched until she had safely trudged back up to her bedroom. When she was certain that Loretta had made it back into bed, Francesca returned to the kitchen to check on the sauce. Humming a tune to herself, she lifted the lid off the pot and gave the now-bubbling red liquid inside a stir. It was a simple sauce, she reflected, nothing special at all, but hopefully the start of something good.

CHAPTER 32

The doorbell rang.

Francesca, who was standing atop a step stool, gazing into one of Loretta's cupboards, looked at the clock and frowned. It was a few minutes past one. Who, she wondered with some consternation, could be coming to the door at that early hour on a weekday afternoon? Having neglected to bring cookies or some other sweet with her that morning, Francesca had been poking around the kitchen, looking to see what might be on hand that she could use to make a treat for Penny and Will when they came home from school. In truth, there wasn't much to be found, but Francesca had just managed to spy a can of sliced peaches up on one of the cupboard shelves and an unopened box of baking mix on another. The refrigerator, she had already discovered, held a carton of eggs and a half gallon of milk, and a bag of brown sugar was hiding behind the coffee canister on the counter. As she was standing there atop the step stool, an idea for something tasty had just been starting to percolate in Francesca's head. The ringing of the doorbell, however, distracted her and chased the nascent recipe from her mind. Annoyed at the interruption to her deliberations, she gave a growl of displeasure, stepped down onto the floor, and went to the front door to see who it might be.

Francesca opened the door a crack and looked out onto the front step, where she beheld a dapper, older gentleman waiting.

The collar of his long gray coat turned up against the chill wind—
it was a sunny day, but had suddenly turned quite blustery—he
held in his hands a cardboard box from which protruded a white
bag holding a loaf of bread. The tops of some plastic containers
were also visible. Francesca always had a healthy suspicion of
strangers, and she eyed this one sharply, but her instincts told her
that she had nothing to fear, especially from someone who came
to the house bearing food. Still, she opened the door only a little further, so that she might scrutinize the man more closely.

"May I help you?" she said tersely, fixing him with a stern,
skeptical gaze.

"Good afternoon, ma'am," he said affably. "Sorry to bother
you. I've just come to deliver this to Loretta Simmons. I hope
this is the right house."

"Who are you?" said Francesca, not at all concerned with
the forbidding tone of her voice.

"My name is Bill Pace," he answered. "Loretta works for me
at the firm."

"And *I* work for Loretta right here," countered Francesca,
narrowing her gaze at him. "Does that mean I work for you?"

The query brought a bemused look to the gentleman's face.
"Syllogistically speaking," he replied after a moment's contem-
plation, "I suppose one could make that deduction, but of course,
I would never be the one to do it."

"You talk just like a lawyer."

"Well, I guess that's because I *am* a lawyer." He paused and
gave her a smile. "So I take it that I have come to the right place."

"Oh, yes," nodded Francesca. "But we have the flu here, you
know. You probably shouldn't come in— *Dio mio, hold on!*"

A great gust of wind had just slammed into the house and
blew a swirling cloud of snow off the tops of the bushes. Despite
his sturdy build, the wind and snow hit Pace with such surpris-
ing force that the box nearly fell from his hands and he from the
top step. When he had regained his balance, the gentleman's face

lit up in a startled smile as he reached his arms around the box and clutched it more tightly. Despite the near mishap, or perhaps because of it, his eyes were full of merriment, as if he wanted to laugh out loud but didn't dare, for propriety's sake. Despite his years, he looked for an instant like a little boy who had just happily picked himself up off the ground and found himself unscathed after tumbling out of a tree right in front of his mother. Francesca herself had almost laughed out loud. Just the same, she maintained her stern demeanor.

"Well, I did get my flu shot, if that helps," Pace finally said once he had collected himself.

"Never mind about that," huffed Francesca as she opened the door wide. "Just come inside before you get yourself blown away."

"Thank you," he said, stepping quickly inside. "It is a bit breezy out here."

As he came in and shook off the cold, Francesca regarded him more closely. He was, she suspected, of the same age as herself, perhaps a year or two different in either direction. He had a pleasant face with bright blue eyes like her own. Time had left its mark on his features, but not so much that he looked old to her. The creases in his forehead and the crow's feet by his eyes were, to Francesca, simply signs of a well-lived life. All in all, he was a handsome and well-groomed gent, save for his thin silver hair, which the wind had made a tousled mess.

"You should try wearing a hat," she observed. "It's not spring out there, you know."

"I had one with me this morning," shrugged Pace, passing a hand over his hair to restore order to the top of his head, "but I couldn't seem to put my hands on it when I left the office."

Francesca clicked her tongue and shook here head disapprovingly.

"So, Mister . . . what was it again?"

"Pace," he answered. "And I'm sorry, your name is . . . "

"Francesca Campanile."

"My, that's a beautiful name," he said.

"Thank you. I've always liked it," replied Francesca, inwardly flattered by the remark, though she would never admitt it.

"I thought when I came to the door that you might be Loretta's mother," Pace went on.

"No, I'm just the nanny," said Francesca.

"How nice," he said. "Tell me, how is Loretta feeling?"

"Not so great," said Francesca. "She's upstairs sleeping right now. Do you want me to wake her and tell her you're here?"

"Oh, please, not at all," replied Pace. "I can only stay a minute, so just let her rest." He paused and gave the air a sniff. His eyes lighting up, he looked past her to the kitchen. "Hmm, it certainly smells like something good is cooking," he said.

"Oh, nothing special," said Francesca. "Just a little tomato sauce for dinner later."

Pace nodded. "Ah, I recognized that smell as soon as I walked in the door," he said in a wistful voice.

Francesca hesitated for just a moment, studying his face to see if he was sincere, before finally giving in to a smile. She nodded at the box. "Why don't you bring that into the kitchen and show me what you've brought," she suggested, "and maybe I'll let you have a little taste."

"Now that's an offer I couldn't possibly refuse," said Pace, his eyes lighting up again. He followed close behind as she led him into the kitchen.

"Sit there," said Francesca, gesturing to a chair. She took the box from his hands, set it on the table, and began to take out its contents. "A nice loaf of bread," she said, giving the bag a sniff; the aroma of freshly baked bread was another of Francesca's favorite things. "What else?"

"That's chicken-and-escarole soup in the plastic containers," said Pace. "And there's some veal cutlets and vegetables as well in the others. I bought it all at Angelo's on the Hill on the way over."

"I haven't been to that restaurant in years," said Francesca in a wistful voice of her own. "My husband and I used to take our kids there sometimes when they were little."

"One of my favorite places," said Pace.

Francesca picked up the containers of food and began to transfer them to the refrigerator. The loaf of bread, however, she set on the counter next to the stove. "You're a nice boss, to bring all this food," she said, reaching up into the cupboard for a dish. She placed it on the counter next to the bread and opened the drawer to find a bread knife.

"Well, there's nothing worse than being all alone when you're sick," said Pace with a shrug. "I just thought some soup would make Loretta feel a little better, and the meat and vegetables would save her the trouble of having to cook supper later for the kids. I hadn't realized, of course, that she was already in such good hands."

"Oh, don't worry," Francesca assured him. "None of that food will go to waste. I'll just heat it all up later and save the sauce for tomorrow. Speaking of which . . ."

Francesca took the knife and lopped off a sizable chunk from the heel of the bread. This she again cut in half to open it up, and set it on the plate. Then she removed the lid from the pot and dipped the ladle into the bubbling sauce. She drew forth a healthy sampling, making certain to collect some bits of meat in the process, and poured it all across the bread and onto the plate. Delighted at the look of eager anticipation in his eyes, she set the steaming treat in front of Pace.

"Now don't get that all over yourself before you go back to work," she warned him, pushing a paper napkin his way.

"I'll do my best," he replied. Wasting no time, Pace pulled the bread apart and lifted a piece to his mouth. Taking care not to let the rich, red sauce drip onto his coat, he sunk his teeth into the bread. He closed his eyes, and a look of pure pleasure came over his face, as if he had suddenly stepped out into the sunshine. "Ooh," he sighed happily. "This brings back memories."

Francesca herself could not have been more pleased. She watched him with interest, noting the easy, practiced manner in which he tore in two the other piece of bread and used it like a sponge to mop up the remaining sauce from the plate. He was, she could tell, a man who knew how to eat and savor the little things.

"Mmm, I love the pepperoni in the gravy," he said, swallowing the last of the moist, warm bread.

"I only cut up a couple of small pieces," chuckled Francesca. She eyed him more closely. "You know, for a Yankee, you have an educated taste in Italian food."

Pace looked up at her and smiled, a twinkle coming to his eye. "Oh, I'm not so much of a Yankee as you might think," he told her. "My mother was a pretty fair cook herself in her day, you know, my wife too. I always insisted on having my pasta with Sunday dinner."

"It's not Sunday dinner without it," opined Francesca, taking a seat across the table from him.

"I agree," nodded Pace with a smile, though Francesca detected a hint of sadness in his voice, one she well recognized. She stole a poorly concealed glance at the wedding ring on his finger.

"Does your wife like to cook?" she asked.

"Well, she did," he answered. "She passed away several years ago, so I'm afraid Sunday dinners haven't been as frequent as they once were."

"Oh, I'm sorry to hear that," said Francesca, her suspicions confirmed. "Children?"

"No, we never had any," he replied. "Now don't look sad. We had lots of nieces and nephews to spoil, so we always had fun. Of course, they're all grown up now and busy with families of their own. I still have a brother who I see now and then, but he moved out to Phoenix a few years ago, and my sister and her husband are down in Florida now, so I don't get to see them much either." He paused and shook his head. "People move around so much these days."

"Eh, it sounds like my family," said Francesca, throwing her hands up. "Everybody's living all over creation."

Pace nodded in agreement, and for a moment, the two sat in downcast silence, something that quite annoyed Francesca, for up till that moment, she had been thoroughly enjoying herself. This change in mood, she berated herself, was just what she de-served for letting her curiosity about his wife get the better of her. Now the two of them were feeling glum. She should have just kept her big mouth shut.

"What can you do?" she finally said with a sigh.

"Not much," said Pace, absentmindedly fidgeting with his wedding ring. He looked up at her and gave a sad smile. "Funny," he said, "but after all these years, I still wear this. I don't know why."

"Ayyy, probably for the same reason I still wear mine since my husband died," said Francesca, seeing her chance to set things right once more. "It just won't come off."

"I know what you mean," said Pace with a sympathetic sigh. "It's like a part of you, isn't it?"

"No, you don't understand," said Francesca, tugging at her own ring. "What I mean is, it just won't come off. I can't get the stupid thing over my knuckle anymore."

It was an old joke that Francesca had told a thousand times before, but it had the desired effect. Pace's eyes lit up once more, and he burst out laughing. Francesca could not help but join him. The two, though, quickly covered their mouths, so as not to awaken Loretta.

When he finally composed himself, Pace gave a contented

chuckle, then dabbed his mouth with the napkin, before pushing himself away from the table. "Well, on that note, I suppose I should be getting back to work," he announced, getting to his feet. He started to bring his plate to the sink, but Francesca snatched it from his hand.

"I'll take care of that," she told him, putting it aside. "Come on, I'll walk you to the door."

As the two walked to the front hall, the wind outside roared again, rattling the windows in the living room. Before opening the door, Pace turned to her.

"Well, thank you, Mrs.—"

"Francesca," she said before he could finish.

"Well, thank you, Francesca," he corrected himself. "That was as nice a lunch break as I've had in quite a while. Perhaps we could—"

"Fix that tie, will you?" Francesca interrupted him once again.

"I'm sorry?"

Francesca clicked her tongue and stepped closer to him. Reaching up, she quickly tightened his tie for him. "What kind of operation are you running that you'd go back to work looking all *sciacquat'* like that?" With a huff, she stepped back to assess her work. "Well, at least you didn't get any sauce on it," she observed.

"So, there's hope for me yet," said Pace with a smile as he buttoned up his coat. "Thank you, Francesca."

"Don't mention it," she replied, giving him only a hint of a smile in return. "Now go back to your office. I've got work of my own to do here, you know."

Pace nodded to show that he understood. "Well, it was a pleasure meeting you, Francesca," he told her before stepping out the door. "Perhaps we'll see each other again sometime."

"I'll talk to my boss," said Francesca.

With that, she nodded good-bye and watched him descend the front steps to the walkway. She closed the door against the blustery wind and went to the window to make certain that he didn't slip and fall on his way to the car. When Pace finally drove away, Francesca gazed off into the distance for a time before looking down at the ring on her finger. She gave a little laugh and looked up toward the heavens.

"Don't worry, Leo," she said. "The ring's still on good and tight."

Then she went back to the kitchen to finish what she'd started.

CHAPTER 33

Three forty-five that same afternoon found Francesca stationed at her usual post at the living room window, keeping watch for Penny and Will. By this time, the wind outside was howling for all it was worth. Bursts of sand and snow leaped into the air like ocean spray, while scraps of crumpled paper and other debris tumbled along the street. Next door, a pair of empty trash barrels lay on their sides, scratching and bumping against a pile of rock-hard snow at the end of the driveway. Another great gust of wind roared through, and the cover to one of the barrels rolled off across the street like a wayward hubcap. The cold, bleak scene and the roar of the wind sent a chill racing up Francesca's spine. From what she could see, there was no letup to winter in sight.

"Where's all this global warming they're always yapping about?" Francesca muttered.

Pulling the collar of her sweater tighter about her neck, she turned from the window and looked back to the kitchen, where the improvised peach crumb cake she had just baked in a cast-iron frying pan was cooling atop the stove. A pan of soup warmed on the burner beside it. The scent of the cake drifted pleasantly throughout the house, but like any baker, having been immersed in the warm, sweet aroma for some time now, Francesca noticed it little. Besides, at the moment, she was more preoccupied with watching to see that the children made it safely home.

Francesca stayed by the window, anxiously watching, until Penny and Will finally came into sight. Leaning into the teeth of the wild wind, they trod gamely up the street, every step a struggle. It seemed to Francesca that all of nature was pushing against them, trying all it could to thwart their progress toward home. As the two drew closer, Will suddenly slipped on a patch of ice and fell to his knees. The old woman was ready to throw on her coat and run out to help, but Penny quickly reached down and helped her brother back up. When at last they made it to the front walk, Francesca unlocked the door and hurried back to the kitchen.

"Oh, my God!" cried Penny when she and her brother clamored in through the door. "It is *so* windy!"

"I thought I was going to get blown back into the bus when I got off!" laughed Will.

As usual, the two dropped their backpacks on the spot and began to peel off their coats and hats.

"*Shush!*" called Francesca. "Keep it quiet. Your mother is upstairs, sleeping."

"Oops, I forgot," grimaced Penny, tossing her hat and gloves on the chair. She and her brother paused and looked up the stairs.

"Is she still really sick?" whispered Will.

"She'll be fine before you know it," Francesca answered. "Now take off your boots and come into the kitchen to get warm."

The smell of the cake was more than enough to entice the siblings into the kitchen. The two rushed in, each of them elbowing the other to get there first. Francesca couldn't help but smile when she saw their rosy red cheeks and wide, expectant eyes. Upon entering the kitchen, Penny still held back just a bit, but her brother came right up to Francesca to get a look at what she had prepared for them.

"What did you make this time?" he asked eagerly, leaning over to take a peek at the cake.

"Yeah, it really smells good," added Penny, drawing a little closer.

"Oh, this?" replied Francesca nonchalantly. "It's just a little something I decided to bake this afternoon to pass the time."

Without another word, Francesca took a spatula and carefully slid it around the perimeter of the cake to loosen it from the pan. Then she covered the pan with a plate and casually flipped the whole thing over, much to the chagrin of the two children, who watched in horror, certain that the precious treat would end up on the floor. Francesca, however, was a practiced hand at this maneuver. She lifted the pan and set the plate on the counter. Perhaps two inches thick, the simple cake had retained its perfect circular shape. Better still, the peaches and brown sugar that had been on the bottom of the pan had caramelized into a nice golden brown glaze across the cake's new top. Though not quite up to her usual baking standards, the sight of it made even her own mouth water.

"Do we get to have a taste?" said Will hopefully.

"That depends," answered Francesca, shooting them glance.

"Oh, no," groaned Penny. "What do we have to do this time?"

"Your bedrooms," Francesca told her. "They're a disgrace. How do you expect your mother to keep this house nice and clean if you two won't even pick up after yourselves in your own bedrooms?"

"But—" Penny began to protest.

"Fifteen minutes," said Francesca, cutting her short. "That's all you have to do today. That's not asking much, but at least you'll make a little bit of a dent."

"Right now?" said Will glumly.

"No," said Francesca, turning her attention to the soup

warming up in the pan. "First you sit at the table and have some soup to warm you up. You both must be frozen like ice cubes."

Francesca filled two mugs, set them on the table, and gave each of the children a spoon.

"Don't you want to have some?" said Will, before gulping down a mouthful.

"No, that's just for you two and your mom," Francesca answered. "So eat up."

"But it's really good," said Penny after taking a taste. "Did you make it?"

"Nope," Francesca shook her head. "That came from a restaurant, but I'll make you a nice soup of my own someday." She sat down at the table with them. "So, tell me about your day at school."

"Numbskull lost his math book," said Penny first.

"And *she's* in love with Jason Maloney," countered her brother.

"Shut your mouth! You don't even know what you're talking about."

"Do so—"

"Ayyy!" exclaimed Francesca, throwing up her hands to silence them. "What do you think this is? Congress? All I wanted was to know how school went, not to start a debate."

"She started it," muttered Will.

"You're right, she did," agreed Francesca, quieting both of them with her glare. "But what's this about your losing your math book?"

"I didn't lose it," protested the boy. "I just can't find it."

"What's the difference?" his sister chimed in.

"Quiet, you," warned Francesca. "This is a serious matter. Are you getting straight As, by the way?"

"Not exactly," admitted Penny.

"In that case, forget about the boys and pay attention to your schoolwork," Francesca told her with a steely gaze that made the young girl sink lower on the chair. Then, turning back to Will, "Now, last I remember, it sounded like you weren't doing so well in math. Am I right?"

"Yeah," he sighed. "And I've got a test tomorrow."

"And how are you going to study for it without your book?"

The boy could only shrug in response.

"You've looked everywhere?"

He gave a discouraged nod in reply.

"Okay," said Francesca, letting out a long sigh of her own and a click of her tongue. "Well, we'll just have to see what we can do. Lucky for you, I'm pretty good with arithmetic, so later on, before I go home, we'll sit at the table, and you can show me what kind of work you've been doing in class. I bet we can get you up to speed for your test. Before that, though, you should go up to your bedroom and, while you're straightening up, see if maybe you didn't lose your book somewhere in that mess. If it's not there, or someplace else in the house, then you'll just have to say a prayer to Saint Anthony."

"To who?" the two asked in unison.

"Saint Anthony," said Francesca, surprised at the curious looks on their faces. "Don't you know who Saint Anthony is?"

"Never heard of him," shrugged Penny.

"Oh, Saint Anthony's a good saint," Francesca explained. "They're all good, of course, but he's the one to pray to when you lose something. Works for me every time. I remember once when I lost a beautiful brooch that I liked to wear on my coat. I searched the house for days, but I couldn't find it anywhere, so at last I gave up and just said a prayer to Saint Anthony. The very next morning, just as I was getting ready to go out of the house, I happened to reach into my coat pocket and there it was. Somehow or other, it must have fallen off the outside of the coat and straight into the pocket the last time I hung it up. Now some people would say it was just a coincidence that I found it that way, but I know it was Saint Anthony. The thing you have to remember, of course, is that if he helps you to find something, like your book, then you have to pay him back by putting some money in the poor box the next time you go to mass."

"Mass?" said Will. "You mean like going to church?"

"Yes, of course," she answered.

"But we don't go to church," said Penny.

This admission really should have come as no surprise to Francesca. She knew from the beginning that their parents had never married, so it stood to reason that they probably were not churchgoers. Just the same, as she looked from one child to the other, the two of them gazing back with innocent eyes that pierced right through her, she felt her heart ache. Francesca had known this little family for only a very short time, and there was much, she understood, that was absent from the lives of these children, but somehow, this revelation truly saddened her.

"Oh, I see," Francesca said thoughtfully after a moment's contemplation. Then, forcing a smile, "Well, I still think it's a good idea for you to pray to him anyway. It can't hurt, right? Now finish up that soup and go get started on your rooms. Then after dinner, you can both have a piece of cake."

Later, when the two children headed upstairs to their rooms, Francesca took the mugs they had left on the table and rinsed them in the sink. Then she took out a pan to use later to warm up the meat and vegetables Mister Pace had brought to the house earlier in the day. Dinner, thanks to him, would be easy, but as Francesca thought about Loretta and her children, she could not help but feel that there was even more work to be done here than she had realized.

CHAPTER 34

The next day, Francesca was sitting at the kitchen table, matching up socks from a basket of colored clothes she had just washed and dried, when Loretta came downstairs. It was midafternoon, well after lunchtime. Loretta had been asleep when she had first come to the house, so Francesca had gone about her business quietly. She had hoped to have all the clothes folded and ready to be put away before Loretta awoke. Now, though, the young woman stood in the doorway, shaking her head in mild annoyance at Francesca.

"Don't say it," Francesca told her before she could open her mouth. "I saw the clothes starting to pile up, and with you in bed sick, no one else was going to wash them, so I just decided to do a quick load myself, to pass the time before the children came home."

"But Mrs . . . I mean, Francesca," began Loretta. "It's really too much of me too ask you—"

"You didn't ask," Francesca cut in. "I just did it, because it needed to be done. Now if you're feeling guilty about it, just sit down and help me fold the rest of this."

Loretta gave an exasperated sigh and took a seat at the table. Reaching into the basket, she pulled out one of Will's shirts, laid it across her lap, and began to fold it.

"You're looking a little better," observed Francesca as she continued matching up the socks. "Not so green in the gills."

It was true. Though still a bit drawn, Loretta's face had regained some of its color and the dark circles beneath her eyes were retreating. The assertive way in which she reached into the basket and tugged out another shirt when she was done folding the first was further evidence that she had turned the corner and was starting to regain a bit of her energy.

"I'm still a little woozy," nodded Loretta, "but my fever's down, so I think I'm going to survive. Two days ago, I wasn't so sure."

"Ayyy, that's the way it always is when you first get sick like that," chuckled Francesca. "You think it's the end of the world. But these things pass."

Loretta looked down at herself and considered the baggy gray sweatshirt and the equally baggy pajama bottoms she had been wearing for at least the past twenty-four hours. "I suppose I should get myself cleaned up and put on some decent clothes before the kids come home," she mused.

"No, no. Don't worry about that," Francesca told her. "Just stay nice and comfortable if you feel like it. If you get yourself all dressed up, you'll be tempted to do too much too soon, and then you'll just end up making yourself feel worse again. You know, just because you're starting to feel better doesn't mean that you're not still sick."

"I suppose you're right," said Loretta. She sat up straighter and rolled her head gently about. "I am still a little achy, but just the same, I feel like I should be getting back to work."

"That's probably what someone else who was sick at your office thought," Francesca pointed out. "Whoever it was came back to work too soon and spread it around. That's why you're sick now. Trust me, you're not doing anyone any favors by hurrying back to the office before you're better. Take an extra day to be sure, and don't worry about it. I'm sure your boss Mister Pace would tell you the same thing."

Loretta gave her a curious look. "How did you know his name was Mister Pace?" she asked.

"He came here yesterday while you were sleeping," Francesca explained, to Loretta's obvious surprise. "He brought some nice soup and bread, and some meat and vegetables too. I had been planning to use the sauce I was making for dinner, but I gave the kids the food he brought instead. I didn't want it to go bad. Anyway, it was very nice of him, I thought."

"Yes, it was," agreed Loretta. "I'll have to call him later to say thank-you. But it's so strange. I don't remember hearing anyone at all come to the house yesterday besides you. I must have been out like a light when he came in. You know, I ate that soup last night after you left, but I just assumed that you had made it. How long did he stay?"

"Oh, just a few minutes," said Francesca. "He didn't want to disturb you, so he went on his way pretty quickly."

"I suppose he must have," said Loretta thoughtfully. "Funny how fast time goes by and how oblivious you are to everything when you're asleep."

"That's what sleep is for," replied Francesca. "It makes you forget about everything so that your mind and body can rest. It's so important, but everybody tries to ignore it. It's like my daughters, who are always complaining that they feel so tired and blue. I try to tell them that they just need to turn the television off, stop watching those crazy shows with all these gruesome murders every night. Or if it's not murders, it's people going into the hospital because they're dying from some ghastly illness or because they got run over by a bus. How's a person supposed to have a good night's rest after watching all those horrible stories? And then they wonder why they wake up in the morning feeling like a wet rag. Forget the TV, and try going to bed an hour earlier, I tell them. They'd feel ten years younger in a week. But young people don't want to listen."

Loretta smiled.

"I remember now that you told me once that you had two daughters," she said. "Do they live in Rhode Island too?"

"Florida and Oregon," Francesca replied ruefully.

"I see," said Loretta. "Do you miss them, being so far away like that?"

"Only every minute of the day," said Francesca. "That's how we old mothers are, you know."

"I'm not sure if all of you are that way," said Loretta, "at least not in my case."

"No? Tell me, where does your mother live?"

"Upstate New York," Loretta answered.

"That's still pretty far apart for a mother and daughter to be," said Francesca. "Believe me, she misses you."

"Well, I don't know about that . . ." said Loretta, her voice suddenly trailing away. She quickly turned her attention back to the basket and pulled out another shirt to fold.

Francesca eyed Loretta for a moment. She had been around long enough to know when someone was holding inside a story that needed telling. There was much she would like to know about the younger woman and her family, but till now, she had been reluctant to ask; it just didn't seem her place to do so. Now, though, as she watched Loretta dutifully folding the clothes, Francesca could not help feeling that an opportunity was presenting itself to her, one which might not come again any time soon. The question that now weighed on her mind was how best to take advantage of it. Pushing herself away from the table, she stood and looked down kindly at Loretta.

"What do you say to my putting some water in the kettle," she offered, "and when we're done with the clothes, maybe you and I can have a little cup of tea? It will make you feel better—

and then maybe I can let you try one of the pizzelle I made this morning."

"I would love some tea," admitted Loretta, "but to be quite honest, I don't know if I have any on hand."

"Oh, you do," Francesca assured her. "I found a box yesterday when I was a rummaging around through your cupboards while you were asleep. Sorry about that—I really should have asked first—but I didn't want to bother you."

"Oh, please," huffed Loretta with a dismissive wave. "Last night I had a piece of that cake you made. It was unbelievable."

"Then tea sounds good?"

Loretta hesitated for a moment, looking as though she were mulling over something about which she couldn't quite make up her mind. At last, though, she simply smiled at Francesca and nodded. "Yes, tea sounds very nice," she said. "But tell me, what in the world are pizzelle?"

"You'll see," laughed Francesca, "you'll see."

The afternoon sun was streaming through the front window, casting a slanted parallelogram of light across the floor, when Loretta came into the living room. She had insisted that, despite her infirmity, she at least be allowed to carry in the tray on holding the pot of tea, cups, and saucers. She set the tray atop the coffee table, while Francesca brought in the plate of pizzelle. The two women sat on the couch, and Loretta filled their cups with tea.

"This is a pizzella," said Francesca, handing Loretta one of the round, waferlike cookies. "You see, it's sort of like a little pizza. You make them like waffles, except these are thinner."

Loretta took the pizzella, noting with pleasure its golden brown color and delicate snowflake design. "It's almost too pretty to eat," she said. "And it smells wonderful. What's in it?"

"That's the anise," Francesca told her, taking one of the pizzelle for herself. "I've always loved that smell too."

As they nibbled on the pizzelle and sipped their tea, the women began to chat amiably about the incessant cold weather they had been experiencing that winter. Soon they were taking turns complaining about the icy roads, the appalling cost of keeping the house warm, and, of course, of the perils of the flu season. It wasn't long, though, before the conversation brought them back around to the subject of their families.

"You were telling me about your daughters before," said Loretta. "How did they end up so far away?"

"Work," lamented Francesca. "You know how it is. Everybody thinks you have to go where there's more money so you can have a better life. Nobody ever stops to think that part of having a better life is being close to your family. My daughters's husbands both had good jobs right here in Rhode Island, but then one of them got a big promotion, and the other decided to go into business out of state, and before you knew it, they were moving all over the country. They had to go where the best opportunities were while they had the chance. At least, that's what they've always told me. But who knows, maybe they were just trying to see how far away from me they could get. I can be a real pain sometimes."

"I'm sure that's not it at all," laughed Loretta.

"Eh, you'd be surprised," she said.

"Well, from what you've told me, at least it seems like your children are all happily married," said Loretta.

"Ayyy, not all," sighed Francesca. "My daughters are doing fine. But my son hasn't settled down yet. That one's still trying to sort out his life. Don't get me wrong, he's a good boy. Smart. Hardworking."

"What's the problem?" asked Loretta.

Francesca hesitated for a moment. "Well, I'll tell you," she said at last. "He was all set to get married a few years ago. To a nice girl, or so, least at, I thought. Everybody seemed happy. Then three weeks before the wedding, right out of the blue, the whole thing got called off."

"What happened?"

"You know, my son would never say a word about it, no matter how hard I tried to pry it out of him. But then two months later, I read in the paper that his fiancée had married some other guy. Six months after *that*, I see the birth announcement for their first child." Francesca paused for effect, then gave a shrug. "So, you do the math."

"Oops," said Loretta with a pained expression.

"Oops is right," Francesca went on. "Anyway, to this day, he still won't talk about it. It's sad." Taking a deep breath, she let it out and shook her head. "But, life goes on. He'll find his way. So tell me about you. What's your story? How did all . . . all this happen?"

"You mean, how did a nice girl like me end up raising two children all by herself?"

Francesca shrugged and nodded.

"Well, it's a long story," said Loretta.

"There's plenty of tea left," noted the older woman.

Loretta set her cup on its saucer and looked blankly toward the window. "Where would I even begin?" she wondered aloud.

"Why don't you tell me about your mother?" Francesca suggested.

"Ah, my mother," Loretta began with an ironic smile. "Well, I guess things started to fall apart for Mom and me after my father died. I was a teenager, and I was really close to him. Mom loved him too. I knew that. But two years later, when I was in high school, she got remarried, and I couldn't stand her husband."

"What was wrong with him? Was he abusive?"

"No, of course not," said Loretta with a laugh. "He was as sweet as could be."

"Then what was the problem?"

"Nothing," admitted Loretta with a sad shake of her head. "Nothing at all, really. He just wasn't my father, you see, and I guess I couldn't deal with my mother just moving on with her life the way she did."

"Life has a way of dragging you forward, even when you want to stay put," said Francesca.

"I guess," sighed Loretta. "Anyway, I went through this strange rebellious phase and pretty much made life miserable for everybody at home. I couldn't seem to get along with anybody. It was always one argument after the other, if not with my mother, then with my brothers or my stepfather. Then I stopped going to church, and that drove my mother nuts, because she's an old-fashioned-Catholic—which I guess is why I did it. I at least managed to keep my grades up in school, so it was probably a big relief for them all when I finally went off to college. And that's where I met David."

"Penny and Will's father?"

"That's right," said Loretta. "David was two years ahead of me when we met. He was young and good-looking, and full of philosophy and all these avant-garde theories about society and relationships and the uselessness of organized religion. I thought he was brilliant. Marriage, of course, was an anachronism to David, which, looking back, was probably a result of his coming from a broken home. But he had me convinced that it was enough for two people to just love one another, without all those useless formalities that society was always trying to impose on people. So, when he graduated, I quit school to go with him, thinking I could always go back someday to finish."

Here, Loretta paused to shake her head. She looked at Francesca and rolled her eyes. "Yeah," she said with a wry grin, "I was a complete sucker."

"It happens," said Francesca sympathetically.

"Well, needless to say, my mother was apoplectic," Loretta continued, "but I didn't care. So we ended up here in Providence because David found a teaching job through one of his friends. We found a nice little apartment on the East Side. I was happy. He seemed happy. Everything was great, and about a year later, we decided to start a family. And that's when Penny came along. A little over a year after that, I became pregnant again, which I'll admit was something of a surprise. I was happy, though, when I found out, but David wasn't. I didn't want to admit it to myself, but I knew that he had been growing distant for a long while, ever since Penny had first been born. That very night when I had planned to tell him I was going to have another baby, David came home from school and told me that he needed to get away. He felt like he was suffocating from work and being a father, he said, and he just needed some time on his own to find himself again. Like *I* never felt the same thing sometimes."

"What happened when you told him about the baby?" asked Francesca.

Loretta did not answer right away. Instead, she bowed her head and stared down into her teacup for a time, before looking back up at Francesca. "He didn't want me to keep it," she said in a voice barely above a whisper, her eyes starting to well up. She glanced at a picture frame on the wall that contained a collage of photographs of Will and Penny together from the time they were just toddlers. "Can you imagine it?" the young mother said, her voice cracking with emotion.

"No, I can't," confessed Francesca, her own eyes growing misty. She reached for a napkin and dabbed the corner of her eyes. "So, what happened next?'

"I was furious," said Loretta, wiping her eyes with the sleeve of her shirt. "I told him to go away and do whatever it was he had to do, and that I would take care of my children by myself.

It probably wasn't the smartest thing to do, but it at least shamed him into staying for a while. It wasn't long after, though, that he finally left—to go find himself."

"And did he?" asked Francesca.

"Oh, yeah," said Loretta. "He found himself all right. He found himself with another woman. She must have helped David forget all about marriage being an anachronism, because a year later, they got married and moved to Europe somewhere."

"Some men," huffed Francesca, shaking her head angrily. "I just don't know what planet they come from that they can do such things. So does he at least stay in touch with the children?"

"What for?" shrugged Loretta. "Penny was a baby when he left, and Will wasn't even born. Now and then, David used to send me money to help me take care of them, but I always threw it away. I guess he got the message to not bother anymore when he saw that the checks weren't clearing—and so I haven't heard a word from him since. It's almost like I never met him at all. If it weren't for Penny and Will, I'd wish that were true."

Francesca nodded, to show that she understood. She sat and listened quietly as Loretta went on to talk about her struggles over the years, trying to raise the two small children on her own. She did not want to interrupt, for the words were now pouring out of the woman, like water finally released from a dam that had for too long been on the verge of breaking. As she listened, Francesca was struck by the unmistakable tone of defiance and steely determination in the young mother's voice. What impressed her most, though, was her sense of responsibility, her refusal to blame anyone else for the circumstances in which she had found herself, her willingness to go it all alone if she had to. Her pride.

When Loretta finally finished, her eyes red-rimmed, she sank back on the couch, seemingly spent from the effort. Francesca could not help but beam a smile of admiration at her.

"You know, I didn't know it when I first came here," she told her, "but you're one tough broad."

Loretta forced a smile. "Oh, I don't know about that," she sniffled. "Most days I feel like I'm barely keeping things together. I worry about everything, especially about the kids. Penny is growing up so fast and needs a father in her life who will be there for her. And poor Will, he just needs someone to toss a ball to him now and then. They've both missed out on so much because of me."

"Listen, honey," said Francesca gently. "Before you go beating yourself up for no good reason, I think you should know that you've done a great job. You have two wonderful kids. They didn't turn out that way by accident."

"Then why do I feel so guilty about everything?"

"Why do you think?" laughed Francesca. "It's because deep inside, you're an old Catholic too. If you want to feel better, try going to confession. Works all the time for me."

"Oh, God, I haven't been to church in a thousand years," groaned Loretta. "The walls would fall down around me the second I stepped inside. I never even had the kids baptized."

"Well, at least you wouldn't be at a loss for words in the confessional," noted Francesca.

"No, I suppose not," sighed Loretta. She gazed pensively out the window for a moment. "But I don't know how I could ever go back," she said, "even if I wanted to. It's too late for me."

"Nonsense. It's never too late for anyone," Francesca told her, "not if it's something you really want."

"I don't know," said Loretta with another weary sigh. "Right about now, all I really want is to go to sleep for a couple of years and just let everything work itself out on its own."

"A couple of years might be hard to arrange," laughed Francesca. "But I think a couple more good days of rest might work just as well. You'll see, things will work themselves out. They always do, and never the way you expected, almost like magic."

With that, Francesca patted Loretta on the hand and began to collect the teacups and saucers. She squeezed them onto the tray along with the plate of pizzelle. and stood.

"Well, that's enough for today," she said. "Now you should go back upstairs and get some rest, while I get dinner started. The kids should be home any minute. If you're up to it, maybe tomorrow we'll chat again, and we can both drag a few more skeletons out of our family closets."

"There's plenty left in mine," chuckled Loretta before adding, "But you know, I'd really like to help you with dinner, if I could. I mean, I am feeling a little better. It wouldn't be too much."

"Well, there's really not much to do," replied Francesca. "The sauce is already made. All that's left to do is boil some water for the macaroni."

"Hmm, boil some water," said Loretta, thoughtfully scratching her chin as though she were pondering some great mystery. "Now I know it's a stretch, but I think that's something I might be able to handle . . . that is, if you show me how."

Francesca caught the mischievous sparkle in the young woman's eyes. "Oh, yes," she nodded, a playful gleam coming to her own eyes, "boiling water's a perfect place to begin if you want to learn how to cook. Come on, I'll show you how it's done."

"Great," smiled Loretta. "And maybe while we're at it, you can tell me again how to make that sauce."

"Of course. Grab a pencil and paper. It's the easiest recipe in the world."

Loretta was just pulling herself off the couch to follow Francesca's lead when suddenly the front door burst open, and Penny and Will, laughing the whole way, came tumbling in. The two must have raced home from the bus stop, for they were all out of breath as they picked themselves up from the floor.

"Hey!" shouted Loretta. "How many times have I told you guys not to come roughhousing through the door like that!"

"It worked, Mrs. C! It worked!" cried Will, beaming with excitement. "I didn't think it would when I went to bed last night, but I tried it anyway!"

"What on earth are you talking about?" said Loretta, turning dumbfounded eyes to Francesca, who looked equally baffled.

"Show them, dopie," said Penny, giving her brother an elbow in the side.

His eyeglasses sliding at an odd angle down his nose, Will pulled open the top of his backpack and reached in. "The bus driver said he found it under a seat," he gushed as he rummaged through the sack.

"Found what?" asked his mother, still perplexed by all the commotion.

"Look!" the young boy cried triumphantly, holding up his lost math book for all to see.

Francesca looked on, and smiled with deep satisfaction. Apparently, Saint Anthony had come through once again.

CHAPTER 35

Having spent the better part of the week in bed sleeping, Loretta awoke on Friday morning as reasonably refreshed as one might expect after enduring a bout with the flu. Unlike most mornings, when the obnoxious buzzing of the alarm clock was enough to plunge her into despair—and back under the blankets—on this day, she casually reached over and turned it off. Contrary to Francesca's prediction, the additional hours of rest from taking an extra day off had not left Loretta feeling ten years younger. Happily, though, she realized that at least she no longer felt ten years older.

Tugging her legs out from beneath the covers, Loretta set her feet on the floor and gazed out the window. Away to the east, the rising winter sun was still only a crescent of embers on the horizon. The rest of the outdoors was bathed in a muted glow, which gave the trees and the houses a soft, velvety quality. As she sat there, considering the scene, Loretta realized that there was a simple beauty to the dawn, one that she had somehow forgotten in her frenetic life. Despite the chill in the house and the temptation to crawl back into the warm confines of the bed, Loretta was glad to be awake to see it. With a yawn and a stretch, she got to her feet and went to wake up the kids for school. They, she reflected with a sigh, would not be so taken with the tranquil virtues of that early hour.

"Come on, guys, up and at 'em!" she called, setting the merry-go-round once more in motion.

When she arrived at work that morning, Loretta stopped by Mister Pace's office before going to her desk. The door was ajar, but as expected, the senior partner was not yet in. Stealing inside, she left the thank-you note she had written atop his desk, leaning against the telephone where he was sure to see it. Then she hurried off to get her workday started.

"What are *you* doing here?" asked a surprised Shirley a little while afterwards, when she happened by Loretta's desk. "It's Friday. I thought for sure you were going to call it a week and just stay home till Monday. Believe me, that's what I would have done."

"The thought did cross my mind," admitted Loretta.

Shirley shook her head disapprovingly. "You know, chances like that don't come around very often," she said. "Well, I hope you're at least feeling all better."

"Pretty much," said Loretta. "I suppose I could have milked it for one more day, but I thought it would be good to come in and get caught up a little bit today so that I'm not so far behind on Monday." Then, taking on a pious air, she playfully added, "But what can I say? I guess I'm just a workaholic."

"Oh, right," chuckled her friend. "My guess, is you're planning to meet someone for lunch."

"I only wish," sighed Loretta.

"Too bad you didn't come in yesterday," said Shirley. "You're old friend Ned Hadley was here."

"Really," replied Loretta cooly. "He didn't by chance trip and fall down a flight of stairs or anything like that?"

"Sorry," laughed Shirley. "He managed to stay on his feet for the whole day, as far as I could see." Then, with an impish gaze, she said, "I did hear that he was asking for you."

"Oh, goodie," replied Loretta, her already-sour expression turning into one of complete disdain.

"So, I take it by that look on your face that you're not going to give him another chance?"

"Oh, please," huffed Loretta. "I went out with him once, and then I got sick as a dog for a week. I'm taking that as a sign to stay away."

"Smart girl."

"As a matter of fact," Loretta went on, "I think I'm planning on staying away from men in general for a while."

"Ha!" scoffed Shirley. "Good luck making *that* last."

"Well, it's at least worth a try," said Loretta, herself skeptical of the odds. "At least for this weekend."

"Don't even worry about this weekend, honey," said Shirley. "All every guy in America is thinking about this week is the stupid football game on Sunday."

"That's right," laughed Loretta. "I forgot all about the Super Bowl. Not that I care anyway. I never even watch it."

"Ugh," groaned Shirley. "It's always such a bore. At least it means the football season is finally all over, thank God. Maybe now the guys will want to discuss something different at the water cooler."

"Yeah," snickered Loretta. "They'll all want to talk about *next* season."

The two kibitzed for a while longer, cheerfully casting aspersions on the male of the species and discussing the latest company gossip. It wasn't long, though, before Shirley went on her way, leaving Loretta to her work.

Later that morning, as it was nearing lunchtime, a golf ball came slowly rolling past Loretta's desk. It bumped up against the wall a few feet past her, bounced back an inch or two, and came to rest. Leaning over to the side, Loretta peeked out of her cubicle. As expected, she saw Mister Pace ambling down the hall in her direction. The old gent seemed less intent on retrieving the ball than he did on inspecting the grip of the putter he was carrying. He turned the club over in his hand, examining it with a look of perturbation.

"Thought I had that putt read perfectly," he muttered. Then, looking up with a half smile at Loretta, he added, "It must be the putter that's the problem, not the man doing the putting, right?"

"Oh, no question about it, Mister Pace," Loretta agreed. "I'm sure they don't make those clubs like they used to."

"Maybe we could file a lawsuit," he mused, giving her a conspiratorial wink. "You can't imagine the pain and anguish I've suffered on a golf course. I could tell you some stories that would have the jury in tears."

"Just give me the word, and I'll start writing up the papers," she offered.

"Well, not just yet," he said, clearing his throat. "For the time being, I just stopped by to thank you for your nice note."

"Thank *you* for all the nice food," replied Loretta. "That was really sweet of you. You shouldn't have gone to the trouble."

"Oh, it was no trouble at all," he said. "Gave me a good excuse to get out of the office. Besides, I enjoyed meeting your Mrs. Campanile. She seemed very nice—and she makes an excellent spaghetti sauce, you know."

"Yes, she does," said Loretta, eyeing him with curiosity. "But how did you know that?"

"Oh, while I was there, she let me come into the kitchen and have a little taste test with some Italian bread I had brought," he explained.

"Did she really?" said Loretta, nodding thoughtfully. "Now that's very interesting."

"Of course, she seemed quite busy," Pace hastily added, "and I had to get back to the office, so I didn't stay long. I don't want you to get the wrong idea, that she was shirking her duties or anything like that. But I rather enjoyed talking to her . . . that is . . . what I mean to say is that she seemed very . . ." The senior partner's face suddenly flushed, and he gave a little cough. Stooping down, he snatched up the wayward golf ball and tossed the putter atop his shoulder.

"At any rate," he said, turning quickly to go, "I suppose I should get back to work before I get myself in trouble. Nice to see you healthy again. Have a good weekend, Loretta."

"You too, Mister Pace," she called after him.

Drumming her fingers on her chin, something Loretta did when she was deep in thought, she watched him saunter back down the hall. A smile came to her face, for a silly, impossible notion had just crossed her mind, one that hadn't the least chance of ever coming to fruition. Nonetheless, the thought of it brought a warm glow to her heart, which would carry her through the rest of the day.

"Yes," Loretta chuckled to herself as she turned her attention back to her work, "that was very interesting indeed."

Francesca and the kids were in the kitchen, sitting around the table, when Loretta returned home that evening. The three had been talking and laughing so loudly that none of them heard her come through the door. She stepped quickly inside and stuck her head into the kitchen.

"Hey, what is this? Nobody comes to the door anymore when I come home?" she said, feigning a pout.

"Hi, Mom!" called Will. "What's for supper?"

"Ayyy, never mind about supper," Francesca chided him. "The two of you, go give your mother a hug when she gets home from work."

With exaggerated enthusiasm, the two hurried over to embrace their mother. Penny rested her head on Loretta's shoulder and looked up at her with angelic eyes. "It's so nice to have you home, Mother dear," she said sweetly. Then, "So, what's for supper?"

"Pizza, you brats," said Loretta, playfully pinching their ears. "How does that sound?"

"Ouch," Penny winced. "Pizza works for me."

"Me too," added Will, rubbing his ear as he squirmed free. "I'm going to play some PS2 while we wait."

"And I'll be upstairs," said Penny, pushing past her brother. And off the two went.

"You know, I would have been happy to cook supper tonight," said Francesca when the children were out of earshot. "You still look tired."

"No, you've already done way too much this week," said Loretta, sitting down at the table. "I'm really grateful, by the way."

Francesca shrugged and gave her a dismissive wave.

"Well, anyway," Loretta went on, "it's Friday night, so who wants to cook?" She paused to assess the older woman's reaction. "That doesn't make me a bad mother, does it?"

"No, not at all," laughed Francesca. "Like you said, it's Friday. Everybody deserves a break. The most important thing, no matter who cooks supper, is that you all sit down together every night to eat it. That's what counts. Believe me, if you do nothing else but that when you're raising kids, you've got half the battle won."

Loretta nodded respectfully. Francesca, she was discovering, was a font of simple wisdom on a variety of subjects. She admired that a great deal about her. Just the same, despite her growing esteem for the older woman, Loretta could not suppress an impish impulse.

"I happened to see Mister Pace today," she said, the hint of a mischievous smile coming to her face.

"Oh, that's nice," said Francesca, betraying no evidence of emotion at the pronouncement.

"Yes," Loretta continued. "He said he enjoyed meeting you— and getting to taste the sauce you were making that day."

Francesca narrowed her gaze at the younger woman. "So?" she said with a touch of annoyance in her voice.

"Oh, nothing," said Loretta innocently. "I just thought it was funny that the first thing you did when you two met was to give him something to eat, that's all."

Francesca, no doubt, caught the knowing gleam in the young woman's eye, for her face reddened ever so slightly. "It just goes to show that you have to be careful who you feed," she said, taking the offensive. With that, Francesca got to her feet and pushed her chair back in place. "Well, I think it's time for me to be going home now."

Ever so pleased with herself for having once gotten the better of her venerable babysitter, Loretta walked Francesca to the door.

"Come say good night to Mrs. Campanile, Will," she said.

"Good night, Mrs. C.," said Will as they passed, his eyes reverting immediately to the television.

"Good night, Will. Be a good boy," Francesca told him.

"Penny!" Loretta called up the stairs. "Say good-bey to Mrs. Campanile."

No answer came.

"Penny!" she called again with the same result. "What is she doing up there?"

"What do you think?" said Will. "She's on the computer."

Loretta shook her head. "I don't know what to do sometimes," she said to Francesca. "I worry all the time about what she's doing up there on that computer, what she's looking at on the Internet, whom she's talking to."

"Why don't you just move the computer down here, where you can keep an eye on her?" Francesca said simply.

Loretta scowled with annoyance at the simple, inescapable logic of the suggestion, her smug self-satisfaction of just a few moments earlier gone with the wind.

"Well, good night everybody," said Francesca, an impish look coming into her own eyes. "See you on Monday." With that, she turned and headed out the door.

Loretta could only stand there, fuming, as she watched the old woman make her way down the steps. She stayed there, tapping her foot, until she could contain herself no more.

"Oh, you think you're so smart!" she finally cried out.

From out in the darkness, she could hear Francesca break into unrestrained laughter. Then, in spite of herself, Loretta broke out into laughter too. She waved good-bye, closed the door, and went to the window. Will put aside the video game controller and stood beside her.

"You know, Mrs C is okay," he said, looking out. "But sometimes, she thinks she knows everything, doesn't she."

"Yes, she does," Loretta agreed.

She smiled, though, because as she watched Francesca drive away, Loretta suddenly realized that something quite unexpected had happened between her and the old Catholic Italian lady who sometimes made her feel guilty.

They were becoming friends.

CHAPTER 36

"**W**ell, hello, Mrs. Campanile," said a yawning Tony. "It's been a while since the last time I saw you in the store at this hour. Cooking dinner for the family today?"

It was Sunday morning. Anxious to get to the market early, Francesca had roused herself from bed the moment the first rays of the rising sun had touched her eyes. With a yawn of her own, she pushed her carriage up to the register and shook her head.

"Not exactly, Tony," she replied as she put the chicken cutlets and the rest of her groceries up on the counter. "My son decided at the last minute to have some friends over to his apartment today, to watch the big football game, so he called me last night and asked me to make a little something for them to eat. Can you believe it?"

"Hey, I don't blame him," said Tony, smiling. "You can't have a Super Bowl party without food."

"Eh, I guess," grunted Francesca, trying her best to sound annoyed, even though she was inwardly delighted. She had never been a particularly avid sports fan, so the game held little interest for her. Just the same, any opportunity to put her cooking skills to work for her son made it a happy occasion. She gave a scowl nonetheless. "It would have been nice if he at least let me know about it a day or two in advance," she griped.

"Ayyy, you know how kids are," laughed Tony. "They're all the same, even after they grow up."

"I'm not sure if all mine are completely grown-up yet," Francesca sighed.

"Yeah, but would you want them any other way?" said Tony.

"Probably not," admitted Francesca. Then, leaning closer, she added, "But don't tell them that."

When she returned home, the first thing Francesca did after bringing the groceries into the kitchen was to put on some music on the living room stereo. Francesca loved music. For her, it was as integral a part of Sundays as was dinner with the family. Good music complemented good food like a pleasant bottle of wine, and Francesca reveled in their blending, especially when she was cooking. That's when a symphony of sounds and smells would fill her home. Ask any of her children to name some of their favorite reminiscences of growing up, and sooner or later all of them would inevitably mention awakening on Sunday mornings to the sound of Verde, Puccini, Mozart, or Strauss playing on the record player in the living room, or sometimes to the voice of Francesca herself crooning along with Sinatra or Tony Bennett. Along with the music, the delightful smell of whatever happened to be baking in the oven would float up the stairs to their bedrooms like notes in an arpeggio, rousing them from their slumbers, so that for the rest of their lives, the sounds of many pieces of music were forever coded in their memories along with that of the warm, pleasing aroma of food.

Later that same morning, as it was nearing midday, Francesca was listening to Beethoven's Ninth while squeezing the juice of a lemon onto the lightly breaded pieces of golden brown chicken she had been sautéing on the stove. The juice evaporated with a hiss when it hit the pan, but it would leave the meat with a nice tangy flavor. Humming along to the music, Francesca tossed a pinch of salt over the chicken for good measure, and covered the pan with a lid. In a separate frying pan on another burner sizzled sliced artichoke hearts, zucchini, scallions, garlic, and olives. Francesca gave it all a stir before turning her attention to the oven. She opened the door and peered in to get an assessment of the two big foil pans baking inside. Satisfied with what she found, she covered each of them, closed the oven door, and turned off the heat.

By the time Joey arrived a short while later, the orchestra had made it to the symphony's fifth movement. Though she spoke not a word of German, Francesca was ramping herself up to join in with the chorus when her son walked into the kitchen. She had been in soaring good spirits all that morning even before he arrived. Alice and Rosie had called earlier; both had talked of a possible trip home to visit in the summer. Added to her elation at the prospect of seeing all her grandchildren together was the distinct satisfaction she felt at how much better things seemed to be going for her at the Simmons house. Loretta had surprised her Saturday afternoon by sending a nice little floral arrangement to say thank-you for taking care of her all week. Displayed in their vase atop of the dining room table, the flowers reinforced in Francesca a feeling of confidence and optimism every time she looked at them. All in all, she had already been in a mood to sing. Seeing her son put her over the top.

"Hey, there you are," she said merrily as she pushed the chicken from the skillet into an empty foil pan. "You're just in time. Listen, they're playing 'Ode to Joey'!"

It was obviously still too early in the day for her son to appreciate the joke, for his only response was a blank look and a shrug. He ambled over to the counter to get a peek at what his mother had prepared.

Francesca shook her head and clicked her tongue at him. "Let me tell you something," she said testily. "That's as good a joke as you're going to hear all day."

"Uh-huh," grunted her son. "So, whatcha got cookin'? It looks good."

Francesca didn't reply right away, but instead took the other frying pan from the stove and pushed all the artichokes and zucchini and olives into the foil pan with the chicken. Humming along to the chorus, she began to mix it all together.

"Listen to that music," she mused. "Imagine how good it must have felt to write a song like that. I mean, the first time he heard it in his head. What was it like for him?"

"I'm guessing he was joyful," said Joey, deadpan.

"Oh, so the brain is finally up and running after all," she chided him, wiping her hands on her apron.

"Oh, yeah," he said. "I remember you making wandies one time when this song was playing." Then, furrowing his brow, he added, "Don't ask me how I remember that."

"Out of my way," said Francesca, elbowing her son away from the stove. She bent over and opened the oven door. Reaching in with a pot holder, she pulled out the two foil pans and set them on the counter. She lifted off one of the foil covers, releasing an aromatic burst of steam. "Here," she said, "have a look. I made you some sausage and peppers. And in the other one is the baked ziti."

"*Madonna mia,*" marveled Joey.

"Hey, watch that mouth," said Francesca, even though she was quite pleased by his reaction.

"But Mom, you cooked so much. The chicken would have been plenty. You didn't have to do all that."

"What, you're gonna be *scumbari* and not have enough food for everybody?" she scoffed. "Just shut up and take it."

"You're the boss," said Joey. He reached toward the pan to sample a piece of the sausage, but his mother swatted his hand away.

"Hands off," she snipped. "Go sit down for two minutes if you want to try some." With that, she nudged him toward the table before reaching for the bag of rolls she had bought earlier that morning at the bakery. She opened one of the rolls and layered the inside with some sausage and peppers before spooning on some of the olive oil and juice from the pan. She put the sandwich on a dish and set it on the table before her son. "So, anybody special coming to watch the game with you today?" she asked, taking a seat across from him.

Joey well understood from experience what his mother meant by "special." "No, Mom," he said with a shake of his head. "I'm just having a few friends over, so please don't start. Just let me enjoy my sausage and peppers."

"Who's starting anything?" huffed Francesca defensively. "I was just asking a simple question."

"Yes, but that was just a different version of the same simple question you're always asking me."

"What," pouted Francesca, "I'm not supposed to want to see my son settled down and happy. Go ahead. Shoot me for being concerned."

Joey let out a little laugh. "Well," he said gently, "it hasn't quite come to that yet—not *yet.*" Then, looking away to the window, he suddenly shook his head, his smile fading away. "You know, it's not like I haven't been looking for someone," he admitted in a weary voice. "Sometimes it feels like that's all I do. I'd settle down in a minute if I could find the right one. But it gets to the point where I don't even want to bother anymore."

Francesca reached out and gave her son a gentle slap across the top of his head. "Maybe you're looking *too* hard," she told him. "Maybe you should try a little less quantity and a little more quality, if you know what I mean. And who knows, maybe let someone find *you.*"

Joey made no further reply, other than to shrug and take a bite of his sandwich. The subject was once again closed.

Later, Francesca packed all the food into a pair of cardboard boxes. While he waited, Joey wandered into the dining room, where he noticed the flower arrangement on the table.

"Hey, what's this?" he called. "Who's sending you flowers? Somebody special?"

"None of your business," Francesca called back, relieved that she had thought to tuck away the little card from Loretta. "Maybe I've a got a boyfriend. What's it to you?"

"Just askin'," said Joey, ambling back into the kitchen, where his mother was stacking one box atop the other.

"Here you go," said Francesca, tucking the bag of rolls into the box before covering it all with a towel to keep everything warm.

Joey reached out and gave his mother a hug and a kiss on the cheek. "Thanks, bella," he said. "I owe you one."

"Ayyy, you owe me a lot more than that," said Francesca. Turning to the counter, she passed the boxes to her son and guided him to the door. "By the way, those flowers are just from a sick friend I cooked some food for last week." This she told him hoping to preempt any suspicions her son might have. "And if you really think you owe me one," she added, "you can pay me back by taking a look at my car one of these days. It's making some funny noises lately."

"Yeah, sure," said Joey. "I'll take a look at it any time you want—that is, any time I can find you at home."

"Very funny" said Francesca, opening the door for him. "Just watch how you go, so you don't drop everything."

Despite her good spirits of just a short time earlier, Francesca felt a pang as she watched Joey walk to his car. She had told her son another white lie, this time about the flowers. It was getting to be a bad habit, she realized. It bothered her for many reasons, not the least of which was her certainty that it was only a matter of time before one of the liberties she had been taking with the truth of late would come back to haunt her. She shuddered to think of the commotion it would cause with her children, particularly her daughters. It would be better, Francesca decided, to take control of the situation and tell them straight out what she had been doing. This she vowed to do very soon—just not today.

CHAPTER 37

As it sometimes does during even the coldest of years, winter finally paused to catch its breath. The north winds fell silent for a few days, and a more gentle breeze puffed out of the south and west, nudging the daytime temperatures into the high thirties and occasionally the low forties, positively balmy in comparison to the bitter weather that had prevailed the previous several weeks. The February sun still climbed in a low arc through the vernal sky, but the days were growing ever so slightly longer. Little by little, patches of dark earth were beginning to show themselves everywhere outdoors; the ice and the snow were beginning to melt.

Francesca was too much a veteran of New England's peripatetic winters to be taken in by this midseason thaw. She had seen it all before, a winter that remained unnaturally warm for weeks on end, lulling everyone into the false hope that it had passed and an early spring was in the offing, only to suddenly return one day and attack once more, with all its wild, freezing fury. Nonetheless, though she trusted it little, Francesca was grateful for the respite from the arctic chill, for however long it lasted. If nothing else, the moderation of the weather put everyone, including herself, in a better mood.

Not to say that Francesca had been feeling downcast in any way. To the contrary, she could not remember a February when she had felt in better spirits. The few hours she spent with Penny and Will each afternoon brought a sense of order and purpose to her days that had long been missing. It gave her a thrill to see the two children come traipsing home from the bus stop every day. She enjoyed baking them after-school snacks and occasionally preparing dinner when Loretta had to work late. Most of all, she loved simply being there, to hear their stories about school, to share in their triumphs, or to comfort them when things did not go their way. She fell easily into the daily routine, for she found in it something comfortable and familiar, a feeling like that of an athlete returning to his training regimen after a long hiatus from competition. Will and Penny had become an important part of Francesca's days, and it gratified her deeply to think that she was becoming an important part of theirs.

This growing familiarity with one another, reassuring as it might have been, was not without its consequences. The children, particularly Penny, had long been accustomed to speaking their minds and easily manipulating their mother to get their way. In Francesca, they found a far less malleable authority figure, one who always insisted on getting her own way. Occasional clashes of will were inevitable, and Francesca's inevitably reigned, a state of affairs that did not always sit well with the two siblings, who decided one afternoon to try their hand at mutiny.

It was a dark, dreary day. A thin, miserable drizzle had misted down from the clouds all morning and into the afternoon, making it damp and foggy withal. It was a day best suited to hunkering down indoors and curling up by the fire, so it was a distinct disappointment to Penny and Will when they returned home from school and did not detect the aroma of something sweet baking in the oven when they walked through the front door. They made their displeasure known by unceremoniously dropping their backpacks and coats on the floor.

"Ayyy, is that where those go?" said Francesca, wagging a disapproving finger at them.

"I don't feel like hanging up my coat," said Penny, slouching over to the computer in its new home on a little table by the bookshelf. Its relocation downstairs to the living room by their mother had proven to be a constant source of annoyance to the young girl.

"Me either," said Will, emboldened by his sister's defiant attitude. With a long face, he turned on the television and plopped down on the couch.

Having anticipated their pique, Francesca said nothing, for she knew its precise source. Instead, she sat quietly at the kitchen table, leafing through a magazine, while the two children sulked in silence.

"I thought you said were going to make us some gingerbread today," Penny finally blurted out, getting straight to the heart of the matter.

"Yeah," brooded Will.

Francesca closed the magazine and came into the living room.

"What I said," she corrected them, "was that I would bake some gingerbread today—*if* you straightened up your rooms last night and made your beds this morning before school. From the looks of things upstairs, you didn't bother to do either, so I didn't bother to bake any gingerbread today."

"But that's not fair!" Penny protested. "You're always making us do stuff we don't want to do. You're not our boss, you know!"

"Yeah," added Will.

"And I'm not your chef," Francesca pointed out. "Now, it's still early. Plenty of time for me to make a treat for you two to have for dessert, after your mother makes supper. But if you really want me to do it, you'll have to ask me nicely and—"

"And what?" the two children asked in unison.

"You'll have to straighten up your rooms and make your beds, like you promised. In any case, hang up those coats and hats before your mother gets home, and start your homework."

There was no hesitation in Francesca's voice, no pleading for cooperation, and no hint in her tone that she was anything less than in complete control of the situation. For whatever reason—perhaps it had been a particularly long day at school—it was all too much for Penny to bear.

"No," the girl said, glaring at the old woman with an expression of open rebellion. "I'm not going to do it."

"Me neither," said Will, though his demeanor was much less convincing. He sat there, cringing, as he waited to see what the old woman's response might be.

"Really," said Francesca, giving them a withering glare of her own. "And just what do you plan to do instead?"

"Whatever we want," declared Penny. "This our house, not yours, so just leave us alone."

"Yeah," murmured Will, but with even less conviction than before.

Francesca folded her arms and scowled at the two mutineers.

A long, awkward silence ensued. No one, Francesca could tell, felt very good about the verbal skirmish that had just transpired, but for the time being at least, it appeared that the rebellion had fallen back to regroup.

"Well, you children do what you think best," Francesca finally told them in a well-practiced tone of voice intended to inflict the maximum amount of guilt on its recipient. With that, she turned away from them and walked back into the kitchen. She sat down at the table and opened her magazine once more, pretending all the while to pay them no further attention, when in fact, she was watching closely out of the corner of her eye, waiting to see what they would do next.

Penny and Will stayed there in sullen silence, shooting questioning glances at one another. A silent debate was raging between them. To retreat to their bedrooms, Francesca understood, would signal outright surrender, but to just sit there doing nothing probably seemed as silly to them as it did to her. Finally, with a communal sigh of frustration, the two reluctantly slunk to the front hall, hung up their coats, and dragged their backpacks into the living room. Will turned off the television and pulled out his math book to start his homework, while his sister returned to the computer to work on a school project of her own. It was, Francesca supposed, as much of a face-saving solution as they could be expected to manage.

Barely a word was spoken in the house, until Loretta returned home from work. By this time, Penny and Will had finished their homework and were sitting on the couch, watching television. At hearing their mother open the door, the cue that they could, with honor, finally abandon their positions, the two jumped up and gave her the briefest of greetings before hurrying upstairs to the sanctuary of their rooms. They were, no doubt, anxious to be as far away as possible when their mother received the report of their attempted insurrection that afternoon. The two were long out of sight when Francesca came out of the kitchen to collect her things.

"Hi, Francesca," said Loretta brightly, though there was a marked look of curiosity in her eyes. "Everything go okay today?"

"Yes, of course," Francesca assured her, though she knew full well that Loretta had been around long enough to pick up on the strained atmosphere to which she had come home. Before the younger woman could pursue the subject, Francesca quickly engaged her in some idle small talk about the weather and something she had read in the morning newspaper while she pulled on her coat and gloves. She was just about ready to get on her way home when Will and Penny suddenly appeared at the top of the stairs. As solemn and contrite a pair of children as she had ever beheld, the two looked down at her with sad, penitent eyes. Returning their gaze, Francesca gave a half smile and nodded to them in a gesture of patience and understanding.

"Are you sure everything is all right?" said Loretta at witnessing this quiet exchange.

"Trust me, everything's fine," said Francesca, patting the younger woman's hand. "Good night, children."

"Good-bye, Mrs. C.," they answered. Then, as Francesca was walking out the door, Penny meekly added, "Thank you."

Giving a wave over her shoulder, Francesca went on her way.

After watching to make sure that the older woman made it safely to her car, Loretta closed the door and turned to face her children, who by now were sitting on the top stair, looking gloomier than ever.

"What's going on, guys?" she asked with growing concern. "What's with the long faces? Did something happen today?"

"Yeah," Penny admitted. "Sort of."

"What? Tell me."

Neither child said anything, until Will finally shrugged and gave a heavy sigh.

"She made our beds," he said.

CHAPTER 38

"Hey, Frannie," said a surprised Peg. "What are you doing here at this hour on a Wednesday afternoon? Aren't you supposed to be working?"

It was two weeks later. For the past few days, Francesca had been hanging around the house, restless and bored. She had come to the library as much for the change of scenery as to pick out some new books to keep her occupied.

"Winter vacation," she said ruefully as she stepped into the library's computer room to chat with her friends. "The kids are out of school, and the mother took the week off from work."

"Then why are you looking like a mope?" said Connie, who was installed at her usual post on the computer next to Peg's.

"Really," added Natalie, turning away from her own monitor. "You think you'd be happy getting a week off for yourself."

"Eh, I guess you're right," agreed Francesca with a shrug, "You think I would be, but . . ."

"But now you don't know what to do with yourself, do you?" Peg finished for her.

"*Mannagia*, I'm going crazy!" cried Francesca. "I don't know what's the matter with me."

It was true. Without fully realizing it, Francesca had built the entirety of her weekdays around the few hours she spent with Will and Penny each afternoon. Those hours had become for her the center of gravity, holding everything else in place. They were the best part of her day, and she looked forward to them with great anticipation. Now, with nothing on which to focus her energies, Francesca's days suddenly lost their shape. Even though she knew it was for only a single week, she felt completely out of sorts, like the wind had gone out of her sails and she was drifting rudderless again.

"I think what you need is a hobby," Connie kidded her.

"Maybe I should take up surfing on the computer, like you three," griped Francesca.

"It's called surfing the Web, Frannie," Peg corrected her.

"Whatever."

"Never mind that," said Natalie. "Tell us about the kids. How's it been going?"

"Ayyy, what's to tell?" said Francesca, hesitant at first to say too much. "I go to the house, the kids come home from school, I wait until the mother comes home from work, and then I go back home again."

"Oh, come on," Connie urged her. "You can do better than that. You can't tell me that all you do is just sit there twiddling your thumbs all afternoon while you wait for the mother to come home."

"Well, not exactly," admitted Francesca.

It required but a little further prodding from her friends to start Francesca talking about her days looking after Penny and Will. She was discreet enough not to go into too much personal detail about the little family, for that's the kind of person Francesca was, but instead she told them of the ups and downs she had experienced getting to know the two children since first coming to their house, and the wonderful feeling it gave her to see that they and their mother were all finally starting to warm up to her. Her face beamed as she recounted some of the precious moments that had already passed between them, and even the recent confrontation about the gingerbread made for a pleasant reminiscence. As expected, Peg reacted unfavorably to the news that Francesca had been baking treats and occasionally cooking dinner for the children, and worse, straightening up their bedrooms—and not charging the mother extra! Just the same, as Francesca rambled on, she caught a faint hint of envy in her friend's eyes. She saw it, in fact, on all their faces.

"So anyway," sighed Francesca when she finished telling her little tale, "I guess things have gone pretty well—better, really, than I had expected. I just don't understand why I feel so inside out today."

Her three friends looked at one another and exchanged knowing smiles.

"Can't you guess what it is?" said Natalie.

"Guess what?" said Francesca innocently.

"It's easy," said Connie. "Go ahead. It's okay. I'd probably feel the same way if I were in your shoes. Just admit it."

"Admit what?"

With a kind grin, Peg leaned over and patted Francesca on the shoulder.

"Frannie, it's as plain as the nose on your face, what's bothering you," she said. "Face it. You miss them."

It was small consolation to Francesca to realize that Peg was perfectly correct, and later, after she had said her good-byes and checked out her books, she left the library feeling just as moody and irritable as she had when she first arrived. That night, home alone once again, Francesca tried calling Rosie and Alice while heating up some leftover soup for her supper, but no one was home at either house—or at least, no one was picking up when she left her messages on their answering machines. When it was sufficiently warmed, Francesca poured the soup into a bowl and brought it into the den.

While she sat on the couch and ate her soup, Francesca scrolled through the channels, trying to find something to distract her, but soon grew impatient with the long list of inane shows on offer. What was the use, she wondered, of having so many cable channels, when there was almost never a single show on any of them worth watching? Disgusted, she turned off the television, tossed the remote control aside, and ate the rest of her soup in silence.

Afterwards, when she brought the bowl into the kitchen and was rinsing it out in the sink, Francesca gazed out the back window into the night. Across the city, the rising moon hovered low over the horizon, struggling to pull itself free from the surrounding dark clouds that partially obscured its orange glow. It was an eerie, beautiful sight, one that might ordinarily have truly captivated her. On this night, however, it did little to draw Francesca out of the doldrums. With no other remedy for them coming to mind, she decided that the only thing left to do was to get in bed early and take a look at the books she had checked out of the library. One, a history of early Italian Renaissance art, had looked reasonably interesting. Perhaps spending a few minutes with Giotto and the rest of them would help her drift off to sleep. And so, with a nod to the heavens, Francesca dropped the bowl into the dish drainer, headed out of the kitchen, and trudged upstairs to her room.

Monday, she reflected glumly, seemed as far away as the moon.

CHAPTER 39

If she could have had arranged things her way, Loretta would have loved to take Penny and Will on vacation to Florida, or Bermuda, or any warm destination for that matter, just to escape the New England cold for a few precious days. Winter had long ago worn outs its welcome with her. Unfortunately, airfares, hotels, rental cars, and expensive restaurants simply weren't accounted for in her budget that winter. As it was, she felt lucky simply to know that she had enough money on hand to pay that month's gas and electric bills.

Nonetheless, despite the lack of a travel allowance, Loretta had managed to keep the kids entertained for the first few days of their vacation week. In truth, she had never taken them to a resort of any kind, so it wasn't something that they missed. The two were content with making little day trips here and there, just to get out of the house. For Loretta, it was a treat just to be able to sleep in as late as she wanted in the morning, without worrying about hustling everyone out the door to school in a frenzy.

Come Thursday, though, the natives had grown a bit restless. Having already made excursions to the Newport mansions, the children's museum in the city, a Providence Bruins hockey game, and a concert at the Performing Arts Center, Loretta had run short of novel ideas to keep Penny and Will occupied. With nothing particular on the agenda, the day was spent primarily hanging around the house, watching old movies on the television.

"I'm bored," Penny announced late in the afternoon.

She was sitting sideways in the big upholstered chair adjacent to the couch. Her legs drooping lazily over one puffy arm and her head resting back against the other, she struck a languid pose. Her brother, meanwhile, was lying on the floor, his chin propped on his hands. He rolled over and stared up at the ceiling.

"Me too," he said with a yawn.

"It's not fatal, you know," said their mother, who was only too content to stay sitting comfortably at the end of the couch with her legs curled up under a blanket while she read the newspaper. "The two of you could try something different, like maybe reading a book."

"Please, Mom," sighed her son. "We're on vacation, you know."

"Oh, right, I'm sorry," said Loretta, flipping to the next page of the newspaper. "What on earth could I have been thinking?"

"Come on, Mom," lamented Penny. "It's getting dark, and we haven't done anything fun all day."

"I'm open to suggestions."

"How about we go to the movies?" offered Will.

"You've been watching movies all day long."

"Then how about skating?" said Penny. "We haven't done that yet this week."

"Well, it's a little late for that today," replied her mother, tucking the blanket more tightly about her legs. She knew full well, of course, that in the winter, people skated under the lights all the time at night at the outdoor rink downtown, but she was feeling too warm and comfortable to budge. "What do you say we go tomorrow morning?"

"I guess," said her daughter, giving a heart-wrenching sigh, as if the agony of having nothing in particular to do at the moment was draining the very life from her.

"What about dinner?" said Will, moving to a subject near and dear to his heart. "I'm getting hungry. What are we having tonight?"

"I haven't made up my mind yet," Loretta told him.

"I wonder what Mrs. C is making for dinner tonight," said Penny, staring absentmindedly into space.

Loretta put the newspaper aside and gazed at her daughter for a few moments. "Now, what makes you wonder about that?" she asked her.

"Nothing," shrugged Penny. "I was just thinking about her today, that's all."

"That's funny. I was thinking about her too," said Will. "It's been kind of weird not having her here every day, hasn't it?"

"I know," agreed Penny. "I mean, sometimes Mrs. C does get on my nerves, but then other times, I don't know. It's kind of nice to have her here."

"Especially when she makes her spaghetti and meatballs," mused Will, "or when she bakes one of her cakes."

Loretta smiled, for she understood how the children felt. She herself had to admit that things around the house had not seemed quite the same without their nanny's daily visits. If nothing else, the burgeoning pile of dirty dishes in the kitchen sink and the untidy state of affairs in the rest of the house were evidence enough of that. Discipline in the ranks had taken a decided fall in her absence. But Loretta knew there was more to it than just the decline of their housekeeping.

"Well, she's a nice person," she said after a time, "and I guess we've all gotten used to having her around, looking after us."

"Hey, I know what to do," enthused Will. "Why don't we call her up and ask her to come over and cook us dinner?"

"Don't be an idiot," huffed his sister.

"Why not?" her brother persisted. "What do you think, Mom?"

"Well," Loretta chuckled, "I don't think that would be quite fair to Mrs. Campanile, do you? After all, it's her vacation week too."

"Yeah, I guess you're right," sulked Will. "It was just an idea."

Loretta turned her attention back to the newspaper and was beginning to read once more, when a different plan suddenly popped into her mind. She set the paper aside once more and looked back toward the kitchen with a thoughtful gaze. The more she considered it, the warmer it made her feel inside. The only question was, could she pull it off?

"What's the matter?" asked Penny.

"Oh, nothing," said her mother, drumming her fingers on her chin. "It's just that I suddenly had a little idea of my own about what to do tomorrow."

"But what about dinner tonight?" pressed Will. "I'm starving."

"First we need to go to the market," said Loretta. "Then later, we'll order out some Chinese. How's that sound?"

"Hooray!" cried Will.

"And tomorrow?" asked Penny.

"Well," said their mother, leaning closer with a gleam in her eye, as if she were drawing them into some playful conspiracy, "for tomorrow, here's what I had in mind . . ."

CHAPTER 40

Francesca's delight knew no bounds when she received Loretta's call on Thursday night. Will and Penny wanted to go skating Friday morning, Loretta explained when Francesca answered the phone, but they were all wondering— if she didn't already have plans, of course —if she would be interested in spending the rest of the day with them, just knocking around the city for a few hours, doing whatever, and perhaps having dinner together later in the afternoon.

There was, of course, no need to ask twice. Francesca's sole condition to saying yes to the proposal was that they allow her to come along and watch while they skated. She did not want to miss out on a minute of the fun, no matter how cold it might be in the morning. Her terms were more than acceptable to Loretta and the children, and arrangements were happily set in place for their outing.

Will and Penny were sitting on the front porch with their skates slung over their shoulders, both of them raring to go, when Francesca arrived at their house the next morning at precisely ten thirty, as planned. A few moments later, their mother bustled out the door, carrying her own skates. The four of them piled into Loretta's car, everyone talking and laughing at once, and soon they were on their way.

It was a bright, chilly morning when Loretta and the children took to the ice with the rest of the colorful crowd already in attendance. The lively music blared from the speakers, and the skaters went round and round, as a brisk breeze blew across Kennedy Plaza, where the rink was nestled at the foot of Providence's fledgling skyline. Eschewing the little shed by the rink, where she might have stayed perfectly warm, Francesca instead stood by the ice's edge, smiling and waving to Will and Penny as they called out "Hi, Mrs. C!" each time they skated by. Loretta, she discovered, much to her surprise, was a marvelous skater. Seemingly with no more effort than a feather riding on the wind, she glided about the ice graceful as a swan, carving one elegant turn after the other as she went. Penny exhibited much the same serene confidence on the ice, and skated easily along, doing her best to follow her mother's lead.

Will, on the other hand, was something of a calamity on skates, and Francesca made the sign of the cross as she watched him tear about. Try as he might to stay upright, the young boy spent almost as much time picking himself up off the ice as he did skating on it. His struggles did little, however, to curb his enthusiasm for speed. Had Loretta not made both him and his sister wear helmets, Francesca would have spent the majority of their time there with her eyes squeezed tightly shut, praying Hail Marys for the boy.

"Did you see us out there?" gushed Will, his cheeks a bright red, when they finally came off the ice.

"Yes, I did," Francesca assured him. "Very impressive. I was . . . amazed . . . at how you skate."

"Did you see me too?" said Penny eagerly.

"Of course," Francesca told the girl. "You looked like a ballerina out there. I bet one day you'll be a beautiful figure skater, maybe in the Olympics."

"How about me?" cried Will.

"Oh, and I think someday *you're* going to be great hockey player. You really like to throw yourself around on the ice."

Both children beamed with pride.

"So," said Francesca, giving their mother a wink, "where to next?"

After dropping their skates off at the car, a unanimous vote resulted in the group repairing to the warm confines of the Providence Place Mall, just a few steps away, to grab a bite for lunch in the food court. As they strolled up the hill to the mall, the majestic State House looming above them, Francesca looked out at Waterplace Park, on the banks of the river just below. Come the warm weather, the little amphitheater would be teeming with people soaking up the sun or enjoying one of the many outdoor performances held there; at night, the river would be aglow with fiery braziers, the light from their flames dancing across the water, while gondoliers skimmed quietly by in their long, elegant boats. For now, though, it was all deserted, the scenes she envisioned asleep like perennials in a snow-covered flowerbed, waiting for their chance to bloom again.

Penny and Will, meanwhile, were in high spirits, the two of them gabbing nonstop the whole time, until they finally came to the mall. Loretta admonished them more than once to stop and take a breath, so that someone else might get a word in edgewise, but to little effect. They were too excited and having much too good a time. Francesca could only laugh, for the two reminded her of her own children and grandchildren. Kids, she marveled, were much the same the world over. It didn't take nearly so much to make them happy as people often thought. In her experience, just spending time together and doing simple things with those who loved them was usually more than enough.

After lunch, the four strolled about the lovely, three-tiered mall, pausing now and then to peek inside the stores. Though she was thoroughly enjoying herself, Francesca could not help but fret about Penny and Will, who insisted on always gleefully rushing ahead of them. With Loretta's permission, Francesca had promised to buy them each a little gift if they saw something they liked, and so the two were eagerly scavenging about to see what they could find. Will soon made his choice when, out on the main floor, they came across a man demonstrating little windup helicopters that soared up into the air, only to circle right back and glide to an easy landing. Penny, however, was not having any luck, and she pouted in growing frustration.

At seeing an empty bench up ahead, Loretta and Francesca stopped to take a break. While the two adults sat and chatted, Penny continued her search, with Will in tow. In truth, her brother was too absorbed in his new helicopter to be of much help, but their mother insisted they stay together and not roam too far. Just the same, the two were soon lost from sight. When a few minutes passed without their reappearance, Francesca began to worry. Even Loretta, who to this point had struck a more casual attitude about their wanderings, looked anxious. They were just gathering their things together to go look for the children when Penny suddenly emerged from the crowd with Will close behind, still ogling his helicopter. Penny was all smiles when she approached.

"There you are," said Loretta, sounding much relieved. "I thought I told you two to stay close."

"Sorry, Mom," said the young girl, bubbling with excitement, "but I found something. I know I can't have it today, but I thought I would show it to you anyway."

"What is it?" asked Francesca.

Just then, the young girl did something quite unexpected. Without the least hesitation, she reached out and took Francesca by the hand. It was the simplest of gestures, an everyday occurrence by anyone's definition, and an onlooker would have thought nothing of it. Francesca, though, knew better. At the touch of the child's hand, the old woman felt her heart melt.

"Come on," Penny told her eagerly, giving her a tug. "I'll show you and Mom."

Francesca happily let herself be pulled up and guided away by the young girl. She had no idea of where she and Loretta were being led, but it mattered little, for she would not have traded that moment for all the treasure in the world.

"Here it is!" cried Penny, leading them to the young ladies' section of a women's boutique. There, displayed on a mannequin, was an adorable blue gown with fanciful lace sleeves and a delicate floral pattern stitched into the collar. The young girl stood there gazing at the lovely dress with dreamy, longing eyes. "Isn't it beautiful?" she sighed.

Loretta and Francesca cooed in agreement.

"Wonderful," muttered Will, who was not so impressed with the find.

"Oh, my God, you'd look just like a little princess in that dress," gushed Francesca, not hearing the boy.

"Wouldn't she?" nodded Loretta.

"That's what I thought," said Penny with another sigh and a demure shrug of her shoulders. "I know I can't get it now," she started to say, glancing at them with eyes that said she hoped she was wrong.

"Well, not today," gulped her mother, after sneaking a peek at the price tag.

Penny curled up her bottom lip, feigning extreme sorrow, and let her shoulders droop back down. "Oh, well," she said wistfully. "I didn't think so. Maybe someday."

"Someday," agreed Francesca, giving the girl's hand a little squeeze.

In the end, Francesca and Loretta helped Penny pick out a pretty little knit tam and matching scarf that happened to be on sale. The distraction of trying them on and looking at herself in the mirror while Francesca and her mother fussed over her was enough to make the young girl forget about the dress. Penny, in fact, was so pleased with the two items that she insisted on putting them on and wearing them the rest of the afternoon when they left the mall.

In no particular hurry to go straight home just yet, Loretta instead took them all on a little driving tour of Providence, letting Francesca act as guide. It had been a very long time indeed since Francesca had last gone for a ride around her hometown just for fun, and she loved every minute of it. The old woman was proud of her little city, and she enjoyed pointing out for the children its historical landmarks, telling stories about its people and places, and describing how very much things had changed downtown since she had been a little girl. As they went along, it seemed to Francesca that, around every corner, she would see something that awoke in her one memory or another of the old days .

"There's where Mom works!" the children cried when Loretta drove them past the building that housed the offices of Pace, Sotheby, and Grant.

It surprised no one, least of all herself, that Francesca had a story to tell about the quaint, dignified structure.

Eventually, their travels brought them across the river and up the hill past the Rhode Island School of Design and Brown University, on the city's fashionable East Side. This was a particular pleasure for Francesca, for when they were young, she and Leo had often taken drives along the area's tree-lined avenues and pleasant boulevards, daydreaming about what it would be like to live in any one of its stately brick homes. Loretta drove aimlessly about the lovely neighborhoods, pausing now and then to gawk at some of the more beautiful houses, until they came to Prospect Park. There, Loretta pulled the car over, and they all got out to have a look at the nice view it afforded of the city. With her camera in hand, Loretta led them down to the edge of the park, where she snapped a picture of Francesca and the children in front of the statue of Roger Williams, Providence's venerable founder, who kept watch over the city below. It was a perfect shot, but there was no time for them to linger and enjoy the vista. By then, the late afternoon wind had picked up considerably, and she hustled everyone back into the car, to get out of the cold.

When at last they returned home, the children, and even Loretta, seemed to be bubbling with eager anticipation as they all hurried out of the car and up the walk to the front porch. Francesca eyed the three with interest, wondering just exactly what they were up to, as Loretta fumbled with the keys to the door.

"Come on, Mom, hurry up," Penny urged her.

"Wait till you see the surprise we have for you!" said Will, who was instantly shushed by his mother and sister.

Her curiosity sufficiently piqued, Francesca followed them inside to the warmth of the house.

"Why don't you just sit in the living room and relax for a couple of minutes, maybe watch a little TV?" suggested Loretta before Francesca had a chance to follow her to the kitchen. "I'll be right back."

At seeing the earnest look in the young woman's eyes, Francesca did as she was told and dutifully settled onto the couch, wondering all the while just what sort of surprise Loretta and the kids had in store for her. As she sat there with Penny and Will, both of whom seemed to be doing their best to occupy her attention, Francesca glanced out the front window, her thoughts turning to dinner. It was growing late in the afternoon—the sun had already dipped behind the roofs of the houses across the street—but no one had yet made mention of any plans to order out a meal or go to a restaurant. This struck her as a bit curious, as did the clattering of pots and pans and utensils, the opening and closing of the refrigerator door, and the sound of running water coming from the kitchen. Looking about, she also happened to notice that the coffee table was remarkably free of clutter. The entire living room, in fact, appeared to be quite spic and span. Francesca puzzled over just what exactly was going on, until a few minutes later, when she detected a very familiar aroma in the air.

"Okay," called Loretta, just at that exact moment. "Bring her in!"

"Now close your eyes," said Penny when Francesca got to her feet. The girl came to the old woman's side and took her hand.

"And no peeking," added Will, taking the other.

Flanked by the two children, Francesca let them guide her to the kitchen. "Okay," they both cried, "open them!"

Francesca could scarcely believe what she saw when she opened her eyes. The entire kitchen was immaculate, not a single dirty dish in the sink nor a stray scrap of paper or homework assignment to be found anywhere. The table was beautifully set with four settings atop a white linen cloth. A pair of candles stood at the center, the light from their flames glistening across the glasses and silverware.

"Oh, my," she exclaimed, impressed beyond words. "Well, I see that you three have been very busy."

"Everybody pitched in," said Loretta, who was standing with arms crossed in front of the stove, smiling from ear to ear.

"And what's for dinner, might I ask?" said Francesca, craning her neck to get a glimpse of what was behind the young woman.

"Ta dah!" announced Loretta, whipping the cover off one of the two pots on the stove to reveal the bubbling tomato sauce within. "I made it this morning," she gushed, almost giddy with excitement. "I followed your recipe exactly. It was so easy! And look," she joked, uncovering the other pot, "I'm even boiling water for the spaghetti! Can you believe it? And I bought some nice Romano cheese to put on it, because I know you like that. And I've also got some garlic bread warming up in the oven. I have to admit, I cheated on that one. I bought it frozen at the market last night. But it smells good, doesn't it? And I've got some ice cream in the freezer for dessert. I didn't have time to bake a cake. Maybe next time. Anyway, I've almost got the salad done, then I just have to throw the spaghetti into the water, and dinner will be all ready!"

Francesca beamed at all of them with pride, but particularly at Loretta, as the young woman hurried to finish preparing dinner. In all her years, she had never seen anyone put a meal out on the table with more pure joy and enthusiasm. When at last they all sat down to eat, Francesca raved at how lovely the table looked and how wonderful everything smelled. Filling their bowls with the spaghetti, and passing them out one by one, Loretta suddenly grew quiet, and only smiled and shrugged modestly in reply, for the moment of truth had finally come. She bit her lip and watched as Francesca and the children all dug in.

The verdict was swift and decisive.

"Wow, Mom!" exclaimed Will, wide-eyed with amazement. "This is delicious!"

"Really, Mom," agreed Penny as she slurped up a strand of spaghetti. "It's excellent!"

Francesca, of course, concurred wholeheartedly, but she could tell by the look of quiet triumph in Loretta's eyes that it was the children's judgment that gratified her most.

"To Chef Loretta!" said Francesca, raising her glass. "Or should I say, *Mamma* Loretta?" "To Mamma Loretta," laughed the children, and everyone joined in the toast.

Later, after dessert, Francesca helped clean up the kitchen, while Will and Penny flopped down on the living room couch to digest.

"You know, that really was very good," said Francesca, bringing the dirty dishes to the sink. "I'm proud of you."

"Thanks," smiled Loretta, "I had fun doing it." Then her expression turned to one of puzzlement as she regarded the big pot of leftover tomato sauce. "I think I made too much," she said. "What on earth am I going to do with the rest?"

"Are you kidding?" laughed Francesca. "You save that for Sunday. Then I'll tell you what to do next. You buy some nice pork chops or ribs, put them on a pan, and brown them in the oven nice nice. Then you take them out of the oven and toss them in the sauce, and serve it all with some nice ravioli."

"Ooh," said Loretta, "that sounds delicious."

"Then, if there's any sauce left after *that*," Francesca went on, "you buy yourself a pound of pizza dough for ninety-nine cents, spread some sauce over it with some pepperoni and a little bit of cheese, and throw it the oven. Trust me, you'll all be in heaven."

When it finally came time for Francesca to go home, Loretta and the children gathered at the door to say good night.

"Thank you so much. I had a wonderful day," Francesca told them, and she meant every word. Then she leaned down toward the children and wagged a finger at them. "And the two of you should give your mother a kiss to thank her for cooking you such a nice meal."

"And then you should also say than-you to Mrs. Campanile for the nice gifts she bought you at the mall," replied Loretta, giving Francesca a nod.

The children started toward her, and for a fleeting moment, Francesca thought that they were going to give her a hug. Unsure of themselves, though, they held back and just stood there smiling warmly at her.

"Thanks, Mrs. C," they both said.

"Oh, you're welcome, children," she told them. "I had a lot of fun. Now be good for your mother the rest of the weekend, and I'll see you again on Monday."

With that, Francesca bade them all a good night and soon went on her way.

The wind outside had subsided, but it was still quite cold when Francesca walked out to her car. As she opened the door and climbed inside, however, Francesca could not have felt warmer. The thought of the long, beautiful day that had just passed left her blissfully tired and happy. She was ready now to go home and climb into her bed and dream about it all night long. With that pleasant thought in mind, she turned the key to start the car.

Nothing happened.

She tried again. The engine made a clicking noise and then once again nothing.

Francesca pumped the gas pedal a few times and then turned the key once more. The engine sputtered and coughed to life, and Francisca breathed a sigh of relief. No sooner had she done so when the engine suddenly died again, this time for good. No matter how often she turned the key or pumped the gas, Francesca could not make the engine start. Uncertain as to what she should do next, she sat there for quite a few minutes, mulling over her options. With a sigh, she looked at the clock and up into the dark winter sky. At last, Francesca came to what she could not have known in that moment would be a fateful decision. Letting out a grumble of irritation, she opened the car door and trudged back up to the house.

"Is everything all right?" asked Loretta with concern when she opened the front door.

"Yes," Francesca told her, "everything's fine. Don't worry. But would you mind if I used your telephone. I need to call my son."

CHAPTER 41

There is something sweetly inexplicable that passes between two people who are destined to meet when one day, after wandering often aimlessly through life, searching without ever knowing for exactly what, the heavens finally fall into alignment and they happen upon one another unexpectedly, as if by magic. It is not quite, though some might call it so, the proverbial fire of love at first sight that strangers sometime experience, for in truth, the two find in one another something extraordinarily familiar and comforting. Before either even speaks, each has the oddest notion that they have already met and indeed known each other since long ago. It is more a feeling of profound recognition, almost surprise, than anything else, one that brings with it a sense of relief, as if their hearts are simply saying to one another, "Oh, there you are. Where have you been? I've been looking all over for you for the longest time."

Such was the case that night when the doorbell rang and Loretta left Francesca and Penny in the kitchen, and Will in the living room with his video game, to answer it. Laughing along the way at a silly joke Penny had just told, she hurried to the front hall and turned the doorknob. Expecting, as she did, to encounter someone quite a bit older than herself—for some reason, she could not envision her elderly nanny's children any other way—she opened the door, her laughter coming to an abrupt halt when she discovered a young man of her own age waiting on the front porch. With his hands buried deep in the pockets of his frayed, gray sweatshirt, the hood pulled up over his head, he was standing there looking about at his surroundings, as if he were not quite sure that he had come to the right place. When he turned his gaze to Loretta and their eyes met for the first time, she felt strangely overcome by a sensation of paralysis, as if suddenly she could not move or speak. From what could she could see, the young man seemed to suffer from the very same affliction, for he stood there equally immobile and mute.

In this way, the two regarded one another in awkward silence for what seemed a very long time, but in truth was for but a moment, after which the young man stepped closer and pulled back his hood.

"Hi, I'm Joey Campanile," he said in a hesitant voice. He turned and quickly glanced back over his shoulder at his mother's car, parked out front. "I'm . . . uh . . . looking for my mother—Francesca? Did I come to the right house?"

"Yes, of course," breathed Loretta, relieved that she had rediscovered her power of speech just in the nick of time. "Please come in."

Loretta stepped back and let Joey enter. There, in the light of the hallway, she saw that besides being younger, he was also taller than she had imagined he would be—for Francesca was far from statuesque—and his features darker and more rugged, but there was no mistaking his striking blue eyes, which came no doubt from his mother. Not quite able to turn her gaze from them, she self-consciously pushed a stray strand of hair from her face, suddenly wishing for all the world that she had taken just a moment to look in the mirror and straighten herself up before she had answered the door.

"I'm Loretta," she said, extending her hand.

"Nice to meet you, Loretta," replied Joey, gently taking it in his own. Though chafed and cold from being outdoors without gloves, his hand nonetheless felt warm to Loretta, and it was only with great reluctance that she released it from her grasp.

"Come on," she beckoned, turning away. "Your mother is waiting for you in the kitchen with my daughter."

"Excuse me for a second," said Joey, touching her shoulder while she was still in reach. "But can I ask you a question?"

Loretta turned back and saw the look of puzzlement on Joey's face. "What is it?" she said.

"Well, I was just wondering," he replied. "What is my mother doing here?"

"She's my babysitter—well, more my like my nanny," Loretta laughed. Then, seeing that he wore the same confused look, she stopped and added, "Didn't you know?"

Aside from a raised eyebrow, Joey made no reply, but simply shrugged and shook his head.

"Oh, well, then follow me," said Loretta, leading him on.

As they passed through the living room, Will, who up till this moment had been thoroughly absorbed in the animated aerial battles of his video game, looked up in surprise at the newcomer. At the sight of Joey, the young boy sat up straight, letting the game controller drop onto his lap. His attention diverted, the simulated combat jet he was piloting on the television spun out of control and crashed into a mountain with a fiery explosion.

"This is my son, Will," said Loretta. "Will, this is Joey. Mrs. Campanile is his mother."

"Hey," said Joey in his quiet way.

"Hi," the boy replied in a small voice, sinking down a bit into the couch, his eyes darting nervously about as if he wasn't sure of what to do or say next.

Joey nodded to the television screen, where the game was waiting to be reset. "Ace Combat?" he asked.

Will's eyes widened in amazement. "Ace Combat Zero," he said eagerly, suddenly much more at ease.

"He's got all the games, every last noisy one," lamented Loretta.

"Oh, yeah," said Joey, jutting his chin out in a way that showed he was impressed. "I heard that's a good one."

"I kinda like it," said Will. Picking the controller up off his lap, he pretended to turn his attention back to the game, all the while keeping a sharp, suspicious eye on Joey.

"Ayyy, *finalmente!*" exclaimed a red-faced Francesca, just then bustling out of the kitchen, her coat and pocketbook in hand. "What took you so long to get here? And look at the outfit he wears to pick up his mother. Didn't I tell you to throw away that old sweatshirt?"

Despite Francesca's bluster, Loretta could plainly see that the older woman was ill at ease and anxious to leave. She suspected, quite rightly, that her discomfoet most likely sprang, for whatever reason, from the necessity of making Joey come to the house and discover that she had been working as a nanny. Though she would never have admitted it, some dark, mischievous side of Loretta was rather enjoying the awkward situation. Something in Joey's demeanor told her that he felt the same way.

"Sorry I didn't get here sooner," he told his mother patiently, "and that I didn't wear a tux, but I was at the gym when you called me on my cell, remember, Mom?" Joey rolled his eyes for the benefit of Loretta, who put a hand to her mouth to hide her smile.

"Hmm, I see you two have met," said Francesca, alternating her gaze between the two.

"Yes, and I was just introducing him to Will," explained Loretta. "And this, Joey, is my daughter, Penny."

Penny had just followed Francesca out of the kitchen and was now standing with her arm wrapped about her mother's waist, gaping up at Joey.

"Hey, Penny," he said.

The young girl did not respond right away, but instead, stood there, still staring at him.

Loretta looked down at her daughter and gave her a shake. "Hey, aren't you going so at least say hello?' she chided her daughter.

"Oh, hi," Penny said at last, shrinking back behind her mother.

"Well, that's nice. We've all met," said Francesca brusquely. "Come on now, Joey. Time to take me home so they can all settle down for the rest of the night. Good night, everybody." With that, she unceremoniously grabbed her son by the arm and oriented him toward the door. Loretta could only watch, even though her first impulse was to reach out and grab his other arm.

"Whoa, just a minute," said Joey, before his mother could pull him to the door.

"What?" she said testily, shooting him a look of perturbation.

"I just need to let them know what we're planning to do with your car," he replied. Then, turning to Loretta, he said, "Is it all right if we leave it here overnight? I mean, I'll come back to take a look at it tomorrow morning first thing and see if I can't get it started."

"Yes, of course it's all right," Loretta assured him. "Come whenever you want. We'll be here."

"Great," said Joey with a smile. He hesitated, as if he wanted to say more but didn't dare. "Well, I guess then I'll see you tomorrow. It was very nice to meet you all."

"It was nice to meet you," said Loretta, returning his smile.

"Okay, let's go," said Francesca, giving her son a tug. Before anyone could say another word, she swept him out the door and down the front walk to his car.

Loretta closed the door behind them and went to the window to watch them go. She was soon joined by Penny and Will, who stood there with her, gazing out with equal interest, as the pair climbed into the car and drove away into the night.

Penny slipped her hand into Loretta's and rested her head against her mother's arm. "He seemed nice," she said wistfully.

"Very nice," her mother agreed.

"Do you think he'll really come back tomorrow?" said Will.

"I don't know," sighed Loretta. "I really don't know." Then, in barely above a whisper: "But I hope so."

CHAPTER 42

They had been driving for some time, and Joey had yet to make a single remark. Francesca had expected him to pepper her with questions the moment they were alone. Instead, lost in thought, he gazed straight ahead, his eyes fixed on the road. His reticence, Francesca knew, should have come as something of a relief to her, but it did not. Was he so upset with her that he couldn't speak, or was he just waiting for the right moment to start the interrogation? Whichever the case, the suspense was killing her.

"Okay, let's have it," she blurted out at last, no longer able to contain herself.

"Have what?" Joey replied.

"You know what," she said impatiently." Come on, out with it. Just say what's on your mind."

"I haven't got anything on my mind," he said.

"Oh, you're going to tell me that you're not angry or upset or worried or *something*, now that you know that I've been babysitting those two children every day without telling you or the others?"

"Oh, that," said Joey with an absentminded shrug. "Wasn't it you who told me once not to ask you about your business?"

Francesca sat there for a moment, glaring at him. "What's the matter with you?" she finally exclaimed. "Is that how you show concern for your mother? What kind of son are you anyway?"

"I came to get you, didn't I?" Joey pointed out.

"And that doesn't bother you either, that you had to come get your mother at a stranger's house? What if these people were ax murderers?"

"I really didn't get that impression of them," said Joey, calm as always.

"Well, you never know," his mother carried on. "You think you would have been at least a little bit worried when I called you."

"Actually, I was mostly annoyed, because I had to cut my workout short," he jested, giving her a sideways glance.

"Nice," huffed Francesca, folding her arms.

"I was just wondering about something, though," Joey went on. "Not that I minded, really, but how come you called me?"

"Who else on earth was I supposed to call to take me home?"

"I dunno," shrugged Joey. "I mean, obviously you've been trying to keep all this a secret. Couldn't her husband or somebody else give you a ride?"

"Did you see a wedding ring on her finger?" snipped Francesca.

Joey did not answer right away, but continued to look straight ahead. After a time, his expression brightened ever so slightly. "No," he said thoughtfully at last. "Now that you say it, I didn't."

"That's because she's not married," Francesca told him. "So, what was I supposed to do? Make that poor girl drag her two kids out on a winter's night and drive them all across town just to take me home?"

"Nope," said Joey with a shake of his head. "I guess you did the sensible thing."

Frustrated by her son's refusal to take the bait, Francesca sat back and sulked in silence for a while. She had known all along, of course, that it was simply a matter of time before Joey and his sisters caught on to her. That being the case, she had spent considerable hours imagining different scenarios of how the dramatic confrontation would play out, anticipating the cries of concern from Rosie and Alice, and preparing ready responses to their inevitable questions. Now that the moment had come, the first engagement of the grand battle she had envisioned had fizzled without a shot being fired, and she felt strangely let down, like a boxer whose opponent has forfeited the match just before the bell for the first round was about to ring.

Joey drove up to a red light and brought the car to a stop. Francesca stared out the window at the familiar surroundings. Just then, something about the place jogged her memory, and she sat there wondering what it might be. Finally it came to Francesca. This was the very same intersection at which she had stalled Leo's car that day long ago, when he had first tried to teach her how to drive. The recollection, despite the present circumstances, brought the hint of a smile to her face. The light turned green, and Joey drove on.

"So, why did you do it?" he said at last, breaking the silence.

"I told you," answered Francesca. "I didn't have anyone else to call."

"No, not that," said Joey with a little laugh. "What I meant is, how come you started babysitting for them? Is something wrong? Do you need money?"

"No, of course not," sighed Francesca, the fight having gone out of her. "It's just something I felt like I needed to do. It's a long story. I'll tell you all about it some other time, but not tonight. Okay?"

"Yeah, sure," nodded Joey. "Whatever you say. I'll just go back there tomorrow and see what I can do about the car."

"Good," said Francesca. Then, climbing back up onto her high horse for just one more moment, she added, "And make sure you wear some decent clothes when you do. I don't want you to embarrass me again. I meant what I said back there."

"Huh?"

"That ratty old sweatshirt. Get rid of it. You look like a *zuz-zuzz'*."

Joey smiled and kept his eyes focused straight ahead.

"Thanks," he told her, "but I like this old sweatshirt just fine."

CHAPTER 43

Loretta was upstairs, watching from her bedroom window, when, true to his word, Joey returned to the house the next morning. Despite it being a Saturday, in a vacation week no less, she had sprung out of bed and dressed quite early so as not to miss him when he arrived. Now that he had, she stood there, nervously drumming her fingers against her chin, quite unable to make up her mind as to what she should do next. The children were still abed sleeping, but she knew it wouldn't be long before they awoke and dominated the day's proceedings. Finally, tiptoeing past their bedroom doors, she hurried downstairs to the living room window and nudged the curtain aside, to hazard a peek at what was happening out front.

It was a raw morning outdoors. The crystal blue sky of the previous day had been replaced by a shroud of heavy, slate gray clouds, and a thin, miserable drizzle hung in the air. Wasting no time, Joey went straight to his mother's car, pausing only briefly to cast a questioning glance at the house before climbing inside to try the ignition. Having no luck, he climbed back out, opened the front hood, and gazed in at the engine, his breath coming out in little white puffs as he assessed the situation. After a moment's consideration, he leaned over and reached inside to fiddle with some part of the motor hidden from Loretta's view. Not that it mattered much to her what it might be, for she had only the vaguest notion of what went on beneath the hood of a car. Just the same, she watched with keen interest.

After a time, Joey straightened back up and walked to his own car, where he opened the trunk and pulled out a toolbox. He returned to his mother's car and, with a wrench in hand, was soon at work once more on the engine. Just then, as he was making whatever adjustments he had decided were necessary, the light drizzle that had been falling all morning suddenly turned into a steady rain and, before long, into an outright downpour.

Loretta rushed to the hallway and threw open the front door.

"Hey!" she called to him. "Come inside quick, before you get drowned out there!"

At seeing her at the door, Joey's face lit up in a warm smile despite the cold rain beating down on his head. He looked up in annoyance at the skies and gave a shrug of resignation before quickly closing the hood of the car and running up onto the porch. With drops of rainwater dripping off his forehead and shoulders, he stopped at the threshold, looking unsure as to whether or not he should enter.

"Come in, come in," Loretta insisted, tugging the sleeve of his sweatshirt, the same tattered gray thing he had been wearing the night before.

"Yeow, it's unreal out there," said Joey, stepping into the dry warmth of the hallway, where he shook some of the raindrops from his head. "Were they predicting this for today?"

"Who knows?" said Loretta. "I don't even listen to the weather report anymore. From the looks of it, though, I'd say it's going to keep coming down like this for a while."

"Yeah," agreed Joey, glancing back out the door. "I think you might be right." He scratched the back of his neck and made a pained expression. "I don't think I'm going to be able to work on my mother's car anymore today," he confessed.

Loretta looked up into his eyes, trying her best to project

outward calm, even though her heart was galloping a mile a minute inside her chest. She was turning things over in her mind, desperately trying to think of a way to entice him to stay for just a little while.

"Do you think you can fix it?" she finally asked, not knowing what else to say.

"I don't know. Maybe," he answered. "I mean, I think I should at least be able to get it started."

"It sounds like you're good with cars," she said, beaming a smile at him..

"I know a little bit," said Joey modestly. "My father had his own shop for a long time, so I learned a lot from him."

It seemed neither of the two knew what to say next, and a pronounced silence ensued, despite the fact that the two never took their eyes off one another.

"Listen," Joey said at last in a timid voice. "I was just wondering—"

"Yes?" said Loretta expectantly.

"Um, would you mind if I left the car here one more day?"

"The car?"

"Yes," he nodded. "I was thinking I'd come back tomorrow and take another whack at it. Of course, if you're tired of looking at it, I'll just get it towed," he hastily added.

"No, it's no problem at all," said Loretta, a bit crestfallen.

"Okay. Well, in that case, I guess I'll just get going," said Joey.

There was a hint of reluctance in his voice, but Loretta was uncertain what the reason it was—a reluctance to leave or to return. She watched stupidly as he stepped out onto the porch.

"See you tomorrow," was all she could think to blurt out as he hurried down the steps and out through the rain to his car.

When he drove away, Loretta stood there at the door, fuming. She slammed it shut and stomped into the living room, where she plopped disconsolately onto the couch. By then, having heard voices at the front door, a yawning Penny had come downstairs and was standing in her pajamas on the bottom stair, scratching her side.

"I am *such* an idiot!" Loretta screeched. "What was I thinking? Offer him a cup of coffee or tea, or a glass of water. *Anything!*"

"What's the matter, Mom?" said Penny through another yawn. "Who was here?"

"Mrs. Campanile's son," lamented Loretta, tossing aside a cushion in frustration.

"Oh, *already*," groaned Penny, clearly disappointed that she had missed him. "So, does that mean we'll never see him again?"

"Yes, we'll see him again" sighed Loretta. "He's coming back tomorrow, to finish fixing that stupid car."

"Really?" said the girl, her sleepy eyes brightening. "That's good."

Loretta sat there for a time, staring blankly into space, before suddenly sitting up straight, for an intriguing idea had just occurred to her. As she drummed her fingers once more against her chin, mulling it over, the makings of a plan began to coalesce in her mind.

"You know, you might be right," she told her daughter at last. "It *is* good that he's coming back tomorrow."

It rained the rest of the day and all through the night, washing away much, if not all, of the snow left over from the storms of that long, relentless winter, before finally tapering off late Sunday morning. By midday, the clouds had started to break apart, and the sun once again showed its face just as Joey pulled up to the house. His timing could not have suited Loretta better. She went to the door and waved to him, while he went to work again on Francesca's car. Penny, resting her elbows on the sill of the front window, propped up her chin on her fists and gazed out at him, while her brother pulled on his coat and hurried outside to watch.

"What's going on out there now?" Loretta called from the kitchen a little while later.

"I don't know," answered Penny. "It looks like he's saying something to Will." A pause. "Wait a minute. He's giving Will one of his tools and pointing to the engine."

"What?" exclaimed Loretta.

She knew nothing about automobiles, but she was alarmed by the prospect of her son causing further damage to the car or, worse, injuring himself. As she rushed to the window, all manner of horrifying, if wildly improbable, mishaps instantly played in her maternal imagination. Crushed limbs, severed fingers, exploding gas tanks, electrocution. It was all too much to conceive. By the time she reached Penny's side, though, she saw to her relief that Joey had already taken back the tool and was leaning once more over the engine by himself. Now and then, he would turn back to Will and say something to which the young boy paid rapt attention. The pair looked perfectly at ease with one another, and Loretta's fears of just a moment prior melted away like the snow and the ice.

Nearly an hour passed before Joey packed up his toolbox and stowed it away in the trunk of his car. Will, meanwhile, ran up the front walk ahead of him to the house.

"Here they come!" cried Penny to her mother.

Loretta, wearing a crisp white apron, was just emerging from the kitchen when Will burst through the front door. Not far behind, Joey came to the doorway and leaned his head inside.

"Anybody home?" he called with a good-natured smile.

"Yes, of course," Loretta greeted him. "Please come in."

Joey stepped into the hallway, just as she had hoped he would.

"Did you fix the car?" Penny asked him.

"Nope, it's busted," answered Will before Joey could open his mouth.

"Is it really?" said Loretta.

"Technically speaking? Yup, it's busted," said Joey with a laugh. "I thought I'd be able to get it started, but I'm gonna have to get it towed. I think it might be the transmission."

"Oh, that's too bad," said Loretta. She had no clue as to what the transmission might be, but it sounded ominous. "Do you have a garage where you can take it?"

"Oh yeah, no problem," Joey assured her. "I'll just—"

He was about to say something else when he paused and gave the air a sniff.

"Gee, *something* smells good," he noted.

"Oh, that," said Loretta, a perfect picture of nonchalance. "I was just getting ready to put dinner on the table. Nothing special—just some ravioli and pork chops and spare ribs." She waited a moment to give the image time to fully settle into his brain. Then, as if the idea had just come to her from completely out of the blue, she said, "Are you hungry? Why don't you stay and have a bite to eat before you go?"

"Oh, no, I couldn't do that," said Joey, sheepishly. "I mean, I wouldn't want to impose."

"Nonsense," said Loretta. "There's plenty."

"Are you sure?" said Joey weakening.

"Yes, I'm sure," said Loretta with an inviting smile. "Come on."

Joey relented and, with a smile of his own, followed Loretta's lead. While she went directly to the stove to finish drawing the spare ribs and pork chops out of the big pot of sauce, he came into the kitchen, washed his hands in the sink, and sat down with the children. The two youngsters sat there, gazing with unabashed admiration at their dinner guest, whose own eyes were drawn at the moment to the stove.

"Well, this a nice surprise," Joey said, giving them a wink. "I hope your mom made enough."

Loretta poured some sauce over the ravioli she had cooked

and set the bowl on the table along with a plate of the pork chops and spare ribs.

"Trust me, there's more than enough," she said before taking her own seat, pleased beyond words that when he had come into the kitchen, Joey had obviously not noticed that the table had already been set for four.

CHAPTER 44

"**W**hat do you mean you couldn't get it started?" said a displeased Francesca later that afternoon. "What did your father and I send you to college for anyway?"

"Chemical engineering," Joey reminded her. He was once again sitting at a dinner table, this time in his mother's kitchen, looking over the front page of the Sunday newspaper. "Believe it or not, automotive repair wasn't part of the curriculum."

Francesca was notoriously frugal and thus loathed to spend money on certain things, automobiles among them, unless absolutely necessary. "Well, you think you would have at least learned a thing or two from your father after all those years he spent repairing cars," she griped.

"I did," her son replied, turning the page. "I learned enough to know when I can't do something by myself."

Francesca let out a grumble and sat down across the table from him. "So now what do I do?" she asked him.

"Don't worry about it," said Joey. "I'll get somebody to tow it tomorrow morning, and we'll get it fixed, that's all."

"That's not what I meant," said Francesca, shaking her head in annoyance. "What I want to know is, how am I supposed to get around the next few days without a car?"

"Oh, I get it," said Joey, his eyes still scanning the headlines.

"You're worried about how you're going to get back and forth to babysit every day."

"Among other things," said Francesca testily, for he had read her mind precisely. "Are you finally going to start on me about that now?"

Joey shook his head. "Nope," he replied. "I was just going to say that, if you want, I can take a late lunch for the next few days and drop you off there, and then come back after work to take you home."

This suggestion was eminently suitable to Francesca. "Are you sure you'll be able to do that?" she said, her tone softening a bit, for she now regretted getting so snippy with him.

"No problem," her son assured her. "Just tell me what time to pick you up."

"Great," said Francesca, feeling much relieved. "You're a good boy, Giuseppe, I don't care what they say."

"Eh, I try," he said with a shrug.

Pleased to have her transportation arrangements settled for the next few days, Francesca slapped her hand down amiably on the table and got to her feet. "So, what do you want to eat, *figlio mio?*" she asked him. "I've got a couple of steaks in the fridge I can cook for you. Maybe a little risotto and a salad?"

Joey gave a nervous cough. "No thanks, Mom," he told her. "I'm really not that hungry right now."

Concerned for her son, Francesca came to his side and put her hand on his forehead. "Not hungry?" she said worriedly. "It's almost five o'clock on a Sunday afternoon, and you don't want to eat? What's the matter? You feeling sick or something?"

"No, I'm fine," said Joey, gently nudging her hand away. Then, in a faltering voice, "It's just that—what I mean to say is that I already had something to eat a little while ago."

"Where did you eat?" said Francesca, incredulous. She had

been looking forward to cooking for him and was keenly disappointed.

"At her house," her son admitted after a moment's hesitation.

"Her? Who her?"

"Loretta," said Joey, hiding himself once more behind the newspaper.

Francesca cocked her head to one side, as if she hadn't heard him quite clearly.

"*Where?*" she asked again.

"Loretta's house."

Francesca stood there, gaping at him. Something about this admission gave her a nervous feeling in the pit of her stomach. Very slowly, Francesca backed away and lowered herself once more into her chair.

"I see," she said quietly. "I suppose that's why it took you so long to get here."

"Yeah, I guess," murmured Joey. "Plus her son wanted to show me his video game."

"But I don't understand," said Francesca, her brow furrowed. "What made her cook dinner for you?"

"She didn't cook dinner for *me*," Joey tried to explain. "She just happened to have dinner on the table when I walked in to say good-bye."

"Uh-huh," nodded Francesca thoughtfully. "So, tell me," she asked him, "just what exactly did she cook for you?"

"Oh, nothing special," said Joey, sinking lower in his chair. "You know, the usual thing. Some ravioli, and pork chops, and stuff . . ."

Had he thought to look over the newspaper, Joey would have seen his mother's eyebrows meet her hairline.

Now, Francesca was inclined to believe that a man—or a woman, for that matter—should be considered innocent until proven guilty, and she was certain that nothing untoward had yet taken place between her employer and her son. Just the same, as she sat there brooding, the sudden silence between them growing steadily more deafening, she could not help but be seized by the conviction that there was something not quite right going on in the state of Denmark.

"So let me get this right," she said, her mind whirring. "The first thing she did when you came into the house was to sit you down and give you something to eat?"

Joey's only response was to turn to the next page.

Francesca's disquiet only grew over the next few days. Each afternoon, Joey insisted on coming to the door, ostensibly to walk her to the car, when he arrived at the Simmons house to take her home. He invariably lingered on the porch, stopping to exchange a few pleasant words with Loretta, who seemed only too eager to delay their departure. As Francesca observed the pair, she perceived a sort of nervous tension hanging in the air between them like a rain cloud waiting to burst. The signs weren't hard to read, and she fretted all the more about the slow pace of repairs being made to her car.

Had one asked her, Francesca would have been at great pains to explain why the nascent amity between Loretta and her son troubled her so. Nonetheless, it was for her a source of deep and abiding distress. It was not until Wednesday evening, when Joey came to take her home, that Francesca's apprehensions began to abate.

As usual, Joey had come to the door to walk Francesca to the car. At Loretta's invitation, he had stepped into the hall. The two stood there, exchanging glances, while Francesca put on her coat.

"Good news," Joey finally announced in a voice that sounded more glum than happy. "I got a call from the mechanic this afternoon. He said your car should be ready tomorrow."

"Hey, that is good news," said Francesca. "See, now you won't have to be bothered coming here every day to pick me up." This she said more to Loretta than to her son.

"Oh, how nice," said Loretta softly, her eyes downcast.

Wasting no time, Francesca gave Joey's arm a tug.

"Well, come on now, Joey," she told him. "I want to get to mass. It's Ash Wednesday, you know."

"That's right," said Loretta, all at once perking up. "I'd forgotten that it was Ash Wednesday." Then, turning to Joey, she added, "My boss, Mister Pace—he's a lawyer downtown—he went to mass at *lunch* today and came back with ashes."

The word "lunch" Loretta said with odd emphasis, but for what reason, Francesca could not discern. For his part, Joey only gave a knowing nod in reply to the statement, before taking Francesca gently by the arm.

Unable to make anything of the exchange, Francesca dismissed it from her mind. In any case, it mattered little to her. The stress of the past three days, worrying about her son and Loretta, had left her insides feeling twisted in a knot. She was content to bid Loretta and the children a good night and finally be on her way. As she climbed into Joey's car and he drove her away to mass, Francesca settled back and finally relaxed, relieved as she was by the thought that, at least for now, Loretta and Joey had seen the last of each other.

Things, she reflected happily, would soon be back to just the way they had been.

CHAPTER 45

The flowers arrived a little after ten the next morning.

Loretta had been at her desk, busy as always, during the early part of the day, when she received the call telling her that a delivery had just come for her out front. Her curiosity thoroughly aroused, Loretta dropped what she was doing and hastened out to the lobby, where a lovely floral arrangement was waiting for her. The young receptionist, at the moment occupied with a telephone call, could only mouth the word "beautiful" and gesture to the flowers with an enthusiastic thumbs up. Hurrying back to her cubicle, carrying the flowers before her, Loretta endured the playful oohs and ahs of her co-workers along the way before setting the arrangement down on the corner of her desk. Wasting no time, she ripped open the little envelope and tugged out the card inside, which read simply:

How about lunch?
       J.

Smiling from ear to ear, Loretta sat there, gazing at the card, while an inquisitive Shirley sauntered over to her desk.

"My, my," her friend said, a bit green-eyed. "Who's your secret admirer?"

Before Loretta could reply, her telephone rang.

"There's a call for you from a Mister Campanile on line three," the receptionist informed her. "Do you want to take it?"

"Oh, yes," said Loretta, shooing Shirley away. "I'll definitely take it . . ."

"So, Loretta Simmons," said Joey, "at long last, tell me about yourself."

They were sitting in the restaurant, leaning across the table toward one another, their hands touching ever so slightly. Theirs was a small table for two, nestled amongst many others in the busy establishment. The room was abuzz with conversation, and the waiters bustled about, taking orders from the patrons, most of whom were businessmen and women who worked downtown. It was not the most intimate of places Joey might have taken Loretta to on their first date, but with only one precious hour for lunch, it had the distinct advantage of being situated just a few steps down the street and around the corner from her office. Not that it mattered much to Loretta. Off in their own little world together, as she felt they were, she would have been just as content sitting outside on the front steps with him, watching the cars go by. Despite the crowd, they were finally alone together for the first time.

"What would you like to know, Joey Campanile?" said Loretta.

"Everything," he said with a smile.

"Well, for starters, I really like getting flowers," she told him sweetly.

"Ayyy, I bet you get them every other day," said Joey with a playful nod.

"Uh-uh," said Loretta, shaking her head. "Not in a very, very long time."

Joey looked straight into her eyes. There was something irresistible about the way he looked at her, an honesty and warmth she saw in his gaze that melted her. She could not have looked away at that moment even if she had wanted to.

"I find that hard to believe," he told her.

"Oh, it's not so hard," said Loretta softly. She gave a shrug. "Such is the life of a single mom."

"I'm guessing that's gotta be tough sometimes," he said gently.

"I'm not complaining," said Loretta. "Things just work out the way they do. I'd like to think that everything happens for a reason, although *that's* hard to believe sometimes. Trust me."

"I know what you mean," smiled Joey. "But if you could do it all over again, where do you think you'd like to be right now?"

"You know, I ask myself that question all the time," she said.

"And what answer do you give yourself?"

"Well, at the moment, I'm kind of happy right where I am," she said, returning his warm gaze. Then, pursing her lips, she added, "I haven't felt that way in a long time."

"I haven't either," said Joey. He let out a long breath and settled back in his chair. "I was almost married once a few years ago," he told her. He rolled his eyes and gave a shrug of his own. "I just figured I'd get that skeleton out of my closet right away, while I had the chance."

"What happened?" said Loretta, even though she already knew.

"It's a long story," he said. "Let's just say that, at the last minute, right before the wedding, things just kind of fell apart. And that was that."

"I'm sorry," she said. "That must have been painful for you."

"It was," admitted Joey. "It hurt for a long time, and it just wouldn't go away, no matter what I did or where I went. It was always there, pulling me down on the inside like a lead weight, you know?"

Loretta nodded, because she understood all too well.

"Anyway," he went on, "then a funny thing happened."

"What?" asked Loretta.

"My mother's car broke down," he told her. "All of a sudden, ever since that night, it just doesn't bother me anymore. As a matter fact, almost nothing does."

"It's funny about that night," said Loretta, giving him a knowing look as she gently rested her hand on his, "but ever since then, I feel the exact same way."

CHAPTER 46

Over the weeks that followed, Joey came to the house almost every day—after his mother had gone home, of course—to have dinner with Loretta and the children and spend some time with them before going home again at night. On the weekends, he arrived in the mornings and stayed the entire day, helping Loretta around the house and horsing around with Will and Penny out in the backyard. It thrilled Loretta to see how happy he made her children. Will, she could see, already looked up to Joey like a father, and Penny adored him.

It was wonderful.

Circumstances being what they were, however, Joey and Loretta decided that, at least for the time being, the best thing to do was to say nothing to Francesca. Both had an inkling that she would be less than pleased by their blossoming affair. It was not the most rational course of action, and completely without merit as a long-term strategy. But like all lovers, Loretta and Joey were far too consumed by the present moment and their incessant need to be with one another to think much further beyond it. The future would have to take care of itself.

It weighed heavily on Loretta's mind, though, that she had burdened Penny and Will with keeping secret from Francesca her son's visits to their home. "Let's just keep it to ourselves," she had confided in them, "and we'll all surprise her and tell her one day soon." It was a rather thin cover to give them, and really not fair. They were only kids, after all, and it was just a matter of time before one of them slipped and said the wrong thing.

Loretta herself suffered from occasional pangs of guilt. She had come to care deeply for Francesca, and the thought that she might do something to hurt the older woman filled her with anguish. There were many days when Loretta came home from work, determined to confess all to her nanny, but in the end, her courage always failed her.

Nonetheless, as nerve-racking a situation as it might have been for all of them, it was also one of the most joyous times of Loretta's life. No matter what might have gone wrong in her day, when Joey walked through the door, she felt whole again, as if she had at last found a piece of herself that had been missing for the longest time. And though their private moments together were always stolen and brief—how could they have been otherwise, with two adolescent children around—she felt their love for each other deepen with every embrace. At night, after the children had gone to bed, Loretta and Joey would lie together on the couch, nestled in one another's arms, until the hour grew late and it was time for him to go home. Both of them yearned, of course, with all their hearts for the time when they could stay together the entire night, and were indeed growing impatient for it, but that longed-for moment had not yet come. Deep in her soul, Loretta knew that her bitter disappointments in love were a thing of the past. But she also knew that what was happening between her and Joey was a miraculous gift, one that she longed to keep forever, and she was determined this time to do everything right.

Given enough time, however, all conspiracies of silence, no matter how benevolent, are destined to fail. The truth always finds a way to show itself.

Francesca was not blind. She was too astute an observer of human nature not to recognize the signs that something was amiss at the Simmons house. More to the point, as the days went by and April drew nearer, Francesca got the distinct impression that somehow, she herself was at the root of it. She had hoped that, with her son and Loretta having seen the last of each other, everything would fall back into the happy routine she had come to enjoy so much. On the surface, at least, such seemed to be the case. She came to the house every afternoon, as always, and the children always seemed pleased to see her. Loretta was as pleasant as ever—vibrant, in fact.

Just the same, there was an evasiveness about all of them, as if they were reluctant to say too much to her. Very often, for instance, when she tried to start a conversation with the children, they would inevitably hurry off upstairs, using the excuse that they needed to straighten up their bedrooms or do their homework where it was quiet. Had she not known the children as well as she did, she might have been inclined to accept these explanations without question.

As for Loretta, the young mother had suddenly found the energy to keep the house in perfect order. Even more, as of late, she had been trying to expand her culinary repertoire by cooking dinner herself almost every night. This, of course, met with Francesca's approval. What dismayed her, though, was that the young woman always waited until after she had left to start preparing the evening meal. It would have given Francesca no end of pleasure to stay now and then, and to pass on some of her expertise in the kitchen, but Loretta always seemed anxious for her to leave. It was all very distressing, and Francesca puzzled over it, until one afternoon when everything became clear.

That afternoon, Francesca had dutifully looked after the children, not that there was much for her to do. It was a pleasantly warm day, and Will and Penny had rushed outdoors to play in the backyard the moment they had returned home from school. To pass the time, Francesca had sat in the kitchen, leafing through some books she was planning to return to the library that evening. The two children were still frolicking outside when Loretta came home at her usual hour, bustling through the front door with a bag of groceries under her arm.

"Cooking dinner again tonight?" asked Francesca, eager to get a peek at what she had brought home.

"Yes, in a little while," said Loretta, hurrying into the kitchen. "Nothing special. Just some hamburgers and stuff."

"It's good to see you cooking so much lately," Francesca told her. "It's healthier when you eat food that you've cooked yourself, not to mention a lot cheaper."

Loretta only smiled in reply as she put the groceries away. She went to the back door and called for the children to come in.

"Wash those hands," Loretta told them when they came through the back door. "And then the two of you can start setting the table for dinner."

With nothing left to do, Francesca went to the living room to collect her things. When she returned to the kitchen to bid them all good night, she happened to notice that Will and Penny had put out four place settings on the table.

"Hey, put that extra plate and silverware away before they get dirty and your mother has to wash them later," she told them.

"What extra plate?" said Penny.

"Yeah, we always put out four," added Will.

"Why would you put out four plates when there are only three of you?" asked Francesca quite sensibly.

The question, simple as it might have been, apparently stumped the siblings, for neither child seemed able to make a response. Instead, the two stood there in awkward silence, exchanging nervous glances, while their cheeks flushed red.

"Mrs. C isn't having dinner with us tonight," said Loretta, quickly coming to their rescue. "Just do as she said and put the extra plate back in the cupboard. Then the two of you can walk her to the door and say good night, while I start supper."

It was an odd moment, but Francesca could read nothing into it, and so she went on her way, intending to stop at the library before going home. After leaving the house, she had driven only a minute or two when she realized that, quite stupidly, she had left her book bag on the floor beneath the kitchen table. Library fines were another expense Francesca loathed, so she pulled into the next driveway she came to and turned the car around. As she drove back down the street toward Loretta's house, she was startled to see a familiar car parked out front and an even more familiar person strolling up the front walk. Suddenly, the fourth place setting made sense to her.

It was Joey.

Francesca was thunderstruck, and her first instinct was to drive straight up to the house and catch them all red-handed. Curiosity, however, overcame her, and she brought her car to an abrupt halt a few houses away, just close enough to watch what happened next without herself being seen. To her astonishment, as Joey neared the porch, the front door swung open and out dashed Penny and Will to greet him. The two children talked excitedly, both vying for his attention, the way children do when a parent comes home. A smiling Loretta soon appeared at the door. Stepping out onto the porch, she took Joey's hand and gave him a kiss. Slipping her arm through his, she pulled him toward the door, and the four of them went inside together, laughing and talking the whole way.

Francesca sat there in stunned silence, her stomach churning and her mind racing. It was as plain as the nose on her face what was happening, but any notion she might have had of staging an angry demonstration had already vanished. Of the thousand conflicting emotions besetting her, anger was no longer one of them. Something else had taken its place. Francesca could not quite put a name to it, but when Loretta and Joey went inside the house and the door closed behind them, she felt an ache deep within her, something akin to what a mother feels on that morning when she leaves her child at school for the very first time.

With nothing else to do and nowhere else to go, Francesca started the car and slowly drove off toward home.

CHAPTER 47

"Bless me, Father, for I have sinned."

It was Thursday, two days later, and Francesca had decided to attend the weekly Lenten penitence service at her church. She had been going through the motions the last forty-eight hours, feigning ignorance of what she had discovered and trying to show a happy face to everyone, especially for Will and Penny's sake. All the while, though, she felt as low and miserable as she could ever remember. It was draining the life out of her. She felt like a wretch, and the worst part of it was knowing that she had no one to blame for it but herself. Such being the case, Francesca had come to the one place where knew she would find a sympathetic ear.

"It's been a month since I last confessed," she went on.

"Ah, Francesca," said Father Buontempo brightly. "I was wondering how long it would be before I saw you this Lent."

"I've been busy," said Francesca.

"That's good," he said. "You need to stay active."

"Whatever," she grunted.

"So, what's on your mind this time?" said the priest, sensing that Francesca was not in the mood for small talk.

"I've lied to my children," she confessed straightaway.

"Hmm," mused Father Buontempo. "Maybe I'm wrong, but haven't we already covered this ground once before?"

"Yes, we have," sighed Francesca, "but this time, it really cost me."

"How so?" he asked.

"It's all my fault," Francesca lamented. "It never occurred to me that something like this could happen, but because of me, my son has become involved with a woman, a single mother with two children."

"Divorced?" said the father.

"No, she's never been married."

"Oh, well, if it makes you feel any better, that actually could make certain things easier," he opined.

"What do you mean?"

"Um, never mind about that for now," he said. "Tell me about this woman. I take it that you're worried for your son because you disapprove of her."

"Disapprove? Why no, of course not," gasped Francesca. "I love her like a daughter."

"Oh, I see," said the priest. "Well then, I suppose the children are the problem."

"They're angels!" protested Francesca.

"Okay, then I guess what you're saying is that you just don't think your son and this woman are right for each other, yes?"

"Who could think that?" huffed Francesca. "All you have to do is see them all together, how happy they are."

There was a long pause.

"Forgive me, Francesca," Father Buontempo finally said, "but I'm having a little bit of a hard time understanding just what it is that's troubling you."

"So am I," confessed Francesca, heaving a heavy sigh. She looked down at her hands and fumbled with her rosary beads. "I guess what's bothering me, Father, is that I came to know this woman and her children because I needed to be a part of their lives, to do something meaningful again with my own life, and I thought that they needed me just as much. It all felt so perfect, and I was so happy. But then this all happened, and at first I was so mad and hurt that I couldn't think straight. Then I suddenly realized something, that after all this time, it wasn't *me* they needed all along. It was my son. And now I feel . . ."

"Left out again?" said the priest. "A little cheated, maybe?"

"Yes, I suppose," said Francesca miserably. "How did you guess?"

"It's why I make the big bucks," he replied, hoping a bit of levity would lift her spirits. It didn't. That being the case, he drew a deep breath and pressed on. ""Francesca," he told her gently, "by now it should have occurred to you that your life has never been just about you alone. It's also about everyone and everything you touch. God has his own plan, and what *you* think you might need to make you happy might not ultimately be what God *knows* is the best thing."

"So, what are you saying I should do?" said Francesca, growing a bit impatient.

"What I'm saying," replied Father Buontempo, "is that if this relationship is meant to be, and if your son and this woman are truly in love, then just get out of the way and let God do his job. Trust Him, and let whatever is going happen, happen. In the end, you might even consider lending Him a hand."

"But how am I supposed to do that?"

"Think about it," he told her. "Something will come to you."

"You know," griped Francesca, "you and God could try being a little more specific now and then."

"Well, if you think it would help," said the priest good-naturedly, "for now, you could say three Our Fathers. And while you're at it this time, let's really try to see if you can't stop lying to your children once and for all."

★ ★ ★

That night, after she had performed her penance and returned home, Francesca sat at the table by herself, eating a plate
of leftover polenta. She was feeling only marginally better, but at
least her appetite had come back. While she ate, Francesca kept
turning over Father Buontempo's words in her mind. Just staying out of the way and passively letting things happen had never
been Francesca's style. Hers was a much-too-active personality.
At the same time, though, she could not decide just how she
could possibly lend God a hand in this situation, or if indeed He
even wanted one.

When she was done eating, Francesca took her plate and
silverware, and rinsed them off in the sink before standing there
for a moment, gazing out the back window. A dark, cloudy night
sky hung over the city, but off in the distance, the dome of the
State House glowed like a half moon, while behind it, the lights
of the houses up high on the city's East Side twinkled like
earthbound stars.

"So, Leo," she said aloud. "What do *you* think?"

No answer was forthcoming of course, and so she went upstairs to bed to crawl under the covers and see what, if anything,
her dreams might have to tell her.

CHAPTER 48

Francesca awoke the next morning with her heart not feeling quite so heavy. As the hours passed, in fact, her spirits brightened quite a bit. The sacrament of reconciliation often had that effect on her. It also didn't hurt that it was a beautiful spring day, a rare pleasure after the horrendous winter just past. Outside, the sky was a brilliant blue, punctuated now and then by enormous puffy white clouds that drifted lazily by. The sun shone bright, and a warm, gentle breeze swayed the trees, whose branches were just starting to show their buds. Meanwhile, in the garden, the perennials had awoken from their slumber and were now stretching themselves up out of the soil. The robins had returned, as they do every spring, darting about on the lawn, which would soon need mowing again, while the little house wrens were happily pecking away at the new bird feeder Francesca had hung out for them. All in all, gazing out from the kitchen at the spectacle in her backyard, Francesca realized that it was going to be rather difficult to stay feeling blue that day when it seemed like all of nature was trying its best to cheer her up.

Just the same, as the day wore on, Francesca's thoughts dwelled on Joey and Loretta and the children. Later, as she readied herself to drive to Loretta's house that afternoon, her mind was still unsettled as to what she should do or say, if anything at all. Such being the case, she reluctantly decided to follow Father Buon-tempo's advice to just stay out of the way and bide her time.

In truth, there wasn't much else for Francesca to do. The moment they came home from school that afternoon, Will and Penny dropped their backpacks at the door and scurried outside to play. On such a fine day, who could have blamed them? Francesca might have occupied herself by straightening up the living room or sweeping the kitchen floor, but the house was al-ready in excellent order, a state of affairs the old woman found strangely dismaying. In the end, Francesca settled onto the couch and contented herself by watching the afternoon talk shows.

As the hour grew later, Francesca began to eye the clock. It wasn't unusual for Loretta to come home a few minutes late now and then, but it was now nearing an hour past her normal time. By then, Penny and Will had come back inside and were hungrily prowling about the kitchen in search of a snack to hold them over till dinner. Growing a bit irritable, as children with empty stomachs often do, the two quibbled nonsensically with each other, until Francesca intervened.

"Where's Mom?" asked Penny testily.

"Yeah, we're starving," said Will.

"Be patient," Francesca told them, regretful that she hadn't thought to bake a little something for them that morning. "Your mother will be home soon."

No sooner had she spoken those words than the three of them heard a car pull into the driveway. Will and Penny in-stantly dashed for the front door and out to their mother's car, pushing and elbowing each other the whole way. As Loretta tried to make her way up the walk, the two pestered her with questions about why she was so late and where she had been and, most importantly, what was for supper.

"Hey, you two, let your mother breathe," Francesca cried to them. She held the door open and let the harried woman in, her still-jabbering children in tow.

"Go back outside and play for a few minutes!" Loretta ordered them. "I'll let you know when it's time for dinner." Will and Penny reluctantly slouched off once more to the backyard, while Loretta went and flopped onto the couch. "I'm so sorry, Francesca, for being so late," she said wearily. "I had to work late, which wasn't so bad, but then the traffic was all backed up downtown because of an accident, and it took me nearly hour just to get home. I tried to call you from my car, but the battery of my stupid cell phone was dead."

"Don't worry about it," Francesca told her. "I don't have anyplace special to go tonight. Just relax for a while before you make dinner. You look frazzled."

Loretta cast a nervous glance at the clock and let out a groan. "I feel frazzled," she admitted. "I think we're going to be eating takeout tonight."

As Francesca gazed at the young woman, she recognized that beleaguered, frenzied look that parents in general, and mothers in particular, sometimes wear on those days when they're feeling stretched a little thin and the kids are making them crazy. She had observed it often enough in her daughters and sons-in-law when she visited them. A little time to themselves, she knew, was all they usually needed to feel renewed. It was good for them, and it was good for the children, to get away from each other from time to time.

Just then, as she was about to collect her things and get on her way, an idea unexpectedly came to Francesca, just as her priest had told her one would. She stood there for a moment, turning it over and over in her mind. The thought of it filled her with an indescribable warmth, and finally, she understood exactly what it was that she was supposed to do.

"You know," Francesca said thoughtfully, "I think you could probably use a little time to yourself. Just a day, even, to relax and be on your own."

"What, you mean without the kids?" Loretta chuckled. Then,

with a sigh, "That's a nice dream. What would I do with them? Leave them home alone?"

Francesca smiled and came closer.

"Well actually, I've been meaning to ask you—that is, if you wouldn't object—if maybe you'd consider letting me take Will and Penny to my house one of these days—maybe even let them stay over the night." Francesca paused for effect. "That is, of course, if you think they would want to," she added. "Maybe they wouldn't."

"Oh, no," said Loretta, straightening up, her eyes widening at the thought. "I know they would love to do something like that with you." Just as quickly, though, she slouched back onto the couch. "But no," she said in a hesitant voice, "I couldn't possibly impose on you like that."

"What do you mean, impose?" scoffed Francesca with a playful wave of her hand. "I'm a lonely old Italian woman. I'd be thrilled to do it. So, what do you say?"

"Well, I'm not sure . . ." said Loretta, weakening. "I mean, when would you want to do something like that?"

"Tomorrow's Saturday," Francesca noted with a shrug. "I don't know about you, but I've got nothing in particular on my schedule."

"Neither do we," said Loretta, staring into space as she drummed her fingers against her chin. Then, turning to Francesca, she said, "Honestly, do you think you would really want to do something like this?"

"With all my heart," said Francesca earnestly, looking her straight in the eye.

Loretta at first said nothing. Instead, she bowed her head and gazed down at her hands. When she finally lifted her head, her eyes were welling up. "That would be really nice of you," she said at last with a sniffle.

"Then it's done," smiled Francesca, patting the young woman's hand.

Loretta took a deep breath and wiped her eyes. "Francesca," she said after a moment, "there's something *I've* been meaning to ask *you*. That is, I've had something that I've been wanting to tell you. It's about—"

"Another time," said Francesca gently, holding up her hand before she could finish. "Right now, I need to get home and get things ready for tomorrow, and you need to go get some dinner for your family. I'll call you later tonight, and we'll arrange everything."

With that, Francesca said good-bye and hurried off, anxious to put into action the second part of her scheme. When she climbed into her car, she sat there for a moment, aware that Loretta was watching from the window. She put the key into the ignition and twisted her arm back and forth as if she were turning it to start the engine. This she proceeded to do several times, before opening the door and climbing back out. Feigning a look of annoyance, she trod back up the walk to the front porch, where Loretta opened the door for her.

"Is there something wrong?" the young woman asked, casting another nervous glance back at the clock.

"You're not going to believe this," replied Francesca, "but my car won't start, after all the money I spent to have it fixed. Could I use your phone? I need to call my son again . . ."

Humming a tune to herself, Francesca was sitting on the porch, waiting with Loretta, when Joey drove up to the house a very short time later. He had arrived just in time. Loretta, Francesca could plainly see, was by this time a bundle of nerves and seemed nearly faint from the tension. For his part, as he pulled into the driveway and stepped out of his car, Joey had the look on his face of someone who suddenly suspected that he might be the subject of a *Candid Camera* episode. Hands in his pockets, he strolled up to the porch and nodded a casual hello to the two women.

"Trouble with the car again, Ma?" he said, making an obvious effort to avoid looking directly at Loretta.

"See for yourself," said Francesca, handing him the keys.

Joey took them and went straight to the car. He climbed in and, just as Francesca knew he would, started the engine with no trouble whatsoever. With a bemused look, he left the engine running and climbed back out of the car.

"Sounds fine to me," he called. "I'll just let it run a minute."

"Well, imagine that," exclaimed Francesca, trying her best to look completely flabbergasted. "What on earth could have been the problem?" She stepped down off the porch and began to walk toward the car.

Just then, Will came bounding around the corner of the house with Penny right behind.

"Hey look, it's Joey!" he cried excitedly.

Joey turned to Loretta with startled eyes. The two, in turn, looked in alarm at Penny, who, at the sight of Francesca, had the presence of mind to clap her hand over her brother's mouth.

"Oh, there you two are," said Francesca nonchalantly. She was so exceedingly pleased with herself. She had them all right where she wanted. "Come over here. I have to tell you something."

"What?" said Penny meekly, looking nervously at her mother as the two drew nearer.

Francesca looked down at the two children warmly before giving a little nod at Loretta, who was on the verge of hyperventilation. "Your mother said you two can come and stay at my house tomorrow. Would you like that?"

Penny and Will looked at each other and nodded enthusiastically.

"Beautiful," said Francesca. "Now the best part is on Sunday, when all four of us"—she paused and looked Joey in the eye—

"or should I say, all *five* of us, will have dinner together. Wouldn't that be nice?"

"Yes!" the two cried.

Joey gave Loretta a sideways glance and squirreled up the side of his mouth. "I'm not sure," he said, *sotto voce*, "but I think she knows something that we didn't think she knew."

Loretta, her jaw hanging open, could only nod in reply.

Francesca, meanwhile, stepped closer to her son and gave him a gentle slap on the cheek. "I'm your mother," she told him. "I know everything." Then she turned to Loretta, who was still too dumbfounded to speak. "So that's that," she said pleasantly. "Now why don't the four of you go inside and have your supper."

With that, she nodded them all a good-bye and climbed back into her car. As she was pulling away from the curb, she heard the voices of Will and Penny happily exclaiming, "Hooray, hooray, she knows!" Then, just before she turned the corner, she heard another voice, that of Loretta, who had finally recovered enough to speak.

"Oh, you think you're so smart!" the young woman called after her.

Francesca gave a wave in the rearview mirror, and the two women burst out in laughter.

CHAPTER 49

Will and Penny were waiting on the porch, giddy with excitement, when Francesca came to the house the next morning. At seeing her pull into the driveway, the two sprang to their feet and ran to greet her with cries of "Hi, Mrs. C!" It gladdened Francesca to no end to once again feel their openness and unabashed affection, the strained evasiveness of the past few weeks gone without a trace. The two took her by the hand and walked her inside, both of them chattering nonstop.

When she stepped inside, Francesca found Loretta standing in the front hall, staring down with worrisome eyes at Will and Penny's backpacks, the ones they ordinarily used for school. Emptied of their books and papers, Loretta was using them as suitcases, and the two packs were astonishingly overstuffed. This being the first time in long memory that she would be spending an entire day and night apart from her children, and considering the changeable New England weather, Loretta had been in a tizzy all morning, completely unable to make up her mind as to what clothes she should pack for them. In the end, she decided it was easier to just cram as much as she could into each backpack and hope it would suffice. The result was that, to all appearances, Will and Penny were now prepared for a month-long sojourn.

"I just don't want them to forget anything," the young woman fretted.

A word of assurance from Francesca that she was taking the children only to her house, and not the far side of the moon, was enough to put Loretta's mind at rest. By this time, of course, Will and Penny were clamoring to leave, and so there ensued a flurry of hugs and kisses, and admonitions from their mother to be on their absolutely best behavior, and, of course, profuse thanks to Francesca, and before long, the three were off.

"How long will it take us to get there?" asked an excited Will as he and his sister buckled themselves into the backseat of Francesca's car.

"And what are we going to do?" Penny chimed in.

"Do?" jested Francesca. "We're going to work, that's what we're going to do."

"*Work?*" they exclaimed. "What do you mean?"

"Don't worry. We're going to have fun," Francesca told them. "Just wave good-bye to your mother, and we'll be there in a few minutes."

As they drove across the city, Will and Penny stared out the windows at the unfamiliar neighborhoods they passed. Now and then, to make them feel at ease, Francesca would point out different places that she knew well: a storefront that had once belonged to her cousin, a house where her aunt and uncle had once lived, and the little shop, now a hair salon, where she used to go to buy candy long ago, when she was just a little girl. Before long, as they were driving down the main street toward Francesca's neighborhood, they came to a red light, where she brought the car to a stop. Nearby on the street corner, a group of teenaged boys wearing uniform dark jackets were rough-housing with one another.

"Who are those guys?" said Will.

"Yeah," said Penny, a bit apprehensively. "They look like a gang."

Francesca glanced in the rearview mirror at the nervous pair and gave a little smile before tooting the horn to get the young toughs's attention. They all turned, and to Penny and Will's stunned disbelief, the old woman beckoned for one of them to come over to the car. The two gulped as the apparent leader, a lanky Asian boy, came to the passenger's side window and leaned his head in, smiling from ear to ear.

"How are you, Phoung?" said Francesca amiably, not the least bit afraid.

"Hello, Mrs. C," he said with great respect.

"Are you boys behaving?" she chided him.

"Yes, yes, we're being good," he assured her.

"Good," said Francesca. Then she gestured with her thumb to the backseat, saying, "Now I want you to do me a favor. If you ever find either of these two children wandering around the neighborhood without me, I want you to bring them straight home to my house. Okay?"

"Of course, Mrs. C," said the young man, giving Will and Penny a nod. "We always look out for the old folks and little kids around here. This is a *good* neighborhood. They don't have to worry."

To Will and Penny's visible relief, the light turned green, and with a wave to the young man and his friends, Francesca had the three once again on their way. It wasn't long before she turned off the main road and drove up the hill to her house.

"Here we are," Francesca announced when she turned into the driveway. "Okay, you two, grab your bags—that is, if you can lift them—and bring them inside."

When she opened the front door and ushered the two children in, they were immediately greeted by the pleasant aroma of a pot of freshly cooked tomato sauce in the kitchen. Francesca had arisen early that morning to make it so that it would be ready when the children arrived.

"Mmm, it smells like food in your house," noted Will as he stood there in the front hall with his sister, looking about at their new surroundings.

"That's what houses are supposed to smell like," replied Francesca, patting the lad's head. "Come on now. Leave your bags here and have a look around, if you like, while I get your lunch started."

Will and Penny followed her lead into the kitchen, quietly taking in the house's high ceilings, its gleaming hardwood floors, and the beautiful old woodwork throughout. Francesca's kitchen was, in truth, much the same size as their own back home, but its glass-door cupboards and cabinets, brightly tiled countertops, and lovely back window with its braid of garlic to one side made it seem bigger and airier. Feeling a bit timid, the two children lingered close to Francesca while she filled a pan of water and put it on the stove next to the pot of tomato sauce. It warmed Francesca's heart to have them near, but she wanted the two to feel at home in her house, so after a time, she shooed them off, to let them explore some of the other rooms. It wasn't long before they found their way into the den, where they looked with keen interest at the family photographs she had displayed on the wall. They were most fascinated by those of Joey when he was just a boy, and they giggled to see how young he looked.

"Hey look, it's us!" a delighted Penny suddenly cried out. She had spied the photograph Loretta had taken of them with Francesca that chilly afternoon in Providence.

"I was hoping you'd see that one," Francesca called to them, smiling, as she poured some pastina into the now-boiling pan of water. She gave it a stir with a spoon and left the stove for a minute to join them in the den.

"And who are these other kids?" asked Will. "Your grand-kids?"

"Yes," Francesca replied. "Those are my granddaughters, Dana and Sara, and that's their brother, Frankie. They all live in Florida. And those two are my other grandsons, Charlie and Will. They live out in Oregon."

"That's right," chuckled Will. "I remember when you first came to our house and you said he and I had the same first name."

"I remember that day too," said Francesca.

"What do your grandchildren call you?" asked Penny. "Grand-ma?"

"No," replied Francesca. "They call me Nonna."

With that, she gave them both a smile and walked back into the kitchen. The two children, though, fell strangely silent, and without another word followed her. While Francesca went to the stove to check the pastina, the siblings stood there in the middle of the floor, exchanging questioning glances.

"What is it?" Francesca asked over her shoulder, her back turned to them as she gave the pan another stir. "Is there some-thing wrong? Tell me."

"No, there's nothing wrong," said Penny.

"Go on, ask her," Francesca heard Will whisper. She turned back around and beheld the two children standing there meek as could be.

"What's the matter?" asked Francesca, now deeply con-cerned that something was troubling them.

Will gave his sister a nudge.

"Nothing's the matter, really," said Penny. "It's just that . . . well, we were wondering something."

"What?"

Penny looked down at her feet and took a deep breath to find her courage. "Well," she said at last, looking back up with the sweetest expression Francesca had ever seen, "we were just wondering if maybe—I mean, just while we're here—if it would be all right if we called you Nonna too."

No words could possibly have expressed the old woman's complete and utter jubilation at hearing that request. Her heart bursting with joy, the tears flowing freely from her eyes, Francesca gathered the two children into her arms and squeezed them close, like she was never going to let them go.

"Yes, my sweets," she wept, kissing them on their heads, "of course you can call me Nonna, any time you like."

"Nonna?" whimpered Will, who like most boys could tolerate being hugged for only so long. He looked up at Francesca, his eyeglasses all askew. "Could we have lunch now?"

Francesca let out a laugh and released the two from her embrace. "Yes," she said, wiping her eyes dry, "lunch will be ready in just a minute. And after, we get to work!"

"Work" consisted of preparing the lasagna Francesca wanted to serve for Sunday dinner the next day. When they were done eating their lunch, and the lasagna noodles were boiling, Francesca showed Penny and Will how to make the filling, letting them mix the eggs and the ricotta, the parsley and the other spices, but particularly the cinnamon, which was her special trick. Next, under Francesca's watchful eye, they took the long, wide noodles, once they were cooked, and laid them across the bottom of the pan, spooning the ricotta filling on top, before adding each successive layer of noodles, until the pan was filled. Finally, they laid strips of mozzarella all along the top, and poured some tomato sauce over the whole thing. Then, Francesca covered it all in foil and stowed it away in the refrigerator, explaining, to their disappointment, that they would have to wait until the following day to bake it.

"What else can we make?" asked Penny eagerly.

"Next, I thought, we'd make a nice ricotta pie," answered Francesca. She had considered baking a rice pie as well, but there was only so much time. Francesca decided that it would have to wait until Easter, still a few weeks away. "The best part is, we get to eat it today," she told them to their great approbation.

Will and Penny thoroughly enjoyed themselves, and the afternoon passed quickly. As the day grew later, and the freshly baked pies were cooling on the counter, Francesca made them wash their hands and faces, while she straightened up the kitchen. When the two were presentable once more, she directed them to put on their jackets, and the three went out to the car.

"Where are we going? Out for supper?" asked Will.

"Well, in a way," said Francesca as she backed the car out of the driveway. A few minutes later, they arrived at church, just in time for five-thirty mass. Francesca got them all out of the car, and the three walked up to the front entrance.

"Are we going in?" said Penny, looking at Will.

"Yes, I thought we would," answered Francesca.

She had expected them to protest, and had been ready to turn around and go back if they did, but in fact, the two seemed rather intrigued by the prospect, and so she led them in. Once through the outer doors and into the vestibule, Francesca quickly brought them over to the holy water, dipped her fingers in, and whispering some hurried prayers, blessed the children, making the sign of the cross on each one's forehead.

"What's that for?" asked Will with great curiosity.

"Maybe it's not official," replied Francesca, "but God knows his own."

"Huh?"

"Never mind," she said, shepherding them toward the entrance to the interior of the church, as the organist was just starting to play the opening hymn. Before they could step inside, however, Will released her hand and ran over to the poor box on the wall. Reaching into his pocket, he produced a quarter and dropped it in the slot.

"For Saint Anthony," he whispered. Then he hurried back to Francesca's side.

After mass, an exultant Francesca led her two charges back to the car, explaining to them, as they went along, the significance of the different prayers and rituals they had observed for the first time. Most mysterious to them was the bread she had received from the priest at communion.

"That's going to take a little while to explain," Francesca told them as they settled into the car. "Speaking of bread, though, gives me an idea for tomorrow. But we have to hurry."

Wasting no time, Francesca started the car and drove straight to the market.

Tony was at the register, ringing up the day's receipts, when Francesca walked into the store. With Will and Penny at her side, she quickly picked out a packet of yeast and two bags of flour.

"Good evening, Mrs. Campanile," Tony said cordially when she brought them up to the counter. "You got here just in time before we closed."

"I know," she said. "I decided at the last minute to bake some bread tomorrow morning."

"Can we help?" Penny and Will asked.

"Of course," Francesca told them.

As he rung up her purchases, Tony smiled at the boy and girl before giving Francesca a nod.

"Cooking for the family tomorrow, Mrs. Campanile?" he asked.

Francesca looked at the children and beamed.

"You know something, Tony," she said. "This time, I think I am."

CHAPTER 50

Night had fallen.

Loretta and Joey were walking arm in arm along a downtown sidewalk toward his car, parked a little way down the street. The two had just come from dinner at a little restaurant Joey knew and were now pondering where they should go next. It was a pleasant evening, with just the hint of a warm breeze sauntering in from the south. It was the kind of gentle night that put everyone in a good mood after a long hard winter, and people were out and about all over the city. The clubs and bars were busy, with people already lined up waiting to get into many of the more popular nightspots. Meanwhile, carloads of teenagers rolled along the streets, their radios thumping like bass drums, while motorcycle riders rumbled in and out of Kennedy Plaza.

All in all, it was a typical Saturday night.

As they strolled along, Loretta rested her head against Joey's shoulder. She was as happy as she could ever remember, and content to just be with him, no matter where they went next. It had been a lovely day, she reflected. It was curious, but when Joey first came to the house to pick her up that morning, she had not been able to stop thinking about Will and Penny. She wondered aloud about what they were doing with Francesca, and if they would be all right sleeping in a strange house for the first time, and if she packed them enough clothes.

Joey had listened patiently, never once trying to change the subject. He simply smiled and nodded from time to time, letting her vent all her anxieties, as he drove along out of the city. The farther they went, the more distant her cares had seemed to drift away from her mind. It was less than an hour's journey, but by the time they had driven through South County and across the bay to Newport, where they had planned to spend the afternoon, Loretta had already found herself letting go of her worries and beginning to just enjoy the moment.

Now, though it was really just a handful of hours later, it felt to Loretta as though she and Joey had been alone together on vacation far away for a very long time. She felt renewed inside. It was a blissful, peaceful feeling, the kind that two people in love experience when they're finally truly alone together for the first time, and she wanted to hold on to it for as long as she possibly could.

When they came to the car and climbed inside, the two sat there for a few moments, neither one speaking.

"Any place in particular you'd like to go next?" said Joey, taking her hand in his.

"You know, there are lots of places I'd like for us to go sometime," she told him, bringing his hand to her lips. "But tonight, the only place I really want to go is home."

"I think that can be arranged," said Joey, giving her a knowing smile as he started the engine.

Later that night, as she was standing in the darkness by her bedroom window, Loretta looked out at the full moon beaming down through the cloudless night sky. She marveled at how its soft light slipped easily through her fingers and across her limbs, like beads of translucent marble that cascaded to the floor and gathered in an iridescent pool about her feet. Joey came up from behind her and joined her in the light, wrapping his strong arms about her and kissing the back of her neck.

Though she loved the sensation, Loretta gave in to a little

laugh, for she realized in that moment how very much it all reminded her of one of her silly romantic dreams. True, she was
not off in some exotic locale, standing on some romantic balcony overlooking a shimmering moonlit bay. The only thing
her bedroom window overlooked was her tiny backyard down
below. Just the same, her heart was pounding with anticipation,
just as it always had in her most vivid dreams. The reason, she
well understood, was because, unlike in her dreams, the man for
whom she was burning was no longer some nameless stranger
whose face she could not see. This man was real, and his love for
her was real, and his touch thrilled her to her soul. There was no
place on earth she would rather have been if it wasn't with him.

Loretta turned to face Joey, entwining her arms around his
neck. He drew her close to kiss her, but Loretta held back. She
stood there in his embrace, the two of them bathed in the
moonlight so that they looked like beautiful works of sculpture.
As she gazed into his questioning eyes and caressed his cheek,
Loretta thought back over the long years to all the bitter expe-
riences of her past, which she knew in her heart were now
coming to an end.

Hope had finally triumphed once and for all, just as she had
always dreamed it would. There was only one thing left now to
make it all complete, and at long last she would be his.

Letting him draw her closer, Loretta arched up and brought
her lips to his ear.

"Tell me you'll stay . . ." she whispered.

CHAPTER 51

Early the next morning, Will and Penny awoke to the vibrant strains of Vivaldi playing downstairs on the living room stereo. Had it not been for the smell of something good wafting up from the kitchen, the two might have blocked the sound out with their pillows and lingered beneath the covers a little while longer. The tug of the pleasant aroma and the grumbling in their stomachs, though, soon won over their drowsy spirits, and the two dragged themselves from their beds.

Francesca was standing at the stove when the two children came down the stairs in their pajamas, yawning and stretching the whole way to the kitchen, where they unceremoniously plopped themselves down at the table. Their eyes still full of sleep, and their hair an adorable mess, they happily reminded Francesca of her own children on all those many sleepy Sunday mornings of so long ago. In her mind, she snapped a picture of them, for there was no way to know if a moment like this would ever come her way again.

"So, what's it gonna be?" she asked, flipping over the bacon she had sizzling in a pan on the stove. "You have your choice this morning, ladies and gentlemen. An egg in a blanket—that's an egg fried in a piece of bread? Some French toast? Or how about blueberry pancakes from scratch?"

"How about all three?" yawned a hungry Will.

"Done!" exclaimed Francesca to their surprise.

In truth, if they had asked her to prepare eggs Benedict or homemade Belgian waffles or a seven-course meal, she would have been happy to do it.

After breakfast, the children went upstairs to get dressed, while Francesca cleaned up the kitchen. When they returned, they found that she had set out the flour, yeast, sugar, and salt on the table, along with a small bowl of warm water. Before long, Francesca had them mixing it all together, and then kneading the big lump of dough it formed, to make the bread. The two worked at it until Francesca put the dough in a bowl, covered it with a towel, and set it atop the oven. Will and Penny, their arms and hands and chins covered in flour, were amazed and delighted to watch how quickly the dough rose, nearly doubling in size. After a while, Francesca took the dough out and had them beat it down and thoroughly knead it again. It was a bit of a struggle for the two, but neither complained once. There is something exquisitely satisfying about working with one's hands, especially for children, all the more so when the end result will be something warm and delicious to eat. Before long, the dough was ready to be formed into a nice classic loaf, which Francesca put on a flat pan and slid into the oven.

By the time Joey and Loretta arrived just after noon, the house was filled with the aroma of the freshly baked bread cooling on the counter and the lasagna simmering in the oven along with a nice baked ham. When they came through the front door, the children ran to their mother and hugged her as if they hadn't seen her in days.

"Wait until you see what we made," bragged Will.

"Ooh, I can't wait," said his mother, giving them both a squeeze.

Meanwhile, Joey walked into the kitchen, in his hand the Sunday newspaper that had been sitting out front on the sidewalk all morning. He came up behind his mother, who was busy putting together a little antipasto to have before dinner, and gave her a little hug and kiss on the cheek.

"Ciao, bella," he said happily, as animated a greeting as he had ever given her.

"You're looking rather well rested," said Francesca with just a hint of sarcasm in her voice.

"Eh, I can't complain," said Joey with a shrug.

There was a certain mischievous gleam in his eye that gave Francesca to wonder just what her son might be up to. She watched him with a skeptical air as he opened the oven to assess the status of the ham and lasagna. A moment later, Loretta came into the kitchen, raving to Francesca about how beautiful the house was, before shooing Joey away so that she could help his mother get dinner out on the table.

When at last the food was ready and the table set, they all gathered in the dining room to start the feast. Everyone was talking and joking and carrying on at once as they all took their seats. Francesca, meanwhile, stood at the head of the table, smiling as she presided over the proceedings, for it was wonderful to once again have her home filled with such happy sounds. She was about to start dispensing the antipasto when Joey suddenly got up and left the room. He returned a few moments later with a bottle of champagne.

"My, my," said Francesca as she watched her son pop the cork. "What's the occasion?"

"Tell you in a minute," said Joey, filling the adults's glasses before turning to Loretta and asking, "A drop for the kids?"

"Uh-uh," she playfully warned him, rolling her eyes.

"I'll get them some ginger ale," offered Francesca, hurrying off into the kitchen.

When everyone's glasses were finally filled, Joey stood and raised his own. "Kids, mamma mia," he began, "there's a little something we—that is, Loretta and I—want to tell you, because we wanted you to be the first to know. We talked it all over last night and . . . well . . . actually, I had already made up my mind, but . . ."

"What?" Will and Penny asked impatiently.

Before her son could say another word, Francesca looked at Loretta and noticed that the smiling young woman was now wearing a diamond ring on her finger. Somehow, she had kept it hidden from everyone until just this moment.

"Oh, my God!" cried Francesca joyously. She jumped up and hurried over to the side of the table, where she kissed and hugged Loretta and then Joey and then Loretta again, and both the children.

"What is it, what is it?" cried Penny above the hubbub.

"What do you think it is, dopie," said her brother. "It's a ring."

"Yes, but what does it mean?"

By now, for the second time in two days, Francesca was laughing and crying for joy at the same time.

"*Dio mio!*" she sighed happily. "What it means, young lady, is that we're all going to be having Easter dinner together. And then, one day very soon, I think we're going to go back to that store and buy you that nice blue dress!"

CHAPTER 52

The first thing Francesca did that beautiful afternoon in August, after Loretta and Joey had exchanged vows at the church before Father Buontempo and he pronounced them husband and wife, was to open her purse and pull out her rosary beads. Rolling one of the dark, smooth beads between her thumb and fore-finger, she whispered a quick prayer for the two newlyweds and made the sign of the cross. Beside her sat Loretta's mother, Jane. The two had only just met the previous evening at the rehearsal party, but they had hit it off at once, and Francesca was looking forward to getting to know her better. She seemed a feisty, high-spirited sort, though at the moment, she was dabbing her tear-filled eyes with a handkerchief while gushing to her husband, Paul, about how beautiful her daughter looked. With Penny as the flower girl in her beautiful new dress, and Will the ring bearer in his little tux, Loretta's stepfather had gladly acquiesced to her request that he walk her up the aisle. All in all, it had been the loveliest of ceremonies, and Francesca herself was moved to tears.

Everyone had flown home for the wedding, and later at the reception, Francesca was in all her glory when the photographer gathered them all together to take a picture with Joey and Loretta. Looking about at her smiling daughters and sons-in-law and grandchildren, she rejoiced in knowing that they were all finally together once again under one roof. Even better, Francesca was looking forward to the coming week, when they would all, Penny and Will included, be staying at her house, while the newlyweds were off on their honeymoon. For seven chaotic days, her quiet home would become a madhouse. There would be daily disputes about where they all should go or what they should do, and they would all drive each other crazy—and it would all be wonderful.

After dinner, when the plates had been cleared away and everyone got up to dance, Francesca sat for a time alone at the table, taking in the beautiful scene. It wasn't long, though, before she spied Mister Pace moving tentatively in her direction. Francesca was happy that Loretta had invited him to the wedding, and a little smile on her part was it all took to encourage the old gent to come and join her.

"Is this seat taken, madam?" he asked, gesturing gallantly to the chair beside her.

"Only if you sit down in it," replied Francesca with an approving nod.

"In that case, I'll do so," said a smiling Pace.

"So, how was your dinner?" she asked, once he had settled in beside her.

"Oh, not bad," he replied in a less-than-convincing tone. "How about yours?"

"Eh, it was okay," shrugged Francesca, "but the sauce on the macaroni gave me *agita*."

"I know what you mean," nodded Pace. "That's happened to me sometimes too."

Francesca gaped at him for a moment. "Really? Now how would a Yankee like you know what *agita* is?" she asked, incredulous.

"Like I said once before," he told her with a smile, "I'm not as much of a Yankee as people think."

"And how is that?"

"Well," said Pace, leaning a bit closer, "I'll let you in on a little family secret. When my grandfather, who I was named for, first came to this country, he realized right away that it would be a lot easier to get along if he introduced himself to people as William D. Pace, pronounced like *space*, instead of his real name."

"Which was . . . ?" Francesca asked, her curiosity piqued.

"Guglielmo Di Pace, of course!" the old man chuckled. "He came from a little town in Abruzzo, just like my grandmother. The two of them wanted their children to do well in America, but they also didn't want them to forget where they came from, so when they began to go by the name of Pace, they made sure to give all of their sons and daughters the letter D for a middle initial."

"Ah, I can see that there is much more to you than meets the eye," Francesca teased him.

"Well, not that much more," he confessed with a shrug.

Just then, the sound of cheers and applause drew their attention to the dance floor, where Loretta and Joey and Will and Penny were holding hands in a circle, dancing together. Francesca smiled warmly at the magical sight and blew them a kiss.

"They all look wonderful together, don't they?" said Pace.

"Yes, they do," said Francesca.

As she watched them happily whirling about hand in hand, Francesca marveled at Loretta and Joey, and how they had finally become a family. In time, she knew, they would discover their own way of doing things, their own way of raising the children, keeping their house, sharing their meals. Their life together would acquire its own unique rhythm, beautiful and perfect in its own special way. It gladdened her to know that, even if unwittingly, she had played some little part in bringing them together. Just the same, Francesca felt a familiar tug in her heart.

"Well," she said with a wistful sigh. "I guess they won't be needing me anymore."

"Oh, I don't think that's the case at all," Pace assured her. "Just look around. I think all of them need you now more than ever."

Francesca looked at him and smiled. "You lawyers always know exactly what to say, don't you?"

"That's why we make the big bucks," he said with a suave air. Then, clearing his throat, he quickly added, "Or at least, why I used to." With that, the old gentleman got to his feet and offered his hand to her. "What do you say to joining them on the dance floor?"

"Oh, I haven't danced in years," said Francesca. "I don't think I even remember how."

"Then maybe now would be a good time to learn again," he noted.

Francesca looked up into his earnest face and warm eyes. She wanted to go with him, but hesitated, for she realized that deep within, something she couldn't quite put her finger on was holding her back. It reminded her of that moment of fear in the airplane, just before it was about to take off. Part of her wanted to stay there, safe alone in her seat, but another part was equally afraid to sit idly by and just let life fly away without her.

"Yes, Guglielmo Di Pace, you might be right," she finally told him, giving him her hand. "Maybe now *would* be a good time for me to dance again."

And off she went, leaving her fears behind. After all, sometimes in life, it was good to take a little chance.

Please turn the page for a very special interview
with Peter Pezzelli!

Where did the original idea for *Francesca's Kitchen* come from?

A year or so ago, I came across a story in the newspaper about an elderly man in Italy. A retiree, the man had no family, lived by himself, and was very lonely. He was longing so badly too be part of a family that one day he decided to take out an ad in the newspaper, describing himself as a grandfather in search of a family. His offer to any family willing to take him in was simple: He would contribute his pension to help the family and cover the costs of letting him stay. In return, he simply asked that they let him become a part of their lives.

Evidently, the ad caused something of a national sensation because responses poured in from all over Italy. Families rich and poor offered to take the man in. His story struck a nerve in Italians who traditionally revere their elders. But the general population is aging and, as their society becomes evermore mobile with younger people moving about to wherever they might find the best employment opportunities, more and more Italian seniors are finding themselves in much the same situation. The traditional family structure is under great stress, and it is becoming a subject of great concern to Italians.

It occurred to me that much the same thing has been going in America for quite some time. Americans have a long tradition of pulling up their roots and moving to wherever the opportunity for a better life might be. The result is that we often have families whose members are spread all over the country, living in isolation from one another. Sometimes it's the children who grow up and move away. Other times it's the parents who decide to retire to sunnier climes instead of staying close to their children. I began to wonder about the cost this arrangement extracts from people, the unseen toll that it takes, and the rich opportunities for fuller, more satisfying lives that go to waste. I started to think about how much all generations need each other, how much we have to give to each other if we're only willing to share.

And that's when Francesca popped into my mind.

In *Francesca's Kitchen*, as well as your other novels, *Home To Italy* and *Every Sunday*, the characters' lives often revolve around cooking, food, and the kitchen. Can you tell us a little more about this culinary preoccupation?

Home is a very special place in each of these stories, and the kitchen to me is the heart of every home. All the really good stuff in family life takes place there. It's the first place you go when you come home after work or school because it's the warmest, most inviting place in the house, and what's better than walking through the door after a hard day and smelling something good cooking? The kitchen is where you sit around the table and eat and talk and laugh and just reunite as a family every night at dinner time. The refrigerator is the place where you hang up your funny family pictures, or leave little notes or reminders, or display your kids' school work. There's something warm and magical about a kitchen that people find irresistible. Ever notice how people at house parties tend to congregate in the kitchen? It's generally where all the action is. It's like a refuge from the outside world.

As for the role of food in my stories, I've always seen food as something that brings people together. Food is a universal language. Preparing and sharing a meal with others can be a profound expression of love, and affection, and friendship. I also think that sitting down at the table and sharing meals together is an important part of the foundation of family life. It doesn't matter how simple the meal might be, the important thing is that you're all there together, sharing it.

Besides all that, I simply love to eat!

You did an amazing job of getting inside both Francesca's and Loretta's heads. Is it difficult as a male writer to create such convincing female characters?

It was a challenge for me, no question about it, especially in the beginning when I was really struggling to understand who these two people were who had decided to invade my imagination. It took a long while for Francesca and Loretta to crystalize in my mind, but once they did things flowed a litte more easily—but it was never easy. It seemed like every time I was feeling confident that I had a firm grip on their personalities, they would become elusive to me, and I would find myself staring out the window for hours, trying to figure out what they were thinking and why they wouldn't talk to me anymore. Of course, that's just what women, fictional and non, have been doing to men ever since Adam and Eve, so it really shouldn't have come as any surprise.

Did you draw from any real life people as inspiration for any of the characters in *Francesca's Kitchen*?

I think I draw inspiration, in some way or other, from everyone I meet, so my characters are often composites of many different people I've known or encountered.

As the general U.S. population ages, and considering that American families are often spread all over the country, do you think Francesca's story might provide a practical model for building bridges between generations? Are there other solutions for keeping the elderly connected with their communities?

I think staying connected with your family is the place to start. We're all different, so I don't think there is any one solution, no single arrangement that would be right for everyone. If people take anything away from Francesca's story, I would hope that it might be the notion that any attempt at all to keep older and younger generations closer, especially within a family, is more than worth the effort. Family members, old and young alike, can annoy us, frustrate us, make us want to scream, but in the final analysis we still need each other. When we drift apart, it diminishes our lives in so many ways, we can forget who we are and where we came from.

What can you tell us about your actual writing process?

It's hard. Ninety percent of it is just showing up at the keyboard every day at the appointed hour. I'm easily distracted, so I have to really struggle sometimes to stay focused when it comes time to get my creative work done. I write little motivational

Post-It notes to myself and stick them on the wall next to me. The most important one has only one word: Produce. It's not enough to just come up with a wonderful story idea with wonderful characters in a beautiful setting. What counts is actually getting it down on paper so other people can read it, and that takes consistent effort. It also takes patience and a certain amount of trust in yourself because the characters and the story don't always reveal themselves to you on your schedule. Some days I write a bunch of pages, other days barely a word. On those days when the story isn't flowing, I try to just think about my characters and what they're experiencing and where it is that I ultimately want them to go. I might scribble down just a few thoughts that at the moment don't seem to fit the story, but might help somewhere down the line. In any case, it's a very hard process to rush.

What, for you, were the most enjoyable aspects of writing this particular novel?

I had a lot of fun with the confessional scenes. I also enjoyed the interaction between Francesca and the two children.

Did you draw inspiration from any particular books or writers while working on *Francesca's Kitchen*?

Not directly. When I read a book, I often find myself wondering why a particular passage was funny or moving, or why it seemed ineffective or superfluous. I try to learn from it. My tastes in reading, though, are all over the place. Right now I'm reading *The Mauritius Command*, the fourth installment of Patrick O'Brien's Aubrey/Maturin novels. I've enjoyed them all so far. He was a great writer. I have several other books on the floor next to my bed which I'm reading in fits and starts. I'll get to them all eventually—I hope. My favorite book of all time, though, is still *The Once and Future King* by T. H. White.

What is your strongest childhood food memory?

Helping my mother make the lasagna for a holiday meal when I was kid. The memory of mixing the ricotta and the eggs and the spices is still very vivid to me. Another favorite memory is helping my Gramma Helen make tapioca pudding from scratch. I *love* tapioca pudding.

Can you tell us about a family celebration where food figured strongly?

I can't think of a family celebration where food hasn't figured prominently. Whatever the occasion, when you invite the family to your house, people come expecting to eat, and eat well. You can't disappoint them.

Certain foods, of course, have special significance. On Christmas Eve, for instance, Italian Americans traditionally eat fish, usually of more than one variety. We might eat fried smelts, baccala, snail salad, shrimp, lobster, scallops, or liguine with clam sauce. Seven different fishes seems to be the magic number that everybody shoots for, but nobody knows exactly why. Some people say it represents the seven sacraments, others say the seven virtues or the days of the week. Either way, it's a lot of fish—but it's really good. On Easter I always look forward to the rice pies and ricotta pies and Easter bread. I love all that stuff.

Do you like to cook?

I enjoy cooking very much, but I have a very limited reper-toire, mostly some simple pasta dishes, frittata, a few meat dishes, things like that.

Who's the best cook in your family?

My wife, she's awesome, which is one important reason why I like to ride my bike, because otherwise I'd weigh three hun-dred pounds!

From where do you derive your love of Rhode Island?

I was born and raised in Rhode Island, and I've lived here my whole life. It's home.

Finally, the question many of your fans have been waiting for: Can you give us any hints about your next book?

Sorry, that's a secret!

FAMILY RECIPES

One of my favorite things in the whole world is to come home, especially after a long day, and smell dinner cooking in the kitchen when I walk through the door. When you're tired and cold and hungry, is there anything better? No matter how crazy your day might have been, sitting down to a nice meal with your family has a way of centering you and restoring your sanity. Sleep might be the balm that knits up the raveled sleeve of care, but good food is what keeps it from falling apart in the first place.

With that in mind, I pass along to you the recipes for some typical family dishes that always bring a smile to my face. Like most Italian cooking, they are all very simple, but very delicious. For appetizers there are my cousin's *arancie e pepe*, and the *fungi riempieni* which were one of my father-in-law's specialties. My wife makes a great spaghetti *agli e olio*, and of course my mother's lasagna is the best! I love frittata, so I asked my sister for her recipe. And for a little sweet after dinner, my mother-in-law's *biscotti* are always a treat!

Buon appetito!

BILLY'S FUNGI RIEMPIENI
(STUFFED MUSHROOMS)

18 large mushrooms or stuffing mushrooms
2 stick pepperoni, chopped finely
1 cup tomato sauce (canned puree)
2 teaspoon red pepper flakes

Clean mushrooms. Remove stems and chop very small. In bowl, mix chopped stem pieces, chopped pepperoni, tomato sauce, and red pepper flakes. Stuff mixture into caps of mushrooms. Place on baking sheet or sheet pan (can line with foil to avoid a mess). Bake in oven at 350° F. Mushrooms are done when they turn brown. Serve hot or at room temperature.

ALICE'S ARANCIE E PEPPE
(ORANGES AND PEPPER)

Fresh oranges
Olive oil, preferably extra virgin
Black pepper

Slice fresh oranges into half moon shapes and place on platter. Sprinkle generously with extra virgin olive oil and black pepper.

CORINNE'S SPAGHETTI AGLIO E OLIO
(GARLIC AND OIL SAUCE)

1 lb. spaghetti
3 gloves garlic
Red pepper flakes
Fresh flat leaf parsley
Olive oil (preferably extra virgin)
Freshly grated Romano or Parmigiana cheese

Using a 6 quart pot, put water on to boil. Optional: add 1 tbsp. salt when water is at a boil.

Use a 12-inch heavy bottom skillet for sauce. Warm skillet on medium heat. Add 2 tablespoons olive oil. Sprinkle in red pepper flakes. Use as much as you like for desired hotness. Chop 1 garlic clove and add to pan. Slice other 2 garlic cloves into large pieces and add to pan. Heat garlic over medium heat until just soft and starting to turn color. VERY IMPORTANT: Do not let garlic burn! Now, lower heat while spaghetti is cooking (remember to stir spaghetti so the strands don't stick together). Add ¼ cup of olive oil to skillet. Add 1 cup of pasta water (water taken from the boiling spaghetti) to skillet which should be at a low simmer now. Add a handful of chopped flat leaf parsley (about ⅓ cup).

Drain spaghetti while still al dente. Reserve the water in the pot. Put spaghetti into skillet. Add another 2 cups of pasta water to skillet. Toss spaghetti to coat with sauce. This will be wet, but not soupy. If you like, you can add more pasta water. Bring skillet to table or transfer spaghetti to a warmed bowl. Drizzle with olive oil (not too much). Serve with freshly grated cheese.

This will serve 4 people. Enjoy!

P.S. To make your basic sauce more interesting, try adding chopped black olives, hot pepper rings, or tuna fish in olive oil or all these together. Add these when you add the first ¼ cup of olive oil to skillet. This can also be tossed with a pesto sauce at the very end while still in the skillet. Be creative. Use the basic Aglio e Olio sauce to make your own signature dish!

NORMA'S LASAGNA

2 pkgs. lasagna noodles, flat or curled edges.
8 eggs
1 large ricotta cheese (12–15 oz. container)
1 bunch parsley, leaves chopped (approx. ¼–½ cup)
1 teaspoon cinnamon
¼ cup grated Parmesan cheese
¼ cup grated Romano cheese
2 qts. marinara or meat sauce. (I prefer marinara.)
2 mozzarella cheeses—medium size (sliced) or 1 pkg. shredded mozzarella

Boil lasagna noodles in large pot of salted water until softened. Drain and add cold water to keep from sticking together. In a large mixing bowl, whip eggs until frothy. Add ricotta cheese and fold together. Add cinnamon, parsley, Parmesan and Romano cheeses, gently folding mixture together.

To assemble lasagna:

Use large oven-proof baking dish, approximately 12x15x3 inches. Start with a layer of sauce to cover bottom of dish to keep noodles from sticking. Take noodles from cooled water, shake off water. Place layer of cooked noodles, slightly overlapping, in bottom of dish. Spoon small amount of tomato sauce over noodles. Spoon ricotta mixture on top of the noodles. Sprinkle on ¼ cup mozzarella pieces or thin slices. Spoon small amount of tomato sauce on top. Add another layer of noodles. Then add tomato sauce layer, layer of ricotta cheese mixture, then layer of mozzarella cheese slices and more sauce.

Continue to layer until pan is ¾ filled. There should be 3 to 4 layers. For top layer, a little extra mozzarella will give a nice browned crust to the finished dish. Put pan on a cookie sheet to avoid spills in oven. Bake in oven approximately 2 hours at 350° F or until bubbling and golden brown on top. If there are any ingredients left over, continue layering in another baking dish. These can be frozen raw or after cooking for an extra meal.

SUE'S ZUCCHINI FRITTATA

1 dozen eggs
¼ cup grated cheese
2 thinly sliced zucchini
2 cloves sliced garlic
olive oil
1 whole chopped onion
2 cups half-and-half cream
¼ cup grated cheese
salt

Spray bottom of skillet with cooking oil spray. Beat eggs and grated cheese together. Saute zucchini in skillet with garlic, olive oil, onion, and salt. Add eggs and cream to skillet. Let cook. Use a spatula to check bottom of eggs. When bottom of eggs is brown, place skillet in oven under the broiler to brown the top. To test, stick a knife in. If it drips, cook a little longer.

Camella's Anisette Biscotti

2 cups flour
1 cup sugar
dash salt
2 teaspoons baking powder
3 eggs
⅓ cup oil
2 teaspoons anise flavoring

Mix flour, sugar, salt, and baking powder. Make a well in center. Put eggs, oil, and flavoring in the well and mix together. Place in bowl and let stand loosely covered for 2 hours at room temperature. Preheat oven to 350°. Grease cookie sheet with cooking oil spray. Shape mixture into two logs on floured surface, then place on cookie sheet.

Bake about 25 minutes until tops brown slightly. Cool and slice diagonally about 2 inches thick. Place cookies on their side on baking sheet and return to oven for 10 minutes more at 360°.

As an option, add ¼ cup chopped walnuts or almonds to mixture. Also, dip ends of biscotti in chocolate before serving.